TAPESTRY OF THE HEART

By Pat Daulton & Grace Hampton

Acknowledgements

Pat Daulton wishes to thank members of her writing group: Lizzie Ross, Geneva Grace Kellam, and Taylor Hallman, and her good friend Frances Zak, for their encouragement, support, and valuable advice.

Grace Hampton wishes to thank her family for their support and Stephanie Sherwood for her excellent counsel.

Antonine Wall

Edinburgh

Lindisfarne

Hadrian's Wall

Jarrow

Durham

NORTHUMBRIA

North Sea

Whitby

York

Rosedale

Highhear

Irish Sea

Buxton

Chester

Stoneheart

Lothlar

MERCIA

Peterborough

CYMRU

Pencelli

London

KENT

Canterbury

WEST SAXON

0   25   50   75 mi

0   50   100 km

© 2009 Encyclopædia Britannica, Inc.

Table of Contents

CHARACTER LIST

HIGHHEAR

Lord Ecgbert married to Alfa
Hilda: the daughter of Ecgbert and Alfa
Bergdorf: sister-son (that is, son of his sister) to Ecgbert
Nurse: Ethel
Caedmon: servant and later Reeve at Highhear, marries Alanya, the daughter of
Aelfwynn, the Lady of the Moors
Hilda has a child by Brother John

LOTHLAR

Lord Bertram married to Pagany
Leova: the daughter of Bertram and Pagany
Leova marries William; their son is Wulfram; William dies and Leova marries Rolfe
with whom she has four children: Riana, Rosaleen, Bergdorf, and Bryan
Nurse: Gwynned
Servant and later Reeve at Lothlar: Jankin

STONEHART

Allmana married first an unnamed nobleman who dies
Roger: Allmana's second husband with whom she has three sons: Robert, Regan,
and Rolfe. Robert marries Wyomina, the child of Ian and Iona.
Rolfe marries Leova with whom he has four children (see above)

BRYNA

Bryna marries Angmar with whom she has five sons: Garamund, Garulf, Golmund,
Garhild, and Gardorf
Angmar also has a daughter (Alfa) whose mother is unknown

Prologue

Folca tosomne,
And mid freondscipe faest gegadrað,
gesamnnað sinscipas, sibbe gemengeð,

þæt hi hiora freondscipe forð on symbel,
untweofealde treowa gehealdað
sibbe samrade

Fellow to fellow   firmly joineth,
So that their friendship   forth and forever
They hold, their faith fast, undoubting,
Their peace unvarying.

Meters of Boethius

In The Beginning (866)

Leova was awakened by a sudden burst of sound.

Men shouting, armor clanking, as horses raced into the courtyard outside her window. The uproar grew in volume, and although six-year-old Leova had never seen a battle, she knew that the screams she heard and the thud of metal on metal had to mean the fortress was being attacked. Before her nurse, Gwynned, could stop her, Leova threw open her door and ran down the hall, flying into the barricaded enclosure surrounding her father's hall. She stopped just in time. A rush of warriors, oblivious to the little girl, jumped from their horses with spears held high and shields close into their bodies, pursuing other soldiers, and forcing Leova to take what shelter she could find. Behind a water barrel, crouching between it and the wooden palings that surrounded her family hall, Leova instinctively stifled both breath and words, attempting to stay hidden as warrior after warrior, round shields across their bodies, spears in hand, ran past her.

A sound that didn't fit with the others, a young voice shouting "Father!" caused her to peek out from her hiding place. A few yards away, she saw a rider fighting off a foot soldier who seemed intent on snatching a small girl, no older than herself, who rode sitting before a horseman on a white stallion. Her dark matted hair, wet with sweat, clung to her cheeks; her arms clutched the neck of the stallion.

As Leova watched in horror, the little girl lost her grip on the horse's mane and slipped, almost in slow motion, from the horse's back and rolled on the ground, stopping only a few feet from the barrel. The soldier ceased his assault on the rider and turned toward the fallen girl, leaning down, clearly preparing to scoop up the limp form.

"No! You shan't have her!" Leova screamed as she threw herself on top of the girl's still form.

Seemingly taken aback by the sight of two little girls where before there had been only one, the pursuer laughed derisively as he moved closer to them. A sudden shout arrested his advance; startled he looked back over his shoulder to where a wild group of fighters struggled toward an opening in the barricade, fleeing onslaught from their enemies. He looked up at the rider on the white stallion as he turned; "I'll be back," he shouted, as he disappeared out of the gate, quickly fading into the night, followed by a rush of horses. The rider on the white stallion looked back at the two little girls, almost as though he were going to stay, but then he turned in pursuit of his enemy.

"Get off!" an irritated voice from under Leova demanded. The girl pushed at her rescuer, giving her a kick in the process of extricating herself.

"Sorry," Leova responded, rolling back to get a better look at the dirty face before her. However, before anything else was said, Gwynned plucked her charge from the ground and set her on her feet. The disheveled child jumped up defiantly and faced Leova. "I can take care of myself." Everything in her tone dared Leova to contradict that declaration.

"He was going to take you, hurt you," Leova stammered defensively although she didn't quite know why she had to be defensive.

The two girls, both frightened but both strangely challenged by the noise, the smell of horses, the metallic clashing of shields and armor and spears, looked each other in the eyes and after a moment, smiled in recognition of what they'd just survived. The smile between the children—blue-eyed Leova and hazel-eyed Hilda— formed a connection that would last the rest of their lives.

Departure (878)

Ne ðis ne dagað eastan, ne her draca ne fleogeð
Ne her ðisse healle hornas ne byrnað"

That is not the light of dawn in the east nor a flying dragon
nor burning horn ornaments on hall walls
                                    As often happened,
Hilda had let her mind create pictures as the words
cast their spell. A tapestry of a female saint
thrusting a sword up toward the heavens, a halo
about her head, had hung in the hall of her
childhood home. She had often imagined herself as
that figure. But now the face that had been carefully
stitched into the cloth became the face of Judith.
The Battle of Finnsburh 3-4

Leova looked around the courtyard, remembering that first encounter with the girl who had become her friend, her sister-in-spirit. Quickly, she scurried outside the compound walls, trying to catch one last glimpse of Hilda. The early dawn glimmered on the horizon even as the company of horsemen faded from view, their armor glinting in the rosy morning glow. Marching in a phalanx, the men almost hid her friend as they took her away from the only home she had known since that frightful arrival twelve years earlier.

As she stared, frozen in place, through the staked barrier and down the long road, Leova silently repeated words, words she had heard many times in her father's hall. How she wished she were sitting there now with Hilda beside her on the benches next to her father, listening to the singer and his harp, caught up in the magic of the poetry and the dreams of excitement and adventure evoked by the muted rattle of armor and the gleam of golden cups passed around to the men by her mother. Sometimes she or Hilda would take the heavy, jeweled vessel from her mother's hands and walk about among the feasting warriors handing it to them and turning youthful eyes away from their sometimes brazen stares which excited at the same time as they frightened.

Leova shook her mind away from reverie to gaze once more down the road leading away from her father's hall, her cheeks streaked with tears, her usually sleek blond hair cascading raggedly down her shoulders over the folds of the loosened cap worn to enclose it. Though it was early dawn, the glimmers on the horizon seemed to fade along with the company of horsemen surrounding an also sad-faced young woman whose dark hair, escaping from her loose hood, framed her face in tangled ringlets which, Leova knew, could not cover the startling flecks of green in the hazel eyes struggling to blink back tears. As Leova turned for one last look, a brilliant gleam from the new sun lit up the horizon, swallowing up the retreating group in its glare and revealing its fading presence only by gleams reflected from warrior armor. The beginning of the new day felt to Leova more like an ending, the ending of a charmed chapter of life.

Her friend's exit couldn't have been more different from the manner in which they had first met. The memory of that first meeting, as dramatic as it had been dangerous, had gradually changed, and with every retelling of the tale, the event that originally had been frightening eventually became the subject of a merry tale, full of laughter and teasing comments about Hilda's stubbornness and Leova's impulsive and fearless nature.

Gradually Leova and Hilda had learned the basis for her arrival at Lothlar: warned that the enemy was advancing north out of Yorvik, Hilda's father, Lord Ecgbert, had decided to foster his only child Hilda. Placing a child with a family was an old tradition, one which not only taught children to be independent but also bonded kingdoms and families. In this case, however, the times rather than tradition promoted this decision. Ecgbert's lands were in the path of the wild men from beyond the northern sea, and his wife, Lady Alfa, had already sequestered herself in a distant monastery. When Leova's father, Lord Bertram, volunteered to foster Hilda, Ecgbert looked upon the offer as a god-send.

And it had been a god-send for the two girls, also. An only child, Leova thrived, having a companion in the hall, especially another girl. The hours spent learning to be a lady—weaving and sewing, overseeing cooks and house maids, playing the harp and ceremonially serving at table—started at an early age. Having another girl to share the learning made it all fun. The tasks, simple at first, became more complex as the girls grew, and although they always had time to play, the importance of their roles as princesses of minor kingdoms often seemed to overshadow even the freest moments of childhood. As children they hated being restrained, scolded gently by their mentors when play interrupted their becoming-a-lady-of-the-household tasks. Leova eventually glided naturally into the new tasks, Hilda often suggesting some other way, almost always not feasible, to accomplish a particular end. At times, Hilda even stubbornly stood her ground, literally refusing to move physically; it was Leova who could entice her out of that refusal. But as they grew older, they both learned to take pleasure in the more formal events in the hall. When visitors arrived for supper, Leova sat beside Hilda on the benches at the front of the great center hall of the house. As princesses, they held a place of honor next to Leova's father.

"All gone now—so quickly," Leova whispered, lost in her memories. It had only been four days earlier that the announcement of their pending separation had fallen on the two friends. However, it now seemed to Leova it had been only four minutes since that arrival of the band of warriors sent by Hilda's father Ecgbert to accompany his daughter back to her true home.

Leova recalled her puzzlement when her father had summoned Hilda to come alone to the great hall, ordering Leova not to come. Unsuspecting of the visitors' mission, Hilda entered the hall and gasped at the sight of the solemn company gathered there. When a tall solder knelt before her and with obvious joy told her that she was being called home, Hilda stood stock still, trying to comprehend his message. Then she turned and ran, desperately looking for Leova.

Leova had turned to her weaving as she often did to settle her feelings, trying to concentrate solely on the pattern she'd decided to try. Hilda's sudden arrival, a wild gaze on her face, startled and alarmed her friend.

Hilda didn't give Leova time to ask what was wrong.

"I'm to return to Highhear! To go home!" she whispered, and stumbled forward to embrace her friend. Hilda's dark hair framed her face in tangled ringlets but did not hide eyes struggling to blink back tears.

"But this is home," she wept as she looked around at the hall, at the tapestries on the walls, at the scenes visible through the hall's open barriers. "I know I should be happy, but I can't bear the thought of leaving you! Of leaving here!"

Leova, too stunned to reply, had simply stroked Hilda's hair as she tried to make sense of this turn of events. Now, she remembered with startling clarity, that morning's parting.

"I'll come to you soon," Leova promised. "We won't be separated forever."

"Perhaps father will let me come back for a visit," Hilda offered, not really believing that it would happen.

Then both girls spoke at once. "When we marry—." They laughed and then hugged each other once again, thinking of the future they knew would shortly separate them.

And then Hilda was gone.

As she turned from the horizon that no longer held her friend, Leova sighed tearfully and shook her head. In the confusion that had followed the arrival of Ecgbert's message, Leova had begged her father to allow her to return home with Hilda. Her father, smiling indulgently, reminded her that it was time for her to be thinking of marriage. Marriage! Leova didn't want to marry anyone; she needed to be with Hilda. She wanted life to stand still around them as they played their harps and embroidered happy, childishly colorful scenes.

"Life won't stand still for me," she muttered to herself, "or for Hilda I know."

Hilda now gone, Leova sat motionless, her small hands folded in her lap. When would she see her again? The girls had hardly ever been out of the barriers of the hall. It was not safe, Leova's father told them, to go beyond the tall stakes which enclosed the hall, its grounds, and their sleeping quarters. Secretly, and more than once, Leova's mother had taken her and Hilda beyond the manmade walls to observe the *auncient woones* perform the age-old rites of spring in a wooded glade before the dawn and on a hilltop after dawn. It had not been far in terms of distance. Her mother had told them they would be protected by the old gods; perhaps she had been right because they had always come and gone undetected and unharmed. Leova smiled despite herself, as she pondered her mother's seeming inability to accept the new ways and give up the traditional beliefs of her people. She loved reminding her daughter of how their ancestors had come from far away over the green hills where the sun disappeared every night. Hilda was not going that way though; she was going toward the land of the rising sun.

After a motionless eternity, Leova slowly dragged herself to her sleeping quarters and flung herself on the bed. Gwynned quickly removed herself at the wave of Leova's hand. She had never seen her lady like this, but she had expected it. She too was going to miss the spirited young girl who had lived with them so long—even though she had been quite devilish and much more likely than Leova to create the unpredictable. Gwynned smiled as she remembered the day Hilda had decided she wanted to climb through one of the narrow windows and onto the roof of her bed chamber. She had gotten stuck and for hours refused anyone's help, screaming that she wanted to be where she was and they should all just leave her alone. Whenever she thought no one was looking, she would wiggle frantically; whenever anyone came into view she started singing what became her favorite song: "This too will pass," adding new verses to its already long sequence of recorded, but tunefully transient, unpleasantness. Finally at nightfall she had allowed herself to be removed, saying that that was the way she had planned

15

it. What a stubborn, iron-willed young girl she had been! And still is, Gwynned thought to herself.

Leova stared unblinking at the ceiling of her sleeping room. Her mind was empty; emotion and loss had drained her energy. Her grief was carried by the wind to Hilda's grief and their combined sadness bowed the trees under, and the tides along the shores backed away from its force. As the room darkened, Gwynned stole in as silently as she could and lit the torches along the wall. Firelight revealed the intricate tapestries covering the wall, holding in the heat against the damp of evening. Leova gazed up at the embroidery she and Hilda had created just in the last four days; together they had made one for each of them to have. Woven into each of the tapestries were stories of their lives together, stories Leova would read from the pictures for years to come.

Chapter 1: Hilda Returns Home (878)

Hilda was as lost in her own thoughts as her friend Leova was; what lay ahead for her? She pushed that question deep into her mind as she looked backward. All those twelve years at Lothlar, she had seen her father twice and her mother only once. Her father had explained to her (though she didn't quite understand) that he and his family and warriors were fighting ceaselessly, struggling to recover the land that had been theirs always, or so it seemed. On the other hand, her mother had imparted information even more difficult for Hilda to grasp: she had told her that she was going with her ardent beliefs into a monastery on a distant coast to fast and pray for the results her husband was fighting for. "I will pray for you too, my daughter, that you will someday be able to fulfill your destiny." Hilda shuttered whenever she recalled the tone of voice in which those words were encased.

Shaking her head slowly to eject both the sound of that voice and her own uncertainties about her present condition, she pulled her horse up to that of the leader who had been introduced to her as Berghorf, not much older than she was her guess.

"Berghorf," Hilda asked, "Are we related?"

The armor-clad horseman smiled down at her. "We're cousins, my lady. I am sister-son to your father; he and my mother are brother and sister."

She nodded, digesting the information—though she had no idea what a "sister-son" was—opting to take the questions in a slightly different direction. Although they had been traveling since sunrise, they had spoken little more than phrases of courtesy, even when they stopped at midday to eat. Hilda had been preoccupied for most of the morning, needing to be warned at several small stream crossings. At first all her thoughts had been about the leave-taking, about Leova, her spirit sister; Gwynned, their nurse; Lord Bertram and Lady Pagany, her fostering patrons; and then about the visits of her father and mother.

Gradually, however—almost forcibly—she pushed her thoughts elsewhere, disciplining herself to look ahead rather than back. Her mind obeyed and she discovered that the farther along the journey they traveled, the more she wanted to know about her destination, about those she would be reunited with. Slowly, a bit to her surprise even, a sense of freedom and excitement took over, and she felt a growing pleasure at ever-changing sights. The world began to seem different somehow, new and inviting...and mysterious, in more ways than one. The crunch of horses' hooves on the dirt, the twittering of unseen birds, the rustle of windblown leaves: all caught her attention. She became aware, too, of the chattering of her attendants as they talked among themselves, realizing, however, that she couldn't understand some of the words that fell from their lips. If she had heard them when she was a child, she had forgotten what they meant. As much as she wanted to understand, she hesitated to ask questions. For one thing, she couldn't yet feel part of their world; for another, she felt she should know. Not knowing made her feel stupid. "I have much to learn," Hilda whispered.

"Sorry, cousin," she heard Berghorf say, "I didn't quite hear you."

Hilda looked up shyly.

"May I ask you questions?" When he looked at her strangely, she hastened to add, "Since we're family?"

"Of course," he laughed. "I might be instructed to guard you from harm, but that doesn't mean I can't entertain—and teach—you as well!"

Hilda took a deep breath and began. "I would know about my lady-mother. Has she left the monastery and returned to our hall? And, now that we are on the road, do we travel to our old hall or to a new one?" She paused, suddenly aware of how little she knew. "I don't even quite remember how big the hall is. I guess it must look somewhat like Lothlar...and I have no friends there. No one except my parents."

Berghorf smiled, almost indulgently, at the slight figure beside him, but suddenly realized how momentous this return home was for Hilda, how radically it would alter her prior ways of being. In order to cheer her, he tried to joke with her.

"Little one, before I answer your questions, I have a task for you. Take a moment and straighten your hair and your veil. Your braids are coming undone and your circlet is sliding dangerously to the left side of your head—soon it will drop to the ground and I'll be forced to chase after it! A proper princess," he wagged his finger at her, "must keep her hair covered and her wits about her."

The joke failed. Hilda's shoulders slumped and she sighed, suppressing the impulse to shout that she was not a "little one." "But would a proper princess ever shout at anyone ever," she whispered sadly to herself. The idea of being a princess had plagued her all her life. She had no natural inclination toward decorum: the rules and customs about proper action and proper dress seemed confining to her. In truth, her foster parents had not exactly demanded that she and Leova be "proper" at all times, usually enforcing standards only for formal events. Ever since she had arrived at Lothlar, the two friends had made a game of running through the courtyard, balancing themselves on the benches lining the hall, and jumping from one to the next. Although they had curbed their childish enthusiasm somewhat, it was more than likely that several times a week they'd find themselves racing each other along the familiar obstacle course, their long hair unbound and free. Still, Hilda had often gazed longingly at the farmers' children who had the freedom to run and laugh and play almost unsupervised outside the barricaded walls of the house. She yearned for that freedom. And, now? Now she felt even more confined, conveyed along by a company of armed men.

Nonetheless, here in the middle of these strangers, she struggled to return her hair to the confines of her veil and her small gold circlet to its "proper" balance on her head. For good measure, she tightened the gold clips that held the thin fabric in place. As usual, the veil felt uncomfortable; fortunately—or perhaps to her elders, unfortunately—it eventually would work loose and slip off.

"There," she announced, looking for approval.

19

Berghorf nodded, his face the model of a gravity he didn't feel. Then he spoke, "Lady Alfa, your mother, has returned home—abandoning for a while the good saint whose nails she had been keeping trimmed—in order to prepare for your return." He shook his head in wonder. "I've seldom seen that good lady so happy. Your father, eager to welcome you home, would have sent for you weeks ago, but your mother convinced him they needed to restore the old hall. The enemy, I'm afraid, stripped it bare."

Hilda started to speak, but he raised his hand to silence her.

"Luckily, once our ally, good Cynge Alfred, drove the marauders back into the sea and even baptized a number of them, we found many of the things you will remember: furniture, cups and plates, cloth and tapestries—some armor as well. Your mother busily set the hall to rights, and now she's set the seamstresses to work." He winked. "Seems she thought there should be covering for your bed—and clothing for your presentation to the people."

"That is indeed good of her," Hilda responded, trying to smile at her cousin, but his words didn't reassure her and she fell silent once more, remembering again the last time she had seen her mother during her mother's one visit to Lothlar. During that brief visit, Alfa had made it clear that nothing Hilda did pleased her. She snapped at her daughter's clumsiness, and disapproved of her tendency to laugh rather than remain silent. And when she had seen her running with her friend around the hall, she had gasped in horror. Somehow her mother had seemed too old. Much older than Hilda expected. And much older than Pagany.

"She won't have improved," Hilda mumbled to herself. "Talking all the time about God. Lecturing about leading a pure life." Another early memory returned, a memory of their trip to a double monastery housing both male and female religious. What Hilda recalled from that trip as a five-year-old was vague; she retained only the sense that the place was quiet, unnaturally so—and a bit eerie. They had spent most of the time inside the chapel, which was dark and musty; pointed windows high up on the wooden walls let in only muted light. The dark room with its elaborate cross frightened her until the priests began to chant. But the music

20

floating over her head seemed to enrich the very air she was breathing. Hilda could still remember that sense of peace. Her mother had never mentioned peace nor even seemed to listen to the music. Always, always, Alfa had emphasized the hardness of monastery life, the strictness of the rules, the need to follow God's commandments and be aware of punishment. She apparently did not find any peace there.

Toward evening, just when she felt she could ride no longer, Hilda spied a small cluster of houses. Smoke rose out of holes in the thatch roofs; chickens and pigs and even a cow stood in the yards. Beyond these humble huts, Hilda could see a hall, not as large as Lothlar, but obviously the solid center of the village.

Excitedly, she turned to Berghorf. "What is this place?"

"The lands of Lord Broadheath, my lady. We stopped here on our journey to Lothlar, and he invited us to stay once again on our return. We will exchange our horses here also." Before she could question him further, Berghorf turned away to order several of the riders to speed up and announce their arrival at the hall.

"Berghorf," she demanded, "Tell me who they are."

He raised his eyebrows at her tone of voice, but quickly understood that she needed to be prepared to greet whomever she was about to meet and, more importantly he assumed, determine how she should act.

"Lord Broadheath is a landowner with fealty to Leova's father, a member of Lord Bertram's kin group. Living in the hall with him are his wife, Mathild, his three young sons, and a loyal group of warriors. His lands are particularly valuable because of the many surrounding salt mines. The Lord and his men fought honorably with your father against the enemy. Your father rewarded them with weapons, and Lord Bertram gave them additional lands in recognition of their courage. Your presence will honor them."

Berghorf, recognizing that Hilda seemed confused and even a bit overwhelmed, sought to make the visit easier for her to contemplate.

"During our stop here, the lord's brother, Bishop Ceolwulf, told us many stories of the early times. Since he had been in

21

residence during our first visit, he might have tarried. He could be telling stories in the hall this evening."

"Stories?" Hilda brightened at the thought. "Tell me the stories—please!"

"Not now, little one. Tonight—if he's still there—he'll be able to tell them himself. And his tales—many of them not religious in the least—are best heard from his own lips."

The hall they approached looked almost identical to Lothlar, though smaller. Just past the small group of huts, a tree-lined path led up to a clearing, and a high staked wall obscured the inner court, visible only through the open gates. Farm animals grazed around the walls and up the gentle sloping hillsides. As the party approached, grooms—alerted by the heralds Berghorf had sent earlier—rushed to take their horses. Having dismounted, Berghorf carefully placed his shield, helmet, and spear against the outer walls of the hall as a sign of peace, beckoning to his companions to do likewise.

"This way, my lady," announced a gentleman who had hurried from the largest building within the walls. "Our lord is eager to welcome you properly."

As Hilda, Berghorf, and her attendants followed the greeter into the manor, she found herself taken back with his use of the word "proper." Would she never escape the need for herself and others to behave in what she tended to think of as a rigid and cold manner?

The great hall, its walls covered by golden-threaded tapestries, sparkled in reflection of the fire at the very center. The official greeter indicated that the attendants should wait at the door and then escorted Berghorf and Princess Hilda to the benches where the Lord and his family were seated.

Hilda, suddenly unsure of herself, tried to pull up memories of the many visitors who had appeared at Leova's father's hall. Patterning their behavior, and taking cues from Berghorf, she bowed slightly from the waist,

"Greetings, My Lord, My Lady," she hesitated for a mere second before continuing. "And many thanks for your hospitality."

Lord Broadheath smiled, "You are most welcome, sweet lady. Do us the honor of breaking bread with us. Sit here, next to my lady-wife." Hilda felt as though she had passed the first test of being a "proper" princess.

The meal passed quickly, food and drink appearing almost instantly. As much as she wanted to devour the abundant roasted meats, fresh bread, vegetables and fruit, she restrained herself, remembering the manners that Pagany had drilled into her. She made sure that she chewed her food delicately and silently and didn't speak before she swallowed the delicious fare. Watching Lady Mathild, she saw her too eating decorously. "Princessly eating," Hilda might have said to Leova had she been there.

Although having consumed very little, Lady Mathild courteously inquired of her health and of the difficulties of travel. "And how did you leave your friends at Lothlar? I've never visited the great estate, but I've frequently heard of the kindness and wisdom of Lady Pagany."

For a moment Hilda lost her composure, so intense was her feeling of loss. Pulling her thoughts back to the conversation, she started to confess her surprise that Mathild had never been to Leova's hall, only a day's travel away. Thankfully, she quickly realized that only those who had cause traveled from estate to estate. She and Leova had seldom gone beyond a tight circle of the land surrounding Lothlar. There had been no need for girls to travel, as there had probably been no need for Mathild to leave her home.

"Men have greater need to see the world," she thought. Almost to prove her point, Lord Broadheath and Lady Mathild's three sons broke into loud descriptions of their latest hunting adventure. From the oldest, a man of twenty, to the youngest, a lad of thirteen or so, they filled the air with loud claims of skill.

"Had I not been quick," the oldest said, "You would not be feasting on this grand deer."

"Had I not alerted you," retorted the lad, "he would have passed underneath your nose without harm."

Their voices joined with others and the noise reverberated throughout the hall, louder and louder until Hilda could not make out the words of her hostess even as she leaned in to ask another question.

Suddenly, however, the clamor began to decrease and gradually silence descended upon the hall. An elderly man, clothed in a long white robe—a thick gold cross on his chest—made his way to the bench where Lord Broadheath and his guests sat. He was bald except for a wild line of hair that rose like a crown above his bushy white eyebrows. Hilda instantly knew that this must be Bishop Ceolwulf and, following the lead of both guests and hosts, Hilda stood in honor of his age and reputation. To her horror, it became evident that he had set his gaze upon her. Nervously, she lowered her own eyes, not sure what to do. Shyness had rarely been her reaction to any happening in her previous life.

"I greet you, Princess Hilda," he announced gravely. She raised her head to acknowledge his greeting and saw that he smiled with genuine pleasure.

"It gives me great pleasure that your father has returned to his rightful place. He has always been generous to my order, and we have prayed long for this homecoming." Ceolwulf paused for a moment. "We rejoice for your mother's restoration, too. Although I must confess that we will miss this most blessed woman. She has given generously to our order and worked among the poor without rest. The most saintly of women, Lady Alfa, a woman valued by God."

In a flash of what she knew was misplaced irritation, Hilda wondered if her mother's sharp tongue had ever been turned against the Bishop. Apparently not, or he might have been less generous with his praise.

At his brother's invitation, Bishop Ceolwulf took a seat next to Hilda, but refused all proffered food. "I observe a fast day," he said to no one in particular.

Hilda imagined whispering into Leova's ear, "The good bishop's girth suggests that his fast days are limited in number." Then, sadly, she reflected that she no longer had someone she could whisper irreverent thoughts to. Her anxiety returned when she realized that he expected her to know what feast day he observed. She didn't.

Hilda had never been religious, at least not in the way her mother was. As a small child, she had found her mother's fierce words and observances frightening, and that fear had alienated her from Christian worship. When she discovered that her foster mother—Leova's mother—had little to do with what she called the "new" religion, she felt a sense of release and relief. Now her throat tightened as she contemplated reuniting with her zealous mother.

"When did you last see my mother? How does she fare?" Hilda asked the Bishop, trying not to reveal her concerns. "I have had no word since she visited us at Lothlar—several years ago."

"She's well, my dear, although she has set aside her work in order to prepare a home for you."

She dropped her eyes, not sure why she felt embarrassed. It was, after all, not her fault her mother had not tried to see her for so many years. Nor her fault that Lady Alfa had left off serving the saint. Hilda's curiosity, however, overcame her discomfort.

"Bishop Ceolwulf, my mother spoke of tending the body of a holy man, but I didn't really understand what she meant. Maybe I was too young," she added, supplying an excuse that felt more like an apology.

"Lady Alfa minds the body of St. Oswald, and his is a long and blessed story," Ceolwulf looked about the hall, "one perhaps all here should listen to." Hilda noticed a sudden glow in Ceolwulf's eyes. "No," he continued, "I have a more apt blessed story for this evening."

Hilda looked about the hall. The reverence that the occupants demonstrated when the bishop had entered faded once he took his seat beside her. The men in one corner lifted tankards and toasted some mighty deed. Across the hall, a young man stood on a bench, loudly telling his own tale of adventure. At the tables, men and women tossed discarded bones to the many dogs that roamed in search of food. Laughing heartily, they speculated about which dog would pick up the bones first. And Bergdorf's men had begun to entertain the Lord's sons with recollections of shared battles.

"They will not hear you, Reverend One," Hilda declared. She stumbled over the title, not quite sure how one should address a bishop. Pagany called holy women "Reverend Ones," so she reasoned that a similar title would work for Ceolwulf.

"The harp will gain their attention," Ceolwulf answered, not at all disconcerted at her form of address. He whispered to an attendant who respectfully relayed his message to Lord Broadheath, who stood up, took the harp lying next to the hall synger, and carried it to the bishop. Such a presentation underscored the honor with which his brother viewed the Bishop; Hilda's mother had always paid such honor to important men.

Ceolwulf received the harp as one familiar with it and immediately struck a loud chord on its strings. The notes resounded through the smoky hall, bouncing off the walls again and again. The priest struck a second chord whose notes blended with the first. As the notes swirled around the hall, the other noises—even the dogs' barking—faded until only the memory of the tones could be heard.

>   *Heard I that Holofernus*
> *Ready drinker of wine   ordered a wondrous feast*
> *To be set up   the lord of men ordered*
> *To it the oldest thanes;   they with much haste,*
> *The shield bearers, went;   they came to the powerful lord,*
> *Traveled to the people's leader.   That was by the fourth day*
> *When there Judith,   the one wise-in-thought,*
> *The elf-shining woman,   first arrived.*

The words soared up to the roof of the hall where they hung for a second before blending with the smoke, the crackling of the fire, and the muted sounds of metal on metal as men stirred slightly on the benches, learning forward to hear better.

Hilda, too, leaned forward, her thoughts traveling back to the many evenings she and Leova had sat between Pagany and Bertram, listening to other syngers. She loved their tales of burning halls and fierce battles and exiled men who were feared and hated by all who encountered them. The two of them especially loved the haunting words which echoed of tragic ends, words from the lips of abandoned women grieving for friends and lovers, words from the hearts and minds of men lost at sea without companions, words from warriors whose troops had all died, words from exiles who could never return to their beloved country.

Hilda had eagerly learned to play her own harp and practiced reciting some of the tales herself. But she and Leova never dared play the harp for anyone except each other. Hilda recalled with a smile a day when she sat in her room, reciting a violent tale of severed heads that continued to resist their tormentors and vow revenge. Leova, who had been sitting by the window, began to giggle. Hilda, insulted by her friend's ridicule, finished her account angrily with a final swift striking of the harp.

"Was I so bad? Did I tell the story wrong?"

"Oh, no," Leova reassured her. "It was wonderful—as good as my father's synger."

"Why were you laughing at me then?" pouted Hilda.

"Hilda, Hilda. I would never laugh at you. Look out the window. Everyone in the courtyard was listening. I giggled because they were trying so hard to act as though they weren't. They were really quite spellbound by your reciting!"

Another strike on the harp brought Hilda's thoughts back to the words of the bishop.

> *Then became Holofernus,*
> *Gold-lord of men,   in great glee;*
> *He laughed and bellowed,   shouted and caroused,*
> *So that the sons-of-men   from far off heard*
> *How the strong one   stormed and rejoiced*
> *Drunk with mead.*

Ceolwulf paused for effect.

> *Then the one steeped in evil*
> *Ordered to be fetched quickly   the blessed maid*
> *To his sleeping place   adorned with circlets*

27

With rings laden.   They quickly did,
The lord's servants,   as their lord ordered
The chief of warriors.   Quickly they stepped forth
To the guesthouse, found   and then quickly
The shield warriors   began to lead
The glorious maiden   to the high pavilion
Where the powerful one   always rested himself.

Those in the hall had become quieter as the tale progressed; some who knew the Biblical story were not as fearful as those who were aware of the possibility of a cruel, merciless conclusion for the holy Judith.

Ceolwulf's voice rose dramatically:

They then to rest
Brought the wise woman.   Then the stone-hearted warriors
Went to the lord to make known   that the blessed maid
Was brought to his pavilion.   Then the well-known warrior
Became joyous, the lord of cities.   He intended the bright
woman
With filth and terror to smite.

Ceolwulf ceased briefly and looked about at his audience. Silence pervaded the hall.

The evil one neared the bed   fell there the wine-drunk
Powerful one.

As often happened, Hilda had let her mind create pictures as the words cast their spell. A tapestry of a female saint thrusting a sword up toward the heavens, a halo about her head, had hung in the hall of her childhood home. She had often imagined herself as that figure. But now the face that had been carefully stitched into the cloth became the face of Judith. She couldn't see in her mental recreation of Judith the halo that the weaver had placed around the elongated and slightly tilted head, but she could imagine the brave woman of Ceolwulf's tale with a halo. She closed her eyes listening to the words and seeing all the events in vivid detail, but as though Leova had whispered into her ear, she suddenly became fully conscious of the narrative and uttered a slight gasp. These men were throwing Judith on the bed of a drunken, powerful king. She realized she didn't want to know the remainder of the story, fearing a horrific ending.

A quiet murmur floated through the hall. Ceolwulf's voice dropped to a whisper:

> *Then was the saviour's*
> *Glorious maiden   eagerly mindful*
> *How she the horrid one   most easily might*
> *Deprive of life   before the impure,*
> *Filthy one, awoke.   The curly-haired one,*
> *The lord's maiden,   seized a sharp knife*
> *Hardened by scouring   and from its sheath drew it*
> *With her right hand.*

The quiet in the hall was interrupted by gasps. Ceolwulf lowered his voice dramatically....

> *She seized the heathen man*
> *Firmly by his hair;   with her hand drew him toward her*
> *Shamefully   the filled-with-evil one*
> *Dragged with cunning   the hated man,*
> *So that she the wicked one   might most easily*
> *Well control.   The curly-haired one struck*
> *The hostile enemy   with the shining sword,*
> *The hateful-thinking man   so that she half cut his neck*
> *With the sword   and he in a swoon lay*
> *Drunk and mindless.*

Approving murmurs came from the listening warriors, even a few cheers and shouts of "More, more, more." Ceolwulf raised his hand for quiet and continued.

He was not yet dead
Wholely lifeless;   *the earnest one*
The soul-rich woman   *a second time struck*
The heathen hound   *so that his head rolled*
Forth on the floor.

The pictures in Hilda's head of the triumphant Judith standing over the bloody head lying on the floor grew stronger. She listened raptly as Ceolwulf concluded his recitation with Judith's triumphant return to her people carrying the head in a bag, then rolling the head out on the floor so all could rejoice at the sight of it.

All others in the hall seemed rapt by the events and the ensuing defeat of Holofernes' troops. But as Hilda reconsidered, she recalled a number of times when a synger at Lothlar had told a similar tale of a heroic man—Beowulf—who saved his people by cutting off the head of an ogre, carrying it back triumphantly to his landsmen. Judith's tale now sounded like the fairy tales Gwynned had told her and Leova. This story now seemed no more credible than those of little girls who after being swallowed by wolves emerge alive or tales of children changed into swans for a thousand years. She became impatient.

"What has this story to do with us?" Hilda muttered.

Ceolwulf had overhead her, and visibly annoyed, he answered, "Wait. Listen."

He turned to the captivated hall, and continued not as a synger, but as a teacher.

"Judith was an Israeli woman. Were it not for her and other heroes of the Old Testament, Christianity may not have become the religion of the world. And, we too, face an enemy who would destroy our religion, an enemy against whom we must raise our swords and pray to our God for victory."

"Yes, yes," Hilda could hear many in the hall respond. She, of course, would admit to no one that she had never heard of Judith and barely knew what the Old Testament was. Nor was she at all certain what an "Israeli" person might be. Still, she admitted to herself, and would have admitted to Leova had she been there, some of the stories Pagany had told them also centered on strong women who had led their people to victories.

Ceolwulf stroked on his strings one more time to bring about silence. "All here should know that women can serve in many ways today also. Hilda's saintly mother has spent many years attending to the body of St. Oswald, an olden time king of our people and martyr for his religion and ours. Hilda is fortunate to have such a parent."

Struggling to answer respectfully, Hilda said aloud, "My mother is a...a devout woman." She almost choked on the words. Despair took residence in her heart. The burden of her feelings couldn't be shared here. Only to someone like Leova could she speak the whole truth. And Leova grew farther away each day.

That night, after the journey, after the feasting, after the stimulation of the stories she'd heard, an exhausted Hilda fell asleep almost immediately. Dreams haunted her at first: disconnected body parts rolling and rolling and her mother struggling under the burden of outsized finger nails. But, finally, the images and sounds departed and Hilda slept peacefully, her tangled dark hair scattered against the white pillow.

No one saw the aging form of Ceolwulf move down the corridor and pause outside the door of Hilda's sleeping quarters. Quietly, he gazed upon the sleeping Princess. The tired bishop sighed and made the sign of benediction. Hilda's sainted mother had great plans for this lively child, plans that might be a blessing—or a problem—for the church they loved so well.

The cloud which had been covering the moon moved and the girl's face was suddenly illuminated by its light.

"It's a sign," he thought. Then he smiled. Surely God was showing His favor to this spirited young woman. As the Bishop closed the door and started toward his own room, he shook his head, praying that Hilda would succeed in her destined course.

Next morning's journey led the small company over an ancient stone road which wound through yet more trees and over more small streams, but gradually their route circled increasingly high hills—and, at times, climbed over them. Hilda welcomed the

31

change, but continued to construct and reconstruct what awaited her.

"How much farther, cousin?" Hilda asked of Berghorf.

"If the weather stays fair, three days," her guardian responded, replying with an even voice so that Hilda would not detect any anxiety to conclude the trip. Nonetheless, she supposed he might be eager to return to this own lands. Hilda settled resolutely back into her saddle. Three days stretched interminably before her, especially since the small group had been joined by Ceolwulf, who wanted to travel to their next destination, the monastery where he lived. Hilda had no idea how to talk to him, especially since he admired her mother's devotion and Hilda found her actions repugnant.

Her thoughts were interrupted as Ceolwulf drew his donkey alongside her slow moving horse.

"Good morrow, my child. May I ride beside you?"

Hilda nodded without much enthusiasm.

"Tell me something of your life at Lothlar," he said curiously. "How did you spend your days?"

Hilda, missing Leova and Lothlar, welcomed a chance to talk about them.

"Lady Pagany taught us to play the harp and the pipe, to embroider and create tapestries." The Bishop seemed less than interested in women's work. Probably thinks it's frivolous, Hilda thought

"And did you see the outside world? Did other folk visit?"

"The children of the servants and farmers came to play—inside the gates. Very few children came otherwise."

"Did you travel often beyond the walls?"

"No, though at times...." She stopped short, fearing the bishop would not approve of the visits to the *auncient woones* with Leova's mother.

"At times...?"

Hilda wouldn't lie to the bishop, but she didn't intend to tell the whole truth. "We visited some friends of Leova's mother."

"And where did they live?"

"In the woods...."

"In the woods? They had houses in the woods?"

"I meant that we met in the woods." She added rather hurriedly, "they had houses elsewhere." Flustered, Hilda fell silent. To tell the Bishop all would be to betray Pagany's friends and cohorts. Peaceful and kind, they blended into the natural world in comforting ways, ways that Christians didn't approve of.

"Ah," Ceolwulf said. He knew Leova's mother did not serve his Christ, and he had often thought that she instead served pagan believers, worshipers of trees, lovers of the dark of the moon. Carefully, he questioned Hilda. "Tell me about these visits. Did these friends have names? How did they entertain you?"

"Pagany called them *auncient woones*—out of respect. When we visited them, they told old stories about people from over the seas...people who settled on an emerald isle and built shrines and temples."

She decided to share one other bit of information. "Some of the *auncient woones'* stories didn't sound so different from your tale of Judith; their stories often spoke of evil enemies and strong women who led their people to victory. Some, even like what my mother does, tended the bodies of the dead who, in fact, were sometimes not really dead."

Ceolwulf indignantly pulled himself up and addressed the girl firmly. "My child, there's a great difference between their old stories and ours. Their stories might have had a bit of truth once, though I doubt it, but they assuredly are true no longer. Our stories are still true and will remain so until the end of time."

Hilda did not agree, but she held her tongue—as Leova would have done.

After a moment, Ceolwulf spoke again. "What else did they do? Did they only tell stories?"

Hilda forgot her caution as she remembered the excitement she'd felt as a child.

"The *auncient woones* sprinkled tree leaves over us and burnt sweet-smelling sticks. Then they chanted tunes in a strange language."

33

The bishop nodded, encouraging her to tell more.

"Once they made marks in the dirt and read them, marks that looked just like lines and crosses, not like the words in books or on stones in the graveyards. And the oldest of the women looked at my hands and traced the lines in my palm with reddened fingernails. She told me things about the future...."

Hilda stopped, seeing the disapproving look on Ceolwulf's face.

"I didn't take any of what she said seriously."

"What did she tell you, my child?"

"That I would give birth to a line of powerful leaders who would bring peace to the people, but that I would only find my peace through old words. Preposterous is it not?"

The question was meant more to please the Bishop than to disparage the prediction. Hilda did not want to believe the prediction preposterous; she cherished it while outwardly ridiculing it.

The Bishop, however, frowned and changed the subject. "Did you and your friend not learn how to read? Were there no books and writing and reading materials at the hall?"

"One of the men who served Leova's father spent some of his early years in a monastery. He could read manuscripts—though we had only two or three. He could also read the letters covering the old marker, too."

"Marker?"

"It stands just outside our chapel. A tall stone covered in writing and in pictures of the Lord Christ and his friends. The writing isn't all the same." Her words took on a higher level of enthusiasm. "Some letters, he told us were of the church, but some were of an older time." She smiled shyly, "As much as I loved the images, I loved the letters more. Often I'd trace them with my finger, wishing I knew what they said. The writing seemed like magic to me, containing secrets which would be revealed only to those who could read them." She paused, "Are there such stones at my father's hall?"

Ceolwulf nodded assent. "Highhear also has manuscripts and books too that you can learn to read—as your mother has."

He continued his questioning: "Did you have a chapel and a priest at Lothlar? And other holy Christians?"

Politely, Hilda prepared to answer, but she found herself irritated by the Bishop's tendency to ask two questions, the second always making the first seem more serious. It felt a bit like a trick.

"We had a small chapel…." She faltered knowing the next answer would displease him. "But we had no regular priest. Sometimes a group of priests would come and stay to baptize the children, perform other rites, and hear confession."

Ceolwulf smiled. "Perhaps I need to return to Highhear with you—begin your Christian instruction. Your sainted mother may be too busy to serve as your teacher."

Hilda, horrified as she was at the idea, wondered if there was some irony in his statement. She couldn't help hoping that the old man would decide to stay at Buxton, the monastery where they planned to stop for the evening. That probably quite silent place seemed more suited to him than the halls of her home. To her great relief, Ceolwulf bowed his head slightly in her direction and fell back to join the conversations of the men behind them.

Relishing the quiet, Hilda saw before her that the road began to rise quite rapidly. The little troop was forced to slow down so that it took some time for them to arrive at the summit where they could finally see their destination.

Outwardly, Buxton resembled more the lord's farmstead they had just left that morning than the important spiritual center that Ceolwulf had said it was. Sheep and several cows grazed on the grass, chickens hunted for food, and a few pigs rooted around in the dirt before doors. Two young boys, clothed somewhat like the bishop, chopped wood, their robes blowing in the wind.

Nothing looked particularly holy.

Pulling up beside her again, the Bishop, pointing to the young boys, announced that they were all acolytes. "Many come to the monasteries when they are quite young, just as the greatest of them all, the Venerable Bede—a man of great blessedness and learning—came to his own monastery when he was only seven."

He looked at the buildings before him quietly, then told Hilda, "I, too, came to my monastery when I was quite young. I saw my mother and father only twice after that." Hilda detected a note of sadness and loss in his voice. Looking sternly at her, he added almost as a defense: "The members of our community serve as my family. We work together, pray together, and learn together."

On the grounds of the monastery, other young acolytes weeded an herb garden, several others milked cows in the barn, and one frail young man tended an oven from which odors of baking bread arose.

"When do they have time to learn to read?" Hilda wondered to herself.

As she dismounted, Hilda found herself being greeted by a motherly woman who emerged from the door. After a gentle kiss, the woman introduced herself.

I'm Abbess Edyth—your mother's aunt by marriage. I am so pleased to welcome you, my lady. Buxton's quarters are rather stark, not the luxury you're used to," Abbess Edyth added as she grasped Hilda's arm and led her through the monastery foregate. "We're a simple people who lead a simple, unadorned life."

Hilda wasn't convinced. Edyth wore a cloth-of-gold habit, and her arm bracelets and the hair clips that held her veil in place were also wrought of gold. However, the rooms to which Abbess Edyth led them were as simple as she had foretold. Hilda's room contained an unadorned bed with a cross on the wall above it and a small table on which she saw a bowl of steaming hot water.

"Evening services begin at six," Abbess Edyth informed her guest. "Dinner afterwards in the refectory. Until then, you have time for prayer and contemplation." After a gentle pat on the shoulder, she left the room.

Hilda found she could uncover nothing she wished to contemplate—or pray about. Throwing a cloak around her shoulders, she quickly found an outside door and entered a quiet cloister. The group of nuns who walked there stared at her openly, but said nothing. Through the opening at the far end of the cloister, she could see trees and the courtyard through which they had entered Buxton's gates. Feeling a strong compulsion to leave the monastery buildings, she put her head down and rapidly walked through the cloister, into the courtyard, and out the monastery gate toward the newly ploughed fields.

On the edge of the field, the soft ground yielded beneath her feet. She removed her shoes to better enjoy the warm, yielding earth. The sun was moving toward the western horizon, that horizon which she had been moving away from for two days now. What lay to the east for her? She sighed, realizing how frightened she was by the unknowns of the life waiting for her. She imagined that her parents would want her to marry. Leova's parents had spoken to both of them about marriage, but marriage had seemed far off and unreal to them. Perhaps now it no longer was.

"We will not force you to marry against your will," Leova's father had said to his daughter. Hilda could only wonder if her parents owned similar thoughts. It seemed that she did have much to contemplate. Being forced to return home brought more to the fore than she had wanted to think about.

In her musings, Hilda had reached the end of the field and, absentmindedly, she turned back toward the monastery, detouring to walk up a small hill and through the tall trees which bordered the monastery grounds. Sighting a tree with branches which dipped almost to the ground, Hilda impulsively climbed up using a lower branch as a step. When she was about ten feet off the ground, she lowered herself onto a wide branch, pulling up her gown so she could straddle the branch comfortably and lean back against the trunk. She giggled in remembrance at how often Leova and she had done the same in several trees left standing within the staked barriers of Lothlar. Climbing a tree was one of the first things she had taught her friend.

Below her, Buxton spread out, its buildings all connected by covered walkways. In the cloister, several groups of women clustered. On the opposite side of the chapel was another cloister occupied by men. On both sides, the occupants held what, at a distance, looked like a book; these seemed to provide a point for conversation, some of it quite animated. The scene was at once familiar and strange. The books and reading were not at all part of her life, but all the activities she knew so well from Lothlar were carried on here. Servants and novices carried baskets and trays between the kitchen and another large building which must be the refectory. Blacksmiths worked outside the barns, and small children combined their play with a very real effort to stay out of the paths of those who worked. A mystical sense of peace brought her calmness.

A movement from the barn caught her attention. Two young peasants, a pretty girl and an eager boy, tumbled over each other in the hay. As she watched, the boy pulled his companion to him closely, one hand pushing her against his body, the other buried in her long, tangled hair. As they kissed, Hilda felt she should not be watching, but still her eyes stayed glued to the barn. The young girl's sturdy legs wrapped about her companion's and his hand slipped under her gown. Hilda knew from Gwynned that men and women "came together" to produce children; she'd sometimes wondered exactly how that came about. Now she suspected that the two in the barn must be "coming together," and the scene became even more fascinating. She leaned forward to see better, but at that moment, the peasant girl rolled away from the boy and taking his hand, she led him out of eyesight. Hilda felt cheated.

The bells began to toll. Then the sound of soft voices emerged from the chapel, growing in strength as they reached Hilda's ears. As it filled the air around her and beyond, quietly filling all the space, the music promised beauty and peace—and freedom. Back in the small room and in the high-walled cloister, Hilda had felt suffocated, trapped. Now, she felt somehow released by the music and the scene below her. She shook her head sadly.

"I feel this way only because I'm up in a tree, on a beautiful day, but I can't stay here. Life won't let me."

The voices faded away; the bells began to toll once again.

Supper that evening marked, even more than the service at vespers, the rigidity of monastery life. Both in the church and in the refectory, women sat on one side, men on the other. Monks read from a large, beautifully bound manuscript on the altar, and a priest prayed in what she knew to be Latin, the language of the church. But he also used words of the people to tell the story of God's people whose flight through parting seas toward a promised land proved they were chosen. Hilda's attention often wandered and she tired of the voices of men—the women never spoke except to respond. However, the musical chanting by a choir of young boys succeeded in bringing her somewhat back to the mystical sense she had experienced sitting on the branch of a tree. When they sang, she felt a presence she had only rarely felt in her previous life and that brought comfort to the young woman who found herself moving farther and farther away from the life she had known.

After breakfast the following morning, her curiosity urging her on, she realized she wanted to see a little more of the monastery before continuing her journey. The day before she had noticed an outbuilding whose many windows made the inside almost as bright as the outside. Inside, rows of monks and nuns, not separated from each other as they had been in the church, had bent over individual wooden tables holding large, partially unrolled sheets of some unknown substance. Now Hilda moved closer and slipped quietly just inside the doorway, curious about their endeavors. Everyone— young men, elderly monks, novices, and wimpled sisters— concentrated on copying the words from inscribed sheets onto the blank sheets lying next to them. Shifting her position silently so that she could peer over the shoulders of the young man nearest her, she gasped a bit at what she saw on the page. Startled, the young man turned.

"Would you like to read, Princess?" he inquired politely.

"He assumes I can read," Hilda thought to herself, wishing with a passion that she could.

"No, no thank you," she replied. "I just wanted to watch for a minute. I'm sorry I disturbed you."

He moved so that she could better see the page he worked upon, and its beauty filled her with awe. She could see faint lines that appeared to guide the writer as he produced a series of letters. But it was the page from which he was copying that filled her with awe. Intertwined flowers, leaves, and what looked like dragon heads and curved bodies, in shades of rose, green, deep blue, and even gold, circled almost totally around the edges of the sheets before the young man, enclosing the already written words. Her swift intake of breath as she absorbed the page caused the young man to look up at her. He smiled at her and went back to his work, carefully forming a group of words with some projecting above the line and some dipping below it. He then dusted the wet ink with a powder. He looked up and smiled, "As you know, My Lady, the powder speeds up the drying." In her mind, Hilda replied: "No, I didn't know that."

But mainly she found herself longing to be able to understand what was written on the page. "Magic," she thought. "Words are like magic. Words are magic."

"Would you like to read one of the manuscripts, my dear?" Abbess Edyth, who had come to stand behind her, spoke quietly, causing Hilda, caught off guard, to jump.

"Yes, very much...but," she shook her head in embarrassment, "I don't know how."

The Abbess pursed her lips disapprovingly. "I'm afraid that your education has been severely lacking!" Then—seeing Hilda's embarrassment—her tone changed, and she added soothingly. "We can remedy that soon enough. Would you like to come to our scriptorium and begin lessons?"

"Yes, thank you, but...," Hilda faltered, not knowing how to remind the Abbess that she had to return to Highhear. At that moment, Berghorf stepped in the door.

"Time to set out once more, My Lady."

Hilda feeling grateful that she didn't have to discuss the matter further, hurried to join him. Abbess Edyth followed her out of the scriptorium and into the courtyard to bid her farewell.

"Think of us when you return home, child." The older woman smiled and kissed her on the forehead, "I'll pray for the time when you come again—for a much longer stay."

Abbess Edyth's words and the experiences at Buxton stayed with Hilda throughout the day, and even polite conversation from Berghorf and Ceolwulf failed to distract her from the confusion she felt. Never had she questioned the life she led. Her only fear had been marriage—and not because of any fear of men, but because marriage seemed to demand the end of her girlhood life. Pagany's light discipline had never constrained what she thought of as her freedom. She and Leova dutifully learned what maidens had to learn. While she didn't welcome the prospect of spending her life as the mistress of a great hall like Lothlar or Highhear, she had no vision of any other life.

At the monastery, she'd had two very different visions of life. One, as she had stared at the sheets of words and drawings, had filled her with an unknown sense of possibilities, but possibilities enclosed by lines, and the other, as she had sat on the branch of a tree, had filled her with a complete lack of constraint and some sense of the power to guide her own future decisions.

"My own decisions," she laughed at herself quietly. "*Now* I will leave the gates of the monastery. *Now* I shall climb a tree! *Now* I'll watch a scribe form letters!" How small her decisions and her freedoms had been, she was beginning to recognize.

After two days on the road and the taste of freedom that her very small adventure within the grounds of the monastery had hinted at, Hilda, now eighteen, found herself questioning—for the first time—what her life as a woman would entail. She and Leova had often pushed against Pagany's and Bertram's demands that they behave as befitted girls of their standing. And they'd taken great pleasure in defying Gwynned's attempts to keep their hair under wimples and their skirts clean.

"*Youngling!*" the harried maid would cry when she came across Hilda kneeling in the courtyard to investigate the new chicks. "Get up! Get up! Look at your dress. Do I need to beat you?"

Hilda had looked at the dirt-covered gown, but instead of being properly chagrined, she only grinned at her nurse. Gwynned never carried out her threats.

With great effort she and Leova had managed to maintain the "decorum" asked of them when visitors feasted at the hall, or when the priests came to perform their duties. Downcast eyes and quiet voices could be held when you knew that you didn't have to keep up the charade once the guests left. And both of them always recognized that it was far more difficult for Hilda to rein in her energy than it was for Leova to whom the strictures seemed more natural.

However, the same trip that found her climbing a tree also had made her aware that she now had come of age, and the temporary restraints she'd practiced as a child were becoming the permanent propriety expected of a woman—and a princess.

"A princess." she whispered to herself. "What do I know about being a princess?" And suddenly she laughed. She knew what a princess should do and why she should do it. She just didn't want to be a proper woman, much less a princess—a grown woman who would have to marry and run an estate and be polite even when she didn't want to be. She might as well be a nun.

"No," she reminded herself. "That life might free me from having to greet warriors and their wives, but it would also mean an even stricter set of rules. Every hour of the day controlled. Women forbidden to speak with the men they lived with except in the course of work. No marriage, no children...."

Snapping back from her musing, she reminded herself that she wasn't ready for marriage and children.

"Home. I'll get home and my father will help me...." She shook her head. How could a man she hadn't seen in eight years possibly help her make decisions about her life?

And so her thoughts continued to turn through the journey. As always, she missed her friend and confidant. "Leova would know what to do. I need to talk to her—she would understand."

The land grew flat, and small stretches of marsh, thickly grown with reeds and cattails, appeared beside the road. At times the water spilled into their path and the horses sloshed through mud, causing streaks of earth to darken the folds of Hilda's skirt. Short trees clustered here and there. Unlike the tall-trunked trees surrounding Lothlar, their wiry branches began at the very ground, almost like bushes.

Hilda became ever more anxious to reach her old home, gripped by a conflux of fear, curiosity, excitement, and wonder.

When Berghorf pulled his large-boned horse up alongside hers, she noticed that he had shed some of his armor, wearing only the short woven burnie over his shirt.

"No spear or shield, cousin?" Hilda teased. "Are we so far from danger?"

"We near home, little one. Traveling among friends now."

"Our enemies are really gone?" she asked. "What if they secretly return?"

Berghorf appeared to take her question seriously instead of dismissing it or addressing her as "little one." "Hilda, it's not likely they'll return. They were firmly routed."

"Tell me about that," Hilda insisted. "We never received word at Lothlar—or they hid it from me—as adults do to protect children."

He looked at her curiously, not really understanding how she could know nothing about the battles that had filled his life. "Alright," he began slowly, trying to decide where to begin. "After seeing you safely to Lothlar, your father found that in his absence, the Danes had taken Highhear. Without a base or supplies, he found himself fighting covertly—more like an outlaw than a lord."

Hilda gasped to think of her father—who had been the law of the land—as a man outside the law."

Even though he heard her gasp, Berghorf did nothing to reassure her. Hilda was secretly glad, for she wanted and probably needed to hear the whole story in order to feel at least somewhat prepared for her new life.

"Lord Ecgbert and the small troop that accompanied you to Lord Bertram's would strike unexpectedly and, as his raids captured supplies and weapons from the enemy, others joined him, even men from those lands known as Mercia—some once loyal to other rulers who had laid down their arms and paid tribute to the conquerors." He laughed scornfully, "Cowards! As your father's band of warriors grew, he became bolder in attacking the enemy strongholds. Eventually, knowing of his success, the troops from the south sought out his help."

"But what of the cynges and lords who remained and paid tribute?" Hilda inquired. "Did they rise and join my father?"

Berghorf tensed. Not even scornful laughter came from his lips. "No, in revenge, the invaders killed all those who thought the tribute they paid would keep them safe. Fools! They paid a price for trusting the enemy!"

He fell silent for a time, and Hilda, sensing how disturbing these memories must be, held her tongue until he chose to speak again.

Shaking himself, Berghorf returned to his story, smiling a little at its happy ending. "Now your father controls all the surrounding lands, and the people remain fiercely loyal to him—farmers, peasants, sheepherders, and even the sons of those dead rulers who deserted him."

"And you, Berghorf, did you fight alongside my father?"

"From the very beginning. As sister-son to your father, just as you were fostered by Lord Bertram, I was fostered by my uncle, your father. Our families protected each other. My brother helped you escape."

"Will I meet him at Highhear?"

"No, no no...he's gone, killed—in the early skirmishes against the invaders." Berghorf fell silent.

"I'm so sorry," Hilda sighed. The two, riding side by side on their horses, dropped into silence. She was beginning to understand that many men had died while she played as a child, unaware of the conflict outside Lothlar's gates. She had, however, often recalled the one scene of battle she had witnessed at the age of six. Something had always bothered her about the escaping enemy. "Berghorf," she asked after some time had passed, "I remember only a bit about the night I was brought to Lothlar, but Leova told me that an armed warrior tried to carry me off after I slipped off my father's horse. Who might that man have been? Why would he have tried to take me?"

"You do not need to know, little one," he declared, turning to her. "It serves no purpose for a woman-child to know the business of the father."

Sparks flew in Hilda's eyes. "I'm no longer a child. You will tell me now." She pulled herself straight in her saddle, determined to show she no longer needed to be protected. "I order you to."

But her stance had an effect on Berghorf that she did not expect. It almost seemed to Hilda that he quashed a laugh; with some effort she quashed an angry retort.

"Perhaps, dear cousin, you are right." he soothed. "However, I swore an oath and may not decide for myself whether to tell or not tell. Your question is for your parents, not for me."

And with that, he slapped his horse's reins gently and pulled ahead of her, falling in with his men and leaving her more embarrassed at her behavior than angry at his refusal to answer her question.

The day passed slowly. After the troop had eaten a quick lunch, the road began to climb steadily. At times the path, obviously a much-used one, narrowed and the horses were forced to move single file. One of Hilda's female attendants began to speak excitedly to a companion about the road. "Here, this road; it ever been here." Hilda listened with interest attracted by the woman's knowledge of the antiquity of the path underneath her feet. "My father comes along this a way through the hills, delivering wood to weavers. He said it be called the Pennine Way, and these" she waved her arms at the scene before them, be the Pennine Hills." Because it was old, Hilda liked the path more than the other roads and ways they had traversed. As she bounced along on her mount, she pondered her love of the old: the pagan ways of the *auncient woones*, the beauty of the manuscripts, even the strange letters on stones and crosses.

Berghorf pointedly, but politely, had deprived her of his company, leaving her to converse with Ceolwulf and the two women who had been assigned to be her attendants. Both sets of companions were unsatisfactory. Ceolwulf spoke of little other than her mother's saintly nature. He only left the topic to ask questions about her foster parents and the manner in which they raised Hilda and Leova. Hilda found herself disturbed by the unstated disapproval that her answers produced. Her attendants whom she had overheard speaking of the path—one her own age and the other much older—had little to say to her once the three of them had spoken briefly about life at Lothlar and Highhear. The girl proved

45

too shy to laugh at the stories Hilda told, and the woman seemed more interested in Hilda's position in the kingdom than in her life at Lothlar. Again, Hilda was brought face-to-face with the realization that lives differed in ways that had never truly penetrated her awareness. Consequently, during the intervals when the path narrowed, Hilda was pleased that Ceolwulf was silenced for a time and that she did not have to make any attempts to talk to her companions.

Toward evening, after rounding a sloping ridge of hills, they reached a small village, defined by two rivers visible off in the distance where they joined and became one. Berghorf had told her earlier that the people of the town, Oderesfelt, were her father's loyal retainers. Hilda felt almost overwhelmed when they rushed out to greet her as though she were a returning hero. She realized that she did not care for attention based solely on her birth; that seemed to her quite undeserved. Once she alit from the steed, the crowd carefully guided her to a table laden with food and drink. Although tired and aching from unaccustomed horseback riding, her body feeling pain and longing for rest, Hilda found herself happily enjoying the food, watching the dancing, and—much to Berghorf's distress—imbibing far too much of the honey beer served with the evening meal. Giddy with the fun, she forgot the cares of the morning and surrendered to her need for distraction. She lost track of the passing hours until finally she gave way to her exhaustion and allowed herself to be led to a small hut and put to bed. On the previous two nights, her dreams had been troubling. After Ceolwulf's tale at Lord Broadheath's she'd been haunted with staggering tyrants, severed heads rolling on the floor, and women struggling under the burden of outsized finger nails. At the monastery, ogres, foreign cynges and great bishops had passed through her dreams, and in between those frightening beings, couples rolled through the hay and gigantic trees entrapped her in their branches. But this evening, warmed by the love of her people and free from thoughts of tomorrow, she dreamed that she joined dancing peasants and spun around with them until she fell to the ground, laughing and happy for the first time since she had left

Lothlar and her friend Leova.

The next morning Hilda woke up early, excited from the moment her eyes opened because before this day was out, she would see her parents again, be back in her own hall, her own home. She felt a tinge of apprehension as well. Not knowing what awaited her in that home, one side of her nature wanted to stop time as much as the other side wanted the day to go by quickly.

Out the uncovered window, Hilda could see and hear people moving about. As she watched, a young girl began strewing kernels of corn about the yard, causing a noisy racket as the chickens rushed to reach the grain before it could be snatched up by the hordes of small birds swooping out of the trees. The larger chickens made short rushes at the birds who only hopped or flew quickly to the other side of the yard. In the background, several cocks crowed. And far down the road, Hilda could espy a sheepherder moving out into the fields with his dog and flock. Human voices began to call greetings and give orders; soon the entire village would be awake.

"It's time to move on," she whispered to herself softly.

Berghorf sensed her impatience, but was unhurried. "Be patient, my lady; our ride today will not be so long; we needn't rush."

Hilda paced unhappily as the horses were fed and watered, and squirmed on her bench while the others enjoyed what seemed to be an unusually leisurely meal offered by their hosts. When she recognized that her horse had been saddled, she accepted the strong arm of one of the villagers and mounted it. The horse seemed as eager as she, and she found herself holding it back.

At long last, the travelers began to mount their horses, but still the party lingered, discussing the route, speculating about the chances for rain, and just making plans for the return to their homes. Finally, irritated and impatient, Hilda ceased restraining her horse and guided it through the group and into a lead position.

"Let us be on our way," she ordered, addressing no one in particular. "I should like to be home before nightfall."

This attempt to exert her authority made Berghorf finally notice her anxiety and give the signal to proceed. Then he came up alongside her and rode silently for a while. Hilda knew he was going to say something quite soon. She had behaved more like a spoiled child than like a lord's daughter. In order to avoid apologizing for her behavior, she decided to reveal the plan that had come to her as she'd waited for the journey to begin.

"A lone rider can make better time than a group, is that not true?" she asked innocently.

"Usually that's the case," he replied. "But only fools—or the desperate—would travel alone. The only safety on the roads is in numbers."

"If, as you assured me, our enemies have been routed, why can't a traveler...why can't *I* ride out by myself?"

He looked at her, astonished at the suggestion.

"You're the daughter of a Lord. You, of all women, need to let us protect you. Our enemies may be gone, but other men, dangerous ones, haunt the woods and the wayside."

"I'm not afraid. So far the people we've met along the road have welcomed us; there's been no sense of danger."

"Don't be a child." Berghorf retorted. "Don't you realize that you've been surrounded by guards who would cut down anyone who dared to harm you?"

"I'm not a child!" Hilda cried, then realized how much like a child the statement made her sound. Berghorf did not answer, so Hilda tried a different tack.

"Berghorf," she argued, "That's true—I've been guarded—but I'm not used to the constraints placed on adults. Must I immediately become an adult? Change on a trip of three days from a girl without responsibilities to a young woman who must take her place as a person of authority? Before I take my place as the true Princess of Highhear, I'd like to be free. I want to arrive at Highhear on my own, see it before I must take over the duties I know I face."

"Alone?" he asked. "Ride alone to Highhear?"

"Yes. Arrive not as a princess, but as an ordinary traveler. Go among the people without all the guards, without the expectations."

"Why?" Berghorf asked, genuinely confused. "What do you expect to learn?"

"I'm not quite sure what I expect. Or if 'learning' anything is my goal." She shook her head and laughed quietly. "I just want—need—to be on my own this last time."

Berghorf turned to her and asked curiously, "Did you and Leova roam about freely at Lothlar? Did you set off on excursions beyond the wall any time you pleased?"

Hilda felt torn. She and Leova had been outside the walls on "excursions." Her lack of fear could be partially credited to the humble but kind souls they'd encountered on those trips to the *auncient woones*. But they'd been accompanied by Pagany and gone in secret. To tell might reassure Berghorf that she had been among the people without guards and survived. However, to tell would also be a second betrayal of Pagany's and the *auncient woones'* trust. She already regretted telling Ceolwulf of their visits: he was far too interested and far too critical of their ways. Perhaps it was best to remain silent about the trips into the woods, concentrate on her own feelings.

"This trip has shown me so much more about the world than I ever expected. I never realized why one might want to get out of the hall. Now I know, and...," she looked at him pleadingly, "Don't confine me, please, not now."

One look told her that her words had not changed his mind, so she tried again. "Aren't there things you would like to do but can't because you're my father's sister-son?"

Berghorf was silent for a moment, and then began to speak quietly. "Much I would like to do is prevented by my position in your father's court. But my life—and yours—allows far more freedom than most people have. Look at the people we've encountered on the way. The priests and nuns go to services eight times a day, and in between prayers they work the land or create goods that the world will buy. And even though they are in a community, they are essentially alone. If the new church rules I've heard prelates discussing come to pass, those who are married will have to give up their loves and their children. Consider the peasants we have met on our trip. Of course they welcome you, it's a chance to leave off their constant work, which they do to pay their dues to their lord and feed their families. Sometimes I find it remarkable that they do greet us so gladly. You know, even in the worst of times, the dues come first. Even if families go without!"

His voice had risen as he spoke, showing a passion Hilda had not known he possessed. However, sensing that he might have gone too far, Berghorf stopped, and looking her directly in the eye, said gravely, "Everyone suffers confinement. Look at the possibilities of the position that God has granted you, not the limitations."

And then he was quiet.

Hilda rode along, silenced but not relieved of her warring emotions. She'd never been good at following rules that she deemed unfair or unwarranted. And Bergdorf's demand that she stay within his protection seemed to her most unwarranted—and quite unwelcome. Her experiences so far had revealed no great peril. The people they'd met along the road had been welcoming and eager to provide everything from food to shelter. However, she reminded herself—they knew who they were entertaining. One of the major obstacles to leaving her guards behind, she suspected, was not that she was royal but that she was a woman. Had she been a lord's son instead of a daughter, she'd suffer little resistance.

Yet she knew that if her adventure shouldn't work out, Berghorf and his men would be held responsible and punished. As sure as she was that she'd be safe, she didn't want the man who had been so kind to suffer because of her actions. She shook her head to clear it of the confusion.

"How irrational I am," she said aloud.

"Sorry," said Berghorf. "I didn't hear you clearly."

"Nothing. I said nothing of value," replied Hilda, annoyed to realize that she'd actually spoken.

For hours they rode along, seldom speaking. The scenery had become unvarying: water, fens, reeds. The road flattened out and the higher hills rose now mostly to the west of them. Pleasant enough, but not as dramatic as the landscape she'd been accustomed to. As the sun moved beyond its zenith, the air warmed up and Hilda began to be lulled to sleep by the motion of her horse. She was

50

abruptly aroused from near sleep by Bergdorf's command to the riders.

"A village lies ahead," he called. "They'll give us food and a place to graze the horses. We have also arranged for them to pilot us across the river as it's too deep for us to remain on our horses. Fresh horses await us on the far shore."

But as they grew closer, the first huts they came to remained unusually quiet. No children ran to meet them; no farmer came forward to wave a greeting. Moving forward cautiously, Berghorf went ahead to investigate. Satisfied that the lack of people didn't signal the presence of danger, he waved the group closer. Not sure of what she was about to see, Hilda approached the structures.

They'd been abandoned. "Perhaps the village once extended out to this spot," Berghorf suggested. Hilda slipped from her horse, eager to look around. At one time, she saw, there had been at least five or six wooden buildings. The largest had once had a stone floor and seemed intact for the most part. The other, smaller dwellings had suffered more damage. While she could still see the walls— visible at spots but hidden by weeds in others—portions of their roofs had collapsed. Vines and weeds grew out of control. Wildflowers had gained root in crevices. Small puddles gleamed in the sunlight.

"What was this place?" Hilda asked, looking at Berghorf for answers.

He merely shook his head, as mystified as she was about the small compound. "On our trip to Lothlar we passed by here, but did not realize the site is deserted."

As they waited for those who would ferry them across the river, they wandered around, looking for clues that might reveal some history and speculating about the decaying properties. The buildings were too large to be simple houses, but not extensive enough to be the buildings for a lord. While a square building with high walls could have been a barn, the doors would never have accommodated animals or a blacksmith's forge. Finally, her curiosity getting the better of her, Hilda ventured into the largest of the structures, a long narrow building almost completely devoid of windows. The only light came from the fire hole in the ceiling. In the semi-darkness, she could see that little of the former inhabitants' belongings remained. As she poked about, however, she came across small inscribed stones, carefully arranged in a circle. She recognized them almost immediately: the *auncient woones* had used similar stone-inscriptions to foretell her future. Pagany had told her that the inscriptions were in the ancient runic language.

"*Auncient woones...?*" She knelt and touched the stones carefully. They weren't embedded in the dirt floor like other objects—cracked cups and broken stools lay half buried in debris but the stones stood out, clean and ready for use. "They weren't left here that long ago," she thought. Something must have caused the women who used them to flee—otherwise they'd never been left behind. Picking up one of the stones, she rubbed it, almost a caress; "Whose fortune did you tell," she whispered as she dropped it into the small bag at her waist.

Ignoring Bergdorf's urging her to return to the waiting troop, Hilda realized that the end of the room had been destroyed by fire. The soil was mixed with ashes and charred pieces of wood. Aimlessly she stirred up the pieces of the conflagration with her foot. As she did so, the wind suddenly picked up and began blowing debris about. Looking outside, she could see that the wind was causing the water on the community's small pond to roil about. Clouds rushed across the sky, blocking the sun and threatening rain. She pulled her cloak closely about her as the air began to chill. She felt quite alone.

Ceolwulf, who had not been at her side most of the day, came up behind her and paused seeing how deep in thought she was. After a moment he spoke quietly, "Princess, we need to journey on."

Closing her eyes as the wind swirled bits of dust and ashes into her face, she bowed her head and closed her eyes, not quite ready to leave this strange place. When she opened her eyes, she found herself staring at an oddity in the midst of the dust and ashes. Filled with curiosity, she brushed away the debris and picked up a piece of parchment much like that the scribes had been adorning in the scriptorium she had briefly visited. Though burnt around its edges, it contained the readable remains of writing.

The old priest looked at the scrap she held.

"Is that the only remains?" he asked.

She handed him the scrap of parchment and he examined it closely. "Not enough left to know what book it came from. The writing resembles Latin..." he mused. "Remember the manuscripts that you saw at the monastery?" he asked as he handed the piece back to her.

"Of course!" Hilda replied. "My mother once told me of a monastery destroyed by the invaders. Is this place the one she spoke of?"

Ceolwulf nodded. Hilda remembered how frightening the anger in her mother's voice had been. Alfa had endowed the monastery. "Now it's just a heap of ashes and desecrated stone," she lamented. "Nothing else remains!"

Seeing the destruction about her, Hilda became conscious of the loss her mother must have felt. But she knew, too, how much more distressed her mother would have been to know that what she considered "pagan rites" had been enacted in this space. Without thinking, she stuffed the stained page into her waistbag, joining it with the stone she had previously taken, and left the shell of the building.

Soon they could see across the wide river crowds of people waving and calling to them. It was not long before several rafts appeared, poled along by men who jumped onto the ground, smiling and holding out their hands in greeting. "We will care for your horses," one told them; "come along to the other side." Hilda was reassured by discovering several makeshift seats on the raft. Berghorf stood beside her with his hand lightly on her shoulder as the raft inched across the water.

"However will the horses come across?" she asked.

"The men of the village will attend to them; there are fresh horses for us on the other side, horses we left there to recover now on our way back," Berghorf assured her. "But they will bring our saddles and horse gear over for us."

"Here they come!" cried several young boys and girls as they ran down the road to greet them. A company of peasants and farmers soon joined the children, some shouting "Welcome," others merely smiling with pleasure.

The morning had been long, and the unexpected discovery of the remains of the deserted monastery had, strangely, left her uncomfortable and ill-at-ease for reasons she could not quite grasp. She recognized and welcomed the opportunity to rest.

For a second time on the journey, Hilda sat at a farmer's table and partook of food and drink. After eating her fill, she felt drowsier than ever and, in a most un-princess-like manner, put her head down on her arms, and promptly fell fast asleep at the table.

When he observed his exhausted charge, Berghorf knew they needed to let her rest. Ceolwulf also needed a chance to recover from the day's ride. So the warrior invited his troop to relax and rest, then retired to a haystack, removed his burnie, lay back and, like Hilda, fell asleep almost immediately.

Hilda awoke with a very unladylike start, not sure immediately where she was. She rubbed her cheek where her head had been nestled in her arm, and looked about while recalling the river crossing that had brought her to this place. Around her, everyone had succumbed to the warmth of the day and the calming effects of the huge meal they'd been served. The troupes slept under the trees and even the animal world appeared lethargic. On the hay stack, her cousin snored peacefully. She recalled their conversation of the morning, and her desire to arrive at Highhear by herself sparked again. Berghorf had made it clear that she would not be allowed to travel on her own as long as he was in charge. But he slept as did the others. She'd never have another opportunity to slip away. She rose from the table where she'd been sleeping and took a step or two into the yard. Still no one moved. It was almost as though everyone but she had become enchanted.

Determined to have her way, but guilty enough to worry about her cousin's reaction, Hilda knew she should not just leave without telling him. However, she had no intention of waking him either. Quietly, she whispered in his direction, knowing full well that he could not hear, "Berghorf, I'm going ahead. I'll be fine; don't worry about me. I need to be on my own. It's important to me."

She turned quickly and headed for the field where the horses were grazing, not knowing how long she had before someone realized she was leaving, She even smiled to herself as she recognized Ceolwulf's mule; what would he do if she took that? But even Ceolwulf had looked uncomfortable on the mule. She looked about at the horses, fearful of selecting one that might be difficult to control, for she had noticed on occasion during their trip that some horses resisted settling down even for a strong man. But how could she possibly distinguish one quietly standing horse for another? She recalled the game she and Leova had created to make a decision when they had no grounds for it. Closing her eyes, she spun around and pointed. When she opened her eyes, she saw her finger pointing at a beautiful white and black steed. She walked over to the horse and patted its rump carefully; it was unperturbed by her touch.

Fairly quickly she was able to pick out the saddle she had used in the morning as she had tucked a frayed piece of her veil under one of the buckles. She had never put a saddle on a horse and struggled even picking it up; it was far heavier than she had thought. Gathering together a strength she did not know she had, Hilda heaved the saddle up on the horse, who skittered a bit in protest but remained quiet. Patting the animal to reassure him, she quickly secured the saddle. The rest was much easier. She guided the horse over to a fence and, by half jumping and half climbing, she took her place as the rider. In less than a few minutes, she had returned to the dusty road.

Berghorf had talked about the end of their journey during the meal, and curious about what lay ahead, she'd insisted on details. She had only meant to learn landmarks that would show her how close to home she'd be, but her cousin had stressed that the remainder of the trip would follow the ancient way, skirting around some hills and crossing the moors that lay just before her father's hall. Now those same landmarks would guide her. Just as he had said, the dirt road gave off onto a side road made of great blocks of stone. At Lothlar, the storytellers maintained that stone roads had been created by the spirits who occupied the country at the beginning of time. In some places, the spirits had erected huge circles of stone as well, many times larger than average men could lift. When she had traveled south to her people's holy places, Leova's mother had seen some of these circles; and upon her return described their mass with awe. Some were built in clusters resembling stone rooms, some stood above ground, others seemed to emerge from lower regions in the earth itself. As she had listened, Hilda longed to see what Pagany had seen. "Perhaps I will someday," she whispered to the overhanging branches.

As Hilda followed the stone road east, she picked up speed, her excitement growing. The horse's hoofs rang against the stone. The landscape again changed and now she traveled through a heavily wooded forest, the road creating a natural cloister where she felt safe. The sound of horses approaching ahead, startled her, making her briefly remember Berghorf's warnings about outlaws; quickly she steered her horse into a heavily wooded stand of trees, rubbing its neck in hopes of keeping it quiet, and watched as a troop of young men galloped by, their horses' hooves ringing musically. They were too well dressed to be outlaws and since they wore no armor and were carrying only bows and arrows, she assumed they hunted game rather than men.

As soon as they had disappeared, Hilda resumed her trip. Glancing sunlight slanted through tree branches, indicating the sun's descent. Surely she could not be far from home. The appearance of the grasslands of the moors just beyond the forest confirmed her rising expectations.

Immediately she again heard people approaching, this time on foot. Once more she drew back into the shadows. She felt a bit like a spirit, a mere observer rather than a participant in life. This group was made up of both men and women, peasants driving a donkey pulling a cart filled with wood. They appeared to be in no particular hurry.

"She be'in here soon," one of the women said to another. "Wonder what she be like?"

"Think her voice like the other one, her mother?"

56

"And such a tongue, too?" The women laughed as though at some secret joke.

"Mock not Lady Alfa," one of the men warned. "She be a charitable and generous woman who grants the necessaries for both monastery and church."

The women snorted with laughter.

"She do be sharp-tongued at times," he argued, "but for such a one, we need make allowances."

Hilda laughed silently: evidently her mother had not changed much in the last eight years. Then she felt a wave of indignation. "How can they think I'll be like someone I've only seen once in eight years?" Hilda asked herself. "How could I possibly be like my mother?" She had only been with Alfa during the first six years of her life, but even then Alfa had frequently been absent, off completing some religious task or journey.

The group disappeared down the road, and when Hilda could no longer hear their talk or see them, she dismounted, realizing that the hall must be nearby or the group who had just passed would not have been on foot.

Pleased that she could not see any signs of life as she hurried down the road, she steered her horse along the path that cut through the ends of the moors. Finally, rounding a turn of the road, she stopped and drew back to where she could not be seen: before her stood the newly repaired and refurbished hall, with its heavy gates wide open so that people from the cottages could enter, but with guards ready to swing the gates closed to protect those inside. And soon, she would not only be inside, she would have a say about who could enter and who must remain outside the protection of those gates. As her father's sole heir, she would have to marry a man strong enough to maintain and defend the lands, and as the wife of the house—a role which might eventually be hers—she would have to oversee the care of the people within the walls. She trembled a bit, suddenly understanding the enormity of her position. She had been right to come to this place by herself. Standing at the edge of her village, her home, looking at her people, she knew it was time to be an adult. It wasn't an understanding she would have had if she'd come guarded by Berghorf and his men. Under their protection, she would have remained too much in the past, too much of a child, considered by others as incapable of acting for herself.

Hilda stood under the sheltering tree for almost an hour, remembering the past, trying to picture the future. When she finally decided to go forward as the sky darkened, she realized that being so set upon arriving alone and undisturbed at her father's hall was the act of a child bent on having her way. The newly aware woman, faced with the practical problems of arriving alone, recognized that it would be quite difficult to slip in unobserved. Not only was she a woman traveling alone, but her dress and bearing shouted out "noblewoman." Her home beckoned to her, but she knew that the moment she started toward the main gate she would be spotted and her chances for solitude would end.

Despite its importance, the village surrounding the hall was small. Three hundred people lived within the main enclosure or inhabited the huts built against its walls. As luck would have it, nearly all three hundred of the souls that dwelled in the village had gathered near the gates, obviously awaiting her arrival. For an instant, she debated returning to Berghorf and her escort. But then, made more stubborn than before by the desire to have at least one thing her way, she resolutely slipped back away from the gate and down a small hillock; when she could no longer see the group of people at the gate. She tied her horse within a thick clump of trees and stole quietly to the walls seeking an entrance she remembered from her childhood.

Hilda had always thought of her secret door as an escape route. She had discovered it not from the outside, but from within. While playing hide-and-seek among the vegetables with her nurse, Hilda had come across the small gate and had been delighted to discover that it led from the garden to a brook just beyond the wall. Then, as now, Hilda had loved adventure and feared nothing, so she had slipped through the tiny gateway, which seemed large for her, and followed the path to the water below. After listening to her nurse call ever more frantically, she had returned to the garden the way she had come.

Even at the age of six, Hilda knew about secrets and the importance of keeping them. Her nurse, more through love and ignorance than through any malignant motives, had filled her head with stories of raids on halls and poor maidens and their families escaping through secret gateways like this one. Hilda, imaginative child that she was, turned the tales, meant to frighten her into adhering to rules and restrictions, into great adventures. The raid would come, the family would need to escape, and she would lead them to safety before she returned to reclaim the hall.

The real raid and escape that came shortly after she discovered the gateway had been nothing like her nurse had expected nor Hilda had imagined. Forewarned of the pending attack, she and her father—her mother being at a monastery—had fled on horseback, accompanied by as many men as they could collect, long before the attackers arrived. Once the enemy had gotten close, the chase had been through the woods instead of through dark passages; and her rescue at the hands of Leova proved far more exciting than any imaginary exit into the dark countryside.

"I was ever an unknowing child," thought Hilda. "More interested in adventure than in the lives lost during the brutal journey." And it was true that even now it was easier to remember her spectacular rescue than the prior fearful day spent mired in the mud. The small gate, which had been her one free passage to the open air was unexpectedly transformed into a symbol of freedom that she was about to lose, or had already lost.

"Well," she decided, "I always supposed the hidden gate to be a means for escaping my lot, but now, if luck holds out, it shall get me in unseen to investigate my future."

She knew there was a chance that the entrance had been closed up sometime in the past twelve years, or that the bushes that grew in close profusion on each side had been pulled up to prevent trespassers from coming too close to the walls, sight unseen. Her luck, however, held. High shrubs surrounded the door, but even though they looked unclipped and wilder than Hilda remembered, the door wasn't blocked. Stepping into the little space formed by the shrub's branches, she placed her hand against the wall but hesitated

59

for a moment: she no longer knew what was on the other side. Some animal might reside behind the wall, or rats might nest there. She looked about anxiously, but a brief, cautious survey didn't reveal any nesting material and the smell from inside didn't indicate that larger beasts were in residence.

This should have been Hilda's clue that the secret entrance was an active rather than a forgotten way into the garden. Nevertheless, her excitement caused her to overlook signs of frequent coming and going. She had barely pushed herself through the small opening and into the garden when a hand shot from behind a bush, locking her arm in a ferocious grip.

Hilda found herself staring into the dirty face of a tall and gangly boy, about her own age she judged, scowling at what he obviously at first believed to be an intruder. He looked her over carefully, taking in her now-soiled dress as well as her face smudged with small lines of dirt, and then he began to nod decisively.

"Good," he mumbled. "Good."

As soon as he pronounced the words, he started to drag Hilda, too much in shock to protest, through the yard. "Quickly, quickly," he insisted when she held back.

Hilda found her voice and spoke out in a tone more indignant than frightened.

"Let me go!" she demanded. In response to the authoritative voice, the boy dropped her arm immediately. He was obviously used to taking orders. She looked at him as carefully as he had her. "Who are you? What do you want of me?"

"Sorry. Sorry, but you should have used the main gate," the boy whimpered, almost apologetically, momentarily taken back by her temper. Then, looking around desperately, he repeated, his voice conveying fright, "Quickly?"

Something in his manner made Hilda aware that, despite his physical appearance, the boy was at the moment a frightened child. "Please?" he put out his hand pleadingly.

"Where?" she whispered.

The boy, obviously realizing that she would not strike him, pointed to a small wooden building near the wall. "There," he whispered, imitating her soft sounds. "In the bur, mistress."

Hilda wasn't altogether clear as to what "mistress" he meant—some woman within, or did he refer to her? The boy was so frightened that she could not get another word from him, so she nodded and signaled that she would follow.

"I've fallen into the hands of an idiot at play," she mumbled under her breath. Suddenly the entire effort to enter her home alone seemed as silly and as childish as a six-year-old's trick rather than the awakening of her adulthood. She had to find a way to rectify her childish behavior, to behave as a princess should. But even as she straightened out her skirts and replaced her wimple, which she was carrying after it fell off, the ridiculousness of the boy's expression— half fear and half curiosity—drove away all thoughts of dignity and she began to laugh. He, in turn, quickly lost his fear and smiled rather shyly back.

"Come here," she commanded. "Tell me who you are and whom you want me to see."

The boy came obediently and stood rather nervously, but he didn't speak.

"Speak up!" she said impatiently, and then immediately regretted it when he backed away and turned to run.

"Come quickly!" he called over his shoulder. "She'll be angry!" And before she knew it, he had pushed aside the tapestry which covered the door of the bur and disappeared within.

Hilda had no intention of following. Curiosity was rapidly being replaced by the desire to extract herself from an uncomfortable predicament, but just then, the tapestry was pulled aside once again and a female voice demanded, "Come, girl. You're wasting time bein' so hung back. She needs care and you should know it. Here," the woman ordered, "take this and brush your dirty face!"

Something in the woman's tone, or perhaps the reference to her mistress, silenced Hilda. She bowed her head, as a more patient woman would have, and entered the bur determined to straighten out the matter at once.

As she entered the darkened room, her eyes went immediately to the crucifix over the bed, softly illuminated for a moment by the light from outside. Her mother's room! It had to be. Alfa always slept under the protection of Christ's cross; his broken body had always managed to both attract and frighten Hilda while, at the same time, that same broken body comforted her mother. Had the boy somehow known she was coming and brought her straight to her mother?

"That doesn't make sense," she thought. How would anyone suspect she would arrive and enter by way of the small door? Hilda's mouth curled into a smile, perhaps the prank had not been such a bad idea after all. If mother and daughter met alone like this, or with just this serving woman present, Alfa might embrace her rather than merely bestow a formal kiss as she had always done whenever they met or parted.

The smile disappeared as quickly as it had come when she saw the woman on the bed before her.

The prone figure was unmistakably her mother. The fleshy face, which had seldom entertained a smile, now appeared to be devoid of any expression and yellow from illness. Never a pretty or graceful woman, Alfa now resembled the witches that Hilda's and Leova's nurse conjured up to scare them. How could this be Bishop Ceolwulf's holy woman? For an instant, Hilda thought of the dead saint Oswald and her mother's ghastly task. Had it harmed her in some way?

"Mother!" she gasped and hurried forward.

Confusion broke out immediately. The stout woman looked up in shock.

"Mother?" Hilda questioned. The woman on the bed stared at her as if she were seeing a ghost. "It's Hilda. I've come home."

"A sign," whispered Alfa. "A sign that my sin has been forgiven!" She looked upward toward an unseen deity and gasped, "Thank you, sweet Jesus for sending this daughter, this sign before my death!" Reaching out and grasping Hilda's arm, Alfa used a

62

strength she did not seem capable of to draw the girl down close, beginning to speak rapidly with a frightening intensity.

"God has planned a marvelous mission for you, my Hilda. Saint Oswald has told me...told me, his handmaiden...." Hilda looked back at the others in the room for guidance and help. With relief, Hilda saw that a man whom she instantly identified as her father had entered the room. He stood quite still watching the scene at the bedside. In desperation, Hilda motioned to him.

"Father! Help me. She doesn't know what she's saying!" The woman on the bed tightened her grip so that Hilda cried out and turned to look back into the stricken face.

"Hilda!" her mother's raspy voice commanded attention, "You will take my place at God's work. It is God's will. I'd planned to be with you, to guide you, but our Lord has other plans—you'll be the stronger for being sent on your journey alone."

For a horrible instant, Hilda envisioned the dead saint's body, fingernails growing, soul fled to heaven. Instinctively she protested. "No. I won't. I'll not serve anyone, much less trim the nails of a body which should have long ago gone to dust!"

She struggled to release herself from the hand of the frenzied woman on the bed, and at last—his own spell broken by his daughter's cry—her father stepped forward to help her. He pried the hand of the sick woman open and after releasing Hilda, gently pressed the agitated Alfa down on her pillows.

"Hush, wife," he soothed. "The child has just come home, and you will not die this day."

Hilda noticed immediately that her father did not promise her mother that she would not die tomorrow. The caution seemed only one of delay rather than of assurance. Her mother, exhausted by her sudden outburst, allowed herself to be soothed, but her own voice overlapped the kind words of her husband.

"Promise, Ecgbert," she murmured. "Promise in front of these good folk, that you will send Hilda to Abbess Edyth. Do not let two suns set on my dead head before she goes. I have promised God and his holy mother that Hilda will serve....If you break my vow, there will be no peace for me in heaven!"

"Let's talk about it when you are calmer," Hilda's father pleaded. "The girl has but now returned home and you do not know her temperament nor her character. Why bind her life if she is not called?"

"She is called! I was told!" Alfa started to rise again, the frantic edge in her voice turning into hysteria even as her head rose from the pillow. "Swear it on your man-bond. Swear it on my deathbed!"

To her horror, Hilda saw her father falter. He cast one desperate look over his shoulder and his eyes, begging forgiveness, met hers. Then he turned to the wraith on the bed and swore. "By my honor as a man, by my power as a father, I swear thy daughter shall go to the Abbess Edyth and learn to serve our Lord."

"Two days after my death," insisted the woman on the bed.

"Two days after your death—and may that be sometime far from this day of her happy return," added the distraught husband and father. The sick woman let go of his arms and sank back on the pillows, exhausted from the effort of extracting the promise. Ecgbert held her hand for a few minutes, waiting until she closed her eyes and began to breathe a bit easier. Then he rose slowly and turned to face his angry and confused daughter.

"How could you...?" Hilda asked. This was not the homecoming she had pictured in her mind.

But before he answered, her father put his arm about her and, motioning for silence, led her from the bur. Out of deference for her mother, Hilda remained silent until they stood once more in the garden outside the hall. Then she shook herself loose from her father's arms and stood facing him, as furious as he was sorrowful.

"I will not go tend the fingernails of a dead saint!" she declared.

"You will learn to serve your God just as your father promised your mother," a deep voice avowed. Startled, Hilda turned to see a figure almost, it seemed, emerging from a mist in the shadowed doorway; Ceolwulf, it was. Hilda wondered briefly how he could have arrived so closely behind her. His words were chilling, his penetrating eyes frightening, his voice ponderous: "A promise such as this must not go unfulfilled or your father will risk his eternal soul."

"But what of me? I have not promised, nor sworn an oath."

"Child, child, be quiet a moment," pleaded her father. "I don't even know how you got here, or why you're in your mother's room. Let me see how you've grown, welcome you properly. Come with me to a quiet place where we can talk in peace."

Ceolwulf took several steps backward and turned to slip to Alfa's side as quietly as he had slipped up behind them.

Hilda allowed herself to be led once more, this time into the great hall. While not as richly adorned as she remembered, the hall somehow felt more comfortable. The subdued finery made the benches softer and the walls warmer. Her father's dogs sat near the cold hearth at the center of the room, gnawing on bones and lounging lazily. Seeing Hilda, they stood up, wagged their tails heartily and came to sniff her shoes and her skirt. As much as she loved animals, she pushed them back. She wanted no distraction from a conversation that could set a course for her life—a life she no longer felt herself in control of.

Turning to look at her father almost caused her to forget her anger. Old and vulnerable, not at all like the mighty war lord that he was reputed to be. He had aged. His beard, which Hilda remembered as black, was now marked with heavy streaks of gray, as was his hair under the heavy gold circlet that held it in place; his face, lined with creases caused by suffering and anger, told her at once that he was no longer the lordly father she remembered. Old, but she hoped not beaten, he was obviously tired, weary to the point of pain. He held out his arms, and Hilda, suddenly weary herself, moved into them. She needed comfort and so, apparently, did he. Taking her hand, he guided her toward the stone benches in the empty hall.

Hilda looked up at her father. "What's wrong with my mother?" she asked. "Was she ill when you sent for me?"

"No, child. She was well and strong and setting about the task of preparing for your arrival until three or four days ago. I no longer remember just when, but she fainted at her work and had to be helped to bed. She hasn't left it since, and as far as the healers can say, they see no end for her other than death."

"Death?" Hilda gasped. "What of? A woman doesn't die of fainting."

"She's suffered fevers and chills. Sometimes she burns so hot that she kicks off all covering and then as swiftly as the fever comes, it goes, leaving her cold enough to shake, her teeth chattering. She grows weaker daily. This day she could not leave her bed—I don't know where she found the strength to hold you to her side."

"Has it a name, this disease?" asked Hilda. "Do others suffer from it? Will everyone be struck down?"

"No, no," her father said. He began to pace distractedly, moving from one side of the great fireplace to the other, picking up objects and putting them down without really seeing them. "No one else in the hall has fallen heir to your mother's malady. She alone has been affected. Mark you how her skin is almost yellow? Her humors are out of balance, and no broths or potions have brought them back into order." He paused for a moment before facing her. "Your mother will die, and not peacefully."

Hilda moved nearer to the cold hearth, and stroked the head of a greyhound while she tried to make sense of what her father had just revealed. A short time ago she had worried that her childish prank would cause embarrassment. Now she could not help wondering if it had presaged more serious consequences. She shook off the thought; no matter how she had entered this hall, the same problems would have arisen.

"Father," Hilda said, almost in a whisper, at Lothlar there are forest women, we call them the *aucient woones*; they have remedies we know little of. Are there such women about? You could ask them to help."

Ecgbert looked at her quizzically. "Remember, my dear Hilda, those are pagans; we here are Christian."

Before Hilda could reply, the increasingly loud noises of horses and men from outside the hall distracted her. She recognized Berghorf's voice, insistent upon seeing Ecgbert, obviously fearful that he had lost his charge. Glancing at Hilda in bewilderment,

66

Ecgbert went to the door and spoke to a servant, who hurried to tell her cousin that Hilda had arrived quite safely and that he would come to welcome Berghorf shortly. Then he settled back on his bench, emotionally exhausted and obviously at a loss for words.

Hilda cleared her throat and stood, ready to explain her behavior, but Ecgbert cut short any sort of statement.

"Would you like to go to your bur?" he asked, clearly not wishing to deal with any more confusion.

"Yes, please," she said with relief, finding herself deeply in need of solitude.

"I will call one of your servants," he rose and moved toward the door, then paused. "I'm sorry, my child. I have waited so long for your return, thought about it so many days, and...." He struggled to regain his bearing. "Despite your mother's health, we will have our feast and our celebration. Go to your room, rest, and refresh yourself. I'll send for you soon."

At his call, a young woman entered, bowed gracefully before Hilda, and then—with the friendliest smile she had yet received in this hall—turned away to lead her mistress to her chamber. Hilda followed and the two women passed out of the hall, crossed the well-trodden ground of the courtyard, and into another section of the grounds where a bur had been prepared for Hilda's return. She had barely entered the small bedchamber when she found herself locked in the energetic hug of a woman she immediately recognized by warm smells and kind words.

"Hilding, my own sweet lady, welcome home!" Only her childhood nurse, Ethel, had used that name. Within Ethel's warm and long embrace, Hilda finally felt at home. A moment later, her joy dissolved and the stress of the last few days hit her full force. She began to cry, the tears running down her cheeks and onto her nurse's shoulder.

"Now, now, little one. No need to cry. You're home. All is well now."

"No, Ethel, all is *not* well." Hilda pushed back from Ethel's comforting hold, and pulling her former nurse by the hand, sat with her on the bed. As they had when Hilda was still a child, the older woman listened to the younger one not only as her caregiver but also as a conspirator. "My mother is dying. My father old before his time...and I'm...lost."

Overwhelmed once again, Hilda buried her head in Ethel's breast. Ethel, lacking any words of comfort, could only stroke the young woman's disheveled hair. Soon Hilda shook herself and looked in her beloved nurse's face, comprehending that the older woman could no longer solve her problems as she had when Hilda was six-years-old. Still, she was overjoyed to be united with her childhood nurse.

"Tell me, Ethel," she inquired earnestly, "how has it gone with you all these past years? I worried about you so much. You were so very old when I left; I was afraid that you'd died long since." Immediately, Hilda caught herself, and for the first time since seeing Ethel, she laughed.

"Oh, I didn't...." Ethel was hardly ancient; Hilda recognized that truth too late to stop her words.

"Do not worry yourself, child," Ethel laughed too. "Twelve years have passed since I was 'very old'! Even though I was 'very old,' in the eyes of a mere babe, I was not much older then than you are now." She became serious, and hugged Hilda again. "I intend to live many more years, and I do not plan to leave your side until death calls me."

Hilda returned the hug, glad once more to feel the comfort of being with her "old" servant, the companion of her childhood. "I have much to tell you, and I want to hear much from you. Please, I've heard nothing about this home of mine for the past eight years."

"How tired you must be," Ethel cut her off, just as she had when Hilda was a child. "Perhaps you would like to sleep?"

"I'm too excited to sleep, Ethel. Let me go to the hall and see the grounds. I remember so little. And my old friends, the ones I played with when I was small—I'd love to find them as well." The old nurse was not listening. Hilda became conscious that her voice was rising and that she was speaking faster and faster. She stopped herself and after taking a deep breath, pleaded simply, "Tell me...."

"There will be time for that, little one, after you have rested."
Ethel brushed away the request as quickly as she had the questions.
"Now it's time to bathe you and replace your traveling clothes with
the beautiful clothes that your women have made—you'll like them
so much!"

Ethel called in two young women who helped her strip Hilda
of her travel worn clothing. They brought hot water suffused with
herbs and sweet smells and washed her hair. In another basin they
soaked her feet; the warmth seemed to move up her legs, through
her body. Her eyelids felt heavy. Finally, they wrapped her in warm
clothing and gently guided her to the bed.

"Oh, your hair," she suddenly heard Ethel moan. "It is worse
than when you were young. Wait a moment, I need to get some
strong combs."

But when Ethel returned, her young charge had fallen
soundly asleep. Ethel smiled and dismissed the serving women.
Then she sat down on a nearby bench to gaze once again at the
beauty of the girl whom she had nursed and raised as her own. She
vowed to tell Hilda everything she needed to know—but not all she
wanted to know. Ethel had learned the value of silence long ago.
When the red-haired warriors had pillaged Ecgbert's hall, Ethel had
been visiting her family. She had returned to the hall to find the
people she served gone and the place where she had lived occupied
by men intent on stripping it of everything valuable. Only by
pretending to serve them had she been spared. She had also,
through her knowledge of the hall's architecture, been able to
secrete some of its valuables. And as soon as she could, she'd
returned to her own village and kept her silence there until Ecgbert
had regained his power. At last she could see her beloved charge
again.

Ethel's smile faded as soon as it had appeared. She knew,
only too well, the vow Hilda's mother had made. "Such a lively,
lovely lass to be locked away in a convent," she murmured to herself,
and then she too fell asleep, planning a way to stay with her young
mistress. She had lost her once; it would not happen again.

The sun had already set when a young servant girl quietly slipped into the room and shook the Princess's retainer by the shoulder. "Everyone is gathering for the feast. Soon they will want Princess Hilda," the young maidservant whispered in Ethel's ear. Ethel shook herself awake, quickly realizing that her young charge was still asleep. She hated to wake her, but knew it could not be avoided.

"Hilding. Little one. Arise, arise." Gently she patted Hilda's arm. The green eyes slowly opened and she spoke with the confusion of one who had been deeply asleep.

"My first dreamless sleep since I left Leova, my friend. I miss her so much! Why don't I dream of her?" The green eyes filled with tears.

"Yes, yes," the nurse distracted her. "I want to hear of your friend and of everything in her world, but you must now get up and dress. Your family and guests await."

It took some time for Ethel and her helpers to tame Hilda's wild hair, but soon it lay shimmering on her shoulders highlighted by jeweled combs. After helping her put on fine sandals which still smelled of fresh leather, Ethel and the two young women helped her into a light green tunic and a softly draped gown with flowing sleeves made of darker green. Ethel brought out two twisted gold brooches—inlaid with pieces of red, green, and blue enamel—and clasped the gown at the shoulders. A golden-threaded belt about the waist completed the first stage of dressing.

Hilda, accustomed to much simpler attire, found herself both pleased and annoyed at the ceremony involved in preparing for a festive evening. She stood as still as she could and endured the clucking and aaahing of her dressers. To finish her costume, they draped a sheer white scarf on her head which hung loosely to her shoulders, acting as a traditional woman's head-covering but not concealing her abundant dark hair as a wimple would. Finally, around Hilda's neck they placed a twisted gold necklace and on her arms two snake-shaped bracelets.

"Your father had the bracelets made for you for just this day, but the necklace is old, very old," Ethel told her. Your mother was given it by a hero, a very famous man in his day—when she was little older than yourself. It's called a torque."

"What a rare name for something so beautiful," Hilda exclaimed. "My mother wore it?" She couldn't imagine the stark Alfa wearing such an elaborate piece.

"No more, not since she decided to serve the saint." Ethel's voice clearly indicated that Alfa's actions were beyond understanding. "She thought to give it to the church, but your father convinced her to save it for you. *I* saved it when the enemy came!" she boasted. "For I knew its hiding place. Now you can wear it as a reminder of the old life, and your new ornaments can stand as signs for the future one."

Perplexed by her own state of mind, Hilda accepted the emblems of past and present. However, the beautiful clothes seemed to be an emblem of the burden that her status placed upon her shoulders. She shook her head to dispel these darker thoughts; refusing to become melancholy, she forcibly shifted her thoughts to the attention she had received—far more than ever before in her short life. With the beautiful clothing, the shining jewelry, came prestige, admiration, and connections to past greatness. She smiled, her heart lightened a bit. Some aspects of being a princess delighted her, she had to admit.

In the large hall, the fire burned brightly in the middle, the tables creaked under the platters of food, and the tapestries hung above all as reminders of heroes, battles, and saints long past. As she stood in the doorway and surveyed the abundance before her, Hilda contemplated the possibility that she was still dreaming.

The people gathered in the flickering firelight to celebrate her homecoming conversed happily among themselves. Those conversations gradually fell silent as, one by one, they recognized and turned to look at the young girl. Hilda, unaware of her striking beauty, stood still, not quite sure what to do. The eyes that watched her did not notice her hesitation because enhancing her beauty was an almost natural regal bearing, enhanced by glowing innocence and youth.

71

Feeling far less regal than she looked, Hilda faltered, overwhelmed by the silence. Obviously the company expected her to speak, but the usually talkative young woman found herself bereft of words. Instinctively, she turned to her nurse. When she was a child, Ethel had often helped her find the right words. Once again, feeling more like that child than an adult, she read Ethel's lips. Turning back to the throng, she said in as firm and clear a voice as she could manage, "Hail, my friends, I return with heart-felt joy!"

A loud hurrah erupted, followed by voices murmuring comments full of praise and approval. Hilda relaxed a bit, confident that she had said what a princess would be expected to say. Glancing back, she wordlessly thanked Ethel before her uncertainty took over again. Ahead of her, following the eyes of the hall guests, she saw her father seated at the primary table. She would need to cross the hall to reach him and pay him the courtesies that he was owed. As she began self-consciously to walk towards Ecgbert, he rose and came down from the dais to greet her. After kissing her lightly on the forehead as a sign of favor and love, he extended his arm to his daughter and guided her up the dais and to the seat next to him.

Hilda pulled back and looked at him questioningly.

"That's my mother's place," she said.

"Your mother wished you to take it since she could not be here," her father answered. Slowly and still reluctant, Hilda lowered herself into the chair. Her mother's wishes had the force of orders. How many more would there yet be?

That question lingered as the festivities continued and, try as she might, Hilda found it hard to fully engage in the festivities. The guests read her silence as an indication that their princess was a pensive young woman, easily lost in thought. Her father, who knew almost as little about his daughter as the people gathered around them, leaned toward his daughter, concerned and caring.

"You do not seem happy to be here, my child."

"I *am* happy, father," she assured him. It's just that....I've never had to be in this position, never had to be the lady of the hall before! I'm afraid I don't know how to act my part!"

72

"No need to act, my dear, you are the most beautiful woman these people have ever seen. And surely your soul is as good as your face is beautiful. Being a princess should not be harder than just being yourself."

Hilda smiled gratefully at her father. He could not know how awkward she felt when forced to display herself before large groups. Leova had always guided her through formal tasks, always knew what a princess should say and exactly how to say it. At this moment, she longed for Leova's help, or even just her mere presence! Grateful for his attempts to reassure her, Hilda once again dismissed her darker thoughts and turned to kiss her father's cheek lightly. He smiled approvingly and gave a sign to the synger, who had begun to regale the assembly with the old tales. While Hilda knew most of the stories, it did not matter: she loved to hear them over and over again. Listening to accounts of feasts—much like the one before her—finally overcame her pensiveness and uncovered a gnawing hunger.

"A young girl who eats like a warrior," Hilda heard one of the guests comment to his companions, as she quickly devoured almost the whole meal set before her. Too hungry to be embarrassed, Hilda ate until she was thoroughly satiated, then leaned back on the cushions provided for her comfort. Idly, she gazed out over the people before her, glad that they had begun to ignore her.

Her old nurse interrupted her reverie—and her peace.

"Hilding," Ethel prompted, "Your mother's not here, so 'tis you must pass the cup."

Hilda had passed the cup around the hall any number of times in her years with Leova, but that had been a game. This time she had to do more than play the cute child. The custom was serious. Serving the warriors present helped bind them as a community. The lady of the hall thus acted as a "peace weaver," bringing a lord's men to recall and honor their pledges to serve their lord. As Ethel backed away and returned to her bench, a young thane brought the golden cup to Hilda. She grasped it securely by the handles on either side and stepped onto the floor, circling around the table to stand before her father's seat. Proffering him the overflowing cup, she paid homage to his power and authority. Then she offered the cup to Berghorf who gave her a stern look. Hilda suspected he was quite angry with her. She then passed among the men, seated in order of their rank and position, offering the cup to each in turn. Approving whispers arose among those in the hall. This was indeed a woman worthy to be a princess! Hilda felt their approval, and she said a silent thank you to Leova, who seemed to be at her shoulder guiding her in every step and word.

Her task completed and the celebration ending, she returned to her father. "I would like to take my leave so that I can go and see mother." He nodded, and they stood together to catch the attention of the crowd. The room became quiet once again.

"I give you thanks," Hilda announced formally but earnestly, "for the happiness you have brought to my homecoming." Again cheers rose from the crowd as they watched the young princess wend her way through the hall. Once outside, Hilda set her sight on the burs that were clustered among the outbuildings, and pulling her cloak closely around her, walked toward them as fast as she could in the chilly night air.

Quietly she entered her mother's room. The candles burned alongside the great bed, casting deep shadows. Her mother's even breathing assured her that the sick woman slept. Drawing a chair next to the bed, Hilda gazed on the still face, now lined deeply around the eyes and mouth and across the forehead. No trace remained of the strong-willed woman she remembered, the woman who demanded—and got—everyone in the hall to comply with her version of religious duty. The years must have been hard for her. Yet she must have done good service to her God. Bishop Ceolwulf praised the work she had done during those years when she had stayed in one monastery after another.

Hilda laid her head on the bed, overcome with the events of the past four days. Her thoughts began to spin and exhaustion reduced her to tears. She longed for the quiet peace of Leova's hall and the soothing voice of Pagany, her foster mother. Despite the fact that she did not want to wake her mother, she found herself unable to contain her sobs. In truth, she did not really know why she was crying—everything mystified her.

A gentle hand touched her shoulder, and Abbess Edyth's voice soft voice broke into her sorrow. "Hush, my child, do not weep for your mother. Her life has been a good Christian one. God will gladly receive one who has served Him so well. She dies content, knowing that you will continue her work."

Slowly, Hilda's body ceased shaking, and she realized with horror that—unlike the Abbess had assumed—her mother had not been the reason for her tears. "Thank you, Sister, for your kind words, but I don't think I *can* continue her work." Nor, her tired brain told her, did she *want* to continue her mother's work. She shivered at the thought.

"You are cold, my dear, whispered Abbess Edyth, misinterpreting the young princess's condition, "Go to your own bed and sleep."

Wordlessly but grateful, Hilda obeyed.

The next day dawned windy and foreboding. Dark clouds sped across the skies; heavy rain came and went. Hilda woke, a bodily chill possessing her; she pulled the bedclothes closely around her and attempted to return to sleep. But in place of the peace brought by sleep, she found only the questions she had set aside the previous night: What was it her mother expected of her? Must she accede to her mother's wishes? What did she want to do? What *could* she do? Knowing the last two questions had no answers denied her any touch of comfort.

The sounds of the awakening day began in the courtyard beyond her door. Sitting up in bed, she felt dread replacing the cold in her bones. Something was wrong. Quickly she threw on the robe lying across her bed and rushed to the door of her chamber. No one seemed to notice her; no one came to help her. She pushed back what her mind and heart were telling her. The anxiety of the night before had never truly departed.

Hilda turned back into her bur and slipped into the everyday clothes she found lying across Ethel's bench. Ethel had not entirely forgotten her. Once she left her quarters, she ventured toward her mother's bur which appeared to be the hub of all the activity in the compound. As she entered the door, the healer at her mother's side glanced up and then dismissed her. Holding several small vials and bottles, the healer bent to observe Alfa who was conscious but not moving. Hilda shivered at the sight of leeches slithering in one of the larger bottles. Her mother's skin was even more yellow than it had been the previous night; her closed eyes, surrounded by large circles, were nonetheless restless, the skin of the eyelids pulsating from the movements beneath them. Her dark gray hair, matted with sweat, spread out on the pillow around her yellowed face. The face itself was a mask, unmoving, except for her eyelids, and vaguely unclean.

Alarmed by the obviously worsening condition of her mother, Hilda drew nearer, and found that the bedclothes were covered with blood. She suppressed a cry at the sight of the engorged wormlike creatures on the bedding. Everyone shifted rapidly between movement and stillness as they tended the sick woman. Periodically, several of her mother's servants attempted vainly to get her to ingest some foul-looking liquid.

"What...." Hilda started to say, but stopped short as she saw her mother's reaction to her voice. As though with one final burst of life, Alfa sat up and stretched both arms out toward Hilda.

"Come, my child, sit by me." Alfa's voice was just above a whisper. Hilda wasn't anxious to get close to all that blood, but her mother's eyes drew her to the bed. Sitting beside Alfa, Hilda felt trapped and resentful. This woman had never mothered her. She had not been there to share childhood adventures and catastrophes. Angry in spite of herself, Hilda acknowledged to herself that Alfa had been far more interested in "doing the work of the Lord" than caring for her daughter, or husband for that matter. Hilda felt faintly repulsed by the yellowed hands clutching at her own.

"Promise me," came the voice out of that mask. "Promise me."

Hilda looked up at the healer helplessly.

"Humor her," she whispered.

"Promise you?" Hilda echoed nervously.

76

"Yes, promise me you'll go with Abbess Edyth two days after I die." She stopped, distracted for a moment, and then continued urgently. "I die today. I can die after you promise."

Hilda did not want to promise this alien creature anything. She wanted to be released from the clutch of those withered, yellowed hands, her own hands struggling against her mother's grip, attempting in vain to be free of the sick woman's grasp.

"Do not be frightened my child," her mother urged, and then she smiled in a ghastly parody of the loving mother she had never been. "Embrace your destiny. Promise me."

Hilda looked around frantically at those gathered about her mother's bed. No one came to her aid. Her father looked ten years older than he had last night. He seemed to feel no connection to her at all, and she could feel no love for him. The only comforting face was Ethel's. Hilda wanted nothing more than to flee this scene, to escape without appeasing her mother. Drawing her energies together, she clenched her teeth and looked into her mother's eyes, but she could not bring herself to speak.

"Promise me!" Alfa's voice and the strident demand for compliance increased. Finally, more concerned for the mother than the child, Abbess Edyth approached and sat beside the unwilling daughter.

"At the monastery you will learn to read, to write, and to recite," she coaxed the young girl. "You can copy manuscripts and study old books. Many are the ways to serve our Lord. You do not have to take your mother's path; we will grant you the freedom to choose your own way."

It was small reassurance.

"I will not rest in heaven if you do not promise me!" her mother snapped. Then she became fearful, "My sin will lead me to damnation. To save my soul I have offered you to God!" Ceasing to struggle, Hilda focused on the frantic woman, but still she refused to speak. Her voice seemed to her the only thing over which she had control.

"Do not worry," Abbess Edyth whispered. "No one can promise another person to the Lord. Each of us must come to Him out of our own faith. Your mother made a vow which the Lord himself would not want you to keep. Just promise her that you will come with me. The rest will take care of itself."

Something rang false in the Abbess's voice, Hilda thought, but she could no longer bear the struggle. She began to gag from the smell emanating from her mother's mouth. All around, the ravages of sickness and bleeding assaulted her senses. She was trapped.

"Mother...." Even the name sounded wrong. "Rest easy," she uttered softly but unwillingly, "I promise to go with Abbess Edyth."

Alfa's eyes closed again; her breathing evened out, and she loosened her grip enough for Hilda to escape. As the sick woman lay back on her pillows, she smiled a twisted smile that lacked any resemblance to one that might be found on a saint.

"She sleeps," whispered the healer, breaking into Hilda's thoughts. Moving away from the bed, Hilda tried to stand up slowly so it would not appear as though she were running away. But she was—she wanted more than anything to leave the room; she yearned to get back on a horse and ride all the way back to Leova without stopping to rest or eat. Moving as quickly as she could, she left the room behind. No one seemed to notice.

Outside the still chilly air helped her to regain her composure. She sat, almost fell, onto a bench placed near the door. She closed her eyes, focusing on efforts to repress a need to vomit. Almost without thinking, she began to rub her belly and recite the words of an old poem which Pagany had used to help her and Leova chase pain away.

"Out little spear, if you be in here....out little spear if you be in here...Out little spear, be not in, spear!"

If Hilda shut out everything but the words, she always began to feel better. The magic—if that's what it was—began to work. At least her stomach calmed down. Her mind remained in turmoil.

That day passed in a haze. No one ate much. No one said much. Even the dogs knew to be silent. By nightfall the winds had tapered off and the setting sun sent out fingers of rays through the bare trees and into the courtyard like a blessing. Soon after, the healer stood before Hilda's father and softly uttered the words they had been expecting all day. "She has gone to her God."

As was the custom, they buried Alfa the next day. Despite the presence of all the families from the surrounding area—nobles and peasants, all Hilda would recall in later years was the dark chapel, the coffin on the altar, and the cemetery where a gaping hole received the body. She had wanted to bury her mother in the torque, but Ethel begged her to keep it for herself. "Your mother has much jewelry of her own that she takes with her. She meant this for you."

Hilda could only wonder why. What use would she have for such a piece of jewelry in a monastery? She laughed bitterly. The torque would go to the destination Alfa originally intended, a gift to God carried by a greater gift—her daughter.

Later that evening, Hilda's father appeared at the door of his daughter's chambers. He gazed in upon his sleeping daughter and sighed regretfully for the promise he had made to his ailing wife. He looked up as Ceolwulf, who had presided at Alfa's funeral, approached him.

"She must go? Is there no honorable way to keep my daughter here with me? To pass on to my own blood the land that is rightfully hers?"

"Your wife made a vow. You made a promise, as did Hilda herself. God will not be pleased if this vow and these promises are disregarded."

"But she and I promised only to ease the pain of her mother!" Ecgbert tried to argue. "Abbess Edyth assured the child that God would not hold her to a promise made under duress."

"The Abbess misspoke," the bishop snapped. "Hilda does not have to enter the order based on her mother's promise; nonetheless, she must meet her obligation to serve."

Ecgbert looked unconvinced, so Ceolwulf repeated his assertion. "I speak with the authority of God's messenger. God will not bind Hilda to the monastery for life, but she must go for at least a period of time."

"I had meant her to be my heir. To marry and assume with her husband overlordship of my lands and people." He had fought to rebuild his kingdom; he had wanted his daughter and the man she married to inherit all of it. He had hoped for grandchildren and the type of legacy that only comes from one powerful lord's passing all land and possessions to his own descendants. He now resigned himself to the loosening of that legacy.

"God moves in mysterious ways, his wonders to perform." Ceolwulf's voice was a bit gentler. "Do not try to decipher His intentions. Your lands will not be scattered. Many a lord lives longer than you—you might marry again and yet bear a son." Seeing the look on Ecgbert's face, Ceolwulf left off that argument and turned to another one. "Should your daughter choose not to return, your sister's son, Berghorf, will remain at your side to protect your land. Such an obligation needs a man capable of battle as well as of planting fields. All will be well."

Ecgbert did not answer, so Bishop Ceolwulf continued. "Abbess Edyth and I wish to leave early in the morning. Hilda will come with us."

"May I send her old nurse and the boy, Caedmon, with her? It will console her in these times when her life has been so disrupted."

"As long as they serve the monastery rather than their mistress," the bishop conceded. The two men moved away from Hilda's bur and walked quietly towards the hall.

Inside the bur, Hilda did not sleep. She lay listening to the voices of the two men outside. Once again, someone else decided her fate. She wondered if Pagany's prayer would work for a sick heart as well as it did for a sick stomach.

"*Ut lydel spare, Ut lydel spare, Ut lydel spare*" she whispered, for indeed the pain she was feeling was akin to that of a stab into her heart from a little
spear.

The magic allowed her to leave the pain of her parent's betrayal behind, but could not release her from the impending changes which she could neither avoid nor control. In her mind's eye she saw the ruins of the monastery she had wandered through on her trip back home. That overgrown world, built so long ago by her mother, offered nothing but devastation and fragmentation—walls which failed to link with other walls—and mind-destroying silence and abandoned rune stones. Yet even as she contemplated the worst, her thoughts turned to the other monastery, the thriving enclave where they had spent the night. Its stone walls had not been so grim. She remembered watching the women as they pointed to pages of a manuscript. Learning to read still tempted her. Even the copying of manuscripts in the scriptorium might be satisfying. And, she thought suddenly, if she could write, she could send a letter to Leova. Someone would read it to her, perhaps even pen a response she knew her friend would want to make. This thought, and the remembrance of the peace in the chapel and the joy of song she had heard there, brought solace. She had at least felt some peace in the monastery and no peace at all in this place which was supposed to be her home. She would no longer fight returning there with the Bishop and the Abbess.

"I will keep my promise, mother," she said into the darkness. "At least for a while."

Chapter 2: Leova Takes Up a Woman's Life (878)

"A distraction!" Bertram shouted, his irritation clearly interfering with his examination of the new sword the armorer had just offered him. He waved the shiny weapon as if cutting down an enemy, then stopped when he saw his wife's troubled frown.

"Wife: our daughter needs a bigger distraction from her grief than sweet treats, new clothes, and pretty jewelry! A trip. She needs a trip."

Pagany agreed with her husband on principle; she was increasingly worried about the change that had come over their daughter. Leova had never been one to be melancholy. When disappointed, she generally recovered quickly and when saddened, she determinedly rose above her unhappiness, well aware that giving into sorrow would not make her feel any better. However, Hilda's departure, more than two months ago, created a sense of grief and loss that the young woman had never felt before. She was listless and found it impossible to become excited about any of the things she had once enjoyed with her companion. Although she moved about the hall and grounds as usual, her mind wandered constantly back to the past. Every step reminded her of happier days, and her eyes constantly sought the friend who could no longer be seen.

But Pagany was suspicious of her husband's call for a trip. "Bertram, if you are thinking of taking her to the wedding of that horrid woman's horrid son...."

"That 'horrid woman's horrid son' will soon rule all those lands that border ours to the north. We'll attend the wedding. It's the wise and politic action to take. And it will be good for Leova."

Although Pagany abhorred the thought of such an outing and she knew her husband quite agreed with her assessment of their neighbors, she was at her wit's end to know how to revive Leova's flagging spirits. Nothing she had done thus far had had any effect. She protested only mildly.

"We are not prepared to go; we'd have to make hasty preparations; we'd have to assemble appropriate gifts and a traveling party...." She waved her hand in confusion, indicating the hopelessness of it all. "I doubt she'd even want to go, but she is our good daughter...."

"...so she'll not refuse," Bertram concluded.

Her parents knew her well. Leova had no desire whatsoever to attend the wedding of young Lord Robert; nonetheless, given no choice in the matter and lacking the heart to protest, she acquiesced. In preparation for the journey to Stonehart, the hall of Lady Allmana, the sheer amount of required effort began to break the depression she'd felt since Hilda left. Although she did not forget Hilda, assembling clothing and preparing gifts prevented Leova from endlessly thinking of her friend.

Pagany had quickly determined that neither she nor her daughter had attire suitable for the wedding. The servants and the ladies set themselves to alter the available wardrobe, adding embroidery to necklines, tassels to belts.

"What about adding pearls to the youngling's blue dress?" Gwynned asked Pagany. "She should shine at this wedding."

Leova looked slightly horrified. She didn't like pearls or elaborate jewels.

Pagany smiled. "Leova does not need pearls. She'll be the loveliest young girl there."

"Still," Gwynned reasoned, "Pearls do make a dress appear regal, and that's all to the good." Seeing Pagany's face, Gwynned stopped arguing. Much to Leova's relief, there would be no pearls on her gown.

While Bertram ordered the gifts for the young couple—two silver drinking bowls and ornamental spoons to accompany them—Pagany supervised the silversmith who created them. After the original design was struck, she sent Leova to check progress, and while the girl cared little for her own rings and necklaces, the beautiful bridal gifts put her in awe of the silversmith's skills. She ran her fingers over the complex ridges of the spoon handles, which were formed with complicated knots.

"Master Smith," she asked, "why did my mother choose this design?"

"They be love knots, lady. No beginning, no end, like heart strings they are...no way to untie them."

The bowls had elaborate crosses engraved on the inside which Leova knew paid homage to the Christian God. The love knots she'd only seen in work made by the forest women or in Pagany's family goods.

"Two powers will bind Lord Robert and his bride," she thought. "The knots bind others too—Hilda and I share heartstrings like these." Then she shook her head and went about her business, wishing the knots could bring her friend back.

At last the clothes were fitted and packed, the gifts secured within an elaborately carved oak chest, and the guards mounted behind the small group of travelers. As the entourage moved through Lothlar's gates and into the countryside and as the sun moved upward, Leova's mood grew light. Once on the open hills, she prodded her horse into a gallop and, much to the distress of her mother, left the others behind. She laughed as she envisioned herself as *Cweane* Boedica, the legendary queen who had avenged the rape of her daughters and driven Roman invaders from her land. It had been rumored that Boedica rode her horse in the nude. "What would it be like to be a woman warrior?" she wondered, relishing the prospect. The sun sparkled on the small lakes that dotted the fields and aroused glints in the stones on the sides of the bordering hills. It was all Leova could do to keep herself from abandoning the intended route and heading off instead to follow Hilda.

"I'd never find her," she thought, her sadness mixed with laughter. "But she'd find me. Hilda's the brave one, the warrior."

Pagany watched her daughter move farther and farther away from them, but even though slightly alarmed, she felt satisfied. The busy days had had a good effect. She smiled to see Leova moving almost as one with the gray steed, her long blond hair escaping from the veil and blowing out behind her. She knew of Leova's fascination with Boedica, and at this moment, her daughter's spirit echoed that of the ancient *cweane*.

As the day moved on toward noon, a storm began to gather on the western horizon. The wind intensified, and the clouds collected into massive gray and white billows, finally obliterating the sun entirely. As the first drops of rain fell, Pagany and Bertram became concerned about shelter: too often what seemed like a light shower transformed into a sky split by lightning and thunder.

"We're in luck—*bothas*!" Bertram gestured toward a small group of structures just at the bottom of the western hills. Leova seemed quite unheeding of the change in weather and had continued to pull some distance ahead of them. Bertram signaled to one of his men to overtake her and see that she turned back toward the huts.

The small complex had obviously been abandoned for some time. However, most of the roofs seemed intact; they could find cover from what was rapidly becoming a full storm. As they entered the largest of the *bothas*, they saw that no furnishings remained, only some dirty straw scattered on the floor. Quickly Bertram instructed two of his servants to assemble as much clean dry straw as they could find and cover it with whatever cloth could be ferreted out of their belongings. As they worked around her, Pagany stood in the open doorway anxiously searching for her daughter and the messenger who was to rein her in. After about ten minutes, she saw not two horses approaching—but three. She recognized her daughter and the messenger, but the young man who rode behind the messenger was a stranger whose tunic and leggings marked him as one of Allmana's house servants.

Leova slipped off her horse, fairly well soaked but glowing from the freedom she had felt for the past half hour. She turned toward the new arrival.

"Mother, this is Jankin, Lady Allmana's reeve. He's been out looking for some sheep. May he shelter here, too?"

Before Pagany could reply, Jankin hurried off, calling that he would return "anon." Within ten minutes, he had returned bearing a pile of woolen blankets.

"We use these *bothas* for shelter when we can't get home before sunset," he explained as he turned the blankets over to Pagany's attendants, "so we store these covers just in case. I'd be honored if you'd use 'em."

"My thanks," Pagany said in appreciation before turning her attention to her daughter.

"You need to get into dry clothing."

Jankin made a hasty get-away.

Gwynned, ever prepared, had already gathered together some of her mistress' clothes and after Pagany shooed the rest of the men off, she and Pagany helped Leova dry off and don a warm tunic and gown. Happily, the young woman settled onto a mound of hay and covered her bare feet with one of the woolen blankets, waiting for the storm to pass.

The storm, however, did not abate. Leova cared not at all; in fact, she found herself rather pleased at the turn of events—until her father, who had returned to the *botha*, dismissed Jankin who had reappeared with even more blankets.

"Father—no!" she protested as she rose from her pallet to confront him. "I'd like to speak with Jankin, learn more about our hosts before we arrive there."

"You already know what you need to know," her father frowned. "He's a servant. What can he tell you, other than gossip?"

Leova ignored her father's obvious displeasure. "Jankin's done us a great favor in providing some comfort in this dismal place. He will not gossip; he's as loyal as any of our own people would be."

As girls, Hilda and Leova had often spent time visiting with what her father would have called "ordinary" people, but Leova had realized for a long time that she older she got, the harder it was to have "real" conversations with any of the farmers or shepherds. They seemed ever more aware of rank and position, and ever more hesitant to share their thoughts with the young women who would eventually be mistresses of their own halls. Jankin appeared to be an exception. He hadn't hesitated to speak when they had met, nor had he waited for Pagany to speak before he went in search of the blankets. He wasn't ordinary. With a little persuasion, he would talk with her; of that she was certain despite her father's doubts. Leova knew somewhat of the lives of the servants and farmers at her hall, but she and Hilda had often speculated about other halls and other ways of living in them. She was curious to know if, despite Allmana's tarnished reputation, life in her hall was anything like life in her own hall.

Her father knew when arguing with his daughter wouldn't resolve problems, and this problem was not such a big one. "Alright, sweetling," he mumbled and went to sit by his wife on the other side of the *botha*.

More than a little bit abashed by the attention, Jankin bowed to show his respect for Bertram and, following the wave of her hand, settled himself warily at Leova's feet.

"I await your pleasure, My Lady."

She smiled to make him comfortable and offered a piece of bread from the basket her attendants had unloaded from the carts.

"My pleasure...." she mused. "It would please me greatly, before I arrive at Stonehart, to know more about you, your family, and...life on the estate in general."

Leova's tone of voice reassured Jankin that she asked out of genuine curiosity rather than idle conversation, so for an hour, or perhaps more, he regaled Leova with detailed descriptions of his home, his family—from the youngest babe to his aged granny—and the activities that filled their days. As Leova had suspected, he proved both funny and serious. On only one subject did he remain quiet: he carefully avoided any discussion of his mistress, the Lady Allmana, or the way she controlled her lands and governed her people—or even what life was like inside the hall. Once or twice, Leova had picked up a bitter tone in his voice and had attempted to discover the reasons for his unhappiness, but she realized quickly that she should not press: Jankin was in no position to speak freely.

As Jankin and Leova talked, the rest of the party found their own ways to deal with the storm and the delay. Lady Pagany dozed, her head against a large bale of hay, a blanket pulled up to her chin. Lord Bertram stood at the doorway with two of his men, anxiously surveying the skies for any hint of the storm's abatement. He and his captain of the guard debated whether they could get to Allmana's hall by nightfall even if the rain did let up. Reluctantly, Bertram came to a decision and sent a messenger to inform their hostess that the weather had delayed their arrival until the following day.

Remaining in the crude huts overnight annoyed him, but he saw no alternative.

"At least my women are comfortable." He smiled as his eyes fell first on his sleeping wife and then on his daughter, who was deep in conversation with the young Jankin. Taking care not to wake Pagany, he moved quietly across the hut and leaned in to speak softly to Leova.

"We must stay the night here, daughter. Best make yourself comfortable and try to sleep."

Jankin rose to go.

"Don't leave," Leova declared, and she put out her hand to stop him. "I need you to tell me about Lady Allmana and her family."

Bertram frowned at her behavior and started to put a stop to this unseemly gossip, but because she was at last engaged in something other than mourning for Hilda, he reconsidered. Shaking his head, he left his daughter with her young companion and went back to watching the rain.

It was fairly obvious to Leova that Jankin was not altogether willing to talk about his mistress, but he soon settled back on the straw and seemed to find a safe place to start.

"Lady Allmana has had much trial and sorrow in her marriages," he began carefully. "She married quite young, but her first husband—the lord whose family owned this land—sickened and died. No one expected it nor understood what took him. Perhaps a miasma?" He shook his head disbelievingly. "Her first-born died, too. I think. No one speaks of him."

"How sad." Leova said.

Jankin paused for a moment, then quickly continued in order to stop the questions Leova seemed eager to ask. "The lady married again—Lord Roger; his family was as rich as hers, but he came to live with her 'cause he was a younger son. This about the time my family settled on our farm at Stonehart. Lady Allmana had herself four sons altogether. You are going to the marriage of Robert, now the eldest. The next, Ragen...well, he doesn't want to be a knight somewhere, so he's there. Rolfe, the youngest, went off to a monastery in the east. Lady Allmana means him to be a priest."

"What about Lord Roger?"

"My lord died some time ago, while the boys were quite young, leaving Lady Allmana in charge. Rumors are...no." He stopped, suddenly realizing how free he had become with his story telling. "I sure must stop—can't talk like this; she'd beat me for sure."

Leova nodded, her feeling about Jankin confirmed. He was a loyal servant, one who knew to not spread gossip. She changed the subject slightly to less sensitive matters.

"And Robert, the son who marries tomorrow? What's he like?"

"Like his mother," Jankin replied shortly.

Leova laughed uneasily. "You don't like any of them, do you?"

"It's not for me to like or not like my betters!" he exclaimed rapidly.

Leova smiled in comfort and compassion. "Your face says otherwise."

He stared briefly into Leova's eyes, then dropped his own to the floor. Quietly, he said, "Telling you rumors not good for me. Beating—or worse—comes from saying what I shouldn't."

"Just think of them as stories about people we don't know. I love stories," she said innocently. Telling stories seemed harmless to her. To share stories with Jankin reminded her of sitting with Hilda, inventing stories. Each night, while others slept, they had invented stories about everyone in the hall—from knights to the lowest of cooks, stable-boys, and every farmer they had ever seen. Even the priests who came to offer mass in the little chapel had been given interesting lives based on the imaginations of the girls.

Jankin knew that Leova had no idea of the consequences he would face if his mistress discovered his loose tongue, but frustration and recklessness drove him to lean forward and speak in a hushed voice.

"Lord Roger wern't a weak man—perhaps a bit of a foolish dolt. He'd not deserve the death he got—no one would."

"What happened?"

"Lady Allman set up a hunting party to celebrate Lord Roger's natal day. The lord and six of his men went off at daybreak but didn't come back. Two days later they were found in a gulch, not looking like their live selves. They'd been robbed: armlets, swords, and rings." His voice dropped to a whisper, "their bodies had the mark of the bloody eagle."

"What's that?" Leova asked, borrowing his whispered tone."

"The body split down the middle and the ribs spread out like wings from the chest."

Leova winced and stifled a gasp.

"I'm...sorry...My Lady. I—shouldn't have! I'll stop."

"No, no. You can't. I'd like to know...everything." Leova lost her little girl fascination with stories, but, as a woman, she sought some explanation for the horror that had occurred so long ago. "Finish the story, please."

Jankin nodded. "It wasn't the killing, not even the robbery that was so strange. The Vikings weren't near us and just going after a handful of men wouldn't really be something they'd do. And more strange, the bloody eagle is really for traitors; treason do bring down awful cruelty just like this. Roger hadn't enemies. He'd not fought in the wars against the red-haired ones, hadn't caused them no trouble at all."

He relaxed a bit, relieved to leave the bloodier details of the killings and move on to the aftermath.

"Some say that Lord Roger and his men were killed by some locals seeking revenge or gain of some kind."

"Surely not! Who would want revenge? For what? " Leova exclaimed.

Jankin ignored that question. "Lady Allmana didn't seem to mind being a widow. On the way back from her husband's funeral she spent more time giving servants orders for the following day than mourning her husband's death. Within a week, people even stopped talking about how sad it were to be a widowed young mother. After a month, it seemed as if there hadn't never been a master. The land grew safe and wealthy for his sons' inheritance— but she'll never let any of them have control. Pity the new bride."

90

Jankin shook his head and stopped to look at his audience. It was obvious that she was eagerly absorbing all he said. Horrified at the tale he'd told, he found himself suddenly without more to say. Leova didn't notice and pressed for more details.

"Why pity the bride? There's more to the story? Tell me about Lady Allmana's sons."

Jankin heaved a sigh, knowing he now had little chance of simply walking away. But he also had to admit to himself that he rather enjoyed telling his stories.

"Robert," he began and then charged ahead. "Like his mother, he is, but weak. He ne'er says 'no' to her." Jankin laughed sardonically. "I'm sure he'll 'cleave' to his mother, rather than his bride!" Jankin shook his head sadly.

"The other two?"

"Ragen...I don't know about Ragen. Not like his mother, at least that's what some say." Leova had already begun to suspect that these supposedly quoted judgments were Jankin's own opinions, not those of some mysterious others. "Ne'er ever spends much time with mother or brother. Not like them much—talks to us like he cares what we thinks."

"And is he married yet?"

"No, no, he t'isn't married."

Leova sensed something in Jankin's voice which she could not pinpoint. But he continued quickly. "Rolfe, the third one, t'isn't there; some say he were sent off to a monastery; no one has seen him for a long time." He looked lost in thought, seeming to gaze into some distant past as he spoke, perhaps remembering a time before he had grown enough to take on the responsibilities of a man.

"My friend, Yffi, and me, we got lost in the woods, and scart that we'd never git home. Lord Rolfe, he were only a bit oldern us'n, found us and brought us back to our mam's. The whole way, he told us stories about Robyn Hode of the forest, and his robbin', fightin' ways to rob rich people and give to poor people."

"After that, he took a notion to look after us—even play with us now and again, liked our company bettern his mam's and that oldest brother's, that's for sure. In all truth, I think he was glad to go.

91

I'd bet the religious folk in that monastery cared for him lots more than his own mam."

Captured by his own reminiscences, Jankin almost forgot that he had an audience. He shook his head ruefully, turned to see how Leova had responded to his tale, and laughed quietly. Worn out by the adventures of the day, she had fallen asleep.

The Wedding

Allmana's hall looked dreary and worn. "Perhaps," mused Leova, "Allmana keeps profits in coins and jewels—not in furnishings."

The tapestries lacked quality and the tables and benches in the great hall could only be described as sturdy, never as elegant. In the room they shared, Leova and her mother rested before preparing for the festivities—which, they soon discovered, weren't as festive as a wedding should be. Fewer than fifty people, none of whom showed outward signs of pleasure or even comfort, stood scattered in the enormous hall. While a few clustered together with friends or family, most of the guests just stood resolutely at the edge of the room, waiting for a cue from the hostess.

"Mother," Leona whispered, "aren't weddings supposed to be happy times?"

"My daughter," Pagany said quietly, "All my instincts tell me that nothing happy can occur here."

Leova couldn't help but agree. Allmana sat joylessly, speaking to no one—not even the groom and the bride. She filled the bench normally reserved for the lord of the hall, forcing the two young people to sit on smaller benches on either side. Behind her, staunchly on guard, stood a burly bearded man. Allmana's features seemed permanently fixed in a frown, her companion's devoid of feeling; but both sets of eyes moved back and forth across the room, looking for something, but what, wasn't clear. The disdain with which the long-time widow observed the people around her was echoed in his face.

As much as they watched the guests in their hall, the guests couldn't avoid looking at them. Stiff and fearsome, the two imposing figures drew everyone's focus to the high dais. No one seemed to dare relax lest the disapproving eyes of the lady and her guardian fall upon them. Even the young couple, who should have been the center of attention, seemed to shrink under the occasional—but disdainful—glance of the lady of the house.

The dark-haired groom bore Allmana's features and a petulant frown. The bride, a girl-woman hardly older than Leova, sat in visible misery in her wedding finery. A small chaplet of flowers circled her head, but her lovely red hair clashed unpleasantly with her rose-colored gown.

Custom demanded that Bertram, due to his high position, stand in for the long dead Lord Roger, so upon seeing him enter the hall, Allmana stood up and greeted him and his family courteously if not warmly. Stepping down from the dais, she took Bertram's arm, then ordered rather than announced, "We will celebrate the ritual of my son's wedding at the chapel door and then go into the chapel for the wedding mass."

Leova winced. Allmana's curt words didn't even dignify her son with a name and made it obvious that the bride's role in the proceedings was altogether insignificant.

Once before the chapel, standing close to the stairs that formed the porch, Leova saw everything that happened—and most of it, from the blessing of the ring to the joining of hands, took place without passion or excitement. The mass that came after the priest's marriage blessing didn't hold her attention. Mass seldom did. Her mind filled with questions that less concerned her soul than the secular world around her. Oddities jumped out at her. Across from her stood a man she had been briefly introduced to as Ragen, the third son. A pleasant enough looking young man, his attention wandered also—he seemed as disinterested in the service as the groom, who slumped against the prayer stool and ignored his new wife. The heavily built body-guard watched Allmana rather than the ceremony. What role did he play in this little family drama? Suddenly she realized that while Allmana had stood at Robert's elbow as he said his vows, the bride had no attendants. Where were her parents? No one in the small gathering paid her the slightest attention.

The wedding feast which followed, while far from joyful, took place in a considerably lightened atmosphere. The food proved plentiful and the wine flowed. As would be expected, Allmana had hired entertainment, and a lively troupe of players provided more delight than the stilted ceremony before the chapel door. Musicians filled the air with light-hearted tunes, while acrobats and jugglers roamed the crowd. One young boy in bright motley colors, teasing the children, suddenly turned to the table where Leova sat and threw a ball in her direction. Just as she ducked, she realized another juggler stood behind her chair.

Leova's laughter rang out. She loved all the action and attention: she'd always had a secret yen to juggle. She and Hilda had begged one of the entertainers who frequently stopped overnight in their hall to teach them how to keep the little balls in the air. Leova threw one ball after another into the air, only to see them drop to the floor instead of into her hand. Hilda, however, could keep three and sometimes four balls in the air. The next time the jugglers performed, she scandalized and delighted everyone by performing with them.

The jugglers finished with a flourish and moved on. Leova listened idly to her parents' conversation and watched the guests as they set about ignoring Allmana and her grim attendant. Gradually, boredom set in and not even the entertainers nor even memories of Hilda's escapades could satisfy her. She rose to move about the hall and almost immediately she found the two sons of the hall at her side.

"I would be honored to escort you about the hall," they said, almost in unison. Leova's eyes fell upon the new bride, Wyomina, sitting alone at the high table.

"Perhaps Lady Wyomina would like to join us?" Leova smiled politely. A scowl passed over Robert's face; he turned curtly, leaving her to his brother, who offered his arm in amusement.

"Your trip here was not a calm one, Pryncess Leova."

Happy to take her mind off the disastrous wedding, Leova launched into a brief tale of the journey, making the storm seem far more dangerous than it had been in reality. She omitted all mention of Jankin's interesting tales, but joked about sleeping in the *bothas* and about the rough blankets which covered the straw.

"All in all," she teased, "I was so tired and cold, the quality of the housing and the bedding seemed to equal those of a regal hall!"

As they ambled along the tables in the hall, the two evoked smiles from the guests. "They make a lovely couple," an old farmer commented to his companions, and found himself greeted with a hearty burst of not altogether kind laughter. Leova blushed, and Regan looked away. Embarrassed, she desired to return to her mother's side, but courtesy held her in place. Regan smiled hesitantly, then grew very silent. A moment later, driven by discomfort and curiosity, she posed what seemed to her to be an innocent question. She looked over toward the silent dais.

"Who's the man behind your mother? Your uncle, perhaps?"

Ragen did not answer; he merely scowled fiercely as he followed her eyes.

Surprised by his reaction, Leova changed the topic. "I should pay my respects to Lady Wyomina's parents."

Ragen answered this time, but with more confusion than the simple question would seem to merit. "Her parents? They...they...could not attend."

She missed Ragen's discomfort. "I'm so sorry. They're aged or infirm?"

Ragen turned from her abruptly, "I've acquired a new dog. He's yet a puppy, but promises to develop into a fine hunter." He signaled to a nearby servant, who released one of the leashes he was holding, and a small terrier bounced forward, jumping eagerly on its young master.

Stunned by his behavior, Leova stood puzzled for a moment, realizing that she had no choice but to forego her questions. "A lively one..." she commented without much enthusiasm, and started back to join her parents. She would not be treated in such a manner!

To her surprise, Ragen hastened to join her, taking her elbow as if to guide her back toward her mother, but before they made much progress, Robert approached leading his young wife.

"My wife thought that you might welcome an opportunity to talk," he said, deliberately removing Leova's arm from his brother's and joining it to that of the young woman at his side. Obviously happy to have the company of another young woman, both girls moved away from the men.

"I wish you joy," Leova said to the young woman who seemed far from joyful.

Wyomina accepted the pleasant congratulations, then turned the conversation in a direction that Leova had not expected. "Have marriage plans been made for you?" the timid bride inquired.

Startled, Leova hastily answered, "Not yet—I feel far too young to marry!" Not soon enough, she realized that her companion was no older, perhaps even younger, than she was.

"I'm only sixteen," Wyomina said, almost as if she had only just realized it. Horrified, Leova realized that the girl was about to cry. "I would have liked to wait a bit, but Robert and his mother insisted and my parents...." Wyomina's voice broke slightly. Leova wanted to comfort her, but had no idea how, so she changed the subject.

"I'm sorry your parents couldn't attend."

"They would have attended had they been invited," came the terse answer. Before she could respond, Allmana interrupted them. Leova found that she was almost glad.

"Come, child," Allmana commanded her new daughter-in-law. "It's time to retire for the night." The older woman took the girl's arm and pulled her toward the waiting, but hardly enthusiastic, bridegroom. Leova hastily sought out her parents, praying silently that she not be accosted by any other member of the hostess' family.

"That was a nice circle you made with young Ragen," said Pagany as she greeted her daughter. Ignoring the comment, Leova grasped her mother's arm and asked anxiously, "Is it too early for us to return to our rooms?"

"No," answered her mother, peering carefully in her daughter's eyes. "As soon as the bride and groom have retired, we too can go. Why so anxious?"

"I don't know," Leova confessed. "This place feels invaded by...I don't know...bad feelings, hurtful emotions. Meanness!" She gestured helplessly. "Everything...seems threatening."

Pagany nodded, confirming her daughter's instincts, "I feel it, too. Strongly." Briefly hugging her unhappy daughter, she pointed toward the main entrance. "We'll soon be free; they've taken their leave."

Leova leaned heavily against her mother, unexpectedly drained by a feeling of dread that wouldn't leave her.

When morning arrived, Leova's desire to escape from the suffocating atmosphere of the hall and its occupants grew stronger.

"It's hard to explain," she told her mother, "but I guess I know now why you called Allmana a 'horrid woman.' Everyone she touches—or even gazes upon—instantly seems afraid."

Pagany had much the same feeling, and while she didn't talk to her husband about matters as vague as "evil," she did urge him to press for an early departure.

"Create some 'unforeseen occurrence' at home," she demanded. "Leova and I can't linger here!"

Since Bertram always felt more comfortable in his own hall and too had no love for Allmana or her children, he obliged his wife and daughter. "We'll leave as soon as we return from breaking our fast. I'll bid our hostess farewell, and we'll remove ourselves from her..." he smiled sarcastically, "*gracious* presence."

When they entered the main hall, they found the servants working quietly to clear away the evidence of the prior night's festivities. Here and there young men still slept on the benches, stirring guiltily only when the servants approached. Ragen was seated at the high table alone, and he signaled to them that they should join him there for their morning victuals. He rose to greet them, and after they were settled, making sure that Leova sat next to him, called for food. As they waited, he turned to her and spoke quietly and sincerely.

"I'm sorry for my behavior last night, Leova. Perhaps in time you will understand why I find it so hard to talk about my mother's business. Everything in this estate is tightly controlled by her: lands, household, who stands where, who comes, who goes." His hands, fingers resting on the table top, grew tense and she sensed that he applied pressure to them to keep his emotions in check.

He stopped suddenly, and looking behind her, Leova saw the black shadow of Allmana's gown as she came to stand behind them. She stood uncomfortably close, positioning herself between them and placing her hands on their shoulders.

"Now, aren't you a lovely young couple so early in the morning?" she asked without an ounce of warmth.

Leova drew away from the woman's touch and the implications of her words. Luckily, as she sought for an additional response, food was placed before her and her father turned the conversation to their plans for departure. Bertram's explanation served quite nicely: a messenger had brought word that relatives of Pagany's had arrived at Lothlar unexpectedly; they needed to return and be gracious hosts themselves.

"However," Bertram concluded, "we would not leave without bidding farewell to you and perhaps even the newlyweds."

"They've not yet arisen," Allmana replied shortly, seating herself next to Leova. She made no attempt to hide her indifference to Bertram and Pagany's departure. Leona suspected Allmana knew her father lied but didn't object because she felt more relief than insult. Maintaining the courtesy of a hostess probably exhausted her.

But as Allmana turned herself to the business of eating, she asked with studied casualness, "Perhaps young Leova might stay a bit? Keep my son company and be a companion to my daughter-in-law?"

Pagany and Leova were struck speechless, but Bertram, quite aware of the horror on their faces, answered quite calmly. "No, no," he shook his head fondly. "My child brings me too much comfort to let others keep her from me."

"Very well," snarled Allmana, angry that he would not defer to her request. "I had hoped to give my son the same comfort." She turned to Ragen, determined not to lose complete control of the situation. "Accompany them to the border of our land. And make use of the opportunity. Our families need to better know one another."

Ragen looked exceedingly uncomfortable, but he nodded in agreement. Leova wondered if he—or any of her sons—ever disobeyed their mother.

The journey home helped to quiet Leova's upsetting encounters with Allmana and her family. While she had not looked forward to riding with Regan, she had little choice, and as the day went on, she began to enjoy his companionship. Making an effort to be pleasant, he strove to entertain her. He played a game that involved naming the plants, flowers, and even small animals. At first he seemed to know all the names and impressed her with his knowledge. Gradually, as the names grew more and more fantastic, she realized that he was inventing many of them. His teasing removed much of the tension that his mother had created and allowed her to forget Allmana, Robert, and the pitiful Wyomina. At the border, he became serious once more, but it was a gentle seriousness, not the distress she'd witnessed the evening before.

"May I visit you, my lady?" he asked with a formal courtesy much different from the teasing demeanor he'd maintained on the road.

Pagany grew alert immediately, suspecting that the question was prompted by Allmana rather than by the young man himself. Bertram, intent on getting home, was altogether unaware of the words.

"You are welcome in our home...I'm sure," Leova responded tentatively and looked to her mother for confirmation. Pagany nodded, Regan smiled, and the moment passed. As the parties took their leave, however, Leova couldn't help but worry about the implications of the question. As much as she liked Regan, she wasn't prepared to accept his courtship, and there was no other reason she could think of for his visit to Lothlar.

As they rode away, her mother, sensing the confusion Leova felt, drew up beside her and reached out to pat her arm. Leova put her hand over her mothers and squeezed it lightly, acknowledging the reassurance.

"Of all the people at Allmana's, Regan seems the closest to normal," she opined, less to her mother and more to herself.

"True," answered Pagany. "Do you want to see him again?"

"As a person or as a suitor?" Leova asked, watching anxiously for her mother's reaction.

"Either, I suppose. Allmana wasn't subtle about her wish to join you to her family."

"Lady Wyomina didn't seem overjoyed to become the wife of Robert."

The question that had plagued her since the wedding popped out. "Mother, tell me, if you know. Why weren't Lady Wyomina's parents there? Whenever I asked, people either didn't answer or made excuses that did not...ring true."

The older woman paused a moment before she spoke, "After Allmana's first husband died mysteriously and her second husband died so violently...." She stopped and looked carefully at Leova. "Jankin told you the story, didn't he?"

Leova blushed to know that her mother had overheard the conversation with the reeve, but nonetheless nodded her head to indicate it was so.

"Yes. Once you know the information I gleaned from one of the wedding guests, you will understand why Jankin was hesitant to talk. It appears that some time ago, Wyomina's parents began to imply that Allmana bore responsibility for both deaths."

Leova gasped. "And they dared say that out loud?"

"You'd think they'd have better sense. But Allmana didn't seem to pay them any mind and ignored them until it became obvious that she had a plan for silencing them altogether." Pagany shook her head sadly.

"You see, they owned a fair amount of land that borders on Allmana's, land she coveted. So, the good lady," Leova detected the sarcasm, "decided to marry her oldest son off to Wyomina, their only child."

"And they agreed?"

"What could they do? They had land, but no money to keep it. Wyomina was their only means of saving it. So, her parents agreed to the marriage. But Allmana had her revenge for their supposed 'slander.' She forbid them to come to the wedding. And given that their daughter's future and their own wellbeing now depend upon Allman's bounty, the parents were in no position to object."

Leova thought about the deep anger obvious beneath Wyomina's submissive appearance. She had not taken her parents' exclusion easily. "Sad Wyomina, she might soon wish that she had stayed poor."

The two women rode silently for a time, then Leova blurted out, "That place, those mean-spirited people are not, not...good!"

She wanted to call them evil, but the word seemed too strong. "I don't ever want to go back again."

The fact that her mother didn't instantly agree, unnerved her enough to make her ask, "I don't have to accept him as a husband, do I?"

Her mother's answer was less than satisfactory, "Of course not." But Pagany didn't look Leova directly in the eye as she uttered the words.

Frightened, Leova tried to change the subject. "That man, Allmana's body guard? Who is he?"

Her mother recovered from her reverie and answered rather crisply. "Steven. He began as a knight of Lord Roger, and when his lord died...," she paused and searched for words. "Steven is not a body guard...he's, well...*close* to Allmana."

Leova remembered Regan's anger and Steven's arrogant possessive stance at his mistress' shoulder. Aware of her mother's discomfort, Leova looked forward toward the road and quietly asked, "Like a husband?"

"Yes, like a husband," Pagany said harshly. And then she fell silent, ending the conversation.

Leova returned to her thoughts about Regan and his family and then slowly to thoughts of her friend Hilda. What would she have made of this strange family? How she wished she had someone to share her reactions and intuitions with.

Learning to Heal

Once back in her own hall, Leova turned again to the routines she had loved when she had shared them with Hilda. Now each day weighed on her heavily and passed with no diversion. The distraction provided by the wedding did not last.

Soon even Pagany lost patience with her. Finding her daughter sighing over her embroidery one day, she snatched the needle from her hand and stuck it firmly in the cloth spread over the frame.

"Enough," she said. "You've learned everything you need to know about thread and cloth and decorating both gowns and walls. It's time you learned more useful skills, skills a woman needs to keep a household healthy."

Leova, surprised by her mother's impatience, felt indignant. It wasn't as if she had no skills. Leova and Hilda had both learned housewifery and the fact that they were royal didn't relieve them of the drudgery of the household. Destined to oversee the men and women in a hot and dirty kitchen, they had first served as apprentices to them. Pagany believed in learning to rule by learning to submit: working side by side with those who worked for you created a healthy respect for the lives of others and, she hoped, kind and reasonable mistresses. So the two spirited girls began, like less fortunate children, by sweeping out the rushes in the enormous rooms, hauling water from the well, and scrubbing down the great dining hall under the direction of the old women who had years before trained Pagany herself.

The "Force of Crones," as Hilda and Leova came to nickname their instructors, had worked in the kitchens of noblemen all their lives. First, and most formidable of the crones was Hannah, Pagany's old teacher. She had arrived at Lothlar when her mistress came as a bride, proud to continue serving as she had served Pagany's mother.

Hannah had been born to oversee the kitchen, just as Pagany had been born to oversee the household. She brooked no disobedience and dealt severely with those who shirked their duties. Even Pagany, from time to time, seemed a little in awe of Hannah and would defer to her experience in matters concerning food, cooking utensils, and storage. Hannah did not have a free rein, however. Pagany had her own ideas about the way the kitchen would be run. No one could raise a hand to another, and the person caught boxing the ears of a serving maid could be sent to the fields to work, a fate considerably harder than scrubbing pots. But that didn't prevent Hannah and her two elderly cohorts, Signy and Freya, from making threats. Pagany might be soft-spoken and gentle on the outside and solid as rock on the interior, but the Force of Crones was shrill and sharp-tongued in their dealings with underlings and soft as butter in their hearts.

"I'll take the poker to ya" Hannah might threaten one of the kitchen maids, but she never did. More than likely she'd slip the victim of one of her tirades a sweet-cake to soothe the tears.

Freya depended more on mental torture. "The mistress will be so disappointed," she'd say in sorrowful tones. "Her trusted you so much." And a guilty scullery maid would take even more care to see that the fire kept burning hot.

Signy took an entirely different tact. "Ah, I'd hate to see such a one as yourself out in the fields…. No nice kitchen with its sure supply o' victuals, no warmth to protect ya from the winds…. Oh, t'would be so unfortunate!" No one doubted she had the power to banish a kitchen maid to the fields, nor could anyone remember when she had sent someone out into that harsh life.

Tough, but loving, the crones didn't spare the young prynces any of the threats or the love that they extended to the daughters of peasants. They couldn't, of course, threaten to remove them from their comfortable rooms or banish them to the fields, but the fear of failing Pagany motivated them constantly, and they knew to assign them the most loathsome of chores because Pagany approved. The girls were often placed in the hands of the baker and the keeper of the herb garden. Those were hard, but far more pleasant tasks. The worst was replacing the floor rushes, especially those in the great hall. The first time they cleaned the hall, Hannah, Signy, and Freya had carefully bound up their long hair, issued smocks, and led them—most unsympathetically—to the great hall. It had been some time since the rushes had been changed, and the room stank with the unpleasant smells of dried food and waste discarded from tables. The rushes, they suspected, hid unidentified horrors. Slowly they began the filthy work, each picking up an armload of the greasy litter and carrying it outside to the bonfire. Removing the floor-covering revealed the leavings of the dogs and well-chewed bones. Worst of all, the girls encountered creatures that scurried up their arms and legs. Occasionally, a rat would rear up when its nest was threatened, causing both Hilda and Leova to scream and jump up on the benches placed against the walls.

As the hours drew on, the young noblewomen longed for the hot baths they knew were their due at the end of the day. The fear of having to repeat any of these distasteful tasks because they did them unsatisfactorily was all the encouragement they needed to keep them busy at less odious tasks. The regimen taught them well. Both girls realized that such duties would not last a lifetime for them—not even much more than a day—and they developed more sympathy for those who had no choice but to perform the dirtiest and most unpleasant chores as part of their daily lives.

Pagany now led Leova not to the kitchen or to the looms where the weavers constantly produced cloth for the estate. Instead she led her daughter outside to a small building just off Lothlar's garden: the herbarium. Inside, the walls were lined with shelves on one side and drying racks full of herbs on the other. The shelves held small pots, some tightly sealed with wax and others merely covered with cloth. The smells that filled the room delighted the young woman. Lavender, tansy, dandelions, and peppermint hung to dry on the racks while less pleasant items—dried eel, nettles, and moss—added a sharp contrast to the garden herbs.

Along with the plants from the garden and the fields, Pagany had stores of honey and poppy syrup, goose fat, and burned bark. Leova had known since childhood that herbs and other natural objects embodied mysteries gathered from the *auncient woones* and passed down from mother to daughter for generations. Often called upon to deal with sicknesses and injuries, Pagany worked with full devotion to the art of healing, and as they stood at the table in the center of the room, she looked into her daughter's eyes and smiled.

"Time has come for you to learn your woman's heritage. I taught you and Hilda the simple tasks of nursing because you will need them as mistresses of households. Your spirit, however, longs for more serious thought and for tasks more difficult than applying bandages and sponging off fevered brows. The *auncient woones* and I will teach you our secrets so that you can serve your people better when they need you."

Leova felt something between joy and horror. That those she so admired would teach her the art of healing brought a sense of pride—they found her worthy. That she would have to become responsible for the lives of others—for there could be no avoiding the fact that her actions could cure or kill—frightened her as nothing in her life had ever frightened her before. The immensity of her mother's statement left her dumbstruck.

"Leova?" her mother questioned. "Do you want to learn to heal? Was I wrong to offer to teach you?"

"No! No, my lady mother," she hastened to respond. "I always hoped you'd teach me, but—to be truthful—didn't think you felt Hilda and I were suited to learn."

Pagany laughed softly. "I've delayed your lessons, it's true. You and Hilda seemed unready to serve as healers. Such knowledge places a great obligation upon the shoulders of those who practice the art. You must study hard, devote yourself to a greater service than most women undertake."

"What has changed your mind? Why do you think I'm ready now?"

The older woman smiled at her daughter, "You've suffered a loss that has made you more conscious of the world about you. You and Hilda lived in an insular world, making your own pleasure, relying on each other to salve your small sorrows. Now you must face larger problems, and someday you'll find that you must deal

105

with them on your own—not even your father and I will be able to help."

Leova experienced a wave of sadness as she thought of Hilda. Her loss *had* changed everything. And she supposed that she should be frightened at the prospect of having to depend upon herself, but even as she contemplated a world where her parents might not be her support, she knew that somewhere her friend still thought of her and their bond would remain.

"I also wasn't sure that Hilda had the patience or the empathy for others that you have always displayed."

Leova started to protest, but stopped, knowing that her mother was right. Hilda was a good person, but she acted on impulse far too frequently and sometimes had to be reminded that her actions affected others as well as herself. "Yes," she said to Pagany, "but she will grow more thoughtful as we grow older! Of that I'm sure—even from a distance!"

"True," said Pagany. "True. You, however, have always listened with an inner ear for the voices of others. I much admired the kindness with which you treated that poor bride of Robert. Everyone else ignored her, including her awful husband, but you spoke to her with genuine concern. What did you think of her?"

Leova reflected for a moment or two before she answered her mother. "She seemed to be a woman of layers—sad but angry, meek but capable of...." She faltered, not knowing quite how to express what she felt.

Pagany solemnly completed Leova's assessment: "There's dangerous fire in that one. Wyomina holds back like a frightened badger cornered by loud boys. But they'd best be careful. Boys think they can taunt such a poor creature, but when they do, it will bite."

"And, my daughter, if you can see that in the bride and also understand your friend's weaknesses as well as her strengths, you have made a good beginning as a healer. Pain and sickness can be made greater or smaller by the nature of the person who suffers. A healer must be able to see more than an open wound or feel more than a feverish brow. Now," she said, suddenly becoming focused on the craft she loved, "Let's begin your first lesson!"

The first lesson took place in the small herb room. Pagany carefully pointed out each of the drying herbs, making Leova repeat the names and their healing properties. Then she opened every jar and pot, every small bag of twigs or pods, every powder and poultice. Some she encouraged Leova to touch and smell, some she placed on her daughter's tongue so that she could begin to identify the contents of the mixtures she created. However, some items Pagany kept locked away in a special cabinet.

"Just as medicines can heal, they can harm, my daughter. When you have grown more knowledgeable in the lore, I'll show you. For now, know that there are darker sides to our art."

Leova, of course, had many questions, but she instinctively understood that Pagany would be a fair but strict teacher: there would be time for questions when she knew what questions to ask. Each day they met to work, at first only in the medicine room but later in the woods outside the hall. They searched out herbs, moss, apple tree bark, and other ingredients that would soon be affected negatively by the coming fall.

"Don't take all the tansy," Pagany would caution her overly enthusiastic student as she eagerly harvested the leafy plant. "If you take it all, we might not be able to find any next year. Always preserve what you can; the spirits will reward you by making it available year after year. And keep in mind how most useful it is for digestive problems."

"What can you treat with mint?" The older woman would query as they stripped the dried leaves from the stems.

"Brewed in a tea, it can settle a sour stomach...." the girl began. "Made into a poultice with a bit of goose fat, it can be rubbed on the chest to help stem a cough or ease breathing."

"Good, my dear," Pagany said, and went on to new questions.

After some weeks, however, Leova grew tired of the constant emphasis on plants and potions. "May I not come with you the next time you're needed for healing? Or visit the *auncient woones* when you go out to consult them?"

"Perhaps you're ready," her mother smiled at Leova's impatience. "Perhaps."

However, she promised nothing, so Leova fell silent. She'd learned as a child that to push or nag her mother would accomplish nothing.

But only three days later, her mother woke Leova before the sun rose. "Come, the smith's daughter has fallen ill, and we're needed."

Leova dressed hastily and met her mother at the medicine room where Pagany placed several small jars in her basket, fitting them between other objects wrapped in cloth.

As they left with their supplies, Pagany provided some background. "The child has been sick for several days, but her parents have tried to ignore it: she's needed to watch the younger children while her mother works in the kitchen. This morning, when her mother tried to wake the girl, she couldn't get out of bed."

"Couldn't...?" Leova questioned. "Why?"

"Too weak. Come, we'll know more after we see her."

The women hurried across the courtyard to the smith's shop, and through it to the back room where the family lived. As one of the more important members of Lord Bertram's household, the smith had privileges other members of the household didn't—he was able to carve out a room of his own for his family in his shop; they didn't have to sleep on the floor in the great hall with most of the other servants. The room was small for a family of five, but in addition to a table and a few stools, Oswald and his wife, Acha, had put together some sleeping pallets of straw for themselves and their children. On one of these, a young girl lay, not sleeping, but not awake either. When they entered, the girl's mother, who'd been sitting over her and applying wet clothes to her forehead, rose and curtseyed quickly. "Thank ye, mistress, for coming. I oughten be in the kitchen helping with the bread, but I so fear for her...."

Pagany soothed the anxious mother: "Never mind, Acha, I spoke to Hannah, and she'll be able to do without you until we find out what's wrong. Now, let me see the child."

Little Audrey roused herself enough to mumble "Mi' Lady," but she couldn't sit up, even though she tried.

"Hush," Pagany said gently. "I'm going to feel your forehead and look at your eyes, then have a look at the rest of you."

Leova watched as her mother examined Audrey, softly asking questions of her and of Acha. Gradually, she became aware of soft weeping behind her and turned to see two small children in obvious distress. Careful not to distract her mother, she turned to the little ones and knelt beside them.

"What's wrong, sweetlings?" she asked.

"Our Audrey's 'bout to die," sobbed the elder of the two, who couldn't have been much older than four. The younger child looked close to wailing from fright. "Dyin', Dyin' Dyin,'" the child shrieked, collapsing onto the floor and pulling herself into a ball.

"No, no. She's sick, that's all," Leova responded, sincerely hoping that her words would prove true. "Come, sit with me and we'll keep watch as your mistress tends to her. Be quiet so that she can put all her attention on Audrey."

Pagany looked over her shoulder and smiled at the trio. "There's honeycomb in the basket, daughter. Give the little ones some to suck on." Then she turned to Acha.

"It's the fever that's making her weak. We need to brew some cherry bark and chamomile and get her to drink as much as we can. I brought some honey to sweeten it and cover the bitter taste."

"Should we bring spring water to bathe her in?" Leova asked, trying to remember the lessons from the weeks before.

"Yes," her mother replied, obviously pleased with the comment. "Just make sure that you sponge her off rather than submerge her. And if the water is too cold, it will drive the fever to her chest and she'll begin to cough."

After Leova had gently sponged Audrey's sweating limbs for close to an hour, Pagany reexamined the sick child, attentive to every change on her face and in her limbs, while Leova occupied the younger children. Finally, Audrey fell into a deep sleep, her color returned to normal, and her body cooled. They took their leave, assuring Acha that she could forego her kitchen duties for a few days to watch over her daughter and keep her eyes on others in the household to make sure no one else fell ill.

"What caused the fever, mother?" Leova asked as they made their way back to the medicine room. "And what were the words you chanted as you brewed the tea and washed Audrey's limbs?"

"For the first question I have no answer," Pagany said. "Fevers sometimes are brought on by wounds both severe and small, and sometimes they are accompanied by a great cough and choking phlegm. But sometimes they seem, as Audrey's fever seemed, to grow from within, having no visible cause. Perhaps an evil spirit latched onto the child, who knows? That's why I chant the old charms. When said by healers as they treat the sick, they help the cure."

"And will you teach me that also?"

"Later, child. Be patient. The healing that is magic can be taught only to those who have proved themselves learned enough to use that which is in the world around them." Pagany smiled. "You'll prove yourself in time, and in time the *auncient woones* and I will teach you charms against the mysteries we cannot see and the curses of unknown origin."

As the season turned towards fall, Leova became more and more included in healing practice. Under her mother's supervision she became competent, and then skilled in her knowledge of medicines. As Pagany had predicted, she became more and more aware that the mind as well as the body influenced the health of her people. A kind and soothing voice could give strength to those who ailed, and a stern word could turn aside the charge that someone had been cursed. The community was small, so she could not practice her skills every day. She divided her time between the house and the medicine room, taking on more and more of her mother's duties in an effort to relieve the burden the older woman carried. Although she continued also to comb wool and weave, she mainly sought on a daily basis to improve her knowledge of herbs and curses. Life became somewhat more satisfying.

In October, as she searched in the garden for the last of the summer herbs, Leova heard a commotion near the gates. Not knowing if there was trouble or if a visitor had arrived, she dusted off her gown and hurried to investigate. Pleased at the possibility of a bit of excitement, she saw Ragen jump down from his horse and hurry toward the hall.

"Regan!" she called, causing him to pause. He waited for her to catch up and bowed quickly over her outstretched hand.

"Greetings, My Lady," he said, "It's good to see you." While he was sincere, Leova couldn't help noticing that he turned to look at the door, anxious to be on his way. His next remark confirmed that this was no leisurely social call. "However, pleased as I am, I must leave you—I come to your father on urgent business."

At her puzzled look, he took her arm and as they walked inside, spoke quietly of his mission. "I've been sent to discover what truth there may be in the rumors that new fighting has broken out to the east."

Leova directed one of the stewards to find her father, and they were soon joined by Bertram, who had been preparing his hawk for hunting. He barely covered his irritation at being interrupted, but Ragen's words soon had him forget his waiting bird.

"Have you heard tell of fighting around the city of Yorvik and to the south and west of the city?"

Bertram frowned. "No. What have you heard? Are we in danger of invasion?" He stroked his beard thoughtfully, "I would think the distance between Yorvik and our territories here in Mercia would keep us safe."

"Perhaps, but travelers have brought word that groups of warriors have been marauding in order to enlarge their holdings. And while they now concentrate on the weakened lands of the north, they may turn west toward our lands in the future. But mainly I'm concerned for my brother Rolfe who serves at a monastery some two or three days riding to the east.

Bertram relaxed a bit; danger didn't lurk outside Lothlar's gate. "I understand your worries, but the news I have heard from travelers is that the region stands at peace. Of course, under that assurance lie some questions. I too have doubts that such peace will last. Still, many of the raiders started settlements and brought over their families.

"Perhaps, however," Regan answered, "they may well want more land, more gold, more stock. Are they willing to kill to get want they want? The region may not be as safe as it seems."

Immediately, Leova thought of Hilda. "My dearest friend lives in that region."

"Does she? Would you like me to find out about her and her family?" Regan asked.

"Yes, please. I long for news of her! Father, tell Regan how to find Highhear."

Bertram took care to map out the route to Highhear, then he quickly excused himself. Since he could see no immediate visible danger to his lands, he saw no reason to leave off hawking. "We look forward to your report and to good news about your brother," he called out as he disappeared.

Pagany turned to the anxious Regan, "It's late, close to nightfall. Stay with us—leave refreshed in the morning. Leova, take our guest to see the garden. Show him what you've done in these months since you last met."

Regan began to protest, but Pagany ignored him and turned to a servant near the door. "Prepare a room for his lordship. See that his men are comfortable, and stable his horses." Ragen protested no more.

"Your mother is quite formidable," he remarked. "I'm not used to such care."

Leova laughed. "Yes, she puts our wellbeing above all else and will not take any resistance to what she feels is best."

"Then let us see your garden. I must say, my own does well this season."

As he and Leova walked toward the garden, Regan gradually relaxed, the mere act of talking about his own garden momentarily pushed aside, but did not dismiss, his concern for Rolfe. He spoke less about what he had planted and more about the minute features of maintaining a garden site: the need for varying composition of the soil, the importance of small ants and almost invisible bugs, the ways to avoid plant damage, and how to encourage the growth of mushrooms in hidden places. Leova grew excited about the prospect of enriching her medicinal herbs as well as her flowers and decorative plants.

"If I'm careful, then," she asked, "I could bring in wild grasses and plants and grow them here. Perhaps in a section all their own? Imagine not having to seek them in the forest!"

Regan looked at her with interest.

"I don't know why we haven't thought of planting inside the walls before."

"Your mother follows the ways of the healers of the forest, and they believe that curatives must be harvested where the gods have placed them. It's part of the magic. Makes the healing more powerful."

Leova looked at him curiously. "You seem to be versed in the beliefs of the *auncient woones.*"

"No, not really." He shook his head. "I would know more, but given my mother's feelings toward them, I'm limited to learning only those things my servants tell me."

"You mother does not believe in the powers of the *auncient woones*?"

"No. She claims that they are godless, but given that she pays little attention to her Christian God, I find it hard to believe that would bother her. I think she fears them."

"Why? They do no harm."

"You know that, as do I," he spoke with an intensity that she found a bit alarming. "But if you craved absolute power as my mother does, you'd fear the influence the *auncient woones* have with the people, both outside and inside our hall."

Leova sat quietly, not understanding how anyone might fear the gentle women from the forest, and not sure what to say to this man who she instinctively felt was her friend.

"We will talk of this some other time," Regan said, flashing her a smile that pushed away her discomfort. "Now I want to hear of your progress as a healer. Worked any miracles yet?" he teased.

They spent the rest of the afternoon talking of herbs and cures and the way the humors could become unbalanced just by grief or melancholy. And Leova's respect for Regan grew. She'd never known such a man—one who would spend time with a woman speaking of what most men thought of as "women's work" instead of rushing out into the forest and fields to hunt. Finally she asked him about it.

"I love our talk, but wouldn't you rather be with my father, hawking?"

He laughed out loud. "I'll confess something," he said, "but only to you."

"What is that?" she asked.

"I don't like hawking or hunting for pleasure—what's the point in killing just for sport? It's one thing to kill for food, but another just to make a competition of it. Many times the game is just left in the field to rot. It's a waste I avoid when I can. When I can't, I pretend to like it. Cheer the dogs on. Drink when everyone else drinks. Tell stories of the *bravery* it takes to shoot down a deer." He laughed unhappily. "Will you keep my secret?"

Up to this point, Leova had taken his "confession" as teasing. Now it seemed most serious. "Of course. But...why would it be a problem?"

Ragen just laughed and squeezed her hand gently before they headed for the hall. "Sweet innocent! Someday we'll talk more of this, for now let's just enjoy the garden and each other's company."

The next morning Regan was gone before Leova rose from her bed. Not long after he departed, the rumors of fighting grew ever stronger. Days passed, then weeks, but he didn't return. By late November, despite the powerful charm Pagany had placed upon him, Leova began to fear for his safety. And as much as she worried about Ragen, she worried about Hilda even more. While she had never thought to hear of Hilda often, she had expected that some word or message would have made its way to Lothlar.

Bertram periodically sent one of his stewards to try to discover what he could about the fighting and whether his countrymen from the north were able to hold back the hostility. Abandoning the hope of ending his days in peace and quiet, he found himself urging his smith to produce more armor. He began to check fortifications and stockpile both food and weapons. Most importantly, he reaffirmed the support of the surrounding earls who owed him loyalty. Crowds of prospective soldiers often filled the hall. Young men slept on the benches at night and spent their days throwing spears, shooting arrows at dummies, drawing their swords to play-act at doing battle.

All the activity proved a good way to distract the residents of Lothlar, but Leova was not so naïve as to forget what all these activities presaged for the future. And another worrisome problem arose. Much of the play-acting and posturing confirmed her suspicions that the sons of the noble families knew that Bertram would be choosing a husband for her before long. Just in case Leova had some bit of control over selecting a marriage partner, each demonstrated his worth as a potential husband and provider, hoping that the beautiful and kind Leova would look upon him with favor. Few, however, proved wise enough to seek out Leova's company and conversation. She was, after all, merely a woman.

But, then, just as suddenly, hostilities ended. A messenger arrived bringing news of the southwest as well as the north.

"Cynge Alfred has pushed the invaders farther to the east. In one battle, he routed a fleet of sixteen enemy ships bold enough to sail into the River Stour. More'n that," he explained happily, "not three days past, I met me a warrior who made claim that his family—and neighbors from his valley—have gone home. They be ready to plant fields and breed their flocks!"

"But what about the fighting?" Bertram asked. "Does it continue anywhere?"

"Not that I hear," the man grinned. "The fighting were not long nor hard this time—found out just afore I started for Lothlar that we soon be released from service. I be on the way back to my wife!"

"But, but, but," Leova stammered. We had been told the fighting was north and east of here, not south and west. I don't understand."

"Yes, that's what I was told first; me and my group went up that way, but there really didn't seem to be any fighting there. Someone said there was some skirmishes or something, even an abbey attacked, but we ne'er saw no fighting. We even went farther east just to see maybe it was there. But it warn't. Then we were told to go south where fighting was going on, but when we got there that fighting was just done."

As welcome as this news was, it did little to reassure Leova. Regan had simply disappeared, and she feared that Hilda had been much too close to the fighting to avoid being affected by it. Desperate to hear about both of her friends, Leova broke into Bertram's questioning.

"Lord Regan of Stonehart rode to join the fighting nearly three weeks ago. Do you have word of his whereabouts?"

The messenger shook his head. "No, my lady. Our paths have not crossed."

"And my friend, the Princess Hilda, who lives at Highhear?" Leova asked. "Is she well? Is Highhear untouched?"

"Highhear? Two nights I spent within those walls. The Danes had left it standing, but wiped out its stores of grain. The Lord of the place went off to see about the fighting too and hadn't come back, but the people were expecting him." The young man reluctantly shook his head as he delivered news he knew would not be welcome. "I never saw the Princess. She were not there."

"Not there?" Leova tried to digest the information and sought the only answer that made sense. "She married and moved to her new husband's lands?"

The messenger looked uncomfortable. "No, no, my lady. She were sent to a monastery, one of the servants said. It be her mother—God bless her soul—pleaded for it from her deathbed."

"Lady Alfa is dead? And Hilda..." she stopped, trying to understand. Then, in a voice that was almost defiant, she demanded, "Why would a mother do such a thing!"

"My Lady, I know not why," he said kindly. "I were there but a short time."

Leova turned to her mother.

"Mother," she cried. "How could Hilda's family make her take on the life of a nun?"

Pagany attempted to calm her daughter. "Leova, we cannot know what happened. Perhaps Hilda agreed to go. She may well be there for her own safety—not to become a nun."

"Hilda? She'd be miserable there." Leova insisted. "She's not fit for such a life. She's been brought up to be a lord's wife, a leader, a...." Leova's voice trailed off.

Pagany remained silent for some time, holding her daughter's hand and looking into her eyes. "Leova, my beloved daughter, we can't foresee what will be. I agree—Hilda doesn't belong in a monastery."

She turned to the messenger. "Might you be mistaken?"

"I only know what was told to me, My Lady," he replied. "And her was not at the hall."

Pagany and Bertram glanced at each other, concerned for both Hilda's and their daughter's wellbeing. Hugging her daughter, Pagany tried to reassure her.

"As ill-suited as we think she is for the religious life, perhaps Hilda will have to find a way to make it her vocation. And she may be there, you know, only for her own safety." Leova began to weep quietly. It didn't seem that was probable since the fighting had ceased and Hilda was, apparently, still at the monastery.

Pagany didn't weep, but her heart filled with sorrow at the thought of the young, adventuresome Hilda in the restricted walls of a monastery. She could only hope that the spirit the girl had always demonstrated would be her salvation.

As the messenger left the following morning, Leova quietly touched his arm. "Please, if you hear more about my friend Hilda, please, please send a message somehow." The young man nodded at the obviously distressed woman as he passed out of the gate and disappeared down the long road leading away from Lothlar.

Chapter 3: Hilda Serves at the Monastery (878)

Hilda punched down the bread in the dough trough with growing force. The chant the nuns had taught her to sing while she baked also helped her work out her frustration.

"Mind yourself, Sister Hilda," chuckled Sister Sewenna. "The Lord wants us to knead his gift, not beat it to death!"

Hilda replied, "Yes, sister," in a voice she hoped passed for meek contrition.

Like many of the young who came from the ruling class, Pryncess Hilda found it a struggle to serve quietly and without question at the monastery. The chores she found herself performing—baking bread, sweeping the floors, tending to the small herb and flower plot within the monastery walls—were the same chores as the other young girls undertook, but most of them had come more willingly to the monastery. Hilda, who could not find it in her heart to forgive her mother and father, more than once received reprimands for losing her temper, and she consistently performed penances for small infractions brought on by her need for fun and adventure. And despite working side by side with her fellow novices, she had made no friends. The monastery rules forbade personal friendships, but she couldn't help noticing that many of the women her age whispered together when they were supposed to be working and chatted in quiet groups when talking was permitted. At first, her sorrow at the loss of Leova had kept her from seeking the comfort of friendship with these strangers; but even if she'd tried to form bonds, it wouldn't have been easy. From the beginning, Hilda was treated differently from other members of the novitiate. The elders of the community paid a subtle deference to her, bringing extra privileges—time alone, easier tasks, and punishment far less harsh than those given the other girls for mistakes and infractions of the rules. Hilda unearthed that truth as the days passed. Within a month it became obvious that no one had any intention of letting her serve only a year and then return home. Everyone else, it seemed, knew that Hilda was being groomed to be an abbess, regardless of the promises that she'd serve "only a little while." The knowledge that she would bypass others who worked harder than she did created resentment in those whom she might have turned to for comfort.

Gradually the routine of early rising, chapel seven times a day, gardening, and plain meals served at the unvarying hours of nine, twelve, and six crept into the rhythms of Hilda's body. Nonetheless, an abiding anger stayed alive despite the illusion of acquiescence she strove to maintain. The longer she contemplated her father's failure to stand up to her mother and Ceolwulf, the more she questioned whether she wanted to return to someone so unwilling—or unable—to defend her. Often in her bed at night, she planned her escape to Leova at Lothlar.

"Caedmon and I will leave after Vigils. Midnight prayers always put everyone into a deep sleep." That late night departure always formed the first step in her plan. The rest of the escape would at first seem simple. On the journey to Highhear, she'd traveled for at least part of the way by herself, she reasoned. Surely with a companion, she could travel off the road to avoid being taken back. They could lodge with the people she had met on the way to Highhear. At this point, her plan began to falter. What if Caedmon proved unwilling to go with her? The road blurred in her memory; they might lose their way. Not everyone on the journey would welcome a small boy and an escaping novitiate—the people she had encountered were pledged to her father. And slavers often took stray children and young women and sold them....

She'd roll over in her narrow bed, wondering whether—if they did succeed in making it back to Lothlar safely—Leova's father would allow her to stay.

"Probably not," she'd conclude, and tears would fill her eyes. Yet that did not keep her from working out a new plan the next night.

Gradually, however, the plans gave way to despair as her resources disappeared. Caedmon had proved useful to the animal keepers; she saw him only intermittently and was never permitted to speak with him. Her father had insisted that Ethel return to the hall to run the household. Snatching her nurse away proved once again to Hilda that her father could not be trusted to put his daughter's needs and desires before his own.

The only way to bear this confinement was the hope of returning to her true friend, Leova. Gradually, however, her hope of escape faded, and life stretched interminably before her—work, prayer, endless isolation from the people she loved, and no chance to find the adventure she craved. One of the priests had cheerfully reported in chapel that "when God made time, he made plenty of it." God had made a mistake, Hilda decided.

Several months after Hilda's arrival, Abbess Edyth sought her out in the garden where she worked. Following close behind the elderly nun was a young man in clerical robes carrying a small book.

"It's important that you learn to read," announced the Abbess, without bothering to explain why. "Brother John, who I believe showed you manuscripts during your first visit, will be your instructor. Spend four hours each day with him and his manuscripts."

Seeing the protest on Hilda's face, she added quickly, "You need no longer work in the kitchen. This does not, however, excuse you from your afternoon work with the herbs and flowers."

The Abbess smiled, not with affection, but with the awareness that she had delivered an unanticipated boon. "Decide what hours best fit your schedules, and tell your superiors to speak with me about the change of tasks." And then she was gone as quickly and unexpectedly as she had come. The two acolytes stared at each other uncomfortably.

"Shall we meet after *Sext*? In the scriptorium?" John asked. His obvious shyness kept him from sounding like a hard-minded teacher.

Hilda could only nod. She had been looking forward to the day her reading lessons would begin. On her earlier visit, the manuscripts and the smell of the ink and the feel of parchment had enticed her. Devoting her time to challenging work, work which had the potential to stir up her mind, promised the possibility of adventure of sorts. Already the world looked a bit brighter.

Learning to Read

The first lesson demonstrated to John that his new pupil had a quick mind and an eager curiosity, coupled with an unyielding streak of stubbornness.

"Why do I have to learn this strange language you call Latin in order to learn to read?" Hilda asked as they started their session. "Why read and write in Latin and limit our own language to speaking?"

"Because Latin is the language of writing," was the only answer John knew to give. Hilda did not look convinced. "And..." he struggled to find a better reason, "monks speak to one another in Latin–especially when their native languages are different. You see," he explained, warming to his own answer, "the people of the church use Latin because it's the same all over the world. All civilized peoples—from Rome to (he gestured vaguely before finding an example) this abbey—can share the knowledge of Christ and his followers. And...most of the knowledge of the past can only be found by reading books in Latin!"

Seeing her stubborn face, he cut her off before she could speak. "Think about it, Sister Hilda, our spoken language, the one that your people and my people use to converse and conduct our business in, differs from the tongues of both the north and west. Surely you have encountered folk from the west—or perhaps the Scots and the Picts who live north of us? They don't talk as we do— the words for common things sound different. And haven't you heard the red-haired ones talk to one another? Trying to speak to them requires making signs and pointing at objects unless you have access to someone who has been enslaved by them for years!"

"Or to someone that *we* enslaved for years," Hilda rejoined.

John halted momentarily at the distraction, then went on with his argument a little more gently.

"If we had a common language, we might be able to put an end to slavery. Sue for peace instead of dealing in war. We need a way for all of us to speak to one another. Latin, what you call the language of writing, makes it possible for nations to speak to each other."

"If they all know Latin," scoffed Hilda.

John lost all patience, and his voice rose in exasperation. "If you want to learn to read, you'll have to learn Latin. That's how it is! Our manuscripts are all *written* in Latin!" He suddenly realized that she was laughing at his passion, and once again resumed with a forced calm, "There's no point in quarreling with the truth."

Hearing the serious tone return to John's speech, Hilda decided to forego her questioning—at least temporarily—so that they could get on with the lesson. She loved reading. When she connected the strange letters to the Latin words, magic happened. Small marks could contain such great thoughts, thoughts that John shared with her, and ideas so new and wonderful that he wouldn't hesitate to explain. John's passion for the words and the manuscripts created an excitement she had never experienced before, and— although it was hard to admit—she valued the looks of approval he gave her when she understood something new.

They had other arguments engendered by the act of reading. Hilda could not be content with merely learning to *read* the words of the scriptures. The passages raised questions, questions she could not refrain from asking, questions which tested John's patience. As they worked though Genesis, she quizzed him mercilessly.

"Why should God make Eve from Adam's rib? Why didn't he make her from the clay of the earth as he did Adam?"

"We are not to question the word of God," he would insist. "He had reasons beyond human understanding for his means of creation. Read the text and accept it."

"Such acceptance is quite beyond me." Seeing his outrage she continued in a voice she hoped sounded inspired by reason. "I don't think your God intended us to just read and be silent. Perhaps he created two levels of reading to challenge us. First, He wants us to know what the letters are and what the words are and how to pronounce and copy them. But, then, He wants us to understand what they mean for our own lives—not just for the lives of the people in the scriptures."

Brother John didn't say so, but he could hardly quarrel with such reasoning. Furthermore, he didn't want to quarrel. His student's enthusiastic application of logic to the texts she struggled with brought him new insights; he was learning as much from her as she was learning from him. She was able to point out to him many of the technicalities of the language which he had not noticed. And as uncomfortable as he found them, her questions taxed all his prior knowledge, providing him with an exhilaration he had not experienced for several years.

One day, a week later, as the two sat on a grassy plot for their daily morning lesson, Hilda stopped in the middle of reading about Babel, the land where God punished an arrogant people by making them all speak a different language.

"John," she blurted out, "this passage suggests that God created all languages. So, isn't our language written in letters, too? Could I learn to read my language as well as Latin?"

"My dear Sister Hilda," replied John in the condescending voice that told her he was once again caught up in his belief in the superiority of Latin. "There is no reason to learn such a common tongue. Everything God requires you to know exists in Latin."

"But, why," persisted Hilda, "shouldn't the words of God be in the language of his peoples so that everyone can understand them. If given my choice, I'd create such manuscripts and teach *all* people to read them!" She hesitated for a moment, weighing whether she should say what she was thinking, but her stubbornness won out.

"And why cannot some of the songs and recited stories we hear be written also?" Her green eyes flashed with determination, striking Brother John with the force of her beauty. He dropped his eyes from her face in confusion; he should not be having these thoughts, he sternly admonished himself.

Misunderstanding his sudden withdrawal, Hilda paused, suddenly sure that she'd gone too far. "Why don't you look at me, Brother John? Is my idea such a bad one that you can't look me in the eye and tell me it's stupid?"

"Hilda, it's an excellent idea, but I don't know how to help. I can't read our own language, nor do I know anyone who could teach us. If manuscripts containing such stories exist, I'm not sure how to find them."

John hesitated, considering the problem and a possible solution. His face brightened, "Brother William might know; he cares for the manuscripts in the scriptorium." He laughed quietly and rather scornfully, "Many of our community consider him dim-witted, but they have never talked with him. I know him well, and know the worth of his counsel. He is my half-brother—we have the same mother."

"Brother John, do others know of your bond?"

"*Sister* Hilda," he replied, emphasizing the word *sister*, "in the monastery we are all brothers and sisters. Worldly kith and kin relationships are never more important than spiritual ones."

Hilda nodded, but curiosity got the better of her almost immediately. "I know William has been here since he was quite young. Your parents deserted him?"

"Not deserted, exactly. His father wished that he be given to the church," John said. "My mother never seemed to object to giving sons to the church. Since we have two other brothers, it's for the best. William has no interest in his rightful inheritance; I came of my own free will. I, as the youngest brother, have no chance at an inheritance; I would only be a burden to my family. Here both William and I feel at home and are contributors to a different family."

His voice faded away, and Hilda, remembering her own mother's decision to give her to the church, felt a growing sympathy for John and his brother.

John continued to speak: friendship that permitted the personal was not something he had allowed himself for many years. He found it difficult to deny its pull on both his thoughts and feelings.

"It's very hard to be shuttled off to a strange place at such a young age," Hilda whispered, but John could sense she was reflecting the pain she felt upon her own—much later—arrival at the monastery.

"William was about four when he was send here; I was told he didn't speak for almost a year," John continued; "Abbess Edyth gave him a little patch of garden, not expecting much, but the first year proved that he could produce more on that tiny plot than others did on land twice its size."

"How did he come to serve in the scriptorium?" Hilda asked. She couldn't quite imagine that the Abbess would let a productive worker spend his time with books instead of vegetables.

"The same way you did," laughed John. "It proved more important—and more profitable—to use his talent for the preservation of books. You don't think the only reason Abbess Edyth has you learning to read is for your own pleasure? Your father hasn't paid good gold to the monastery so that his daughter can pull weeds. Neither had my mother paid for William's care so that he could be a laborer. She might have use for him later, so he needed to be educated."

Hilda couldn't help but see the logic behind setting the children of nobles to work in high preference tasks. "But if all here thought he was simple...?"

"What I was told was that he remained very quiet, speaking only as his needs required, but as he grew older, he began to linger about the scriptorium, and the monks set him about small tasks, allowed him to retrieve manuscripts for them. Within a few months, he had begun, with occasional guidance from others, to read. As his language skills grew, he reordered the manuscripts on the shelves, arranging them by content, then name. He finally devised a map which showed each manuscript's location—he called it his catalogue—so that scribes could retrieve manuscripts far more quickly. No more shuffling through stacks of dusty pages. William now serves as reeve for all the books."

"And do the other monks now respect him?" Hilda asked.

"They consider him odd, but can't deny his talents. They call him 'different,' but in truth, he merely keeps his thoughts to himself, preferring isolation to company. Reading to praying."

"As far as I'm concerned, that's not odd at all." Hilda smiled. "Let's seek him out tomorrow—see if he knows of a manuscript in our language."

That night, for the first time since her arrival at the abbey, Hilda did not go to sleep planning her escape. Instead she thought about ways to decipher the mysterious words on the page. After morning prayers and the minimal breakfast time, both of which seemed an eternity to Hilda, she eagerly sought John.

"Perhaps," Hilda whispered, "there may even be a manuscript wholly in our language." Quickly she ran to William, followed by John.

"And how may I help you?" William asked in a quiet voice.

"Brother William," said Brother John, with clear affection. "Do you have any manuscripts—not in Latin—but in the language of everyday people?"

William's face lit up and he immediately went to a dark shelf in the corner of the scriptorium and returned with a dusty book. "I think this is a Bible," he announced on his return as he gently placed it on the table and opened it to a center page. The page had been marked with a small leather patch decorated with an elaborate interlaced knot that had seemed to have no beginning and no end.

"An 'eternity' knot," he said smiling at the pure complexity of the mark.

"Thank you, thank you; we will treat it well." Hilda said as she and John turned to a work table where they carefully opened up the cover, gasping at the beauty of the page itself. They then transferred their eyes to the text.

Quickly Hilda recognized that most of the letters were the same as the letters in Latin. They found that when they gave the letters the sounds of the Latin letters, they knew what the words were.

On frymðe wæs Word, and þæt Word wæs mid Gode, and God wæs þæt Word. Þæt wæs on fruman mid Gode.

Immediately both of them knew they could read the sentence, checking it against the Latin just to be certain. Slowly they read together

In the beginning was the Word, and that Word was with God, and God was that Word.

John pointed to the first of the non-Latin letters in the English text. "Now we know how to pronounce that symbol whenever we see it."

"Yes, yes," Hilda replied excitedly. "And there are two more odd symbols that we can recognize too." She was silent for a moment, studying the English words intently. "Of course," she whispered, "those are symbols for sounds Latin doesn't have and English does."

John could only marvel at the quickness of his student's mind. He began to read aloud the English text stopping only briefly at the new symbols. But soon, he had no need to do so. He turned to Hilda: "Now it's your turn to read to me."

Hilda read as easily as he had. "Oh, John, I haven't been this happy about anything for months and months!"

Impulsively Hilda threw her arms around John's neck and hugged him tightly. John, feeling the breath of a young woman on his cheek and the warmth of Hilda's body against his, pulled away. Looking into Hilda's eyes, he carefully removed her hands from his shoulders and just as carefully moved them until they rested on the book before them. He couldn't bring himself, however, to immediately let go. Hilda stared at him quizzically, taking pleasure in the weight of his hand on hers, but suddenly feeling as awkward as her companion. Saying nothing more, she turned back to the manuscript pages before her, carefully ignoring the eyes of the others in the scriptorium.

To cover his discomfort, and more importantly, his pleasure, John put distance between them by once again becoming the teacher. "Let us continue with this important work," he stated stiffly, much too aware of the averted eyes of others in the scriptorium, including those of his brother.

The next weeks passed swiftly. Hilda arose early every morning, attended morning vespers, ate her sparse breakfast, then joyfully went off to the scriptorium where she and John together learned to read the language they spoke. The scribes in the scriptorium looked at the two often as they laughed joyfully over some new discovery. Some smiled. Never had learning and knowledge seemed so joyous and blessed. Others shook their heads in disapproval and reported the young people to the Abbess. While their reports displeased her and made her uncomfortable, she did not stop the process. The work Hilda and John were doing would enhance the reputation of the monastery as a site of learning, and perhaps eventually bring in money from wealthy lords who wished to have copies of the manuscripts they deciphered and passed along to William to copy. Besides, she reasoned, what could happen when the young couple was always in plain sight, chaperoned by everyone in the scriptorium.

Slowly, however, something did begin to happen. As John and Hilda worked, their hands touched more frequently, as did their shoulders and arms. Often they would lean against each other as they studied a difficult passage, forgetting that such physical contact broke most of the rules of the monastery. And Hilda began to feel an attachment to John that she'd never felt for any friend except Leova. She tried to imagine another life in which they could be together, but despaired of escaping the monastery. Even if she could leave— which she hoped would happen eventually—John seemed devoted to God and his work. She fancied that if she could talk to him alone, he would choose her over the monastery and they might return to her father's and provide him with an heir. But any attempt to gain some privacy ended in frustration. Everyone—from the Abbess to the older monks—seemed determined to prevent them from having any contact with each other except in the scriptorium.

One late fall afternoon, about a month after the work on the manuscript began, John took advantage of the hour set aside for meditation and left the monastery grounds, climbing to the top of a small hill directly behind the row of trees where Hilda had once listened in peace to the voices from the chapel. As he looked at the abbey, he realized Hilda was climbing up to meet him.

"John, look what I have," she cried, her eyes bright with pleasure. Hilda held out a single page of manuscript on which was written over a dozen lines in the common language. "What do you think?" she asked eagerly.

John's eyes ran down the page. "*On angynne gesceop God heofon and eorðan,...*" he read. "These are the first lines of Genesis, but the page is not from a manuscript I've seen before. Where did you find it?"

Hilda granted him a teasing smile. "I wrote it *myself*—did you really think it was one of the real manuscripts?" She laughed at his perplexity, "That's wonderful! I do believe I'll become a scribe!"

John too began to laugh, which heightened his cheekbones and lightened up his eyes. "We'll not soon be separated then. I intended, my scholarly friend, to present this to you. Not only is it akin to yours, the words also bring you the Bible's first mention of the creation of males and females. From under his robe, John drew an almost identical piece of vellum and held it out to Hilda.

> *God gesceap ðonne man to sylfre licnes*
> *To sylfre licness he hie gesceap*
> *Man and wifmann he gesceap*

Pleased to know that God had shaped both men and women in His own likeness, Hilda grinned as she read what he had written, "You were doing the same thing. Isn't it remarkable how much alike we think, how much we enjoy the same things?" As they compared their writing, they drew closer. Hilda leaned gently against John's shoulder as he pointed out the elaborate "G" that headed his page. Hilda's face turned up to his to ask a question, her cheeks blushing with pleasure. Impulsively, John kissed her cheek.

"Why, Brother," she taunted mischievously, "If you can reward the student with a kiss, then I can gratefully kiss the tutor."

Hilda pulled his face down toward hers, but her lips found, not John's cheek, but his lips. To her joy, he pulled her body against his own and kissed her lips again as well as her eyelids, her cheeks, forehead, and neck. Breathing just as deeply and quickly as her companion, Hilda felt dizzy. She stepped back to regain her composure, tripped on her robe, and with a short laugh of surprise, slipped to the ground. John, trying to break her fall, also became tangled in the skirts of her robe and his own and he, too, slid to the ground, finding himself closer than ever to Hilda. As if it had a mind of its own, his hand ran up her arm under the loose-fitting robe, found her bare shoulder, and drew her closer. They kissed again, this time with deep resolve; the knowledge that they shouldn't even be touching increased their pleasure.

Abruptly, John drew back, aware of the sin they were about to commit. "Hilda, stop. Please, let's stop."

"John, we've both been so lonely…. I love you—more than I thought possible to love anyone." Her eyes met his with a steady and passionate gaze. "I don't want to stop."

In answer, he leaned forward and kissing her gently, he pressed her to the ground. There could be no stopping for either of them.

Hilda, amazed by the act of lovemaking, felt a peace and fulfillment that far surpassed any she had experienced before. John, however, as he looked down on the now calm face pressed against his shoulder, felt his own peace melt away.

"What have we done?" he groaned. "What have we done?"

Hilda's eyes slowly opened. "What we have done is no more nor less than what Adam and Eve did!" The innocence of her voice struck John to the heart.

"And they lost God's grace for all humanity!! Hilda," he whispered softly, "We have sinned against God and against the vows taken by all the good brothers and sisters of this monastery."

Hilda could not understand the quiet despair in his voice. "John, neither you nor I have taken our final vows. I'm not a nun; you're not a priest."

"Nor, my little one, are we married."

"But, we could be…surely, there can be no sin in something so beautiful, something we both had such pleasure doing. Do you not love me? Does this not seal a pledge between us?"

John was silent for a long time. Finally, halting the conflict between his desire and his duty, he spoke to Hilda. "I love you more than words can tell, but being together will be difficult—it's not something we can just stroll into the dining hall and announce."

Hilda drew away from him, not speaking, but knowing he was right. He smiled at her and pushed her tussled hair back from her forehead.

"We need to return…. I heard the songs from vespers some time ago. Everyone will be at supper, and we'll be missed. For now no one must know."

He kissed her gently, but firmly, his eyes showing love and determination. He wanted—no, needed—to find a way to be with her, but as yet had no idea how to manage it. As they stood, brushing the grass from their clothes, John realized that his pocket held one of the small eternity knots that had served as a page marker in the manuscript. He pressed it into Hilda's hand.

"Keep this," he said to Hilda. "No one will miss it from the manuscript; it will mark my devotion to you." He kissed her one last time, "Hurry now, we will be missed."

They separated so that they could descend to the abbey from different paths and slip into their places without seeming to have been together. However, the sharp eyes of the Abbess had studied John and Hilda as they hurried into the refectory, flushed and agitated. Her disquiet about the young people's relationship returned threefold. Dismissing the comments of the monks in the scriptorium might no longer be an option. The connection between Hilda and John needed to be severed, but discreetly. Angrily, she shook her head. "I'll have to see to this problem—immediately."

Hilda could not sleep that night. She wanted John next to her. It seemed natural to feel his body against hers, his breath on her face, his kisses on her breasts—not a sin. And she wanted to talk to another woman about her feelings: Leova. No one else would listen without judging. The distance between them frustrated her. For a moment she considered using her new skills to write her friend, but then she realized that the letter might fall into the wrong hands and betray her and her lover. That word "lover" took on magic in her dreams, circling around every scene her sleeping mind created.

"My lover…" thought Hilda. The complexity of that love overcame her as she considered all the problems as well as the joys of being with John. Finally, she fell into a deep sleep, so deep that she did not hear the rushing horses and excited voices that rose as a group of warriors entered the abbey courtyard several hours later.

The insistent whisper of her childhood nurse awoke her.

"Mistress Hilda! Wake up. Wake up now!" Ethel sat on the side of her bed and the moment Hilda woke, the nurse placed a quieting finger to her lips.

For a moment Hilda forgot where she was and thought she was back in her own hall. She sat straight up, suddenly frightened.

"Ethel? What are you doing here?" The old woman's eyes shifted anxiously from her mistress's face to the open door of the chamber where Abbess Edyth stood.

Alert to danger, Hilda spoke quietly but with force. "Something's wrong. My father?"

Before Ethel could answer, Abbess Edyth interrupted.

"Quick, my child," she commanded. "There's no time to explain. Come with me—and put this on." Edyth threw a monk's cowl at Hilda.

Hilda hesitated, looking at Ethel questioningly. What she saw in her old retainer's eyes silenced her. Responding to the Abbess, she rose, slipped the rough robe over her head and put on the sandals Edyth handed her. Impatiently, Abbess Edyth seized her by the arm and started toward the door. When Ethel attempted to step in, she was waved away.

"You must not be seen here," the Abbess told Ethel impatiently. "Hide in the cook's quarters."

Without a word, Ethel vanished.

Edyth guided Hilda across the grounds, through the cloister, through the kitchen quarters and into a small room in the monks' sleeping area. Finally she turned and faced the bewildered girl.

"Hilda, your cousin Bergdorf came, bringing Ethel with him, to tell us that a troop of warriors has been ransacking monasteries, apparently seeking you. He and his men left quickly to confront the marauding group, tracking them down to end their crusade—though he admits he doesn't understand it. We'll hide you for the night. Everyone at Buxton will leave in the morning, but you cannot come with us. You will leave separately."

"Leave...where?" Hilda stammered.

"No more questions. You'll need a disguise in the event they arrive here before morning. To stay in the monks' quarters, you'll need to look like a monk. This disguise will also protect you once you leave."

Frightened into absolute silence and compliance, Hilda allowed the older woman to remove her garments and wrap her breasts tightly in broad bands of cloth. The Abbess then seated her on a small stool and—to Hilda's horror—pulled a pair of shears from her pocket and began to hack none too gently at the dark curls. Hilda could only watch as her hair fell to the floor, swept up by an unknown servant. At last the Abbess stopped, brushed the stray locks from Hilda's shoulders, and indicated that the girl should once again put on the coarse garment worn by the lowliest of the order.

"The disguise isn't perfect, but it will have to do," the older woman pronounced unpleasantly. With no real attempt to explain more or give comfort to the frightened girl, the Abbess spoke in a voice that was as cold as it was dismissive. Hilda could sense that Edyth blamed her for the attack. Perhaps she was right, Hilda had to acknowledge to herself. But if she were captured, undoubtedly the enemy would force her father to pay dearly for her safety.

"Stay here in the monks' quarters until we can move you. Don't speak to anyone. Don't leave the room. Take your place on the bed and stay still. Act like a sick acolyte."

At first the girl could not force herself to lie on the crude bed that was little more than a mattress on the dirt floor. She walked back and forth in the small room, trying to relieve the sense of panic that she felt and understand the events of the last hour. At last, however, worn out with pacing, she sought what little comfort there might be on the bumpy pallet.

There was no comfort to be had. Everything about her seemed rough—the straw which stuck through the mattress, the monk's robe, the very floor and walls. She listened for sounds from the outside, hoping first that someone would come and then hoping she'd remain undiscovered. Nothing seemed to move. Through the small window, she could see only darkness.

She wasn't sure when she slept, but she woke to the sound of excited voices and running feet. Dawn had barely brightened the sky when she sat up. "Whatever is wrong now," she whispered. Just as she decided to go out, she heard someone in the hallway. Frightened, she retreated to the pallet again and pulled the covers up over her head. Hoping that she appeared to be asleep, she lay as still as possible. Someone entered the room, moving stealthily toward her. All she could hear was the sound of his breathing and her own. Again she could not stand her ignorance. Inching the blanket down so she could see, she found herself looking into the startled face of Caedmon.

"What are you doing here?" they said almost in unison.

"Shhhh'" cautioned Caedmon.

"Caedmon, what is happening? My own ignorance is frightening me!" Hilda whispered.

"What, in the name of heaven, did they do to your hair?" Caedmon cried out and then immediately put a finger to his own lips."

"Tell me something, Caedmon," Hilda threatened.

"I can't tell anything when I know nothing."

"Then you must go with me to find out."

No sooner had Hilda spoken than Caedmon, as frightened by touching his mistress as he was by what might happen to them, laid a hand across her mouth and pointed to the door. Someone was coming. The two on the bed froze into one figure as they listened to the stealthy footsteps approaching. As a figure came through the door, they breathed a sigh of relief. Hilda threw off Caedmon's restraining hand and sprang from the bed, throwing herself at William.

"Brother William!" she gasped. "Thank heaven, you've come! What's happening? Did Abbess Edyth send you?" Hilda hesitated, and asked the question she know she should not. "William, please, where is John—I mean, Brother John? Is he safe?"

"No time for questions," he answered tersely. "Come with me and be quiet." Turning to Caedmon, he continued, "Caedmon, go create a disturbance of some kind—scream or yell or chase the chickens into the yard. Anything to distract everyone."

Caedmon looked at Brother William quizzically for only a moment, and then obeyed. As William and Hilda waited, he ran out behind the kitchen and scattered the sleeping chickens who began to flap their wings and squawk in great distress. At the same time Caedmon began first to bleat like a wounded lamb and then howl like a victorious wolf, attracting the attention of the warriors who stood in the courtyard.

Taking Hilda's hand and keeping close to the wall, William led her to the shed behind the abbey where the cows were brought to feed on piles of hay. He pulled her behind the largest pile and began to burrow into it, beckoning her to follow. Hay stuck her on all sides and felt like needles against her tender feet; somewhere she had lost the sandals. But soon she worked through the hay and into a small box-like enclosure. The two fugitives pulled the hay up over the entrance and huddled into a corner of the small enclosure.

"Quiet now," cautioned William. "We must be still for a while, then I will see if it is safe."

Hilda never knew how long the two of them sat there up against one another for comfort, saying not a word. After what seemed an eternity, William signaled that he was going out to see if it was safe for them to crawl back out. Another eternity passed before he returned.

"We will need to stay here for now," he said kindly, handing her a chunk of bread. Tears came to her eyes as she realized that it now seemed as though her lovemaking with John had happened in another world. Maybe John had been right: they were being punished by an angry God. Forcing back tears, she leaned against Brother William, and wearied by all the hurry and subterfuge, she fell asleep again despite her efforts to stay awake.

When she woke, she found herself wrapped in William's arms, the blanket she had snatched from her crude mattress wrapped around both of them. She also found herself no longer surrounded by hay, but looking up into the angry face of Abbess Edyth.

"What is this? I've searched everywhere for you! And now I find you with one of the brothers, hiding in the hay." She crossed herself before continuing. "You should have waited in the room!"

Edyth did not stop to hear Hilda's answer. Pulling Hilda to her feet, she shook William and motioned him to leave them. As they walked through the darkened cloister, Hilda shook the hay out of her clothing, instinctively reaching up to brush back her hair. But suddenly remembering that it was gone, she instead pulled the cowl up over her bare head. As she did so, she heard the familiar voice of Ethel. Behind her was Caedmon. As she turned to them, a heavy hand fell on her shoulder, and she nearly screamed before she turned and once again looked up into the face of the angry Abbess.

"You must leave. Now! You will all go to Northwich, to my blood sister, Abbess Moira—it's farther west and south from Yorvik. It should provide sanctuary. All the others here have gathered what they can; we are leaving in the hope that the enemy will not harm Buxton once they know it's empty. We will go north."

Hilda had to restrain herself from asking about Brother John, but she stopped the question before it was fully formed. Not only would asking about him bring him grief, instinct told her that Abbess Edyth would not answer. Her only hope was that soon she'd have the freedom to return for him, to find a way for them to be together.

"Then who's to accompany us on our trip to Northwich?" was her only question.

"You'll have to go alone and on foot. We have no guards to spare and no horses for you to ride on. I'm sorry; it can't be helped. And even if we could provide horses and guards, it would be unwise; you three will not attract attention; a larger group would. Caedmon and Ethel will see to you. You'll travel in disguise. Being on foot will make it easier to hide if you need to. I've given Caedmon directions."

Hilda knew instinctively that there was something else behind Abbess Edyth's actions, but she wasn't sure what that was. And she was in no position to argue.

She turned to Ethel and Caedmon. "Cease your worry, young one," whispered Ethel. "The two of us will keep you safe."

Abbess Edyth allowed herself a twisted smile. Although she knew that Hilda's father would be horrified when he learned what she was about to do, sending the girl away seemed like a quick solution to several of her problems. Not only would the move to

Northwich get the girl away from the temptations of young love; it saved her the trouble of confronting Hilda about her sins— apparently not just with one man, but with two. Edyth crossed herself again as these thoughts went through her mind. And no one need be the wiser about her motivation. God had sent her an answer to her worries, she thought grimly.

Early that morning, anyone sitting up in the tree where young Hilda had perched so many months ago would have seen three rather unremarkable figures leaving the monastery grounds over a stile. A young monk walked swiftly, eyes intent on scouting the surroundings. Following close behind came a slightly older monk carrying a provisions bag slung over one shoulder and a blanket draped over the other. And lastly, an older woman made her way, leaning on a cane. As the group made its way through the herd of sheep, the young monk turned back often, searching the horizon as if seeking another lost member of the party. When no one came, he returned his eyes to the path ahead and continued trudging forward.

Soon they disappeared over the horizon, no longer visible to anyone at the monastery who might be straining to keep them in view.

Chapter 4: Leova Reluctantly Accepts a Proposal (878-879)

With the news of peace confirmed, Leova tried to put her worries about Hilda and Regan aside and, difficult as it was, she returned to her work. Her mother had continued to give her more and more responsibility for the care of Lothlar's occupants, and soon the preparation of tonics and bandaging of cuts and scrapes became routine. Several months passed during which Leova became increasingly competent as an herb-mistress. Bringing health and comfort to others brought a degree of comfort to her, a different sort of comfort but—in a sense—almost its own reward.

While trying to convince one of the smith's children to take a swallow of a tonic she'd brewed from comfrey, Leova heard the harsh sound of voices and horses riding into the courtyard.

"Bring help!" someone cried. A moment later, Bertram appeared at the door, calling his stewards and servants.

"Pagany, come. There's injury here. Bring water and bandages!" Her mother rushed to help, and after insisting the child she was tending stay put, Leova hurried to join her mother.

Near the gate, a small group of warriors had placed a pallet bearing a young man. Utterly silent, he seemed oblivious to the commotion about him. One fist opened and closed compulsively, the other clutched a bundle of white rags to his chest—rags which were slowly being stained with bright blood. At one end of the pallet was Ragen.

Pagany barked orders to the warriors while Bertram and his men took care of clearing the horses from the scene.

"Hurry, hurry. Bring him into the main hall," she bade them, then turned back and called to her husband. "I need strong drink for the boy. Will you fetch it?"

He nodded sharply and leaving his men to tend to details, headed toward the buttery. Pagany paused a moment to whisper something in the ear of an old retainer. He quickly disappeared through the gate. Leova, meanwhile, hurried to seek out blankets, ordering those who had gathered at the door to begin gathering up the bales of straw stored in the corner and arrange them into a bed.

"Good," Pagany observed as she took the blankets from Leova. "Help me here, daughter." Together they spread several blankets on top of the straw, and Pagany directed the soldiers to place the wounded man on the makeshift bed where she and Leova spread more blankets about him.

"We must bundle him up warmly and keep talking to him." She glanced up at Leova, "See to Regan: he's distraught. I'll work with this one."

Startled by hearing Regan's name, Leova looked more closely at the men who had carried the wounded man's pallet. Her friend stood quite close, his eyes on the scene before him. Leova moved to Ragen's side and gently touched his arm. The eyes that turned to her were red and staring. "It's my brother, Rolfe," he whispered and then fell silent.

Leova squeezed his hand and stood silently, not speaking because she feared she would upset him further. She knew he'd speak when he could.

Bertram rushed into the hall carrying a large flask. They all watched as Pagany drew a small tube from her belt and squeezed a few drops of liquid into the flask, then held it against the wounded man's lips. After a few sips, his body seemed to relax and his fist opened and remained quiet.

"We need to rub his arms and legs to keep his body warm and the elements flowing," she ordered, showing the warriors how to rub his limbs through the blankets. They worked silently until Pagany's messenger returned, escorting an indescribably old woman who bore a great bag over her shoulder.

"All peace, Angmar," said Pagany, bowing respectfully. "Thank you for coming."

The old woman bowed in return, then turned aside to assess the situation. Kneeling at the side of the wounded man, the crone pulled back the covers to look at the wound. Making no sound or comment at all, she quickly opened her bag and drew forth several bags from which she extracted a variety of dried herbs.

"I need water," she said to no one in particular, but when Pagany sent one of the serving girls off to the kitchen, Angmar called out to her as she hurried away: "See that it's boiled before you bring it." Then removing a small bottle from her bag, she held up Rolfe's head and had him take a few sips.

"You'll sleep now, sweetheart," she said softly. A few minutes later, his breathing grew slower and softer, and she turned to other tasks.

When the water appeared from the kitchen, Angmar turned suddenly to Leova. "You, girl. Scatter these herbs in the water and stir them until the water turns dark." Leova hastened to do so.

"My Lady," the crone said a little more gently to Pagany, "Will you prepare the bandages?"

As soon as the potion was ready, the wise woman dipped clean cloths in it and carefully washed the young man's chest, paying special attention to the ugly wound just below his ribcage. Satisfied that the area was clean, she opened a jar and began to rub the contents on the wound. As her hands moved, a soft chant came from her lips:

Against the red venom, against the foul venom,
Against the white venom, against the blue venom,
Against the yellow venom, against the green venom,
Against the black venom, against the vile venom,
Against the brown venom, against the purple venom.

Having completed the chanting of the charm, Angmar covered the skin around the wound with additional salve, bandaged it and sat for a moment watching Rolfe's face for signs of pain. Satisfied at last, she turned to the men standing around. "Leave us. The young lord needs rest and your fears will disturb his spirit."

When they made to protest, she shook her head. "He'll live; he'll live. But your watching will not help him heal. Go now."

Leova, prompted by the old woman's request, turned to Regan. "Please," she urged him, "You've done what you can for your brother. Angmar is known for her gift of healing—heed her advice. Take food and drink. After you've told us what happened, you can lie down and rest."

Gratefully, Ragen allowed her to guide him out of the hall and to the solar where the morning sun warmed the air. Bertram followed closely, but he didn't wait for Ragen to rest or take food and drink. He asked the question that everyone wanted to know.

"How did your brother come by his wound?"

Regan slumped down on a bench and looked up wearily at the older man.

"My brother, Rolfe, has been in the monastery at Buxton for these past two years. He would be there yet, but several weeks ago, raiders appeared at the walls of the monastery, and all there were forced to flee."

"The invaders?" Bertram queried.

"I believe so. No one else had threatened the area." Regan resumed his story. "Rolfe returned as soon as he could, but the monastery was virtually deserted."

"How did he find you?" Leova asked.

"By search and luck, My Lady," Ragen replied. He paused for a few moments to drink deeply from the wine that a servant brought.

"In December, the bishop assigned new nuns and priests to the abbey—and some of the others who had fled returned, as did Rolfe. Slowly the new occupants repaired the walls, refilled the food stores, and restored the scriptorium so that they could have a way to raise money for other restorations. A brother from the east, where the fighting had ended, told Rolfe that I had been looking for him. By this point, he had begun to feel unsure of his calling, I'm afraid, and he decided to strike out and find me."

Bertram nodded his head. "A good decision for the lad. He's young to make such an important move. Luckily, he has a brother such as yourself. God knows that your mother's no help to him."

Rolfe sighed and looked deep into his cup.

"Perhaps—but before he had the good luck to find me, bad luck found him. Not more than a day after he and a friend took to the road, a roving band of marauders attacked...."

"The Danes?" asked Leova.

Ralph shook his head. "Who knows? Perhaps straggling members of the enemy's troops. Perhaps outlaws. No matter which, the results were the same. They killed his companion and left Rolfe for dead—stripped both of anything of value."

"And how did you find him?" Bertram asked.

"Fortune favored him and me—perhaps to make up for the ill luck she brought before." Regan stood and walked across the room, his fatigue obvious. He turned and smiled at Leova.

"One of your forest women found him, nursed him back to consciousness—almost back to health. There we found him, and there we wanted him to stay until he was stronger. But, stubborn fool that he is, Rolfe insisted on setting off again. We, however, feared for his health. For two days, we rode through cold and wind; then his wound opened again, and despite anything we could do, he began to bleed." Regan sighed again and paused for a moment before he continued. "Soon he slipped into delirium and couldn't ride. My men constructed a pallet out of branches and rope, spread blankets on it and the four of us and our horses managed to carry him."

"Why did you come here?" Leova asked.

Her question drew another tired smile. "Lothlar was nearby and I, knowing the healing powers of your mother and—well—," he hesitated briefly, "of her companions from the forest too, we came here as quickly as the path and the horses could allow."

Ragen stopped, finally overwhelmed by his exhaustion and his fear for Rolfe.

"You must rest, my boy," Bertram insisted, rising. "Daughter, see that a room is prepared for this lad. I've given orders for his men."

"But, Rolfe needs me..." Ragen started to protest, but Leova put her hand on his shoulder to calm him.

"Don't worry. While you sleep, I'll sit by him. I'll come for you if there is any change."

The crone, Angmar, looked up as Leova entered the hall to keep her promise to Ragen. Rolfe slept peacefully now, but the lines of pain still etched his face as he slept. Even in his pain, however, Rolfe was handsome almost to the point of being beautiful. The herb-woman had been rubbing his brow, but now she stopped to place a wet cloth on his forehead.

"I transfer my strength to him," she whispered, answering Leova's silent question. "He needs the power of a healer."

"Can I help in any way?" Leova asked gently. "You are weary and need to renew your strength for your own sake."

The woman turned gratefully and removing the cloth from Rolfe's sleeping form, placed it in Leova's hand. "Your strength—that of the young—will nourish him more than that of an old woman like me," Angmar said. Patting the young woman on the arm, she left the room to seek her rest.

Leova turned to the task and carefully soaked, then wrung out the cloth for his head. The water smelled of parsley and basil, whose gentle smell would calm restlessness. As she placed the cloth on his forehead, Rolfe opened his eyes. Leova drew in her breath slightly. Rolfe's eyes sought the source of his care. When his gaze met with hers, she felt more than the usual sympathy of a healer for her patient. He smiled and slipped back into sleep, but Leova found herself wanting to know more about this stranger.

As the days wore on, Leova spent many hours sitting by Rolfe's side, all the while telling herself she was lending her "strength" to the man she longed to know. She embroidered linens to pass the time and, when he was awake at intervals, talked a bit about how he came to be there. He could recall almost nothing about any of the attacks or the trip with his brother to Lothlar. Leova also played quietly on her small harp. To encourage him to sleep, she sang some of the songs that she and Hilda had learned as children. Rolfe, enjoying the attention greatly, often pretended to be restless merely to hear her voice. He was not loath to stay where he was.

Twice each day, one of the forest women arrived and spent some time forcing Rolfe's legs and arms up and down, refusing to heed his groans. One of them explained to Leova that if he did not move his limbs, they could decay and instructed her in ways to work with them.

Eventually, however, he could linger no longer in bed.

One bright morning, when Leova had just finished a song, Angmar appeared and stood staring at the two young people. She

143

put her hands on her hips, her mouth set in stern disapproval. "Time to stop entertaining him," she said to Leova. "You'll do more harm than good if you coddle him."

Turning to Rolfe, she issued a sharp command. "Get up. You must work those legs of yours, build some strength in your back muscles. Do you want to be a weak man? One who has to depend on others for the least bit of business?"

Leova started to protest, but the old woman silenced her. "If he doesn't walk, his legs will wither. Help him to rise if you want to be of use." She smiled a bit before she went on. "You can sing to him after dinner if he works hard this morn."

Frightened by this dire prediction, Rolfe swung his legs over the side of the bed, determined to show the old woman his strength and was alarmed to find out how right she was. His legs would hardly bare his weight. Angmar called for help. Two brawny servants appeared, ready to lift Rolfe to his feet and steady him for the few steps he could take.

"There," said his healer. "There's a start. A few more steps each day and you'll return to your old self. Think of it as training for battle...or as a feat you perform for that God of yours."

For several days Rolfe needed the support of Bertram's servants, but in a short time, he could walk with the aid of only one, and finally it was balance, not support he needed. As the wise woman insisted, Leova appeared with a cleanly whittled cane in her hand, and with its support, he needed to lean only slightly on Leova's shoulder to move about.

However, as Rolfe's health returned, so did his anxiety. He longed to know how those at the monastery had fared. He appeared to value the friends he had made there far more than his mother or brother. Surely some of them had escaped the raiders. Had they returned to its safe walls? Regan had told him that the abbey had been somewhat restored. Heartened by that news, Rolfe continued to insist that he had to return.

But Regan, too, had an unwelcome matter to contend with. Although he had sent several messengers to Stonehart, only one had returned—with troubling news. It was common knowledge that

Regan had been the true leader at Allmana's hall for some time. As young as he was, he remained more responsible and more level-headed than the other men of the family: Lord Stephen, his mother's lover, and his older brother, Robert. Lady Allmana let him take on more and more responsibility without acknowledging his role as manager of the estate. Since Regan had left Stonehart to search for Rolfe, his mother had barricaded herself in her rooms, refusing to emerge or to see anyone who sought her help or advice. Stephen and Robert took advantage of Regan's absence to lay waste to the wine stored for the winter. Neither of them bothered to see to the day-to-day care of the estate. Only Jankin tried to tend the farms and protect the grounds. The manor had been raided, however, not by the enemy, but by Allmana's own servants. Everyone from the cook to the tenant farmers fought over food, bedding, and what little wool for clothing remained.

Ragen, torn between his love for his brother and his duty to Stonehart, did not want to leave until he knew that Rolfe would recover. On the day he watched Rolfe rise and walk without aid, he met with Bertram and Pagany.

"I must return to Stonehart and save it for my family. My mother has showed little concern for Rolfe and me, but I owe her my fealty. He paused, I cannot give her my unquestioning love, but I would protect what property we have."

"I agree," replied Bertram. "Someone must see that your legacy is safe. I'll send some of my men with you in case of trouble." And so the young man set out for home with Pagany and Leova's assurances that they'd watch over his brother.

Winter set in, but despite Rolfe's growing anxiety, the February days passed pleasantly for both Leova and him. Winter's cold confined them to the hall except for an hour or so at midday, but once again Leova had a companion who enjoyed what she enjoyed and who was full of stories she had never heard. She could not, however, ignore evidence that his anxiety did not abate and, in fact, became more intense as the days passed.

One afternoon, as they sat before a roaring fire, she watched as he lost his temper over the chess piece he was carving. "God's Blood!" he cried and threw it across the room.

"Rolfe! Whatever is the matter?"

Shamefaced, he walked across the room to recover his carving. "Many pardons, Leova. I just cannot bear one more thing I can't do!" She looked at him, puzzled. He ran his hand through his hair and turned to face her. "That's not what I mean...I mean.... I can't bear staying here and doing nothing while Regan deals with our mother and brother, and while my friends at the monastery toil to rebuild what was lost."

Her heart sank. She knew what he would say next.

"I must go back and help them," he said quietly.

"Oh, I wish you wouldn't," she blurted out and immediately blushed, for she knew her words were far too brash and forward.

"I must," was his only answer.

"Why?"

"Because...because," he seemed to be talking to himself more than to the sad-faced woman by his side, "I left behind matters I need to attend to." He looked away refusing to meet her eyes, "And I need to know what happened to those I worked and worshiped with. It may be that I belong there."

"You left because you weren't certain you should be a priest!" Leova blurted out.

"True," he looked up, surprised. He did not remember revealing that struggle to her.

"And now do you wish to be?"

Rolfe could see the pain in her eyes. "Believe me, Leova, I really don't know. And I fear that only at Buxton will I find an answer to that question."

Leova turned her face away so he would not see the tears in her eyes, but he placed his hand gently under her chin and turned her face back to his. Bending down, he kissed her lightly on the forehead. She was surprised to see that tears filled his eyes also.

"Matters are not always as we would wish them to be," he whispered.

The herb-woman reluctantly let her patient go. Although she knew full well he was healed sufficiently to be on his way, she had grown to like this young man and had been watching the growing affection between him and Leova with pleasure.

Bertram sent off a messenger to Ragen, to let him know of his brother's decision, and to everyone's surprise, the messenger returned accompanied by Ragen himself.

That afternoon, as they gathered before the fire in Bertram's great hall, it became obvious that Regan was much distressed about affairs at home.

"Brother. I know you wish to return to Buxton, but I need your help at home."

"Our mother? Robert?"

Turning his back to Leova's family, Regan cast a meaningful look at his younger brother. "Let us talk as we make the journey back; these good people do not need to hear our tales of woe."

Rolfe hesitated, not willing to force his brother to speak, but aware that something momentous must have happened.

"Rest here a bit and let us help you with your concerns," interrupted Pagany. "There's no hurry, surely."

Regan looked out the window at the darkening sky. "None but that which you can see over the hill. Snow and wind approach, and if we delay we will not be able to return at all." He took her hand in his, and kissed it. "Thank you for your kind hospitality, but we should ride immediately." He stopped and took a good look at Rolfe. "Are you fit to ride?"

"Yes, of course." Rolfe replied impatiently. "I was going to leave tomorrow for Buxton."

"Then, we go. At once."

Rolfe nodded in agreement, and the two brothers rose, embraced Leova lovingly, and paid their respects to Bertram and Pagany. Then they strode out of the hall, shoulder to shoulder.

Not an hour later, all the preparations for the journey had been completed, and the brothers departed. Leova, standing next to Angmar, watched from the gate as they rode away. Her heart feared that she would never see Rolfe again, but there was nothing she could do to keep him close.

The herb-woman, seeing the young woman's sorrow, had no need to ask which brother Leova most yearned to see again. "Do not weep, young one. You and he will meet again, even though you may spend some time apart."

Leova nodded allowing herself to believe the old woman and sending a silent blessing toward the man she had come to love.

First a Surprise and Then a Betrothal

Jankin stood in the great hall of Lothlar, looking as if he'd rather be any place other than before Leova and her parents. "My Lord Regan has sent me with news from Stonehart," he said solemnly to Bertram.

He paused, and looked at the floor.

"Tell us, pray tell us!" said Leova, anxious at his delay and fearing that Rolfe had fallen ill again.

"I fear it is not good news."

Ignoring his daughter's interjection, Bertram spoke carefully, "That, perhaps, is even more reason to tell us at once."

"A terrible tragedy has come to his family."

Leova's body went cold and she felt her legs weakening beneath her. "Rolfe has once again fallen ill?" she asked.

"No, my lady," Jankin managed a weak smile. "My Lord Rolfe prospers." He hesitated again. "The matter concerns his brother, Lord Robert. And his wife...."

Leova felt instant relief, followed by a feeling of guilt since she had put Rolfe's safety and health before that of anyone else's at Stonehart. "Lady Wyomina is ill?"

"Leova!" her father demanded. "Be silent and let the man tell his tale!"

Jankin shook his head in distress. "Not three mornings ago, their servant found Lord Robert in his bed, a knife in his chest, and his Lady dead also. Poison in the cup by her bedside. They're both dead!"

"And who has done this thing?" Bertram asked.

"Lady Wyomina. It appears that she went mad and stabbed Lord Robert, then took her own life."

"And the reasons for this desperate act?"

"Lord Regan did not say."

"What do *you* say?" Bertram pushed harder.

"I know only what their servants told me," answered Jankin.

"Well, servants usually know the truth first," Bertram said, somewhat sardonically. "Tell us how the household explains these deaths."

Jankin once again hesitated and then carefully began to explain what he knew. It was dangerous ground he tread—even a servant as important as he was could be punished for revealing secrets of an estate. "Sir Robert beat his wife. The bruises on her face were not easy to hide, and even though he often locked her in their quarters, her servants saw."

Pagany soft voice revealed her horror. "And Lady Allmana? Why did she allow these assaults?"

"Lady Allmana has long refused to care what happens in the hall. She only speaks to her sons when there is urgent need, but at least she addresses them civilly. She talked to Lady Wyomina as if she were the lowest of servants, when she bothered to speak to her at all. There was no help for Robert's wife—or hope Allmana would intervene for her."

"And Lord Regan and Lord Rolfe? Did they not help?" Pagany queried.

"They confronted Lord Robert, constantly admonished him about his behavior, but he ignored them, said he was now Lord of Stonehart and could do as he wished."

"Poor Wyomina," Pagany shook her head in bewilderment. "A woman unhappy on her wedding day will only become more so."

"The lady asked if she could return to her parents, but my mistress refused to allow it. Nor would she allow them to visit Stonehart. The poor woman had no friends. No comfort made her life easier. These deaths were surely born of cruelty."

"What will happen now? Are Ragen and Rolfe taking control

of the estate?"

"They work to bring the manor back to order. Everything has been in chaos since the Lady Allmana ceased to care about what went on around her."

Pagany broke in. "Wasn't Rolfe to return to the monastery?"

"Yes, My Lady, clearly he is eager to leave, but he knows his responsibilities and will stay, I am sure, until matters are straightened out. Poor man, he had the unpleasant task of telling Wyomina's parents."

"And did they get satisfaction from your mistress?" Bertram asked, aware that by law Allmana would have to compensate them for Wyomina's death.

"No," Jankin replied. "When they came to fetch the body, they confronted Allmana, blaming her and her son for their daughter's madness and death. Lady Allmana insisted that they must pay the penalty for Robert's death, and that their land would be forfeit. Against Lord Regan and Lord Rolfe's wishes, she had them driven off their own property. They're not only grief stricken, but homeless."

"She is as heartless as she is strange," Leova murmured, turning to her parents.

"There's stranger news yet," Jankin hastened to add. "No sooner had one matter been settled, another arose. This new event may help solve the problems my mistress has caused."

"Explain," Bertram demanded.

"In the midst of the confusion, William, Lady Allmana's first husband's son, arrived at Stonehart, demanding that she give up control of the lands—turn them over to him and the other two sons."

"Another son?" Pagany inquired. "Where has he been?"

"At the monastery at Buxton, where Lord Rolfe had served. She committed William to the church when he was quite young. Naturally, Lady Allmana refused to acknowledge him and demanded he be thrown off the grounds!"

"And what prevented that?" asked Bertram, always interested in the conflicts created by power.

"His brothers. Allmana's behavior has been so bizarre that they can no longer tolerate it. Rolfe and Ragen intend to strip her of

150

the power that lets her corrupt Stonehart."

Everyone was rendered silent by the enormity of what had come to pass.

At last Bertram broke the silence. "I have many questions, Jankin, but I think your masters must speak for themselves. These are serious matters with grave consequences."

Leova, seeing that Jankin was to be dismissed, decided to ask the question she most wanted answered. "Jankin, will Rolfe remain at home now?"

"Only until the family is once again settled—then he'll return to the monastery."

Leova felt a moment of pain. She did not want him to go far away. She wanted to see him again. Then, a bit of hope crowded its way into her mind. Settling the family might mean that he would stay long enough to change his mind about the religious life.

Jankin returned to Stonehart, but weeks passed with no further news from their unfortunate neighbors to the north. Soon Leova and her parents resigned themselves to hearing nothing. As winter began to lose its grip, an ill wind seemed to blow on Bertram's hall also. In the late fall, an unknown sickness had begun to affect the sheep and cattle. Efforts to isolate the healthy livestock had failed, and the disease had moved relentlessly from one farm animal to another—few survived. In desperation, Bertram called in the herb-women, but even they could not help. Angmar believed that a malevolent spirit moved across the lands, one so powerful that her herbs and charms were useless. That spirit also slowly entered Bertram's anxious and flustered heart and mind, causing him to weaken.

Lothlar's occupants faced the end of winter without badly needed wool and without hope of healthy new stock in the spring. Slowly but surely, the farmers began to seek shelter on the grounds of the hall, knowing that their efforts alone would not be enough to survive the winter. The added responsibility and the loss of valuable stock weighed heavily on Bertram, and he began to sink into a dark mood which had no relief. He watched painfully as his goods and prosperity slipped away from him. Finally, he took to his bed.

Pagany and Leova despaired as their efforts to bolster Bertram's well-being turned to naught. His illness frightened them more than the condition of their lands. "I fear," Pagany confided to her daughter, "your father will die."

"Is there nothing we can do, mother?"

Pagany had no answers. Both women felt paralyzed; and while they still went about their daily tasks, in their minds they waited for Bertram's death.

Help came from an unexpected, and not entirely welcome, source.

In mid-March, Ragen, Rolfe, and their older, but new-found brother, William, appeared in the hall. They discovered Pagany and Leova in the great hall, sewing before the fire. Pagany, worn out from tending Bertram, threw back her shoulders and immediately assumed her role as a hostess. "My lords, welcome. Come sit by the fire and let me bring you refreshment."

Regan, speaking for all three of them, accepted her greeting with thanks, but his quick eyes took in Pagany's thin frame and tired eyes. "Are you well, my lady? I had heard there was sickness here, and I am concerned for your health."

"No," Pagany said firmly. "I am but tired. It is Lord Bertram whose health you should worry about. He is weakened in mind and body." All three of the young men expressed sympathy, their eyes and voices revealing that they were not merely being polite. Both Ragen and Rolfe considered the older man a friend as well as an elder.

Leova, happier than she'd been in months, eagerly tried to catch Rolfe's attention and was dismayed by his coldness. To her great confusion, her friend studiously avoided looking in her direction.

A servant appeared with a pitcher of ale and a few sweet cakes, all that the family could offer at such short notice. After a few moments of courteous conversation, the small group grew silent. It was obvious that they had come for a purpose.

Ragen looked around at his brothers, nodded, and then spoke directly to Pagany, "As you might guess, we've come on rather serious—but we hope favorable—business. We had hoped to go into the matter with Lord Bertram and you, but if he is too ill...." His voice trailed off, not sure what else to say.

Pagany, hesitant to disturb her husband, made a quick decision. "I will speak with you first. If I decide that Bertram should be involved, we will then include him. And Leova?"

"May we talk privately?" Leova felt the urgency in his voice. A small trickle of fear coursed down her spine, but she sat quietly by the fire while Pagany moved to the bench with the three young men.

The conversation among the four of them became quite intense. Both Regan and William looked in her direction from time to time, but Rolfe sat stone-like with his back to her. With growing anxiety, she began to suspect that she was the subject of their conversation.

Finally, Pagany arose from the bench. "I must talk to Lord Bertram; he must be part of these negotiations. Leova, see that the young men are attended to," she requested and moved to the door, disappearing through it without so much as a smile for her daughter.

"Negotiations?" thought Leova. Why would her parents "negotiate" with Allmana's sons? Surely they would not give up any of their land despite its failing condition. Once again a sense of unease descended upon her. She rose reluctantly and moved toward the guests. Seeing her discomfort, Ragen rescued her by asking if she would walk about with him for a while. Taking his arm, she looked back at Rolfe, who seemed to be making himself small and perhaps invisible. Skillfully, Regan led her away from the others, engaging in a senseless conversation about one of the wall tapestries.

After they had exhausted all possible conversation about the tapestry, they fell silent, and Regan looked about the room curiously. "Your hall appears to be in need of repair," he commented, more in concern than criticism.

"My father's illness has worked a hardship on us all." She couldn't help but offer excuses, even though she knew Regan did not expect them. "With the sheep and cattle diseased, everyone has been too busy to make minor repairs. All will be right soon," she ventured.

"I'm sure it will," Regan offered, hearing the note of desperation in her voice. Desperation and fright, he thought. That fright didn't disappear even after her mother returned. Gently, Pagany asked Regan and his brothers to wait, then, even more gently, led Leova to her father's room. Bertram sat up in bed, pale and wan, but still somehow forceful. "Sit here beside me, my child," he beckoned. "Listen carefully."

A glance at her mother told Leova that Pagany was as intent as her father.

"Lord Regan and his brothers have come with an offer of marriage for you." He took her hand in his and held it tightly. "We have accepted it."

"Mother?" Leova questioned, but Pagany could not quite meet her daughter's gaze. When she spoke, she seemed to talk to the wall as much as to Leova. "Your father and I are in agreement, to object would be to dishonor us."

"Marriage?" Leova thought. To Rolfe? Why should she object? Her parents knew how she felt about him.

"Lord William and you will be betrothed next week and married as quickly as our two families can arrange it."

The cold announcement of her fate hurt even more than the betrayal of her hopes, and her emotions boiled over. "I will not!" she blurted out. And then more slowly, she repeated herself. "I. Will. Not!" She stood and turned away from her parents, frantically trying to restrain her tears.

Her father would not release her hand. "You will, my daughter." Her father's voice, suddenly stronger than it had been for weeks, brooked no argument. "You *will* do as we say. This marriage will save our land."

Leova sat back down and directed her gaze to her father's face. Bertram continued in a kinder voice.

"We insisted that William take up residence here after the wedding, and he has agreed. We don't want you to live under his mother's roof; the terrible events that have occurred there will not be repeated with you. Here we can protect you, if need be."

154

"And why would he agree?" Leova asked.

"As your husband, William will take over the maintenance of these lands."

Pagany tried to explain, "He insists that he is the heir to Stonehart, but his mother refuses to acknowledge that claim. As she grows more and more unstable, she makes his life intolerable. Regan and Rolfe have accepted his heritage, but know that as long as Allmana lives, she will strive to block every order he makes. This marriage serves a dual purpose for her: she can rid herself of William by sending him off, but at the same time keep alive some possibility that, were he to prove his claim to her land in some way, she could convince him that our lands were sufficient for him. And, if he continued his claims, she might, as his mother, claim overlordship of both our land and hers."

Bertram took up the narrative. "The three brothers agreed to this plan in order to bring peace to their home, and to make both our estates strong by combining them."

"And what about my plans? Who is looking out for me?" Leova asked.

Pagany leaned over and stroked Leova's hair. Almost in a whisper she said, "The arrangement works for the three of us, too. You will stay safe at home. We will not lose you."

In a soft voice that matched her mother's, Leova turned to her father, "You once told me that you would not force me to marry against my wishes."

Bertram smiled wanly. "Young women's wishes are often guided by their hearts, not their heads."

Defeated, Leova turned her head away from her parents, and stared blankly out the hall door. After a few moments she spoke in a voice meant to sting. "I will be your most obedient and most unhappy daughter. My presence is obviously not needed; I leave you to inform my groom."

Her words struck home to her parents. Before they could protest, she asked, "May I go to my room?" Then without waiting for permission, Leova fled to her quarters, throwing herself on her bed and trying with all her strength to hold back the tears. She failed.

Later in the evening, determined to create a bond between Leova and William, Pagany ordered Leova to dry her eyes and appear at the table. Listlessly, she allowed herself to be dressed and pampered by Gwynned, who secretly sorrowed for her young mistress. "Don't envy my mistress her position," she thought. "Glad none of mine would have to marry for land. Almost makes being poor a good lot." Straightening the veil over the sad-faced girl's hair one last time, she gave the miserable bride-to-be a brief hug and sent her to the great hall for a celebration, one she wouldn't enjoy.

"My Lady," William said, bowing over Leova's hand. "It pleases me greatly that we will be wed. I pledge you my loyalty and protection forever." Leova looked into his eyes, keenly aware that he did not pledge his love. How could he? How could she?

He had been first to greet her when she entered the hall, and now he led her to the table where Pagany and Regan waited. Leova was relieved to discover that Rolfe had excused himself, claiming that he needed to prepare for his return to the monastery. The small group shifted awkwardly while they waited for the first course to be served.

Even with low provisions, Pagany somehow placed hardy food before them, but food could not make up for the depression that hung over the occasion. William, having delivered his obligatory speech, said very little else during the meal. He and Leova barely looked at each other. An observer would conclude that both members of the couple were clearly unhappy about the marriage. Feeling the lag in the conversation acutely, Ragen turned to William in an attempt to create a jovial atmosphere to lift the great gloom. "I've never understood our brother's love of the religious life!" he began boisterously. "You had no choice in the matter—our mother deserted you on the abbey's steps. He, however, rushes back to the hard beds and long prayers of Buxton. And he changes a perfectly *elegant* name for a plain one. Why does Rolfe want to call himself Brother *John*?"

With a smile as artificial as Ragen's, William answered the question. "Taking on the name of disciples or early saints symbolizes an end to one life and the beginning of a new one. Rolfe probably chose the name John because the divine author of the last of the gospels bore the name John."

He fell silent again, unable or unwilling to continue the conversation.

"Were you and your brother at the same monastery, William?" Leova asked.

William started at the question as if he were surprised that Leova had any interest in his life. These were the first words the now-espoused pair had exchanged. "Yes, until the marauders came and destroyed much of it. John—that is, Rolfe—came home; I found refuge in another monastery and then was able to return to Buxton. I had pledged myself to continue working with what manuscripts we had been able to save. Many were destroyed or are now beyond repair."

"And now you pledge to repair my father's broken estate," Leova thought. But hearing the sadness in his voice, she held her tongue and listened as he continued.

"The family tragedies brought me home...."

"Would you prefer to remain at the monastery? Your family long deserted you; you could have remained among your manuscripts."

"God has other plans for me," he said.

Despite her wish to know more, Leova did not continue her questions. There would be many years in which they could learn more about each other. Besides, by the tone of his voice, she knew he would not reveal more to an intended bride who was still a stranger.

Taking advantage of the pause in conversation, Pagany excused herself. "My pardon, sirs, I must attend to my husband. He takes his meals in his quarters."

Regan and William rose in respect. "Please thank him for his gracious consent to our offer of marriage." Leova could not help but notice that Regan said "our offer," and William only nodded. No one looked her way.

"We also must leave, so we will not be able to thank him personally," Ragen explained. "And you, too, have our thanks.

Without you, matters would not have been settled to the satisfaction of all."

Leova and William caught each other's eyes and then quickly looked away. But then her new betrothed, remembering his pledge, stepped forward and again took her hand. "I'm sorry, but we must carry the good news to our mother. We'll return soon to discuss the settlements between us. Perhaps then we can begin to know one another."

And then they were gone.

Leova, left to her own thoughts, surrendered to being unhappy. When her mother returned to the main hall, she found Leova still sitting at the high table. Tears slowly drifted down her cheeks and onto the food she had hardly touched. Pagany sat down silently next to her daughter and took her hand. Leova turned a tear-stained face up to her mother's and laying her head on her mother's breast, broke into quiet sobbing.

"Mother, I don't want this marriage." Although she fretted about her mother at times, the young woman unequivocally adored her, and no one doubted that Pagany returned the adoration. Nor did anyone doubt that the mother would fight fiercely if she felt her daughter threatened in any way. In this matter, however, Pagany did not see the marriage as a threat.

"Yes, I know. Believe me, I did refuse the offer at first. But...."

"But you did not fight for me," Leova whispered.

Pagany stopped, drew herself up and placing her hands on either side of her daughter's face, spoke to her earnestly. "Leova, you know the troubles we face. Your father weakens daily. No herb, no wise woman can help. He's allowing himself to die. He has no will to fight." She paused, and turning from Leova, dropped her hands into her lap and stared into a future only she could see. "I couldn't bear it if he died. And...this union appears to be giving him back his will to live. Someday, I hope, you'll understand."

It was true. Pagany had not agreed to the marriage easily. "Turn down the offer, husband. That house is more than an unhappy one," she argued. "It's cursed. Would you have our daughter drawn into such misery?!"

158

"Women's reasoning!" Bertram had snorted. "Unhappy? Of course it's unhappy! The woman's a bitter widow who's turned inward—what would you expect?" He worked himself into more of a rage than she'd seen in a year. "And her sons are no help. That dolt of an oldest son mistreated his young wife until she had no recourse but to kill him...and herself. The second son cares more for herbs and flowers than for battle, and the third son wants to be a priest! If that's not bad enough, from nowhere comes yet another son who claims authority over her. The house is unhappy, but it's not cursed!"

He calmed himself a little and attempted to reason with his wife—as he saw reason. "Be assured. As matters stand, Leova will become mistress of that whole household some day; she'll reverse any curse and bring happiness to both their family and ours."

He smiled at Pagany. "We could hardly ask for more for our daughter."

Not at all convinced, Pagany resigned herself to the marriage. She knew the final decision was not hers.

"I'll trouble you no more with my 'woman's reasoning'," Pagany said solemnly. "But take care with Allmana. Her sons may think they have taken over the lands, but she accedes to no masterful hand. I suspect she has plans for your future grandchildren's inheritance—just as you do. When uniting kingdoms, one family always profits more than the other."

Pagany herself had united two great kingdoms, an act which made Bertram the most powerful lord in their borough. Fortunately, Bertram was a good man, determined to make his family whole and strong without destroying Pagany's heritage. He had wanted sons to create a dynasty, and Pagany had borne him two: one died at birth, the other was sickly and lived for less than two years. When Leova was born, she was a joy to her father, but the land needed a son and Pagany never conceived again.

Young William seemed like a decent enough man, she attempted to persuade herself. More like Regan and Rolfe than Robert—or their mother. The marriage would serve many purposes: rescue Lothlar from its decay, provide stability for Leova, and perhaps, in the future, produce a grandson who would continue to hold the lands Bertram and Pagany had inherited from their ancestors. And, although not a good woman, Allmana was powerful. She commanded many well-trained men, men who would protect the land from invaders.

And above all, Bertram seemed to breathe with new life. This marriage brought hope and energy.

As Leova listened to the passion and intensity in her mother's voice, she came to understand that her personal grief did not matter. In the end, land ownership and the power it bestowed outweighed her own wishes...and Bertram's illness outweighed both.

Leova kissed her mother, then rose and started toward her room, feeling less a child and more a woman. "And a woman attends to the business of her household," she told herself, smiling sadly at the thought that tending to a household often resulted in sacrifices a woman didn't choose to make. And she recognized also that were her refusal listened to and her father slowly died as the land died, she might well never forgive herself.

The following days, determined to settle her emotions, she shrugged off feelings that could easily turn into self-pity and went about her daily chores. Although she would rather have gone to the herb hut to check the winter supplies of tonics and medicines—a solitary task—she forced herself toward the weaving room where she'd have to encounter other women of the hall. Pagany had turned the responsibility of overseeing the weaving for the hall and its people to her daughter and, while the cording of wool and the spinning of yarn held no joy for Leova, the creation of tapestries to cover the walls brought great satisfaction. Enough satisfaction that she could bear the making of shirts and cloaks and other items of daily life.

In the middle of the room, before a great loom, she paused to look at the wall tapestry that was her favorite possession. The design featured a great tree of life, its branches soaring up to serve as a home for a virtual kingdom of birds. It had been years in the making and at last was ready to be hung. Hilda had helped make it, fighting thread and shuttle as if they were enemies to be conquered.

"This," she thought, "I will have in my chamber."

"Mistress," called one of the women working on smoothing the fine edges of the great piece, "Come look—this edge will not hang straight, no matter how I coax it."

Indeed, the upper corner bulged rather obviously, the warp and weave misshapen just enough to disturb the regular flow of the rest. The woven bird which nested in the tree branches bulged also. Leova laughed in spite of her misery.

"That's Mistress Hilda's handiwork. She was determined to create a wonder of a lark to sing through the cold winter days."

"Looks more like she created a chicken caught in a trap," commented the weaver.

Leova pushed aside the sadness of that image. "Yes, it does seem a bit lumpy for a lark," Leova mused. "But it was a labor of love, not an exercise in re-creation. Weaving was not Mistress Hilda's talent."

"And what was her talent, pray tell?" asked Leova's mother who had followed her daughter, hoping to somehow console her. At the sound of her mother's voice, Leova turned to find her mother watching her as she traced Hilda's work on the tapestry with a slender finger.

Leova compared her own slight stature with her mother's. Leova was small, taking after the women on her father's side of the family; Bertram himself was only minimally taller than his stately wife. They complemented each other in ways that Leova and William would not. Pagany was fair, pale and blonde with eyes of blue that bespoke her heritage. Bertram was as broad and stocky as Pagany was slim, but before Bertram's illness, they had both borne themselves with a presence that made everyone who saw them standing together in the hall say, "Here is a Lord and his Dame!"

Leova could not see herself and William as "Lord and Lady" of the hall. No matter how proficient she became in housewifery, she could hardly take her mother's place in her own home. And William, although she could find nothing to criticize him for—except, of course, that he was not Rolfe—did not appear to her as the lordly type. The mere thought of becoming a couple like her mother and father brought her thoughts back to their one meeting. He had been respectful, but she suspected that he had not even wanted to stand next to her for long. Was he just shy? Did his distance merely reflect a modest nature? Or –she thought in a moment of panic—perhaps he did not want her by his side, as her father had wanted her mother.

"He has yet to know me. We will grow close," Leova said to herself, adding "God willing," a phrase she had often heard from visiting monks. Quickly she dismissed her disquieting thoughts and answered her mother. "Hilda's talents all reside in her head and are demonstrated by her tongue! And I would venture that were she here, she'd be raising laughter and hackles at the same time."

Silently she considered the ingenuity of her old friend. "Maybe she'd even find some means to console me. And, perhaps," she thought wistfully, "She'd find some means for me to marry Rolfe instead of William."

Pagany, dismissing her daughter's mood in hopes of cheering her up, became caught up in the memories of Hilda. "Your father would be frothing because she'd imply that she'd steal William's heart and elope with him. You and I would laugh because we know that she's not interested enough in marriage to give it the slightest effort."

She paused to smile at Leova, who suddenly realized what would make this marriage bearable.

"Mother, could we please send a messenger to find Hilda? She might be able to come to the wedding." Leova didn't really know whether women who went into monasteries could leave to go anywhere, well-nigh to a friend's wedding. But if Hilda could come—her mind opened to the possibility of adventure—maybe they could find a way to help her escape from the monastery! Her mother spoke softly, bringing Leova back to reality.

"The coast is still not safe, sweet one. And we do not know where the abbey she was sent to is. We can't know whether it was attacked or spared."

"An abbey!" Leova became distracted from her own woes. "Can you imagine Hilda at an abbey? How could her mother think of her as a 'gift to God'—if that's what she's supposed to be? Her mother does not know Hilda at all. I can't imagine how a mother could just give away her daughter!"

"I'm giving you away," Pagany reminded her ruefully.

"But—but—that's different. I always thought I'd be a wife. I *knew* I would, but I had hoped...." Leova's voice faded away then returned to its indignant tone. "Hilda never even considered entering an abbey, being a nun shut off from the world."

Pagany attempted to put the best light on Hilda's situation. "Perhaps the discipline will tame those unruly manners of hers. It might not be all bad. Many nuns aren't in cloistered orders. And few elevate the vow of poverty to the point of suffering. In truth, high-born ladies often retire to abbeys or monasteries when their lords are killed in battle and continue to live much in the same style as they had in their own halls."

Pagany was just as concerned about Hilda as her daughter was, but, not wanting to add to Leova's grief, she continued to think of ways that Hilda would profit. "She might be allowed to study. She always wanted to learn to read: remember how she would beg the visiting priests to point to words as they read them."

Leova remained unconvinced. "Can we at least send a message, Mother? Surely a messenger could find the right place if he starts at her home—please." Leova's voice was close to breaking.

"I'll speak to your father," her mother said softly. "If I ask it as a bridal gift for you, he'll not refuse. Besides, he sees saucy Hilda as his own and was no more pleased to learn of her fate than we were."

She hugged Leova fondly. "Meantime, let's take a look at this tapestry. Perhaps we can make this chicken look a little more like a lark so that when Hilda sees it again she'll be amazed at her own skill."

Later that evening Leova lay on her bed staring at the ceiling. She had known since childhood that marriage was her duty, a blessed task assigned to women. She had always wanted to be the best of wives, like her mother, and more than that, she wanted to be the best of mothers, like her own mother and, she supposed, like the Virgin Mary. Leova was not very attached to any religion, old or new, but she had been taught by the priests that the Virgin Mary was the ideal Christian mother. What little religion Leova had consisted of ideas that she liked and valued from both the old religion and the new. In the old religion, a woman grew old and wrinkled, some became wise and honored. Some grew helpless and unloved. Christian women had much the same lot. The Christian God had not saved Wyomina, had He?

Life could be hard on real women. She'd seen that in the fields and even in the halls of her own home. Somehow, however, she had come to believe that striving to be good and pure brought safety from abuse. No one dared mistreat the Mother of Christ, whose goodness served as a model for Christian mothers. As a child, Leova decided that if being good could keep her free from mistreatment, good behavior was a fair bargain.

Hilda had not agreed in the least. In one heated conversation, Hilda berated her friend, calling her naïve.

"Leova, you dolt," Hilda had insisted, "No one *rewards* virtue, especially the 'I'm-a-good-girl-here-at-your-service' kind. Look at your mother—she isn't loved just because she's *good*! She's not a quiet little housewife. Pagany *runs* the house—she doesn't just serve it! Even your father defers to her judgment."

"No, Hilda," Leova would insist. "You're wrong. Mother is honored *because* she serves and she serves because she's good. All her actions are for the good of the household."

"If you stretch a point you could say that," Hilda conceded. "But it's her intelligence more than her virtue that earns her honor. If she were good and stupid instead of good and smart, she'd be treated quite differently. Don't you remember when your cousin came with his wife: her name was Chosy or Chitzy or something like that."

Laughing, Leova corrected her, "Chaladry."

"Whatever—she was a *good* woman, as most would define 'good woman.' Serving her husband consumed her every thought. She couldn't bring him a glass of mead quickly enough, but she was so unthinking that she forgot to ask if it has been strained. So he chokes. And they laugh. He boxes her ears. See…there's no honor or safety, in that sort of goodness."

During these good natured arguments, Leova had learned to pause and think long and hard before countering Hilda's pronouncements. The two were proper matches for each other as far as wit was concerned, but Hilda's tongue was quicker and the sheer barrage of words that flowed from her lips could overwhelm those she argued against. It had taken Leova the first few years of their friendship to learn to use time before she spoke so that Hilda's passion would settle enough for Leova's more thoughtful reasoning to counter the weight of her ardor.

"I didn't say that *goodness* was the only virtue. Certainly a wife must be wise as well as conscientious. Virtue does depend somewhat upon wisdom. Lady Chaladry isn't a good example. She's like one of those mocking pictures you draw, all out of proportion to humans but true to their nature."

Hilda had chuckled and grabbed her drawing slate; instantly the Lady Chaladry appeared: big eyed, confused, and piously posed as the Virgin in the tapestries which lined the chapel. "Like this?" she had grinned wickedly.

"Like that." Leova had grinned back. "She has none of the substance mother has—you and I have more substance. Of course your substance is mostly the result of the hardness of your head."

"And what about the softness of yours?" her friend laughed. "You probably still believe that your mother can make decisions and have them stick, even if your father objects. Foolish girl!"

Now Leova realized that Hilda had been right. Yes, her father did defer to her mother in many ways, but in important cases his will overrode the "good" woman's. He had made the decision, and mother and daughter had to abide by it.

She couldn't rest easily with his decision, even though she instinctively wanted to believe her parents had more concern for her happiness than their sudden decision suggested. "William seems to be a nice person, not at all like Robert. I doubt I'll end up killing him or myself."

Nonetheless, nice as he might be, she had no desire to marry him. Trying to make the best of things, Leova forced herself to concentrate on William's polite and gentle demeanor and his admittedly handsome face. Looming in the background, preventing a simple acceptance, was his horrible mother, Allmana.

Leova shuddered at the thought of her prospective mother-by-marriage. Even her parents' insistence that she remain at Lothlar after the wedding didn't seem like enough protection. How could she join that haunted family? That thought had barely surfaced when she had to admit guiltily that she would have been happy to be part of that family if it were to Rolfe she was pledged.

"Oh, Hilda! I need you here to help me reconcile myself to this marriage! Or help me run away!"

Leova sighed out loud as the truth of her situation settled in once more.

She would marry William and that was the end of it.

Chapter 5: Hilda Escapes from Buxton (878-879)

The journey to Northwich Abbey revealed two things to Hilda: how ill-conceived her earlier plans to escape from Buxton had been and—surprisingly—how strong she had become during her stay at the monastery. Caedmon had vague directions from Abbess Edyth, so they knew their destination was located some three or four days away, but nothing had prepared them for being on their own on a strange road traveling through strange hamlets as winter began to release its cold and wind. Ethel wearied quickly, and the fear of leaving her unprotected slowed their progress. Sometimes either Hilda or Caedmon would stride ahead to see what lay just out of their immediate sight, but if they spotted another traveler or came across a farm, they kept close together. Knowing that Hilda's light voice would give away her disguise, Caedmon took charge of asking directions.

The spare furnishings of the monastery began to feel luxurious and the simple food served nightly delicious beyond compare. Exhausted and aching, they spent the first night in an abandoned shed that had been converted into a winter shelter for shepherds. The straw they spread out on the dirt floor was far from fresh, but they slept soundly, protected from the elements. The second night, lacking any other option, they slept in an open field, covered only by the few cloaks they had managed to slip out with. Hilda woke up before the sun appeared and walked around in circles, rubbing her body vigorously and stomping her feel to revive the circulation. When Ethel awoke, Hilda insisted on rubbing her arms also and forced her to stamp her feet too.

Even though their walking made them ravenous, they rationed the meager hoard of bread and fruit Caedmon had managed to scrape up before leaving the monastery. Each evening they told themselves that the journey would soon be over, and each morning they despaired at the long trip still ahead.

Slowly, however, Hilda began to fear that the food or the walk was weakening her body in some way as the strength she had felt at the beginning of their trek faded. The second night she had even had to get up and walk a bit apart from the others as she felt her stomach pushing up the little food she had eaten. The vomiting only increased her anxiety, but the following day she said nothing to either of her companions.

Late in the afternoon of the third day, after fearing they had lost their direction in what seemed to be an endless stand of trees, they came upon a small thatched building in an opening. It bore all the signs of housing a family. Chickens pecked at the grass near the door, a stout pig with several pudgy piglets snorted about in a fenced sty, and a cow grazed at the edge of the clearing. Smoke rose from the little building. As they hesitated just under the trees that surrounded the clearing, a woman emerged from the doorway, obviously wary of the strangers.

"Good eve, Mistress," Caedmon called as he approached slowly and humbly, his hat respectfully in hand. "Might we sleep in your shed tonight? My mother can travel no farther, and we still have a way to go."

"And where might that be, boy?" the woman inquired.

"Northwich. My brother is to serve at the abbey there, and we think to settle near him."

The woman looked sympathetically at Ethel and suspiciously at Hilda.

"Come," she beckoned to them. "You shall eat with us, and we will find a comfortable place for your old mother to sleep. I am called Bryna, and you?"

Caedmon, caught off guard, started to stutter, "M-m-my name...name...."

"His name is Tom," Ethel broken in. "And the younger is Martin. Friends call me Alys."

Bryna looked each of them up and down, but said nothing more than "Follow me then, Alys. I'll get you settled first." She led Ethel into the cottage and signaled for her to sit on the bench by the fire. Gratefully, Ethel discarded her cane and sank down on the small wooden seat. Hilda followed and sat on the floor, leaning her head against Ethel's knee. Just as she fell asleep, Caedmon shook her slightly.

168

"Bryna offers us a meal. Come, partake."

Hilda shook herself and moved to the table where several roasted chickens emitted enticing smells. Famished, she sat, ready to eat, but Bryna cuffed her lightly and put a trencher in her hand. Pointing to Ethel, she spoke sharply, "Take food for your mother, ungrateful child!"

Chastised, Hilda filled the trencher and placed it respectfully before Ethel. She smiled to herself, ashamed of how self-centered she was and thinking about how good it was to treat Ethel as her mother. And then she turned back to her own trencher and dedicated herself to the chicken, starting to eat as if she might never be offered another meal, but all too soon her stomach became queasy and she tried to look as though she was eating while just picking at the food. Her hostess looked at her quizzically but said nothing, trying to determine what about the little party of travelers bothered her. Her acute intelligence of people warned her that these three were not what they professed to be. Her thoughts were interrupted by the noise and laughter of what seemed to be a whole troop of young men.

"Mother!" they called. "We've returned with enough food to make us fat!" Sure enough, several young men stood framed in the doorway holding up a clutch of dead rabbits for their mother's attention and brandishing a pole hung with at least a dozen silver-scaled fish.

"My sons," Bryna announced proudly to Ethel. Hilda counted five, possibly from fourteen to twenty-five years old, who greeted their mother fondly. Apparently curiosity was in no danger of killing them, because they acknowledged, then ignored, their guests. Settling themselves on the floor, they began a loud and teasing account of their hunting and fishing adventures. Hilda kept silent, knowing that if she spoke, her disguise would weaken.

As the sun set and Bryna's sons finished up whatever food was left on the table, Ethel was led outside to a small attached building at the rear of the main cottage.

"Rest in my bed, goodwife," Bryna invited, pointing to a small bed. "The road will not be as long tomorrow, but you'll need your strength. I can bed down near the fire." Ethel gratefully laid her weary body on the proffered bed and was almost immediately asleep.

Returning to the cottage, she signaled to Hilda and Caedmon and pointed toward several mattresses spread in a corner.

"Sleep here, with my sons."

Hilda looked at Caedmon helplessly, then—far too weary to worry about the sleeping arrangements—she pulled a blanket around her and fell asleep almost immediately. Within what seemed like seconds, she was awakened by a gentle touch on her shoulder. Looking up, she saw Bryna's kindly concerned face. The older woman beckoned to her, so she rose and followed her hostess outside.

"Go sleep with your mother, child—if indeed she is your mother—and call me if you are not feeling well." Hilda, too tired and sleepy to wonder about Bryna's concern, lay down next to Ethel, pulled some of the blanket over herself and immediately went to sleep.

When she awoke the next morning, the sons were already off on their hunting and fishing, and Bryna was busily disemboweling the rabbits and scaling the fish foraged the day before. As Hilda approached, she smiled.

"Did you sleep well, girl?" she asked.

Hilda opened her mouth to explain—obviously her secret had been discovered. Bryna, however, silenced her with a friendly wave of her hand.

"Don't bother to tell me. I imagine that your brother feared to travel with such a beautiful sister. Cutting your hair works as long as no one looks too closely. Those out to do plunder or worse might miss the fact that you're a woman." She frowned. "It was a wise decision to cut your hair and disguise you as a monk."

"How ever did you know?" asked Hilda. Hearing Hilda's voice for the first time caused Bryna to raise an eyebrow, but she let that pass.

"Something wasn't fitting together, so I looked closely as you slept on the floor," she laughed. "I'm just glad my sons didn't!" Hilda smiled at her, happy that the woman didn't know all of the secret.

"Your mother still sleeps," Bryna continued. "Bless her bones—though I don't think she is as old as you would like strangers to believe. Let her rest; Northwich is only three hours away. Leave after the noon meal. Let the sun burn off the chill."

She gathered the game in a sack, "I must get these meats into the cooling basket at the spring and collect wood for the fire. Watch the bread in the oven. Don't let the loaves burn." And with those instructions, Bryna headed for the woods, beckoning to Caedmon to accompany her.

Hilda felt better than she had since her nightmare had begun. At least for the moment danger seemed far away and her stomach was not calling attention to itself. Her blistered feet, however, ached mightily. Never had she walked so far, and never had she appreciated riding a horse so much!

"Being the daughter of a lord has its advantages," she whispered to herself and then quickly laughed, pausing to contemplate what she'd just said. "Bryna walks all the time, and her rough sandals seem a luxury. Why should I complain about my lack of a horse?"

Leaning back on the bench, she relived the past three days. Her father's fate worried her, but she hoped and prayed that he would have help from cousin Bergdorf and his men. But John?

"Where are you, my love? Did you return to your family?"

She opened the small pouch that contained what earthly goods remained to her and after a brief search, drew out the leather eternity knot. Wrapping her fingers about it, she attempted to recall John's face, John's touch. As long as she had this treasure, John would never be completely gone. She sighed, realizing that she might never see him again. "No, no," she said aloud, shaking her head determinedly. "I will find him. We will be together."

Lost in reverie, Hilda only revived when the smell of the burning bread and her hostess' shout returned her to reality.

"Girl, you've let the bread burn!"

Hilda jumped up and rushed to the oven. Pulling open the heavy door, she reached in, hardly feeling the burning crust as she pulled the loaves out. Three were burnt beyond saving.

"I'm so sorry," she cried.

"If you're going to be working at that monastery once you get there, you better learn to keep your mind on what you're doing. They'll throw you out, young lady." Bryna snapped. "That's good flour gone to waste, not easily come by out here. Good that the boys will be away till dusk. I'll have time to make more."

Hilda, remembering the bread-making skills she had acquired with Leova and later at the monastery, had never, however, considered what would happen if there were no handy larder where loaves would be stored and thus always available. Even her experience working in the monastery kitchen had done little to make her appreciate her daily bread. Not so with Bryna and her family. It was another revelation.

"I will do without, but if you would, please feed my mother and my brother. They don't deserve to suffer for my carelessness." Humbly, she waited for an answer from Bryna, feeling far guiltier than she had ever felt for other lapses in behavior. Caedmon had never seen his lady with contrition written in her posture.

Bryna's anger melted as she looked at the repentant young girl, head bowed as she stood in the over-sized monk's robe, her bare swollen feet showing just under the ragged hem. "Just do better the next time," she admonished Hilda, a smile creeping across her face.

Hilda nodded earnestly, now newly aware that her actions had consequences not just for herself but for others, too. After a noonday meal, during which Hilda refused to eat any of the bread left from the day before, the three travelers took to the road in the direction pointed out by Bryna whose sons followed them for most of their journey.

Northwich Abbey

In the late afternoon, the sun's sharp light made Northwich Abbey seem twice as large as Buxton. However, Hilda soon realized, gazing from the hill where the three of them stared down at this new haven, that it was actually smaller as she counted only five buildings and three garden plots. Sheep and cattle grazed in the nearby fields, their slow movements in contrast to the purposeful movements of the monks and nuns who moved about the clearings, bent on their work. As much as she wanted to be back with friends and family, the long journey from Buxton made her feel glad—and relieved—to be where she could rest her weary feet.

Their arrival had not gone unnoticed. As the small group arrived at the gates, Abbess Moira herself met them, pulling them into the small gatehouse almost as if she didn't wish them to speak to anyone else.

"My Lady," she nodded politely but without warmth. "I've made preparations for your stay, but I've made conditions that you and your servants must agree to if we are all to be safe and well."

"Safe and well?" Hilda repeated. "Have our enemies been looking for us? Is there danger of invasion?"

"No. But I intend to keep us free from the hazards that providing refuge to one such as yourself will invite." She paused and looked intently at Hilda and the others. "Do I make myself clear?"

The three nodded their heads, suspicious of what was to follow.

"First, no one is to know you are Princess Hilda. You can keep your name so that you won't be confused by having to answer to another. However, you'll live and work exactly as everyone else. No favors, no special accommodations."

Hilda, who had expected neither, looked at her quizzically. "How did you know we were coming?"

"A messenger arrived yesterday from my sister," replied Moira shortly, leaving Hilda to wonder why she had to travel by foot if the roads were open enough to permit a messenger on a horse to pass. Seeing the question on Hilda's face, her new Abbess seized the chance to issue her first order.

"No more questions. Be quiet now as your fellow acolytes must be! You'll be introduced as a new novitiate from the north country, one who wishes to renounce her family and position. That will explain your strange attire and your hair—or lack of it. The sister in charge of the dormitory will find you appropriate clothing and a scarf to cover your head."

She turned unceremoniously to Ethel and Caedmon. "You people will be settled in with the other help; do not speak to your mistress from this day forth."

Ethel started to protest, but the Abbess Moira, giving her a hard look that silenced the woman, turned again to Hilda. "From this day on, these two cease to be your servants and become servants of the abbey. Do you understand?"

"It's hard not to," thought Hilda, her resentment growing, but she mumbled, "Yes, Abbess" as meekly as she could.

"Good. Now come with me. I'll take you to the dormitory." She grasped Hilda none-too-gently by the arm—just as her sister had done four days earlier—and guided her into the courtyard. Signaling a passing monk, she instructed him to take Ethel and Caedmon to the kitchens.

"As soon as you're clean and dressed properly, join us at prayers. Tomorrow, your work begins."

Abbess Moira spoke true. The next weeks brought Hilda nothing but hard work—work which helped her understand how protected she had been at Buxton. Like the other acolytes, she cleaned out sheds, swept the yard, fed the chickens, and milked the cows, a task which, however, she had difficulty executing. Only one task brought her pleasure—baking bread for the congregation. At Buxton she had resented the short time she had been forced to spend in the kitchen, but here the baking of bread was by far the most rewarding of her tasks. The old monk, Brother Paul, who oversaw the kitchen noticed her interest and took her on as an apprentice, instructing her in the secrets of varying recipes. At his request, Abbess Moira assigned her to the kitchen full time. Hilda longed to work in the scriptorium, but she feared that manuscripts no longer had a place in her life.

Exhausted by the almost unceasing work, Hilda found herself wondering how others continued day after day at such labor. The bouts of stomach pain and vomiting continued though she told no one. In the mornings she could often not drag herself out of bed; she soon came to fear that something in the food or the work was making her ill. She was certain of it the morning she awoke so ill that she could not stir herself. She sent word to Brother Paul, who reported her absence to the Abbess, who soon stood at the door to Hilda's cell. Abbess Moira was obviously not pleased; Hilda's illness more irritated than concerned her.

"Sister Hilda. Stop this malingering immediately. There's work to do," the stern matron said.

Hilda felt as though she were going to vomit again but, with great effort that almost made her black out, she repressed the urgings.

"Abbess, I can't stand, much less work. I need herbs to settle my stomach and rest!" she said quarrelsomely. "I've tried to move about, but I'm too weak."

Usually, the Abbess ignored such claims, routed acolytes out of bed and sent them off to work—that was the best medicine. However, something in the young woman's voiced protest seemed legitimate—and unwilling to be bullied.

"Stay abed, then," Moira said shortly. "I'll send the herb-woman. Can't afford to have a princess sicken and die under my care."

After the Abbess departed, Hilda slept, waking to find herself eye to eye with an old woman who sat on the floor next to her bed staring at her. Startled, she struggled to sit up, and then waited for the woman to speak.

"Tell me, young one, how you feel." The herb woman queried.

"Weak. Tired. For days now, my body aches—and I've been vomiting for several mornings past."

"Is this type of sickness common with you, my child?"

"No. That's why I'm worried; I have seldom been sick—and never afflicted with fatigue."

"Show me where the aches are." The woman addressed her in a kindly manner, so Hilda indicated her breasts, which had been sore for several days and her legs, which hurt far more than they should have.

The old woman stepped back and bowed her head for a few minutes before asking the next question. "What of your courses? Have they come to you as they always have?"

Hilda thought for a few moments, then replied. "No, I don't think so. Truthfully, I haven't paid attention." The woman nodded her head gravely.

"What is it? What is wrong with me?"

"Hush, hush," the herb woman soothed her. "I must ask a hard question—will you answer honestly?"

Puzzled, Hilda nodded yes.

"Have you had ought to do with a man? Lain with one as if in marriage?"

Blushing with embarrassment, Hilda nodded once more and then turned her head away from the woman's gaze.

"I thought as much." The woman laughed. "I'm afraid you no longer look like an innocent."

Hilda's eyes flashed and her voice took on a sharper edge. "What 'look' could mark a woman who has been with her love but once?"

The woman laughed again at her patient's sudden anger, and patted her arm affectionately to indicate she had meant no judgment. Taking Hilda's hand she looked at her directly and openly.

"Your body bears the marks. It tells me that you are with child," she said quietly.

All Hilda could do was stare at her. Abruptly, she pulled away from the herb woman and stood up.

"I...I...I...I can't—that can't be. No...no...it...only happened once...." Hilda's voice trailed off as slowly she understood the enormity of the old woman's words. Covering her face in her hands, she began to cry. She struggled with her emotions, frightened by the fact that she could see no future that included a pregnancy, much less a baby. Suddenly the image of her father's face and John's, and the face of everyone who loved her came roaring up—no one smiling, no one proud anymore. She sank to her knees.

"I must tell the Abbess. You'll need special care." The old woman gently touched Hilda on the shoulder as she passed her, then she disappeared through the door. Hilda pulled herself up and sat stiffly on her rough bed, frightened, alone, and almost paralyzed.

"What have you done, girl!" Abbess Moira burst into the room. Hilda stared at the floor, trying hard to gain some composure and to put some distance between herself and the imposing woman before her. Her superior halted directly in front of her and speaking in a tone devoid of kindness or sympathy, began to interrogate the seemingly intimidated young woman.

"How can this be?" She waited for a reply, but Hilda said nothing. Vexed by receiving no explanation, the Abbess went on in an even more stringent voice.

"Princess Hilda," the stern woman spit out her title and name as if she were unworthy of that address. "To be guilty of such a common sin—the daughter of a most noble and holy mother! This act brings shame and censure to our monasteries! My sister rightly warned me about you." Her voice vibrated with harshness. "Who is the father? Tell me."

"I cannot," Hilda whispered.

"You mean you will not," Moira retorted.

"By God's grace, I will not," Hilda swore, looking her tormentor full in the face. She felt her strength returning and at that moment, knowing the consequences for John, she resolved never to tell.

The exasperated Abbess Moira turned to leave the room, but paused as she reached the door and turned for one last verbal slap. "Then you must bear your shame and your punishment alone. I will not have you sully the name of this holy order or this holy place. No one outside these walls, not even your father, will know of your disgraced state." And with that, she left Hilda alone to contemplate her sin and imagine her punishment.

177

Several hours later, however, the Abbess returned with even more determination evident in her face. As she strode into the small room and stared at Hilda, her obvious disgust distorted her features.

"If we declare you've petitioned to be an anchoress, your condition will be hidden." It is a deception that God will forgive."

"An anchoress—one who is enclosed in a cell, who desires only to commune with God and reject all humanity?" Hilda listened in horror. "I have neither the calling nor the nature to live so strictly apart."

"You don't have to have the calling. We're seeking to hide you—one such as yourself deserves harsher punishment, but the best we can do is isolate you so that your shame is not evident."

If she had been able, Hilda guessed, the Abbess would have cast her out. But even the Abbess could not afford to deny a princess shelter and care. Hilda's father would have destroyed the abbey, whether his daughter was a sinner or not. Furthermore, her abbey and many others depended on the largess of the lords of nearby lands.

Hilda knew that her father would defend her, but she also knew that he would be humiliated to know—and have others know—that his unmarried daughter was with child.

"Must I live in the anchorhole at the back of the church?" she asked. Hilda had been aware of the anchorhole at Buxton and knew it to be a small room attached to the church in such a way that an enclosed woman could see into the church through a small "squint" window—one designed to allow her to receive the sacraments without being seen by the congregation. It was a stark cell, but *Ancrene Wisse*—the Rule of Life by which an anchoress lived—mitigated the isolation slightly by allowing for two windows to the outside world: one through which an assistant could deliver food and take away refuse and another through which petitioners could come to seek out wisdom, prayers, and advice.

"Of course not!" exclaimed Abbess Moira. "A true anchoress must be qualified for such a position. You'll live in the hideaway at the edge of the monastery walls. I'll announce that you've taken a vow of solitude. You may walk around in the dark of night, but only if

178

no one is about to see you." Seeing Hilda's look of distress, she added viciously, "Who knows, contemplation of your sins might help you curb your rebellious nature and teach you humility."

Punishment and Friendship

From the moment she entered the tiny hut that stood near the back border of the abbey, Hilda felt sorrow and some guilt but not humility. The isolation allowed her to contemplate her life in a way that had not been possible before. And the longer she examined the events that brought her to this lonely, cold, stone prison—for it was closer to a prison than a refuge—the more it became evident to her that those who should have valued her had sorely failed to protect her. Her mother had pledged her to Buxton with no care for her own wishes; her father had allowed Abbess Edyth to take her; Abbess Edyth had cast her off at the first opportunity, but—it would seem—had told no one who she surmised was the second person in the forbidden tryst.

"My true family resides at Lothlar," Hilda thought. "Lord Bertram and Lady Pagany tended me as if I were their own child, and no natural, or spiritual, sister could be closer to my heart than Leova. But no one has inspired my thoughts more than John. Or my heart."

Periodically, Abbess Moira would visit, not to see to Hilda's wellbeing but to pressure her to reveal the name of the baby's father. Hilda remained silent. The Abbess tightened what little punishment she could administer. First she reduced the amount of food that a silent servant delivered to the door daily. Then, even knowing that winter approached, she cut back the allotment of wood that warmed the stone building.

As Hilda grew weaker from the harsh regimen, she began to worry that the Abbess intended her to die, to relieve the abbey from its "disgrace." Her sorrow and anger slowly turned to despair. Then one evening, Caedmon appeared at the door, and his smile brightened her outlook. He and Ethel both knew of the rumors whispered by all in the corners of cloisters and in the dark of the night. Abbeys, in fact, were famous for spreading tales, some true, some not.

179

"Where is your fire?" the boy asked.

"I save the wood for the cold that will come later," Hilda replied.

"I'll bring more," he said and disappeared quickly, returning with an armload of logs, and built and lit a small fire. By the light from the flame he studied her drawn face, and as she drew her cloak tightly around her shoulders, he realized how thin she had become. "What do they feed you?"

"Abbess Moira seems to have decided that I must fast for my sins—experience the pain of hunger in order to become aware of the pain I caused God by my actions."

"No, no, no. That must not be!" Caedmon shouted, as he grasped Hilda's arm, forgetting that she was a princess and he was merely a serving boy. "No. I will not stand for it!"

"Hush, hush," Hilda patted his hand to calm him. "I have broken serious rules; the punishment is just. Go back to your place now; being here might bring you trouble." The boy, clenching his fists and stomping, went from her, and despite her troubles, she found herself happy that someone near still cared for her.

The next morning, a gentle rap at the door revealed Brother Paul, who presented her with a loaf of warm bread. "God would want you to have this," he said.

Early on in her days alone, Hilda had made the decision to stifle every emotion. Her still rebellious heart would not let anyone see her vulnerability. But this elderly monk, holding out the gift from his kitchen undid her, causing tears to run down her cheek before she could stop them. And bringing the loaf was only part of the comfort he gave her. He insisted upon sitting with her as she ate, gossiping about the petty intrigues which helped fill the days at the monastery.

Hilda found herself laughing for the first time since leaving Buxton. But as their visit drew to a close, she found herself needing to ask Brother Paul a question. "Do you know why I am confined here?"

"I know the reasons the Abbess gave and I know what the herb-woman told me." He smiled, "I trust the herb-woman more than I trust the Abbess."

"And still you reach out to me? Your kindness could bring you trouble. My so-called sin could blight your life, too."

"Perhaps," he replied. "But I find that the Abbess is far too fond of my bread to do me any permanent harm. And I don't share her view that a child conceived in love is full of sin. Nor is the young girl who will bear it."

"You are truly my friend," Hilda said, and impulsively hugged the kindly monk, who blushed to be the object of such an emotion.

The next night held the most welcome visit of all. A familiar figure appeared in the doorway, causing Hilda to abandon her vow to show no emotion as she rushed, tears flowing, to embrace her longtime nurse. "There, there," Ethel crooned, gathering up the crying girl. "I've left you alone too long. I'm so sorry—thought they'd treat you with the respect a lord's daughter deserves." She caressed the young girl's face, wiping away the tears. "Caedmon let me know how wrong I was. I came as soon as I could slip out."

Hilda pushed back from Ethel's embrace and began to plead with her.

"Ethel!" she choked on her tears, "I...when you didn't come to find me, I thought you had returned to Highhear."

Realizing that her former charge thought that she had been deserted by the very one who loved her best, Ethel's heart ached. "Worry no more. I'll not be parted from you now."

Hilda frowned, "But the Abbess...."

Ethel gently touched her lips to silence any protest. "The Abbess may have hidden you in this rough place and denied you comfort, but I owe her no obedience. I'm not a 'saint' like she fancies herself. We'll await your babe together, and I'll tend to you as I always have. I'll find a way in spite or her."

Ethel's resolve restored a bit of happiness to Hilda's life. During the day, she was alone, but each evening Ethel appeared with stories gleaned from the abbey's servants. And other comforts found their way to the hut at the edge of the abbey property. Brother Paul, continuing to bring fresh bread from the kitchen, came more frequently; Ethel supplemented the meager daily meal left at Hilda's doorstep with fresh eggs and milk. Before long, she found a large basin, and Caedmon hauled enough fresh water for a small, but satisfying bath each week. Between times, Ethel bathed her face, hands, and feet. As her body changed, Ethel told her women's lore about birthing and taught her ways she could bear the pain when the baby arrived. Ethel's most charitable gift, however, was her loving presence. When it was dark, they'd walk together, and to distract her, the older woman would relive the adventure of their escape from Buxton and coax out of her mistress stories of Leova and Lothlar. There were matters that were never discussed, however. Hilda would not speak of her life at Buxton, nor her love of John. She determined to keep that secret from everyone, even her beloved nurse. Ethel, knowing the young woman's resolve and, respecting her independence in ways others had not, never asked.

Even with Ethel's presence, Hilda suffered the frustration of being idle and enclosed. Her mind desperate for stimulation, she asked Abbess Moira, on one of her rare visits, if she might be allowed to work with manuscripts from the scriptorium.

"Absolutely not!" the Abbess declared. God's word is not for the likes of you."

Hilda, however, had been prepared for this answer. She had asked Brother Paul to question the master of the scriptorium about manuscripts in the people's language and had made a most welcome discovery. "God's words are not the only words contained in manuscripts," she began, hoping that her quiet tones would impart a humility she didn't feel. "I traveled to my home with a learned bishop, Ceolwulf, who has long been known for his learned tales of saints. Not all his writings are in Latin, so they are often ignored by church leaders."

"Yes," replied the Abbess, "I know of Ceolwulf. He has often visited our abbey and once spent a summer recording the story of St. Helena for us."

"I am well versed in both Latin and the written language of the people. I could translate the manuscript into Latin as a gift for the Christian fathers."

The Abbess sneered. "And what benefit would we gain that would offset the expense of such a project?"

"At Buxton, the scriptorium brings in many fees for reproducing their works for other abbeys and churches. Since I would work in Latin, the book could be sold throughout the Christian world; Latin is the language of the church. The church needs more stories of its saints."

"And would the story of Saint Helena be the best of Ceolwulf's tales to translate?" asked Moira, obviously intrigued by the idea. "He also recorded the life of Saint Juliana, whose refusal to marry a pagan brought about her death."

Hilda knew at that moment she had succeeded. "Why not both? I can translate and prepare the manuscripts. I learned to write a clear hand at Buxton."

"Perhaps God does see a way to teach you. Working on the stories of these good women may inspire and school your own life. I'll see to it that Sister Martha, head of the scriptorium, delivers a manuscript and writing materials tomorrow morning. Consider this work part of your penance."

Hilda settled into her task, eager to be at work again, and while working could not completely alleviate the sorrow and heartache she felt, for much of the day it allowed escape. In moments of peace, even remembering the manuscripts from Buxton brought her more pleasure than she had expected. At first she worried that she only loved reading them because she had read with John. Certainly, she had to admit, his laughter and keen intelligence had been part of the attraction. However, working even in isolation made her realize that the reading and deciphering of the manuscripts at Buxton had helped her forget her unhappiness and brought an end to her ceaseless dreams of returning to Leova's home.

"Or was it John that put those thoughts of escape out of mind?" she asked herself. Hilda struggled to understand what had happened to her. And gradually, as she felt the first movements of the baby in her womb and began to think of her future, she came to the realization that the past did not matter as much as the future.

As Ethel sat on the bed one night with her hand on Hilda's stomach, feeling the life inside, she looked at the princess and asked the question she had wanted to ask for so long.

"Little one, what shall we do once the child is born?"

Hilda sighed, and looked into the eyes of her companion. "I'm not certain. I've thought of several paths, but none seems easy to follow."

"Will we seek out the baby's father?" It was the closest Ethel had come to asking about the coupling that had brought about such trouble.

Hilda shook her head sadly. "No. No. He doesn't know about the child and—unlike me—entered the abbey willingly. He's likely to stay." They sat silently for a moment before Hilda continued.

"I think I should like to return to Lothlar and raise my child there in the midst of people whose hearts allow them to love children freely, without using them to fulfill promises they had no part in making."

Hearing the bitterness in Hilda's voice, Ethel asked quietly. "Then you do not intend to return to your father's hall?"

Hilda laughed harshly. "And what is there now? Does he still possess it or is it occupied by his enemies? Would he welcome an errant daughter?"

"He would welcome you, I'm sure."

"And the babe? Abbess Moira doesn't want him to know. How could I explain a baby to him without admitting my so-called sin?"

Ethel shook her head over the biggest obstacle. "A babe would come as a great surprise."

"Yes," said Hilda quietly, then fell silent, faced with the enormity of her problem.

Seeing the lines of care on the young woman's face, Ethel hugged her soothingly and got her to lie down on the bed. "Sleep, little one. Soon this will be over. And we'll find a way! We will!"

As the weather showed signs of spring and her body grew more awkward, Hilda worked longer and longer hours on the story of Saint Helene, who rescued the True Cross for her son, Constantine. At first she admired the saint because her strength allowed her to lead warriors and take action against her enemies. Slowly, however, she realized that Helene's strength was her faith; she believed in her cause, sought to bring Christianity to heathens regardless of the dangers inherent in invading a foreign land. But of the two books she worked to transcribe, it was the tale of Juliana—forced by her father to marry against her wishes—that affected her the most.

"Where did she find the strength to say no?" Hilda wondered. "I'd find it—I found it impossible to defy my father, and I didn't face the threat of being beaten or beheaded!" The tales recorded in the old manuscripts helped her in ways that her father's defense of his actions had not, and surprisingly, as Abbess Moira had hoped, the manuscripts helped her calm her pride and consider the consequences of her actions, but the Abbess would not have been pleased that Hilda grew stronger in her belief that she had a right to decide her own fate.

As the spring brought warming and the trees sprouted tiny bits of green and her time grew near, Hilda decided she could no longer keep all her thoughts to herself. She decided to write them down and send them to Leova, the only person she trusted to understand. She could only hope that some trusted friend of Leova's would read the letter to her.

"I'll not tell her of the baby," she decided. Hilda didn't think that Leova would condemn her, but if the letter were read to Bertram and Pagany, they might forbid their daughter to renew the old friendship. "Bertram, not Pagany..." she reflected. At Lothlar, a number of young women had conceived without marrying and neither they nor their offspring were ostracized. The old ways did not think it a sin for men and women to lie together without marriage, and babies were always welcome regardless of the path to conception.

Carefully she began to compose her letter. All the letters she had ever read in the scriptorium began with formal greetings: "Dear

Brother in Christ the Lord who died for us...." She doubted that Leova cared much about Christ or his saints, so she wanted to find a warmer way to speak her thoughts.

"Sister of my heart"... she began, and wrote about her stay at Buxton, her escape to Northwich, and her work with the stories of the saints. Deliberately, she left out her resentment at being given to the church, her joy of being with John, and the disgrace that had brought her to virtual imprisonment. There would be time later, when they walked together in the gardens of Lothlar, to talk of the pain and sorrow of betrayal as well as the force of love. Only one problem remained: how to get the letter to Leova.

Brother Paul came up with the answer. "Traveling friars often stop in the kitchen for bread and ale before they travel on to their next destination. I'll find one who goes toward Lothlar and entrust him with the letter. Even if he doesn't make the entire journey, he'll pass the letter on to another journeyer. It will take a while, but the letter should find its way to your friend eventually."

And so the letter began its journey, and Hilda continued her work with the manuscripts.

The Baby

Several months later, after hours of restless sleep, Hilda awoke, brought to consciousness by strong pressure in her abdomen. The pressure soon became a pain that came and went in waves. At her first moan, Ethel was at her side. As the pains increased and the waves came closer and closer, the older woman bathed her forehead with cool water and encouraged her to walk back and forth in the small room. Finally, she sent Caedmon— always, it seemed, at a doorway when needed—to fetch the herb woman.

For the next several hours, Ethel and the herb-woman saw Hilda through her travails, hampered by the small space in which Hilda had been confined and the need to keep their young charge silent. The Abbess had given instructions to keep Hilda quiet so the baby's birth would not become known to the abbey's community.

The Abbess wished to create a small pocket of secrecy within a milieu where secrecy could not take root.

"The woman knows no mercy," the herb-woman said in disgust. "God said women must bring forth life in blood and pain, but he didn't forbid Eve the relief of a good scream or two."

"Eve had nothing to hide," Hilda whispered, weak from pain. "The Abbess decided to keep me a secret and commands me to be compliant. I have no wish to scream so that she can find yet another fault in my character!"

And so just after dawn, Hilda delivered her child, keeping her screams between tightly clinched teeth. "Give me my child," she insisted.

The herb-woman stood up and walked to the other side of the room, carrying the tiny, squalling baby. She motioned to Ethel to take the baby; then picked up a cup from the small table and brought it to the bedside.

"Drink this, please. The herbs will let you sleep."

"I don't want to sleep. Bring me my baby," Hilda insisted again. "Is it alright? Is there anything wrong?"

"No, no," coaxed Ethel. "Listen to these cries! You've been through much more than most women these last hours and your strength is almost gone. You need to rest so that you can feed your babe later."

Suddenly Hilda realized that she was too tired to argue, and so she drank the bitter potion, and—vaguely aware that harsh whispers mingled with her baby's cries—she lapsed into a deep sleep.

When she finally returned to full consciousness, the old herb-healer was gone, but Ethel sat close by her bedstead. Hilda attempted to sit up, but found it too much of an effort. She instinctively put her hand on her stomach, which no longer felt stretched by the small creature she had carried for these many months.

"Ethel?" she asked. Ethel turned her face away as if she could not look Hilda in the eyes, and following the direction in which her nurse looked, Hilda saw the Abbess standing at the door, anger evident on her face.

"Where is my child?" she asked quietly, fear rising up in her heart.

"That creation of your sin is gone, Princess Hilda. Did you think your punishment would be so simple as staying out here? Your contaminated child will be sent to a family who will raise it as a good Christian and guide it away from the evil of its birth."

"No!" Hilda gasped, and attempted to sit up only to fall back weakly against her pillow. Surely this was part of a terrible nightmare.

The Abbess came a step closer, her hostile eyes boring into Hilda's face. "You have brought disgrace to my monastery, to my sister's monastery, and to your family. Just as your child has been sent from this holy place, so will you."

She paused, waiting for a reaction from Hilda.

"Where am I to go?" Hilda asked. "Why should I be separated from my baby?"

"I suggest you return to your father. He will not know of your disgrace, and no one here will tell him. Abbess Edyth tells me that Highhear is now safe, that your father's enemies have been driven away. Caedmon and Ethel brought you here; they can take you away."

"I want my child," Hilda repeated again.

"You're not fit to be a mother! I thank heaven that your own saintly mother did not live to see what has come to be. Let a better mother raise the child. You must be gone as soon as you can travel. May you have the good grace from now on to live a life free from sin."

And with these words, the Abbess stormed out the door.

Hilda found her anger and turning to Ethel exclaimed, "How dare she!"

Ignoring the pain, she struggled to her feet and attempted to follow Moira. Weakness overtook her limbs and she fell back on the bed. Her crying was almost silent.

Ethel, freed from the paralysis that Abbess Moira created, found her voice and offered what comfort she could.

"Shh, little one, soon we'll be going from this place." She paused. "I did not know they were planning to take the child. I tried to stop them, but couldn't."

The enormity of her position completely overwhelmed Hilda, wiping out any plans she might have made for traveling to Lothlar with her child. She could only nod as Ethel took over the planning of her future.

"Alright, be calm now. I'll help you bathe and put clean sheets on the bed. You can sleep a little more and tomorrow we'll plan." The old woman babbled on, almost as if she believed that continuous talk would distract her charge from the horror that had befallen her. "I have a warm dress for you to wear, and I'll gather provisions tomorrow—Brother Paul will provide good bread and the cook will give me cheese. If you're strong enough, within a few days we will leave this place while everyone is at prayer."

"Ethel," Hilda grasped the other woman's hand to stay the flow of talk. "I do not think I can walk very far."

"Don't fret. I'll see to it that the Abbess provides a donkey for you. If she refuses...well, I'll steal one!"

Even as tired as she was, Hilda laughed at the thought of Ethel sneaking about and stealing a donkey. Then her thoughts once again turned back to the last few hours. "Ethel," Hilda asked as sleep claimed her once more. "Where is my baby? Was it a boy or a girl?"

"Hush," Ethel smoothed back her hair with a tender hand. "We will not talk about that now. Think about going to your father, about going back home. Caedmon is here to guide us." Hilda turned to smile wanly at her faithful servant hovering in the doorway.

Conditioned now to having people refuse to answer her questions, Hilda allowed her worry, her fear, and her aching body to pull her into oblivion. As she sank into a deep sleep, Ethel could hear her whisper: "My love, my love, where are you, John?"

Ethel, heartbroken at the events of the day, stored the name John into her memory and waited until she knew her mistress slept soundly and then whispered into her ear.

"I've carved one of those eternity knots on the baby's foot while the midwife tended you." Caedmon nodded his head at this news. Ethel continued, "the poor babe cried, but at least she has a mark we can use to find her. And we will...someday.... I believe that after we're away from this awful place and you've regained your strength, God will bring you and her together—and maybe her father, too." Ethel's voice became angrier. "God is merciful and forgiving even if abbesses are not!"

Chapter 6: Leova Marries (879)

Three days after Leova found herself with a prospective husband, her family had to negotiate with his mother. William, his brother Ragen, and the fearsome Allmana arrived together to determine and confirm the legal details of the marriage contract, and while relations between the young couple were uncomfortable, the tension between Allmana and her sons was palpable. Allmana, unstable as she might be, had to be present to finalize the proceedings. William and Regan worked together to keep her input to a minimum, but occasionally she would break out with a demand so unreasonable that it took everyone's efforts to avoid the complete disintegration of the negotiations. Luckily, the brothers had insisted upon bringing a scribe, who had recorded beforehand outlines of the land and lists of goods and servants, and having him read back what had been written kept the woman in check. William oversaw the scribe's actions—carefully correcting the writing in spots and pushing him to clarify all points. Allmana was not allowed to dictate to either the scribe or to her sons.

"That's good," thought Leova, relieved to see how the sons controlled the mother. "They can't silence her, but at least they can balance her spleen and soften her attacks."

If Allmana had been able to control the mediations, Bertram would have lost everything he had built. Even in the estate's declining condition, Leova brought much into the marriage, not the least of which was a fortified compound. Not many men had had the power, as Bertram did, to build from stone, nor the bravery to raise impenetrable walls. Such walls marked a lord as having much to protect; stone anchored a man to a plot of ground and to other men, women and children who became the lord's responsibility. Bertram held the position of *Bretwalda*, a king in a kingless land. In his position as warrior and overlord, he had been able to demand deference from his peers and instant obedience from his inferiors. Like the great *bretwaldas* before him—Alla of Sussex, Ceawin of Wessex, Ethelbert of Kent and Raedwald of East Anglia—Bertram had ruled firmly, most would even say fairly. His extensive lands, with views of the plains to the east and hills to the west, suited Bertram greatly.

Lothlar sat on one of the low hills in the north. Offa's Dyke, built by Romans centuries before, provided a bulwark to which Bertram added. Like the Roman soldiers, Bertram cleared land and built great shrub-free ditches, almost as wide as they were long. The uneven ground, covered with rocks of varying sizes and sharpness, running alongside the ditches provided another deterrent to an enemy. Any approaching man, horse, or wagon would be seen long before nearing the heavy timber walls and the great stone gates of Lothlar. From his vantage point on the dyke, Bertram could survey much of the area where flocks fed and, if he wanted, could watch his lady as she surveyed the fields that provided stores for the winter. The farm land was not as good as that farther south, but what it lacked in fertility, it made up for as grazing land, and wool brought good trading prices on any market.

That abundance, unfortunately, had passed. The sickness that had attacked his livestock and proved particularly deadly for the sheep, had all but depleted his ability to trade. No longer productive, much of Bertram's land was now uncultivated and uninhabited and thus unprotected. Regrettably, all he really had left to barter with was that depleted land itself. He knew the land represented the only way to gain any advantage in his dealings with Allmana.

Leova had taken her embroidery into the hall in order to listen to as much as she could of the negotiations, but she had been able to hear almost nothing because she had not been granted a place at the table. Sitting near the fire, the thread and needle useless in her tense fingers, she grew more and more angry as she listened to hours of discussion—some of it quiet, much of it rancorous. At last the negotiators rose from their seats, apparently in agreement on most points. Angry, but helpless, Leova stared into space.

"The issues of my life have been debated without any question aimed in my direction, or any comment made more subtle because I was in the hall." She punched her needle into the cloth she held and dropped the project on the floor beside her chair. "I am no more important—perhaps less important—than an acre of land!"

Pagany appeared and motioned for Leova to join her. She had ordered food and drink to be placed on the high table, and the two women of Lothlar took their places as mistresses of the hall.

"We have no time for dining!" the Lady Allmana blurted out. "We've spent enough hours in this uncomfortable hall."

Bertram looked angrily at his guest and would have spoken out had not his wife interceded.

"Surely, it is fitting that we celebrate this joining?" Pagany said courteously. She phrased her comment as a question, but her tone of voice made it clear that she would not allow the group to so quickly abandon Leova.

"If you must rest, my husband, our guests will understand," she said pointedly to Bertram. And seizing upon the suggestion, he excused himself, barely taking time to quickly bestow a kiss on Leova's forehead and nod farewell before he fled. Regan took his glowering mother by her arm and led her to the table, seating her between Pagany and himself and safely away from Leova and William.

The meal didn't bring about the friendly conversation that Pagany had hoped for. Allmana and her sons ate silently, despite their hostess' attempts to engage them in conversation. Allmana replied with short, almost rude, answers to any question directed her way, and William and Regan seemed too distracted by their mother to comfortably enter into conversation. As the meal continued, the high table grew quieter and quieter, and the servants, sensing the tension, became silent also. Even the dogs lay quietly unmoving.

Leova, more annoyed than hurt, proved herself her mother's daughter when she took on the task of reviving the conversation. She was suddenly determined not to let the occasion turn into a dismal affair; she would keep her new family from setting a tradition that would keep them from engaging with each other. Taking a deep breath and forcing a smile to her lips, she began with her betrothed.

"Tell me of your journey from your hall," she asked William. "Did you find it difficult? There can be layers of ice and snow at this time of the year."

William, seemingly uncomfortable at this mildest of questions, replied hesitantly, "No. No...Lady Leova." He paused, then realized he should say more. "The hills have never presented any problems."

She wouldn't let him get away with such a brief response. "And did you find shelter from the wind? I remember my one trip to your hall; the rain and wind were rather wicked. Were you not cold? Did you need to find protection?"

He looked down at his plate in either shyness or desperation. "We had no need for protection. As I said, there were no problems along the way."

Making conversation had become a challenge Leova wasn't willing to let go. She put on her best hostess smile and turned to Allmana. "My Lady, do not return to Stonehart today. Stay overnight. The journey home will surely be tiring, especially if you come and return in the same day."

Allmana did not answer. She glared at Leova and then reached for more bread, attempting to end the conversation by blunt force.

Ragen, intent on maintaining civility, answered the question that had not been directed at him. "We can return today without tiring any of the company. And the trip is not without its pleasures. If we depart soon, we can watch the sun as it disappears. Often it imparts a rosy glow to all the trees and hillsides."

"Fool," Allmana injected harshly. "It's just a horseback ride."

"Beauty is never foolish, I think," Leova snapped. Allman's back stiffened, but she said nothing more.

Ragen and William looked startled at Leova's remark, somewhat surprised at the vehement response to his mother's comment. Hurrying to keep the conversation going, Regan asked, "Do you love beauty so?" he asked.

"Of course, My Lord," Leova answered, somewhat amazed. "How can one *not* love beauty?"

"And must beauty always be sunrise or sunset or hills in fog— or can beauty be found in objects made by men and women?"

William interjected.

Pleased that he responded, Leova warmed to the question, "I think that beauty has many forms. That which your God creates cannot be surpassed, but that which humans create can hold the eye and heart."

William cocked his head a bit quizzically at the "your God" in Leova's response, but he left the comment unquestioned.

"More foolishness," muttered his mother, casting a dark look at her sons.

"Perhaps," responded William, turning toward his mother. "Perhaps not. Horses are beautiful, are they not? I admire their beauty. Don't you?"

"Horses are well-formed creatures, but their *beauty,* if there be any, is in the fact that they are obedient," she paused and scowled at Regan. "Unlike other living things, they eat what you put before them, do not demand coats of velvet, and work when told to work."

Mother and son glared at each other for a moment or two, each prepared to get in the next word, so Leova, peacemaker that she was, hastily stepped in to smooth things over.

"Your horses are legendary for their beauty, My Lady. The mount you rode in on was exceptional."

Allmana turned to her as if Leova had suddenly arrived from a distant star. "My *best* horses remain at home," she snapped, "only the simple minded would ride them through such cursed country at this season."

Leova, startled by the tone of disdain in the older woman's voice, fell silent, inwardly infuriated that this woman would go to such trouble to gain control over "cursed country." Leova silently thanked her parents for keeping her out of Allmana's hall, a hall in which family conversations evidently tended to turn spiteful in very short time.

Having delivered her insult, Allmana rose abruptly. "Enough. The day grows long and we must hurry to avoid the night that follows any sunset...beautiful or not."

As she headed toward the door, William stood his ground. "I will stay longer and learn more about my bride-to-be."

Leova was as surprised as Allmana at the sudden turn of events.

"There will be plenty of time for that, once you're married," Allmana asserted in a voice which indicated that she expected to be obeyed.

"Nonetheless," responded William quietly, "I will stay for another hour or so and return later in the afternoon."

"And the possibility of snow and bluster? You would tempt fate?"

"I have been out in far worse weather than today's."

Allmana, obviously displeased, turned from her son, and left the hall without even a nod of her head as a farewell.

As soon as the door shut behind Regan and the troublesome woman, Leova felt the tension drain from her body; even William seemed more at ease. Wanting to avoid the courtyard where the grooms were collecting the horses for the ride back to Stonehart, the young couple left the table and walked slowly about the hall, each shy and awkward but willing to make conversation. William pointed to a small harp braced against one of the outer walls. "Do you play?" he asked.

"Yes," Leova found herself blushing. "Poorly, I'm afraid."

"Play something for me? Please." William hastened to make his request seem less arbitrary. "I'm fond of music."

Somewhat reluctantly, but with a growing lightness of mood, Leova picked up the small harp and seated herself on a nearby bench. Holding the small instrument in her lap, she plucked skillfully at the strings and began to sing in a clear, pure voice.

I arise today through the strength of the skies,
the light of the sun and the glow of the moon,
the sparks of fire, the quickness of lightning,
the speed of the wind and the depths of the waters,
the stability of ground and the firmness of the rocks.

Although William seemed pleased by the song and the singer, Leova could see his mind drifting from the present moment. For some few minutes, he was elsewhere. "You do the music more than

196

justice," he finally said, a kind smile showing that he wasn't just being polite.

"It's the first song I remember my mother singing to me. Music can be as lovely as the sunset, can it not?"

"True, my lady, I do think so. But both, like the day, are gone too soon, and too permanently. If I choose to dismiss the singer—which I certainly would not do in your case—the song disappears without a trace; when the sun disappears in the evening and fades into night, the sunset vanishes."

"Doesn't the sunset return the next evening? The singer might retire, but can be summoned again—as can the song."

Surprised at her willingness to debate, William paid attention. "But it might rain, or the synger—not you, of course—might be drunk and sour the sweetness of the notes. Music and sunset are transitory; I prefer more permanent forms of beauty: illustrations in the manuscripts we had at the monastery, objects such as your brooch." He reached out and fingered the dragon pin on her shoulder, following the intricate knot its body made with the tip of his finger. His eyes shone, but then he realized how close he was to Leova and tried to regain his composure.

"This excellent piece reminds me of the manuscript illustrations. It's one of the best objects of beauty that I've ever seen."

It took a moment for Leova to reply. "I'm pleased that it pleases you," Leova confessed. "It's of my own design."

"You designed this?" William marveled. "I have gained an unexpected prize with my new wife!"

Leova smiled, happy with his compliment and glad to be talking more easily with her soon-to-be husband. Mercifully, William seemed quite unlike his mother. His years at the monastery had apparently kept him from absorbing Allmana's poisonous heart and mind.

"The beauty I admire is in craft," William continued. "I have three fine Italian paintings of saints—one shows the Virgin greeting the wise men, and the two others depict the martyrdom of Saint Stephen and Saint Catherine."

Leova was unsure what made a painting "Italian," but she was now listening intently, fascinated with the possibility of learning something new.

"At the monastery, there are many beautiful and worthy books. Those who crafted them bring us art as meaningful as the words they illustrate."

"Can you read?" Leova asked with genuine curiosity. She had heard from several of the traveling messengers that some of the scribes in monasteries could only copy, not read, the manuscripts.

"Of course," returned William, slightly perplexed at the question. "You do not read?"

Leova blushed and shook her bowed head in embarrassment. "I've long wished I could read and write, but only the priests who come here ever so often could teach me. But they tell me that there is no need."

"No need?" echoed William. "How will you keep accounts? And how will you bargain with traders and others in the region?"

"My father and my mother have dealt with those matters quite well without reading," Leova retorted defensively.

"True," William acknowledged, trying to repair any insult he had unwittingly made. "But life is more than managing an estate. Reading opens that world of beauty you love." He smiled gently, "Would you like me to teach you?"

Leova smiled, "Yes, I should like that very much." For the first time, she realized later, she hadn't regretted that William, rather than Rolfe, would be her husband.

During the awkward and unpleasant matrimonial deliberations, Bertram and Allmana had agreed that the wedding would occur six weeks after the bans were read. Those who had to prepare for the nuptials couldn't understand the reason for such a swift conclusion to the agreement, but nothing could dissuade them.

Much in the way of linens and woven goods had been completed over the course of years and stored away for Leova's future home, but since she was to remain at Lothlar, the bride goods ceased to be a problem. However, no provision for wedding clothing had been made, and food for the wedding feast had to be found and prepared as well. For the wedding garments Leova and her mother had very little help; only Gwynned and three of Pagany's closest female companions were skilled enough to work on the bridal goods. Strange women appeared ever so often to embroider fine details on Leova's wedding gown. Although they were obviously women from the forest, women from the old religion, Bertram decided not to "see" them because their help was invaluable. The same women who came to sew brought preserves and sweetmeats for the enjoyment of the guests. And food appeared from unexpected sources also. Regan sent stores from Stonehart: flour and butter, smoked meats and cheese. These gifts would allow Pagany and Bertram to prepare and set forth a worthy feast despite the hardships of the previous year.

As the wedding day grew near, news came about two prospective guests. To Leova's relief, Rolfe's activities at the monastery would keep him from attending. She no longer wept because he would not be her husband, but she didn't want the awkwardness between them to mar what happiness she could derive from marrying William. It grieved her terribly when no messenger could find Hilda. Indeed, her childhood friend seemed to have vanished completely. Envoys from Lothlar had sought her first at Highhear and then—to her amazement—at Buxton where Rolfe had resided. The returning messengers told them that no one knew what had happened to Hilda after the raid; they could only hope that she had found shelter in some other abbey. The news startled Leova. She hoped that her dearest friend was safe, preferably in a spot where she wanted to be. She smiled slightly as she remembered how often Hilda had spoken of escaping into the woods and finding a new world. But she was taken aback somewhat by the possibility that Rolfe, William, and Hilda had been in the same monastery for at least some length of time; Leova knew she had many questions to ask. A time might come when she could question William about Hilda, but now it was time to become a bride and then a wife responsible for a household.

Not the least of Leova's problems was convincing the servants that she could carry out the duties of a mistress. The day before the ceremony, she found herself in mortal combat—and losing—with one of the oldest members of the household staff.

"No, you may *not* serve watered wine to guests at my wedding," Leova said firmly to Hannah, still the most awesome of the kitchen crones. Even though Leova was only too aware of the hardships which had dangerously reduced her family's wealth and resources, she was determined that the wedding not be a poor one. Leova had her pride.

"Bless your h'art, child. You *do* sound like someone's mistress!" the less-than-intimidated keeper of the kitchen cooed. "I'm sure if you ruled your own home, they'd all snap right to you when you took overn the kitchen. Why, even I would quake a bit if'en I'd not trained you."

Leova decided to change tactics.

"Hannah, think of the disgrace if you won't listen to my orders. Lord William and his family may decide I can't keep a decent household, and they'd blame my good mother. Surely you don't want that, no matter what you might be willing to let them think of me, she doesn't deserve to be disgraced."

Hannah reconsidered. Putting young Leova in her place was one thing, tarnishing the reputation of Lady Pagany quite another.

"As ya wish," she shrugged, then smiled warmly. "Neither you nor your ma'am shall be disgraced account of my table. Heaven knows what will happen once they discover the hellion they've broughtn to their family. I shall whisper to your new lad that he must beat ya—otherwise, he's lost!"

"Who needs the beating?" laughed Leova happily and kissed her tormentor on the cheek. In some ways, she was actually pleased that Hannah felt secure enough to challenge her on occasion. There were matters about the kitchen that Leova would probably never understand. However, she never really feared that Hannah would fail her. Still, buried just below the surface of her consciousness, lived a fear that she'd never have a household of her own to control—and, if she did, if she would be able to make it a happy productive place like the one she had grown up in.

The day before the wedding, mother and daughter spend the

entire afternoon in preparation, moving from the kitchen to guest quarters to the great hall itself to make sure that all their plans were being carried out. By mid-morning, the women of the household had already worked for almost five hours straight, aware that William and his family would arrive in the early afternoon. While they stood and admired the decorated hall, Pagany could not overlook the weariness that burdened her daughter.

"Leova, rest now. You must be prepared to meet your guests."

"Mother, I can't. There's still much to do," Leova said wearily. She hadn't slept much the night before, but she couldn't bring herself to stop working.

"Nothing that the rest of us can't finish," her mother replied curtly. "Your main task from this point on is to be a bride."

Leova knew it was useless to argue with her mother when she took on that tone of voice, and so, accompanied by Gwynned, she made her way to her own quarters and allowed her faithful servant to bathe her, comb her hair, and rub her body with sweet-smelling oils. Before the massage was complete, Leova was sound asleep. Gwynned looked down at the young woman to whom she had been a second mother. With her golden hair spread about her on the bolster, Leova looked just like one of the angels in the tapestry on the chapel walls. Gwynned did not have much to do with the new religion, but that did not keep her from knowing that there really were angels—maybe, of course, they were fairies—in the world, visible only to those blessed enough to see them. How she hoped that her young angel, her young mistress, would find some happiness in her marriage—though she had first given her heart elsewhere.

Leova awoke to the sounds of horses and voices in the open yard outside her sleeping quarters. Once fully awake, she realized that her bridegroom and his family must have just arrived. Reluctantly she tapped the shoulders of her faithful servant who was nodding on a bench in the corner. "Gwynned, we need to prepare to meet our guests." Gwynned awoke slowly at her mistress' gentle touch.

"We still have time," she muttered, looking out through the small window high on the wall of the bur. She turned back to her mistress, "unfortunately for them, it does appear as though our guests have had to travel through wind and lightly falling snow. They will go off to their own quarters and recover from their trip; they might not reappear until the evening banquet."

Leova went to the door and managed to peer through it unobtrusively so she could watch the activities in the yard. Allmana, as formidable and disagreeable as ever, had dismounted with the help of Stephen. She supposed that everyone knew him to be her bed companion. The pack horses, she realized, were loaded with unknown packages and goods. "What on earth could Allmana be bringing here?" Leova wondered.

As if reading her thoughts, Gwynned replied, "Perhaps Allmana thinks we don't have goods and possessions enough for her son, but I guess he probably has much that he wants—or needs," she added almost apologetically, not wanting to seem critical of Leova's new relations.

At first Leova did not see William, but as the horses and people cleared away, she spotted him standing alone just inside the gate. He seemed quite pensive and alone. Leova felt her heart ache a bit for him. He did not look happy. As she watched, he turned slowly and moved away, walking slowly and aimlessly toward the out-buildings on the other side of the hall. Gwynned broke through her mistress' reverie. "Come, come, no time for dawdling, now. Let's get you dressed."

This evening's meal was not to be as lavish as the actual wedding banquet. When evening approached, Pagany appeared with Bertram who was determined to participate regardless of the weakness in his legs. Shortly thereafter Allmana appeared with Stephen, Ragen, and William. And, as they settled themselves at the high table, Leova appeared in the doorway accompanied by Gwynned and several young servant girls. William rose to meet his bride and escorted her to her seat next to him, and all those in the hall broke out in cheering and clapping. Leova could not keep herself from blushing; the color in her cheeks only enhanced her beauty.

Once the meal actually began, however, Leova felt quite lonely. Allmana was as difficult to talk with as she had been at earlier occasions, and despite his interest and courtesy when they'd been alone together, with his family present, William had almost nothing to say. Ragen was, as in the past, the one with whom she felt most comfortable, but Pagany and Ragen spent most of the evening in conversation. "Is my life going to be like this from now on?" she could only wonder.

Leova fell back into her reverie, and William fell into his own until the touch of her mother's hand forced Leova back to the present. Her mother had apparently asked her some question. Leova had to ask her to repeat it. "Would you care to join me, Leova, as I pass the cup around to our guests?"

"No, mother, you are still the sole mistress of this house."

"But soon you will be the mistress also," her mother replied sadly.

"Tonight I am just your daughter, and I will not take your place."

Pagany grasped the cup, offering it first to her Lord, Bertram, and then, passing along the high table, to Allmana. Stephen, and Ragen. Then she moved down to the table where some of the lesser nobles and retainers were seated, graciously greeting and offering the cup to one and all. "How frail she looks," thought Leova. Bertram's illness had taken its toll on his wife. Having completed the circle of the hall, Pagany returned to stand before William and Leova, offering the cup first to her daughter and then to William.

"May the blessings and good will of all here stay with you always and may the gods of the earth and the creatures of the forest serve you well." The priest at the end of the table frowned slightly, but Pagany and her beliefs were protected by Bertram.

Leova felt suddenly very tired. Turning to William, she whispered a request. "My Lord, may I retire to my quarters now? Today has been very busy for me, and tomorrow will be even busier. I shall probably not get much sleep."

As soon as the words escaped her lips, Leova blushed and

noticed a slight smile on William's face. She was glad she had been whispering so that no one else had heard her ill-chosen words.

"Please, do as you wish," he replied. His kiss to her hand and the smile that came with it reminded her of the hope she'd begun to have when last they met. However, she couldn't quite dismiss the fact that this marriage had not been her wish at all.

"Do as I wish," Leova said to herself bitterly. How she longed to be able to.

A Company of Women

She had been sleeping only a few hours when she heard her mother's words whispered into her ear. "Leova," her mother's voice called. "Leova, get up and come with me...quickly!"

Deep in sleep, Leova gradually woke to her mother's voice. The darkness and the depth of her sleep indicated to her that this was no morning call to rise. She stumbled to the door and let her mother in, wondering where Gwynned, who usually slept beside her bed, might have gotten to. Despite the early hour, Pagany, dressed in her warmest cloak and obviously ready to leave the hall, pushed her way hurriedly past Leova and immediately began to gather up clothes warm enough to withstand the winter chill.

"Put these on quickly," she commanded, in a voice Leova did not often hear from her mother. "We've precious little time!"

"Where are we going?" Leova questioned. Challenging her mother's commands would get her nowhere, but if she asked patiently, she'd get answers. "What can be so urgent?"

"We're going where a woman must go on the morning she weds."

Instantly, Leova knew their destination and felt an impulse that floated somewhere between resistance and anticipation.

"Mother," she tried to say firmly, "You promised father I would be brought up in the new faith." The "new" faith she had been promised to had not been much in evidence at their hall—only an itinerant priest several times a year.

"Please, get dressed, we're a bit late as it is," her mother ordered. "I follow your father in most things, no matter how strange or unfitting they may be. However, this one thing cannot be ignored. I ask you to honor my desire and my gods as well as your father's."

"But the priest...he's here," Leova began.

"He'll not know lest you tell him," countered her mother. "Priests are men. And no man knows the world that you're about to enter. Priests are hampered even more than ordinary men. They do not sleep with a mate nor father a child—much less bear one."

She paused long enough to grasp Leova by the shoulder and look deeply in her daughter's eyes. "Women need women to celebrate with in times of joy, to comfort them in moments of sorrow, and to support them as they make the steps toward true womanhood. So the old religion taught, and so women have learned to share life's turning points with one another."

Leova paused only a moment, then nodded her consent. She could not gainsay her mother's wisdom. She had not easily taken the first step toward womanhood, the start of a girl's moon cycle, when the young girl's body came to move in tandem with those of the women of her household. Without the women's help, it would have been even more difficult.

Leova had been twelve when her courses came, a full year before Hilda. While Leova had not greeted with joy what the priests called her fate and her mother called her destiny, Hilda had raged against the bleeding that came each month.

"Maybe, I'll never have a baby! I'll stay a virgin all my life! So! I don't need this discomfort!" she'd ranted.

Pagany had patiently arranged for Hilda to go through the Ceremony of Becoming, just as she had arranged Leova's ceremony the year before. Together mother and daughter welcomed Hilda into the company of women in a ritual carefully hidden from men.

The day of marriage was the day that a girl made her second step towards true womanhood. Leova, eager to make her mother happy on this day of all days, drew her cloak close about her in preparation for the journey to the forest site where the ceremony would be held.

Since the spirits of the earth would not enter a place built to confine animals and shut out one sort of woman from another, rituals had to be held far outside the walls built by men. She knew that women of the old religion, long used to ignoring the demanding curiosity of their husbands, sons, and brothers, would have left their beds early this morning and moved quickly and quietly into the countryside toward a natural shelter in the forested hills. From various parts of Bertram's land, points of light from small and fragile oil lamps appeared in the darkness, guiding the groups of two or three women as they moved toward their meeting place.

As was the custom, Leova and her mother arrived last at the gathering place.

In the center of a small stone circle, a fire blazed steady and bright. The twenty or so women who surrounded it made a place for Pagany, but left Leova on the outside, cut off from the warmth of the flame and from the gentle murmur of voices as they chanted the ancient supplications to protect those in the hall and its environs. They passed small packages from woman to woman as they sang, pausing in mid-phrase to kiss the curiously shaped bundles, then resuming the song. After all the packages reached Pagany, she took her daughter by the hand and made her a part of the circle. Handing the woman next to her the bundles, she then drew Leova into the center of the circle, their empty spaces now creating a door into the circle. The women fell silent. All that could be heard was the crackle of the fire and the sounds of the hills about them.

"Welcome my daughter, women of the circle."

Pagany spoke quietly, turning with out-stretched arms of supplication until she had looked into the eyes of each participant.

"We welcome her," came the reply as a chorus.

Turning her gaze to the sky, Pagany asked in the same quiet voice, "Goddesses and Gods of the Sky and Water, bless her. Let the sun shine upon her and the rain nourish her crops." Kneeling on the ground, and placing her palms against the hardened earth, she prayed once more, "Goddesses and Gods of the earth, bless her. Make her path easy to walk and her fields abundant. Goddess of the fire, warm her hearth as long as she lives," she continued.

Mother and daughter now stood together in the firelight and the circle closed around them. From each woman came a fervent cry, half demand, half plea. "Bless her. Bless her." One by one the three eldest members of the group came forward with the sacrificial gifts. Kissing the bundle briefly, the watchman's wife handed a small package to Leova. Unwrapping it, Leova found a wreath woven from wheat stalks, the full grains of the head fanning out from the graceful knots which held together firm as any basket.

"Place it in the fire, child," the woman whispered. "Ask the *auncient woones* to bless your union."

Not speaking, but being ever so careful to do as she was told, Leova silently kissed the earthly token and placed it on the edge of the fire where it quickly flared up and began to burn.

As the woman stepped back into the circle, the next figure moved forward and Leova found herself looking into the eyes of Hannah, elevated from her position in the kitchen to one of honor in the ceremony.

"Place this in the fire, child," she said with dignity. "Ask the *auncient woones* for many children, delivered safely."

Leova opened the package from Hannah and found a small wooden image of a woman, belly rounded with child, breasts full with milk, hips and thighs already broadened by childbearing. She kissed it briefly and placed it on the last burning stalks of the wreath.

The last of the women, her own Gwynned, stepped forward. She, too, had a package that she placed carefully in her mistress' hands. Inside this parcel was a collection of herbs, grains, and fruits as well as barley, figs, licorice, salt and dried pork.

"Place it in the fire, child. Ask the *auncient woones* to keep you and yours from the curse of illness."

Again, Leova did as she was told, then paused waiting for the next step of the ritual.

Now three of the youngest of the group came forward, women who had married in the last two years, one of whom was obviously with child. They draped a light and finely woven scarf over Leova's hair, each kissed her and returned to her place in the circle. The company chanted as one, "May the *auncient woones* protect you from the rains and winds."

Three women of Pagany's age came forward and fed her a

piece of honey-cake, a bit of fresh bread, and a sip of wine. "May the goddesses and gods provide for your table, even in times of hardship," intoned the women in one voice.

Pagany now stepped forward and tied a cord of finest silk about Leova's waist. She kissed her daughter tenderly and spoke the last words of the ritual. "May you be connected to each of us as we are connected to you. May knowledge and love pass from mother to daughter, from woman to woman, in an unbroken line till the end of time."

"May it be so," went up the plea that was in truth a demand, into the sky above, into the vast darkness.

"The *auncient woones* bring you joy!" cried Hannah, and the solemn nature of the ceremony was broken in an instance. The holy circle disintegrated and Leova found herself being hugged and kissed by all those who had been remote only moments ago. The oldest women passed around more honey-cakes, and Hannah moved from woman to woman with the wine sack. Laughter started up as women began to tell ribald tales of the marriage bed and the foibles of husbands.

"Better ask the goddesses for salve to soothe the loss of your maidenhead, Leova," joked one of the young women.

"And add a prayer that your husband will leave you be after you give him a son; mine got six more on me after the first one!" added another woman.

Everyone broke into giggles obviously aware that Leova was blushing.

"I don't know," protested the most recently wed, "I find comfort in the embrace of my man. I don't know that a child is a price too high for an act that does so well by me."

"Wait until your belly swells up," pouted the woman with child.

"Or wait until you must push out the little wretch," snickered another, pregnant with her third child.

"Or wait until you must bury your babe," came a voice that broke the gaiety of the moment.

"Sweet Susan," Pagany chided, "Do not curse my daughter's

joining. Put aside your own sorrows so that she may have joy on her wedding day."

Susan, who had borne six children, none who had lived past the first year, pushed her way toward mother and daughter. She brought her face, still young but worn beyond its years, up close to Leova's and lightly touched her face with a hand hardened by work in the kitchens. "I wish you no grief, child," she said. Her eyes searched Leova's face as she spoke. "But best know that joy can be short. These women will bear you up if need be, as they have helped me bear my sorrows. We have a bond blessed by the *auncient woones*—that is our dearest gift. Don't forget about that as you give yourself to serve your husband."

"Never," replied Leova, more drawn by Susan's words than by the incantatory words of the *auncient woones*. "I will seek to be strong for those of you who have been strong for me."

Pagany moved suddenly between Leova and Susan, "The dawn comes soon; we must return to Lothlar before the new day starts.

The Ceremony

When morning arrived fully, Leova's wedding day was as bright a day as shone on any bride. The chill wind that had hung on for weeks disappeared, leaving the sky fresh with clouds and the air as comfortable as one could hope for in winter. The vows and priestly blessings would be read before noonday in front of the little chapel where all who wished could witness the ritual. The family would then take its place inside for the nuptial mass, after which a lavish banquet would take place. Everyone in the countryside looked forward to attending the feast; everyone but Allmana. True to form, the disagreeable woman insisted that she would return to her own hall as soon as the two young people were wed. Leova was not the only person who was secretly pleased.

Having risen early and having bathed in scented water prepared by Gwynned, Leova waited patiently for her mother to bring her dress. Although it was traditional for a bride to make her own garment, Pagany had insisted upon preparing Leova's gown herself. From the time the match had been determined, Pagany had set apart some portion of her day to work on the dress, shutting herself in her room and working by the light of the window. On her insistence, a small loom had been placed in her room, so that she could see to every stage of the garment's creation. After spinning the wool herself, she had woven the fine cloth, carefully stitched each seam and embroidered the bodice and sleeves with colorful threads.

Leova, tempted as far as was humanly possible, had kept her curiosity under check and her nose out of her mother's closet. Now she needed not to remain patient any longer, and sighed gratefully at the sound of knocking on her door. When her mother entered, carrying the garment, Leova found her patience well rewarded. Almost shyly, her mother helped her to dress, letting the younger woman take the time to examine each piece as she donned it.

The shift was of a pale blue that only Pagany knew how to produce. Around the neck and the long flowing sleeves, knots of gold thread interlocked with colorful cornflowers, roses, yellow daisies, and forget-me-nots. A number of small golden bees seemed to fly across the bodice in search of the honey those flowers would yield. The weskit of soft green featured an overall leaf pattern in a thread just slightly darker than the cloth itself. As she dressed, Leova followed the delicate patterns with her fingertips, marveling at the intricate threads and her mother's skill. Then Pagany draped about her head the white wimple designed to cover her hair and neck, and placed upon it a crown of flowers and ribbons created from stiffened silk touched with gold. A little bee almost hidden in the center of a delicate pink rose delighted the young bride.

"The knots signify eternal happiness—all lives like the knots are endlessly intertwined. The flowers represent the beauty your life will continue to hold, and the bees," Pagany laughed, "stand for fertility."

Leova blushed and looked down at the multiple bees that swarmed across her chest.

"I expect granddaughters and grandsons aplenty," her mother said seriously.

Leova knew that her mother grieved greatly for both the son

who was born dead and for the other who had lived so briefly. "I'll do my best to please you, mother," laughed Leova who began to feel herself at the dead center between the past and future of her family.

"Come now," Pagany said. "Your father waits in the hall, and your bridegroom waits at the chapel door. We mustn't keep them waiting." She took her daughter's arm and, wrapping it in her own, led Leova out the door and down to the great hall where Bertram, William, Allmana and Ragen waited.

"Such a beautiful woman," said Stephen, standing at Allmana's shoulder when Leova and her parents entered the courtyard.

Allmana frowned. Stephen, well aware of his lady's every emotion, immediately caught himself. "Young *bride*, I meant." He bowed briefly to the woman beside him, but she was not deceived.

Bertram, like the rest of the men of the wedding party, was outfitted in the short tunic and robe of a warrior. At his waist, he wore a heavy gold belt which held a ceremonial sword. At his shoulder, an elaborate brooch of garnet and gold held back the folds of his cape.

Lady Pagany was only slightly less dazzling than her daughter. Her shift of blue was so dark that at times it appeared black. Like her daughter's gown, heavy embroidery, this time of silver rather than gold thread, covered the neck and sleeves. Emblems of the night—stars, moons—caught the light as she moved. And from the hem rose a magical comet that seemed to move as she walked. Her weskit needed no ornamentation because the deep red acted as decoration enough against the elaborate dress. Her hair, still free of gray, had been dressed in elaborate braids. And the plain wimple that covered them was held in place by a circlet of pure silver which had been ornately carved and studded with blue and red stones. As a new bride, Pagany had worn it at her own wedding.

Pagany looked at Leova, and silently raised a prayer that this beautiful daughter would someday wear the circlet in honor of her own child's marriage.

The journey to the chapel presented an opportunity to share their joy with the people who had cared for Leova as she grew up. As

211

they emerged from the hall door walking arm in arm, one parent on either side of their daughter, a great shout went up. Both young and old had been waiting for a glimpse of the wedding gown. Although only a few steps separated the chapel from the hall door, Bertram led his family around the perimeter of the yard, giving each of his people a chance to see their princess and the splendid clothing that the three of them wore. The sight of fine wool and jewels set in gold and silver after a year of hardship represented more entertainment than the people of that community had enjoyed in years. As they moved in a sweeping circle around the yard, Leova espied Jankin, gaping at her open-mouthed. When she raised her hand to let him know she had seen him, the crowd turned to see who merited such a reward, and afterwards, Jankin was treated with new respect.

Smiling happily, the threesome stopped before the chapel door where Father Aidan stood on the highest of three steps; just below him stood William with his mother and brother. Allmana's plain gray dress, adorned with indistinguishable silver thread, did little to impress the crowd, but her only concession to the day—a genuinely stunning crown of gold, silver, and enamel—rested over her graying hair and marked her position as a landowner. William's tunic was a simple blue, but his robe was outlined with shining silver and gold threads. He carried no sword.

The crowd grew quiet, waiting for the priest to speak. Excited by the attention and by the wealth and power displayed about him, Father Aidan took his time before he began the blessing. As the priestly words of the church's Latin swept over the marriage party and the gathered audience, everyone became absorbed by the musical sounds of the words and the strangeness of the language. William's face as he attended to the priest's pronouncements showed that he was not an idle listener. Leova felt the power of the words, too, and thought them as magical as the words of the women of the forest the night before.

The priest smiled, and unlaced Leova's arm from her mother's and placed Leova's delicate fingers in William's hand. Reluctantly, Bertram disengaged Leova's other arm and stepped back to stand next to his wife.

The priest continued in Latin for another few minutes and then, in Englisc, asked William if he had a token for his new bride. William released Leova's hand for a moment to pull an elegant gold ring with an intricate design of locked hands and flowers from the little finger of his hand. His smile revealed his happiness as he slipped it on her finger.

"Let this ring serve as a sign that I pledge my life to you and promise to treasure and protect you as long as we live."

Watching his face as he made his pledge allowed Leova see his sincerity. "His words are true," she marveled. "He values me as a woman rather than as a piece of property." Impulsively, she squeezed his hand.

The priest turned to Leova, "Have you a token with which to pledge?"

She nodded and reached into the tiny pocket sewn into her weskit, producing a heavy gold ring carved with a powerful winged horse in flight. A horn protruded from the center of its forehead, and a large ruby rested under one wing, sending out an almost magical source of light.

"With this ring, I pledge to be a loyal wife, a helpmate who will honor you as long as we both live." And with a smile equal to his, she helped William slide the ring into place.

"Now I welcome you into God's house to share together your first mass as man and wife," the priest pronounced solemnly.

"God bless!" someone shouted, and a chorus of voices repeated the hearty sentiment.

William and Leova looked out at the people who now would think of them as master and mistress of Lothlar and grinned happily at the enthusiastic blessings. Then William bent to kiss Leova briefly on the mouth, setting off another round of whole-hearted merriment.

"Good luck to you, good sire! Keep her happy and keep her with child!" an old man called out. His wife, poked him with her elbow.

"Give them a chance to know each other before she has to produce an heir, you rude dolt!"

Leova felt a strange sensation as his soft lips met hers, another promise that went beyond property agreements. They would be partners and perhaps friends...perhaps even true lovers rather than bed mates. Blessed by the women of the forest and by the Christian priest, she knew that they had the power of two great religions behind them. Nonetheless, Leova remained unsure of the future. Could conflict grow out of the differences in their upbringing? She was a child of her mother's religion as much as he was a child of the church. And while her mother's religion gave power to women, William's God demanded men rule their homes as well as their countries.

"Unless we can find a way to meet as equals," she thought, "life might become unpleasant for us and those we love." And then, with the hope that characterized her being, she shook off any harsh fear for the future and entered the church with her new husband.

Later in the hall, Leova listened to the sweet music of the scope, thinking not of her new husband or her lost love, Rolfe, but of her friend, Hilda.

> Sweet loved-one, I pray thee,
> For one loving speech;
> While I live in this wide world
> None other will I seek.

Once they had promised to attend each other's weddings, but now, she reflected, "I sit alone and Hilda is lost, perhaps never to be found." A round of raucous laughter interrupted her thoughts.

"I'm hardly *alone*," she thought, looking around. Bertram had used almost all the wealth he had left to produce the wedding feast. In addition to the food and elaborate dress, he had hired singers and a scope to sing the praises of his family, instrumentalists to accompany them, and acrobats as well as jugglers and tricksters. All of the entertainers were performing at once, creating little pockets of noisy people around the hall. In fact, because of the commotion of the spectators and the playful—but loud—yells from children, Leova could barely hear the words of the songs. She was anything but alone.

The festivities had been in full swing for over two hours, and no one seemed to be tiring. Leova put aside her one moment of sadness and concentrated on the happiness evident in the faces of those she loved. But suddenly Allmana rose and spoke irritably to Regan. "See to the horses. We're leaving."

Her rudeness stunned everyone. Regan sat almost paralyzed at her abrupt outburst, and others close to Allmana stopped talking, waiting to see what would happen.

Pagany stood and moved toward the disagreeable woman.

"I entreat you, My Lady. Let us continue to honor this new bonding of our families. Stay until the morrow."

Allmana barely acknowledged her invitation, "No, I'll return home."

Taken back, Pagany paused and then turned to Regan. "I'll see that your horses are prepared and your bags loaded on the wagons."

"Thank you, most gracious Lady," he bowed respectfully, and with embarrassment tried to excuse Allmana. "Please forgive my mother...she has never felt comfortable in great crowds."

Pagany nodded with sympathy. She was not sorry to see Allmana go, but she regretted that Regan must be deprived of the happy celebration. Joy could be rarely found in Allmana's home, and Regan deserved better. She looked in Allmana's direction. "Good riddance," she thought. "Your presence in this house undercuts the blessings of the good spirits—and we need them."

Bertram was not pleased. He, too, disliked Allmana. Still, there were traditions to be upheld. He would not be dishonored in his own house by foregoing them.

"We have not yet drunk from the cup of peace," he said forcefully to Allmana. "You and your sons must join with us and drink to symbolize the uniting of our families and people. My daughter—now your daughter also—will serve us."

Allmana snorted, but knowing she could not refuse and keep the goodwill of her sons and Bertram's household, she irritably mumbled. "Then let's get on with it," she snarled, beckoning Ragen to return to her side.

Bertram waved his hand at the gathered company, said a few words to his servants, and turned to lead the lords and ladies present. Quickly, guests and hosts alike formed a ceremonial circle with Pagany, Bertram, and Allmana at the high table. William and Regan, who both felt discomfited by their mother's swift and disagreeable halt to the festivities, stood on each side of the elders, as appropriate to their positions as heir to the lady of Stonehart and new lord of Lothlar. Stephen was not visible.

Leova, donning the role of lady of the hall for the first time, grasped the ceremonial drinking horn filled with its well-aged mead, and took what had previously been her mother's place of honor. Walking gracefully toward the dais, she bowed and offered the cup to her father, who returned her bow and drank, obviously proud of his gracious daughter. Then Leova continued around the table, serving first her mother, and then Allmana and Ragen. She moved graciously from the high table, her blue gown enveloping her like a mist, and circled the room, offering the cup both to the men and women of her father's hall as well as to Allmana's company. As she moved, the people about her silent and respectful, a harpist quietly strumming a gentle tune, Leova felt like some rogue female priest preforming a ritual just as sacred as the earlier one in the chapel.

At last, as she completed the circle, she came to stand directly before her new husband. Taking a sip from one side of the cup, she offered it to William. Smiling at her, he turned the cup so that he placed his lips where hers had been and took his sip. Now surely, she felt, they were as married as anyone could ever be!

After the swift departure of Allmana and Regan, the festive feeling returned to courtyard and hall. As the laughter and talk swirled around her, Leova could only watch in amazement. Her marriage occasioned all this merriment, yet she felt detached from everyone around her, from the people she had lived with all her life.

Husband and Wife

But if she felt detached in the midst of the celebration, she found herself grounded once she and William entered the bridal room. Tonight, instead of sleeping in her familiar bed, Leova would share a new room and a new bed with a man newly her husband. Their sleeping chamber had been furnished with objects from around the manor. The curtained bed frame, carved with leaves, flowers, and berries, had been her grandmother's and the matching chests had stored generations of clothing and linens from Pagany's ancestors. Across from the bed, against an outer wall, hung the tapestry she and Hilda had woven, and while Hilda's lark still looked a bit like a chicken, it brought comfort as well as a smile to Leova's heart. Gwynned and Pagany had adorned the room with fresh-smelling herbs and dried flowers that almost helped cover the fact that winter still ruled outside. On the bed were sprigs of bayberry, a blessing of the forest women and a charm for fertility. A new gown, white with red trimmings and sinuous vines, had also been spread out, ready for the bride to wear.

Leova, uncomfortably aware that she and William had never been alone together, looked nervously around the room. When they had talked in the hall, others had always been in the immediate vicinity; as they strolled through the grounds of her father's properties, Gwynned or one of the other servants trailed behind at a respectful distance. Now no one could step in and smooth an awkward moment, as her mother had often done, or ruin a conversation by sighing deeply and commenting on the cold winds in the garden.

Timidly, Leova, who had been holding William's hand tightly, dropped her hand from his and approached the window. She knew what would come next—her mother had been careful to explain the act of joining—but she had no idea what to say or how to gracefully indicate that she was prepared to become his wife in every sense.

William walked over to the bed and fingered the delicate sleeve. "A fine cloth, worked by a talented hand," he said. "A woman couldn't hope for a lovelier garment."

She dipped her head in agreement, and he blushed, realizing that this was no ordinary work of beauty he held in his hand.

An uneasy pause occurred as they tried to think of something else to say. At last William made a clumsy attempt to break the silence. "Shall I wait in the anteroom while you dress for bed, d-dearest?" He stumbled over the word, but Leova knew he was trying to put her at ease.

"Dearest...," thought Leova. "I'm to be his 'dearest.' And he mine."

Even as she nodded to him gratefully, her mind searched for a term of endearment that would show she wanted to return his affection. None that she knew felt comfortable, and for a moment she panicked. Would these words of affection come naturally after they had been together a while?

Gathering her wits quickly, she came toward him and touched his arm gently, hoping she could find a way to address him. He stopped her by bending to kiss her lightly on the lips and then moved toward the small outside room attached to the chamber. But, suddenly, he returned and pulled her close. Tenderly, he removed the circlet from her head and as the wimple slipped to the floor, he extracted the clips from her hair. Her blonde-red hair ringlets unwound and settled about her shoulders.

"You," he said, "are so beautiful. I am blessed to be able to look on you each day. And your goodness only increases your beauty." He kissed her again, but this time, not so lightly as before. Then he turned and left the room.

Leova sank down on the bed, overcome by the passion of his kiss and confused about her own reaction. Then she pulled herself together and tried to be practical. "I'll get myself out of this wedding gown and into the nightgown. Then we'll see what happens." Accustomed to being dressed and undressed by Gwynned, getting out of her layers of clothes proved more difficult than usual. After she slipped into the beautiful nightgown, she pulled her hair back again with a clip so that it hung down her back. Immediately, she released it again. "He liked it this way, I think."

Still unsure, she drew back the heavy locks on one side of her shoulder, and left the other side hanging freely over her breast. Examining her reflection in the polished disk that served as a mirror, she had a moment of hesitation, but stopped herself before she bound her hair again. "This will have to do," she declared, and then laughed lightly at her own nerves.

The candles which lit the room had been carefully arranged to give enough light to see but not so much that every corner of the room was illuminated. Leova circled the room, extinguishing almost all of them, leaving only two on a small table near the door. The light from the fire cast a soft glow. The room felt comfortable now, peaceful.

"May I come in?" William asked from behind the anteroom door.

Leova breathed deeply and answered, "Yes, My Lord. One moment." Then she hurriedly brushed the herbs and flowers from the coverlet, climbed into bed and positioned herself against the pillows. Just as he opened the door, she grabbed the linen sheet and pulled it up to just under her breasts.

William stood for a moment in the doorway, and then with a wry smile, he spoke. "My night shirt fails to meet the standard for beauty that your gown sets."

They both laughed. "Yes," Leova observed. "I fear that it is quite...silly." The laughter helped them relax.

"Shall I put out the candles?" he asked. His voice sounded unsure.

"Perhaps you should leave those by the door lit," she whispered.

William reached the bed, lifted the edge of the coverlet, and slid in, moving ever so slightly toward her. He took her hands in his and bending his head, he kissed them. For a moment he stared at their clasped hand, and then looked into her eyes.

"I know," he whispered, "that we did not choose each other, but my pledge is true. We can, I hope, come to love each other."

They kissed, this time Leova willingly returned his feeling. They pulled apart, and William suddenly declared, "I'm not like Allmana!" and fell silent, waiting for her to respond.

Leova was touched. "I've never seen her in you—not by word nor by deed. You've been quiet, understanding, and most kind."

"Do you think we can be happy together?"

She gave a rueful laugh. "As long as your mother stays at Stonehart." Leaning back on her pillow, Leova answered him more

219

seriously. "My mother told me that she and my father learned to love each other dearly. I hope that will be true for us too."

William lay back next to her and began to caress her gently, taking time to let her become accustomed to his touch. "I don't want to hurt you, Leova. I've been told that when a girl is a virgin, the first time she makes love can be painful. Tell me if I hurt you. I'd rather stop than have you remember me as unkind on this night. We have many years before us, and being with you is more important than taking your maidenhead."

"I thank you," Leova whispered gratefully. She pulled his face closer to hers and kissed him. As he responded, caressing her shoulders and her breasts, she shivered a bit at the strange sensations. William pulled back a bit.

"I'm fine," she said, then whispered in his ear. "I think I will learn to love you very quickly."

Chapter 7: Hilda Seeks a Place of Solace (879)

Hilda knelt at the altar in her father's house, Highhear, her head buried in her hands as she petitioned what she hoped was a forgiving God. At present she was unsure that there even was such a God, but having no other source of possible solace she offered up her prayers. Lost emotionally, and physically weak from the birth of the baby and the journey from Northwich, she had arrived at her father's house only to find herself unsure of her place. Too old to be cared for like a child, and only barely old enough to take her mother's place as mistress, her recovery was hampered by her uncertainty. Only Ethel and Caedmon knew about the baby, but after weeks of evasive and uncertain answers, she had left them in peace: neither could tell her what might have happened to the baby nor would she tell them the father's name, though Ethel suspected who it might be.

In desperation, Hilda turned to the one thing that had remained stationary and unswerving in her life in the past year. She faithfully followed the routine she had become accustomed to at the monasteries. Rising at four or five o'clock in the morning, she went to the chapel for prayer, then returned again at each liturgical hour of the day. What had once been a mere exercise for the frivolous young girl now became a comfort for the heartbroken woman she'd become. As she knelt alone in the half light of the candles, she prayed the same earnest prayer over and over again: "Please, Heavenly Father, reunite me with my child!"

That God had not immediately answered her prayers didn't discourage her. The sermons she had attended, the tracts she had copied, all had helped her understand that God creates plans for believers, but each believer must discover that plan for herself or himself. As she began to heal, however, and looked around at the unfamiliar world of her family home, she recognized that her father's people suffered greatly; their lives had been disrupted by the wars. She found some comfort in bringing food and clothing to the little houses that peppered the countryside, and sent workers to begin the process of rebuilding rundown homes.

Seeing the grateful faces of those who had lost even more than she had, Hilda gradually began to find peace. The color returned to her face and, as she regained her strength, a spring began to develop in her step as she bustled about seeing to what now seemed to be *her* hall's upkeep and *her* people's care. As summer moved toward autumn, she felt even more strongly about continuing these activities, but somewhat uncomfortable about her father's lack of attention to any of her charities. She found herself wondering if her mother had caused her father to turn away from the religion and its message to help others.

But she began to appreciate too that her ability to help people came from the power inherent in being her father's daughter. Princesses have power. She grudging acknowledged that her experience at the monastery her father had abandoned her to had helped to make her strong. However, her anger at Abbess Edyth and her sister Abbess Moira did not abate; nor did she pray for it to abate. It might be sinful to carry such ill will for the abbesses, but she made no effort to forgive.

In her absence, much had changed in her father's country. The violent battles had stopped. Most of the looting had stripped small kingdoms such as Ecgbert's of what wealth they had; sons and husbands had fallen, and there were fewer and fewer men to work the land. Weary of chaos and loss, the owners of large estates turned over much of the land to the enemy, and surprisingly, many of those enemies—perhaps also tired of the chaos of war—brought their families from across the sea to settle in and around the city of Jorvik. There they built villages, farms, and ports along the coast or, just as often, married the women whose men they had killed and whose land they had taken over.

As the former warriors spread inland, it became obvious that they needed the cooperation of the English lords to keep the peace. Ecgbert had been quick to see that working with his former enemies would guarantee safety for his lands and income for his estates; he put down his sword and began to make alliances with those who had once been the enemy. In doing so, he became a figure of controversy. For those who wanted peace at any cost, he was a crafty leader. To those who could not endure the thought of Viking overlords, he was a turn-coat. To his daughter, struggling to deal with a more personal loss and almost oblivious to the politics of war, he remained the father she needed: the father who had welcomed her home with no questions about her time in the monastery. Out of need for his comfort, she forgot his willingness to agree with her mother and banish her to a vocation she had not wanted.

Her father had aged during the years she had been gone. Wrinkles now appeared where none had been before. His chain-mail hung loosely about his body. And above all, the comfortable manner in which he had once faced life had disappeared. He might have survived the wars, but he did not rest easy in his alliance with the enemy. Hilda felt his despair as surely as she had felt her own. Being leader of the Englisc weighed heavily upon him.

One morning in early summer, as Hilda returned from the chapel to the hall, head full of chores to complete and devotions she wished to offer to God, Ecgbert greeted her at the hall entrance.

"My daughter," he said quietly, "come talk with me a moment."

Puzzled by his strangely subdued demeanor and his attention, Hilda complied. Her father seldom had time for her and, for the most part, their conversations had been limited to discussions of matters that pertained to the keeping of the hall. She suspected that he did not find the conversation of women as interesting as he did those of his compatriots.

"Is something wrong?" she asked.

He nodded wearily, "Your cousin Berghorf is dead."

Hilda gasped. She had known Berghorf for only a short time, but on the journey from Leova's to her father's, he had been a kind and pleasant companion. She'd seen little of him since.

"How?" she asked. "How did he die?"

"Foolishly, foolishly," her father replied, his voice raspy with grief. "He refused the orders of the Jorvik council to turn over his land. He fought a battle he should have known he'd never win."

"And his family?" Hilda asked.

"Scattered and in hiding. His actions cost them everything! And by virtue of our kinship, he could have done incredible damage to our own." Ecgbert waved his hand as if to brush away the pain he was feeling. "I've more to tell you, sweetling. Give me a moment to gather my thoughts."

He fell silent as they entered the hall and moved toward a bench placed near the fire. Hilda waited patiently until he spoke again, anxious to know what would come next. Although he sat beside her and reached out to cover her hand with his own, Ecgbert did not look Hilda in the eye. Instead, he lowered his head and began to speak quietly and earnestly.

"Your mother's insistence that you be dedicated to the convent distressed me deeply—more than you will ever know. Through you alone can my line be continued, and her decision endangered my heritage." He paused, and both of them remembered the struggle in the small bur and the promises extracted by the dying woman. Then shaking his head as if to free himself of the memories, he continued.

"While you were lost to me, I consoled myself that my heritage could be rested on Berghorf. As my sister's son, he could have seen that our line continued. Now he's dead." Ecgbert turned to look at his daughter and smiled sadly. "Thankfully, God in his goodness has seen fit to bring you home. You will marry and bear a son; my duty to my ancestors and my dream of a great realm which carries our name can be fulfilled!"

Hilda starred at her father in disbelief.

"Let me tell you of my plans. During the times of terror, while you lived at Lothlar, I lost my old comrade Aldred in battle. Held him in my arms as he died. The loss was even greater because the two of us had pledged that by means of his sons and my daughter we would build a great kingdom the like of which no man had seen before. His death brought me to desire peace at long last. Now his sons, Alwid and Amwahl, have joined me in my attempt to bring peace to our lands and build that kingdom."

Hilda drew back and tried to turn her eyes away, dreading what he would say next. Ecgbert, with no awareness of her distress, hurried on, determined to impress upon her the importance of his plans.

"When you were sent to the convent, Aldred and I knew our plans would be fruitless, though I always had Bergdorf and so…. But now…." He gestured with confidence, his face bright as he attempted to come to terms with new possibilities. "But now—even as I received word of sweet Bergdorf's death, news has also come from Aldred's sons. With Berghorf dead and you returned to me, Aldred's sons have agreed to fulfill their father's wishes, and you will be able to fulfill mine!"

Hilda opened her mouth to protest, but her father, not seeing the look on her face continued with his plans for securing his dynasty.

"They visit within the next few weeks, but I wish to give you some warning before they arrive." He smiled and hugged her as if he had given her a great gift and continued with what he seemed to feel was fatherly love. "You may marry the one you fancy."

Hilda pulled away, appalled at her father's declaration. Ecgbert, on the other hand, beamed. In his mind, he had made a generous concession: what other daughter could choose her husband?

"God willing, before many months you'll be carrying an heir, blessing the lands of your fathers with a son."

Overwhelmed, Hilda turned away, and when Ecgbert gently turned her head to face him once again, the look in her eyes surprised him. Realizing her reluctance and fearing an obstacle to his dream, his voice changed to one of frosty paternal authority. Looking into her eyes, he insisted forcefully, "You cannot deny me this."

"My Lord," began Hilda, her voice soft but as determined as his own.

"No," Ecgbert stopped her, "This is my decision. You will greet Alwid and Amwahl with the courtesy due their rank and bravery, and choose one of them as your husband." Then greatly disturbed, he rose swiftly and without taking leave or giving her a chance to speak, strode from the hall.

Stunned by her father's declaration, Hilda began to shiver with indignation. How dare he use her so carelessly! John, who might well be dead, was the only man she'd ever wanted to marry. She had no intention of marrying another, especially a man she had never met, a man who like her father saw her as a means to retaining property, not as a person with a destiny of her own.

Head down and hands clasped, Hilda rocked back and forth, her feelings bouncing from indignation to sorrow and back again. Ethel approached the bench and, ready to bring comfort to her lady, placed a soft hand on her shoulder. Turning to her old nurse, Hilda felt her anger rising.

"You heard?" she asked.

Ethel nodded.

It took all Hilda's energy to check herself before she spoke again. And when she did speak, her words were firm, not hysterical. "No. There will be no marriage. My place is at the monastery, serving my God."

Hilda stopped, as startled by her own words as Ethel was. She had not yet acknowledged the desire that had arisen from all those hours at prayer. Ethel grasped Hilda by the shoulders and sat down to face her.

"Your father's wishes, my child, are no more than any other father's," Ethel said as gently as she could. "Marriage is woman's fate and should be a time of happiness." Hilda's back stiffened and she made to rise, but Ethel held her steady and almost willed her to listen. "My lady, meet these young men before you rebel against his lordship's desires. They're young men who are well thought of; I hear that it's hard to decide which is more handsome! Embrace your good fortune. Build a good life, have many fine children."

Hilda shook her head sorrowfully. "I already have a child; I do not wish for more," she whispered. Then her voice grew louder and stronger as she finally said what her father had not allowed her to. "Nor do I wish to devote myself to yet another person's vision of a 'good life.' My mother's demands that I atone for her unconfessed sin, whatever it might have been, failed miserably. Now my father commands me to ensure his legacy, and I will not." Little did he know that an heir might exist, but.... She paused for a moment before speaking further. At last she understood God's plan for her. She stood, and this time her hands grasped Ethel's shoulders. "This body, this mind, this *life* belong to me—and I choose to give all to God."

Hilda turned and made her way to the small chapel that had lately been her only source of peace. Despite the fact that it was early afternoon, darkness obscured most of the interior. Taking up one of the candles always ready by the doorway, she carried it to the front and lit the altar candles illuminating the frescos of Matthew, Mark, Luke, John, and Peter that covered the north wall. In the flickering light, the saints' figures seemed to come to life. Their faces looked down with compassion, not condemnation.

Kneeling, she gazed at the ornate cross behind the altar—so like the crosses in the graveyard by Leova's hall—and as she contemplated it, she was able to slip into deep peaceful mediation and leave her anger and her anxiety behind. As she prayed for guidance, her resolve grew, and for the first time since being banished from Northwich, she felt the beginnings of a strong connection to a forgiving God.

After some while, she stood up, brushed her skirts off, and smiled at the cross one last time. Turning, she walked quietly toward the door, where she paused at the octagonal font and dipped her hand into the holy water. Slowly and with feeling, she blessed herself with the sign of the cross. In all the days and months since she had started coming to the chapel, she had avoided the font, feeling unworthy of the holy water and of the goodness it symbolized. Now, however, with her realization of the plan God had for her, she knew she could once again participate fully in the life of God's church. She was blessed and worthy of that blessing.

The Suitors and an Unexpected Guest

Two weeks later, Hilda, her father, and Alwid and Amwahl sat down at the long table at the head of the hall. As the servants loaded the tables with food, Hilda marveled at the quantities the young men seemed able to ingest. As Ethel had claimed, the two were quick of tongue and handsome enough to win almost any heart—both seemed worthy of a lord's daughter. They'd not have difficulty finding wives, but she doubted that other lord's daughters would bring the fortune that came as her wedding compact.

At the end of what turned out to be a pleasant feast, Alwid and Amwahl excused themselves from the table, claiming they must check on their horses. As they bid Hilda and Ecgbert good evening, however, the jovial looks between the three men made it clear that their departure had been prearranged.

"It's like a game," thought Hilda, well aware that she was the prize.

The door had hardly closed behind them before Ecgbert turned to his daughter and, ignoring the people at the tables below the dais, happily posed the question he'd wanted to ask all evening.

"Well, what say you, my dear? Did I not provide handsome lads for husbands? They know I've given you the choice, and they've promised to honor your decision." He smiled broadly and leaned closer in anticipation. "Now tell me, which will you have?"

Knowing what effect her answer would have on her father, Hilda took his hand in both of hers and watched his eyes as she answered. "Alwid and Amwahl are both good men, father—fair of face and full of energy. But I can't marry either of them, no matter what they bring to our family or what dreams you have of a line of heirs reaching down the ages." She paused for a moment and then firmly faced him. "I choose God. I dedicate my life to His church." Hilda had little time to reflect on this conviction which seemed to come from somewhere deep inside her and had now found words whose truth she recognized at once.

Dark with rage, Ecgbert pulled his hand from his daughter's and rose to stand threateningly above her. "Heed me, daughter," his voice was piercing, quiet but strong. "Your dedication to the church ended when you returned here. You took no final vows. You came home. Now, accept your responsibility to that home. As the sole heir of this family and protector of these lands, do your duty. Choose a husband!"

228

She looked up, not afraid; and speaking calmly, once again she confirmed her choice. "No. No earthly husband. Christ will be my bridegroom; his church, my home."

Ecgbert loved his daughter, but his own desires and the traditions of his people outweighed any vision she might have of a vocation. Keenly aware that the hall was still full of people, he fought the urge to shout and bring her into submission. The two stood at a stalemate, until finally, he spoke.

"If you will not select, I must select for you. The older brother will do. Tomorrow, you'll be formally betrothed to Amwahl." His stern demeanor softened a bit, and he placed what he hoped was a comforting hand on her shoulder. "You'll come to see my way of thinking, sweetling. Amwahl is a good man; he'll treat you well."

Hilda did not respond, but she watched sadly as Ecgbert strode off to join the two young men in the stable. To her surprise, a rueful smile came to her lips, thinking of their reactions. No doubt Amwahl would be pleased, but she need not fear that his brother would be afflicted with a broken heart. Neither had an emotional stake in the outcome; marriage concerned lineage and property, not love. Carefully avoiding the eyes of the diners below the dais, she drew herself together, rose from the remains of the feast, and returned to her only refuge: her mother's small chapel.

The flickering candlelight once again provided comfort as she knelt at the altar. She felt safe, strong in her decision, ready to move on from the secular life to the sanctified one. Lost in thought, she started in fear when she felt a hand on her shoulder, but whirling about she saw only the elderly face of Bishop Ceolwulf contemplating her. For a moment she believed that the saints had brought him. Rising from her knees, she gripped the bishop's hand and kissed it humbly, then let him lead her to the front pew.

"My Lord Bishop, has God sent you? Have you spoken with my father?" The bishop nodded, but in her eagerness to present her situation, Hilda didn't pause to give him time to answer. "My father would wed me to a stranger in order to ensure that his line continues. I cannot accept his decision—I've come to understand that God has called me to return to the monastery and devote my life to the work there."

She went on hopefully. "Could you speak to my father? Explain why a person with a calling can't—shouldn't—marry."

The bishop looked unhappily at Hilda's pleading face, torn between the church he loved, the lord whose family had generously supported it, and his horror of Hilda's grave sin. The three elements warred in his thoughts. Ecgbert wanted a legacy, a desire the bishop understood and a state that the church had always found advantageous. The children of families who traditionally supported the church generously were likely to continue the support when they grew to adulthood. However, to side with Ecgbert because of his wealth was unfair to the girl, who was herself a treasure of sorts. The intelligence and potential service she would bring to his beloved church would enrich them all. But her sin. Her sin made him reject her request. Both abbesses, Edyth and Moira has enlightened him about the nature of Hilda's transgression. She had not only, in his estimation, seduced a member of the monastery, she had borne him a child. He shook his head gravely and without acknowledging her claim that God had revealed to her a plan for her life, he focused on the greatest impediment to her acceptance into holy orders.

"Child, you have sinned greatly. How can you expect the church to embrace you whole-heartedly?"

Taken aback by the word "sin," Hilda faltered but did not back down.

"God forgives, Father. My mother committed a sin so shameful that she hid it from my father—and you. Yet even she believed God would forgive her. I, too, trust that He has forgiven me." She paused to gather her thoughts before she continued. "In His forgiveness, God calls me to devote my life to His work. I'm not a perfect human being; no one is. However, my sin has made me more compassionate and more understanding of other sinners. That knowledge should make it possible for me to help them understand that like me, they too have a place in the church." She admonished him gently, "No one should feel they cannot return to God's embrace."

Recognizing the reprimand, Ceolwulf could not help but smile at Hilda's earnestness, her conviction of her own worth to the church. She was not wrong, but he felt strongly that perhaps she was wrong-headed. "You can devote yourself to God outside the church as well as inside its walls. God has many who serve him, and many who think they know his will. Your duty is to serve Him by serving your earthly father." The old man rose, "Come, let's tell him that you'll comply with his wishes."

Hilda drew back, her mouth set in a firm line. "I would not want to disobey you, Father Ceolwulf, but I will not accede to the marriage, and I will not remain at Highhear."

"Ecgbert will force you."

"We will see," Hilda answered calmly.

The old man looked grim. "Don't let your stubborn heart lead you even farther astray, Hilda. God punishes the sin of pride."

"And He rewards the virtues of forgiveness and dedication," she replied as she turned and walked away.

Another Journey

Before sunrise, Hilda was gone. Beside her empty bed sat the distraught Ethel, holding three letters that she was to deliver —one for Ecgbert, one for Alwid and Amwahl, and one for Bishop Ceolwulf. The messages were simple; Hilda had worded them as carefully and kindly as she could. She had wished her suitors good fortune, begging them not to think of her rejection of them as any indication that they wouldn't make fine husbands. She had vowed her love to Bishop Ceolwulf and had assured submission to his authority in all but this matter, promising that their paths would cross again. But she left no such promise for her father. As much as she loved him and understood his desires, she at last comprehended his nature. Like her mother, he was a man obsessed with his own plans, his own needs. No one else's mattered. Her message to him was short: she had wished him good health and regretted that she had to disappoint him so, but for her there was no other decision possible. Hilda doubted that she would ever see him again.

Then dressed as a peasant, Hilda set off into the darkness carrying only her small icon—the "eternity" knot she treasured because it was a gift from John—and a small pouch containing a few mementos of her mother and Leova, food sufficient for two days, and the stone and scrap of manuscript she had retrieved from the ruined monastery so long ago, items she treasured for reasons that eluded her. Determined to completely cut ties with her father, she left behind everything else associated with his care and his control. Her destination was to the east coast, where Whitby stood. The abbey, made famous by the nun whose name she bore, seemed the perfect place to begin her vocation. The community there valued learning and reproduced manuscripts important to Englisc Christians. With her skills, surely the community there would take her in, she reasoned, even if only as a servant. If she could not serve God as a nun, she'd serve those who worked for Him on a higher plane.

The moonlit landscape made even the most familiar sights strange; she had never traveled east from Highhear. Keeping the stone road beneath her feet, she moved slowly, often stumbling on its rough surface. She reasoned that, if she got far enough away from Highhear before dawn, it would be difficult for her father to find her. She hoped he would assume that she was fleeing to Buxton and seek her there first. Maybe he might think she was escaping toward Lothlar. He'd never suspect that she would move in the opposite direction, and she doubted he even knew of Whitby's existence.

Slowly Hilda became aware of a brightening through the trees before her, confirming that the road she traveled headed eastward. "If I keep the morning sun before me, and the evening sun behind me," she thought to herself, "I'll find the coast—and begin my new life."

The morning passed quickly, and despite the fact that her night journey had made her weary, her heart was light. The songs of the birds and the wind through the trees entertained her, and with each step she gained confidence that she'd made the right decision. When the sun reached its full height, she heard the sound of a small stream just off the path, and decided to rest a bit near the water. Not long after she spread her cloak under a tree and rested her head on the soft turf, she heard someone approach. She had been grateful that she had encountered no one on the road, but knowing that a woman alone on the road was vulnerable to all forms of danger, she gathered her belongings and hid herself deep behind a double row of bushes and watched through the leaves to see who was coming. To her surprise, Caedmon appeared, leading two donkeys and peering anxiously down the path ahead of him.

"You followed me," Hilda said, stepping from her hiding place." Her voice was stern, but in reality, she was far from astonished to see him. Caedmon seldom let her get too far out of his sight. She'd long suspected that he slept close by her bur, removing himself at dawn.

"Don't be angry, my lady," Caedmon pleaded, but the grin on his face proved that he didn't expect to be admonished. "I heard you leave and since Ethel had been fretting for days about your desire to join a monastery...." He stopped suddenly, aware that he may have said too much. "I'm sorry, but you can't travel alone. It's too dangerous." Startled by his own audacity, he hung his head for a moment. When she didn't say anything, he looked up sheepishly. "I fear I stole these donkeys." Hilda tried to look disapproving, but within seconds lost the battle.

"Caedmon, you're a miracle," she laughed, now fully aware of how happily she welcomed his familiar face. "It's good to see you. How long have you been following me? How did you decide which road to take?"

"Shortly after I found that you weren't in your room, I loaded the donkeys and set out. Ethel had heard you talk of Whitby which is on the coast; so I decided you would have to take the road east." Caedmon was most pleased with his reasoning. "It took a while to catch up, but I had the advantage of the donkeys and once I'd sighted you, I fell back, keeping out of your hearing range so that you'd believe you were alone." He shook his head. "Perhaps, too far. I didn't realize you'd stopped and hid."

"You've not been followed have you, my friend?" Hilda asked, looking down the road they'd both traveled.

"No, I think not. No one saw me leave. And they will just be waking now. Your father, when he finally misses you, will believe you're making your way back to that first convent or to your friend, Leova." Caedmon suddenly blurted out, "He does not know you well, my lady, nor understand your heart's desire—he won't know where to look."

Surprised but pleased by his observation, Hilda sighed in relief. She didn't want further confrontations with her father. Gratefully, she put her arm through Caedmon's and drew him to her hiding place by the stream.

"Come, sit with me, have something to eat. It's been a long night, and we should rest."

The young man agreed readily. As he led the donkeys off the road, he pointed to the bundles tied on their backs. "I brought food and some blankets for sleeping; we'll need them as we travel, and the air grows cooler."

They ate in silence, then Hilda leaned back against a tree and fell fast asleep. Caedmon retrieved a bundle of clothing from one of the donkeys and gently moved his lady so that her head rested on it. He lay down close by and soon he, too, was asleep. When the two young people awoke in late afternoon, they decided to travel as far as they could before darkness prevented them from seeing what was ahead.

"I have no idea how far it is to Whitby," she confessed. "But I believed it was no longer than another day's journey. Perhaps I was wrong. We'll seek directions somewhere along the way." Stretching her back to relieve the aches that came from sleeping on the ground, she laughed, "And search out a better place to sleep."

"The journey will go faster if we ride the donkeys," Caedmon suggested, and Hilda, readily agreeing, gathered up her skirts and climbed on the nearest of the gentle beasts.

They covered quite a bit of ground before nightfall. Others on the path, they only encountered once: a group of farmers carrying produce to a market, probably at Highhear. They nodded as they passed, but exchanged no words, fearing that a conversation might lead her father to find them.

Neither Whitby nor the coast appeared as quickly as they had hoped. For the next two days, they traveled from dawn to dusk, walking when the donkeys seemed to be tired, riding when their legs could no longer bear them up. At night they slept soundly just off the road in the protection of the woods, exhausted, but still not discouraged.

On the third day, they awoke to the sounds of horses and the loud voices of men. Instinctively, both of them remained still, glad to be safely hidden. A troop of about twenty red-haired men came into view, singing as they rode. They did not appear to be warriors. Instead of being dressed in the heavy leather which protected men in battle, they wore short belted tunics and hooded cloaks fastened on one shoulder by elaborately wrought metal brooches. Clearly they expected no challenge. Following close behind the men on horseback were several servants guiding carts drawn by oxen. Instead of weapons, the carts were laden with goods for trade.

Caedmon and Hilda both remained quiet until the group disappeared from sight. "Those men seem peaceful; still, we must be on the lookout," whispered Hilda, her fear causing her to lower her voice. "They're still the enemy, despite my father's efforts to appease them, and we don't know what they'd do if they discovered me. They might deliver me back to my father's control."

Weary, and certain they had somehow lost their way, Hilda and Caedmon had mixed emotions when they finally came upon a small town. "Should we circle around?" Hilda asked cautiously. Caedmon shook his head.

"My Lady, we're almost out of food."

"I'm such a fool," Hilda berated herself softly. In her desire for independence, she'd even left without the small bag of coins her father had given her when she had returned to Highhear. She'd imagined that the journey would be short and hadn't thought at all about the fact that the country through which she'd pass would be peopled mostly by the north men. Now she recognized the need to be more wary as these men might look upon her and Caedmon as enemies. "Alright, my friend," she sighed. "We'll risk passing through. But we have nothing to exchange for food. We'll need to see if we can work for provisions."

"I have some good leather; I planned to make some new shoes, but we could offer part of it for trade."

"Don't be foolish. You'll need shoes!" Hilda exclaimed. "You can't give up good leather!"

"We need not trade it all; it's a big piece. Besides, it's unlikely that we'll find work—people tend to distrust strangers."

"We can give them a piece of my mother's jewelry—it has no use other than to feed my vanity," Hilda argued.

"And it will make them kill us to find more: unlike the leather, jewelry can be sold for a great deal of money," Caedmon countered. "So it's the leather, agreed?"

Reluctantly, Hilda nodded her agreement, and they followed the road through the heart of the town.

Although the few people they saw stared at them curiously, as Caedmon had predicted, no one seemed inclined to interrupt their own conversations to speak to strangers. Hilda listened to snatches of conversations, trying to determine who might be the kindest of these strangers, and before long she realized that almost all the men, unlike the women, spoke a language she'd never encountered.

"We've stumbled into an enemy settlement," she realized. "Not a war camp, a village like those around Highhear!"

Stopping at the public well, they filled their water skins, smiling at the others in the village square and looking for a chance to trade their leather.   Finally, Hilda spotted two women occupied with a child's leather shoe. As they handed the worn object back and forth between them, they argued about the best way to repair it. Spurred on by the fact that the women spoke their own language, Hilda urged Caedmon to offer to exchange the leather for bread and cheese. Nervously, Caedmon retrieved the leather from his pack, then turned in a slight panic to Hilda.

"What if they ask who we are? What should I tell them?"

"Tell them you're my brother and we're traveling to Whitby to see a relative."

Caedmon nodded and turned again to approach the women, who had stopped their own talk to stare openly at the two strangers.

"Good morrow, mistresses, "he said politely, "Forgive me, but I overheard you talking about your problem with the shoe, and thought I might help us all. You need new shoes; my sister and I need food for ourselves and the animals. Are you willing to give me five days food for us and the beasts in return for this leather? It's soft but sturdy, needs only cutting and sewing." Caedmon stopped. "Truly," he assured them. "It's a good bargain."

The two women looked at each other; then one of them took the piece of leather from Caedmon and examined it closely to see if the high quality bit would serve to make a pair of children's shoes. Eyeing Caedmon suspiciously, they talked quietly to each other, but neither commented about the source of such quality leather. Hilda held her breath. But at last the older of the two smiled at Caedmon and spoke enthusiastically.

"We have bread and dried fruit, some vegetables, grain for the animals ready at hand. But, maybe you have another piece of leather? If so, we have another trade in mind. You and your sister can stay the night, and after our men leave for work on the morrow, we'll provide you with what's left of the cooked meats from dinner."

Caedmon looked questioningly at Hilda who shook her head. Never before had Hilda had to worry about what she was going to eat, much less about whether she was going to eat at all, but she stubbornly refused to allow Caedmon to part with both pieces of his leather.

Caedmon approached Hilda. "We must have the food, and I can get another piece of leather somewhere."

"No" Hilda responded firmly and stubbornly, "you will not give up both pieces of leather." She turned from her companion and leaned against the donkey.

"Is your sister all right?" one of the women asked.

Caedmon gestured in exasperation. "She doesn't want me to give up another piece of leather, but she's not being practical. We need the food; we've still several days of journey before us."

"And where might you be going?" asked the second woman,

"To Whitby, the monastery on the shore, where our aunt serves the good sisters. We hope she can find us work."

"You'll need every bit of food you can carry. The monastery is much farther north than you might think—*if* the nuns are still there," said the taller of the two women. She shifted uncomfortably. "We've heard rumors that the monastery has been destroyed."

Hilda turned with a gasp. "Who spreads this rumor? Surely it's not true?"

The woman moved closer and leaned in, speaking firmly but a bit harshly, "Our husbands told us. They raided up and down the coast."

Hilda couldn't keep a look of shock off her face. The younger woman continued, "Don't judge! Now they're honest men, not raiders—and they treat us well." She paused and the older woman took up the defense. "What else could we do? Our first husbands died in battle; women like us—with no land and children to raise— need a man's protection!"

"Forgive me," Hilda said quickly. "I didn't mean disrespect...I just...." She stopped, not knowing what to say, but realizing that these woman might have been forced by necessity to marry the very men who killed their fathers, brothers, and even their husbands. The apology had an almost immediate effect. The women nodded, and conferred for a few moments.

"Let's end this bargaining; we've all needed help at one time or the other. Keep the other piece of leather; stay the night. We'll put together what you need for your journey."

Caedmon, relief evident on his face, bowed gratefully, "We're in your debt, mistresses. Thank you for your help." The women waved away his thanks and set about the serious business of introductions.

"I'm Alfgif," said the elder of the two cheerfully. Slapping her companion playfully on the shoulder, she reported, "And this tall hulk is my neighbor, Olwinda."

"Come into the house," Olwinda insisted. "By the looks of things, you've been on the road long, and could probably use a bit of ale and a roll or two."

Olwinda led them to the closest cottage and seated them at a crudely built table. The dark room had only a few chairs and a set of shelves for provisions, but it was clean and fresh-smelling. Hilda and Caedmon had to force a tight rein on their manners to keep from downing the fresh bread and cheese immediately. The strong drink, far different from the ale at Highhear, washed down the food, but made Hilda choke a bit after her first gulp. The older women did not question the young people much; it was obvious that they had something to hide, but then again, who didn't in these times of strife? After Olwinda had seen to feeding them, Alfgif then led the two pilgrims out to a small shed behind a larger cowshed which was amply supplied with straw for cushioning their sleep. Hilda thanked her carefully, not looking directly at her. It seemed strange to lower her eyes to anyone, but Caedmon had warned her several times that looking others straight in the face was considered insolent for a young girl.

Hilda was beginning to realize that she had much to learn about Caedmon's world. His life and the lives of the peasant women who shared it held dangers the protected princess had never imagined. She thought about the women who seemed so defensive about their marriages. Although she had been shocked that a woman would marry someone who might have murdered one of her landsmen, she understood why such a marriage might be necessary. What choice had they? The marriages might have seemed to be betrayals, but if a woman had children to care for and a man ready to provide for them, who could blame her for seizing upon such support. Had she faced scorn from her own people? For a moment Hilda found herself wondering if their gift of shelter and food were some form of atonement, an apology of sorts for marrying the men who may have killed their fathers and brothers. Hilda stopped short. And who was she to judge? She well understood the need for atonement and felt linked to these strange women who lived lives so different from hers and, yet, like her, were victims of men's laws and wars.

Might it be possible, she conjectured, that people who had been enemies for decades and decades could live peacefully and banish war? She lay down on the soft straw, weary beyond measure, but before she could reflect more on such heady matters as betrayal, recrimination, necessary choices, and reconciliation, she was asleep.

Caedmon, who had been working to bring more hay from the larger cow shed to this smaller shed, cleared a section for their own animals. Once he was satisfied with his efforts, he stared down at his sleeping mistress. Distressed as he was for her, he was just as impressed by her strength and endurance, and her ability to adapt to wholly unfamiliar conditions. Hoping to give her some undisturbed rest, Caedmon quietly left their shelter and sought out Alfgif's dwelling, where he found their benefactor busily preparing food.

"My husband will come shortly," she warned in a voice which sounded more matter-of-fact than worried. "It would be best he did not find you here. A young man of my people in his home might seem a threat."

"I don't want to cause you trouble," Caedmon said anxiously.

"Don't worry," Alfgif smiled reassuringly. "I'll not go back on the promise Olwinda and I made. The bargain stands. I've already begun collecting bread and cheese for you, and the meats will be cooled by morning."

"I'm most grateful, especially for the chance to rest safely. My sister is unaccustomed to travel. I'm not sure what we'll do if the monastery has been abandoned...."

Seeing the distress on his face, Alfgif shook her head and again tried to defend her husband and the men of the community.

"My husband, his brothers, and their companions are not men who share our beliefs. What did they know—or care—about monasteries and nuns..." she paused awkwardly, attempting to find words to explain. Then threw up her hands in frustration. "Believe me. They're good men. It grieves me that...."

"Stop," cut in Caedmon quickly. "It's past now." He placed his hand on her shoulder gently to assure her of his sympathy.

Alfgif smiled gratefully, patting his hand and then swiftly turning back to her work; she wrapped up a small parcel of food and poured ale into a pitcher. "Here, take this. Go to your sister. Sup and sleep—just be quiet. My husband leaves early for the field.

When he's gone, I'll come to you. Perhaps I can bring news—he may know more about the monastery."

Hilda woke to the voices of men laughing and talking in their odd-sounding language. She lay quietly until the voices disappeared and the door to the shed creaked open, revealing Alfgif's cheerful face.

"Come to the house now—have some food before you leave. The packs for your donkeys are almost ready." The slight adventure of hiding two people seemed to have made her quite energetic. "Olwinda's packed food, too. Some dried fruits, fresh vegetables, and grain for your beasts."

Hilda shook Caedmon gently. "Let's go, my brother." How easily "brother" came to her lips. It seemed right to her. Caedmon sat up quickly, immediately on guard.

"Not to worry. We're safe," Hilda said quickly, realizing she'd frightened him. "Our kind hostess has food for us. Let's pay our respects and thank her for her generous hospitality. Then we must be on our way." Quickly she retrieved the long strip of linen she had been using to cover her head completely and refastened it.

Upon entering the house, they found Alfgif chatting excitedly with her friend Olwinda. "Come in, come in, my children," she beckoned to Hilda. "We have good news—the monastery's not been abandoned." Excited to offer more good news, Olwinda broke into her friend's talk.

"And we've found a way to make your trip more comfortable and safe. One of our friends has a relative there; she's actually made the trip more than once!"

"Wonderful, wonderful news! Thank you for your kindness!" Hilda exclaimed with relief. She'd been afraid to admit it, but she had begun to believe that they might never find the way.

While Caedmon and Hilda broke their fast, Alfgif shared what she had learned from her friend.

"As you go north, you'll come to the heath country. It should take two days, maybe three, to travel around. The distance as the crow flies is shorter, but don't be fooled. The heath's dangerous. No shelter exists. Any tree you'll see won't give cover; the most

241

protection from the weather will be a few large rocks scattered here and there. If you stay on the western edge of the heath and head north, you'll come across a river; you'll find a way to cross it if you travel toward its source. Once across, it's a short distance to the coastline and the monastery." She spoke more and more quickly and began to watch the door. "Others will guide you. Just remember, speak only to the women. It's safer."

Alfgif smiled sadly and hugged Hilda, who marveled at the quiet strength of the two women who had borne the children of the foreigners. She found herself perplexed, however. To whom would these children owe allegiance? Hilda wondered.

"Remember, Olwinda said, "if the path you are following should split before you reach the river, keep to your left and go farther north."

Alfgif paused and handed them the bag of provisions. "May God be with you."

Hilda was a bit startled by the benedictory sound of those last words. "And with you," she replied. The words came easily to her lips; it was a blessing she understood.

Caedmon embraced them in his leave taking.   "Enjoy my leather, mistress. I'm glad your son will have new shoes. May he grow to be a healthy young man, and may he...." Caedmon hesitated a moment. He had intended to say, "grow to be a good man who'll honor our people."   Given the nature of the women's lives, he thought better of it, and instead quickly said, "grow to be a man you're proud of."

They resumed their journey, greatly rested and well fed. Deciding to spare the donkeys until they reached the heath country, they walked down the cobbled road. Any passerby might have thought them to be two young servants carrying food to some market down the road—or they might be brother and sister, even a hard working husband and wife. No one would have suspected their true identities.

As the day lengthened toward dust, the expanse of grayish-purple heather Alfgif had described appeared like a shadow on the hills before them. Hilda found herself both anxious and glad to see the rough country.

"We should reach the edge of the heath by nightfall." she said to Caedmon. Without a hint of concern, she added, "And we'll start across it first thing in the morning."

Startled by his lady's declaration, Caedmon quickly objected. He found it difficult to understand why she would be so willing to ignore the advice they'd been given. "Alfgif and Olwinda warned us against crossing the moor. It's better to stay at the edge and circle round."

Hilda shook her head stubbornly. "Crossing the heath would be less dangerous than prolonging our journey. Who knows what we'll encounter if we spend longer on the road. And, too, winter is approaching. Besides, if we cut across, we'll come out much nearer to Whitby and our journey will be shortened."

Caedmon reluctantly agreed to the change of plans, knowing that Hilda would likely cross on her own if he insisted on going around. But he didn't think it wise. Not at all. Before them stretched a deserted countryside where thick, twisted heather and bracken covered almost every inch of land. They had not seen another person for several hours, nor had they seen any signs of human habitation. As the sun sank to the horizon, the miles and miles of the purplish-gray heather seemed to ripple like a large lake in the dying afternoon breeze, interspersed here and there by tall slender spears of green grass and grey-black, sharply pointed rocks. Caedmon said nothing, but his tension increased. Anyone could see that Alfgif had been right; no sheltering trees stood out against the horizon. Nothing would protect them if it rained or snowed.

"Let's look for a place to spend the night," Hilda said cheerfully, ignoring the fact that her companion had been silent for some time.

"Yes. Of course," he replied and led his donkey off the road and into the brush. Hilda watched him go, and soon saw him beckoning. "This way, My Lady."

Hilda laughed. "You had better stop calling me that; someone will hear you."

243

"I doubt it," answered Caedmon. "There's no one to hear, not even animals." Caedmon avoided telling her that he had been warned about snakes.

"Good," Hilda replied, carefully ignoring the unease in her companion's voice. "We're making good progress, I think. Whitby can't be that far away now!"

Crossing the Heath

Whenever Hilda looked back on the trek across the heath, the days blended into one long nightmare. They rose the first morning, after sleeping in a natural shelter under some bushes and began to struggle along the path, the heather catching on their stockings and shoes. The sun provided no warmth, and the skies promised rain. Like their human counterparts, the donkeys moved sluggishly, but unlike Hilda and Caedmon, who tried to keep moving, the animals often stood still, stubbornly refusing to move at all.

Soon the path begin to disappear, making them search in a wide circle to discover where to pick it up again. At mid-morning, the sun disappeared and the steadily darkening clouds released hard rain. Lacking shelter from the driving pellets, they continued to move. That night they slept fitfully in wet clothing on wet ground.

Now that it was too late to turn back, Hilda realized how her stubbornness had once again led her into trouble. Perhaps their misery resulted from yet another sin—pride. But if this wet and hard ground was punishment for her "sin," why should Caedmon suffer also? To make her punishment heavier?

"Caedmon shouldn't be here, caring for me," she thought. The miserable girl began to cry softly, and when at last she fell asleep, she found no comfort in dreams. Caedmon, worried less about himself than about her, pulled his mistress close in a vain attempt to comfort and protect her.

The second morning the sun shone once more. Taking stock of the condition of their clothes, Caedmon opened one of the small pouches he'd placed on his donkey and pulled out his extra cloak and short tunic, and rough strips of cloth which were slightly drier than the garments Hilda wore.

244

"Here, My Lady," he mumbled. "Change into these clothes; you'll be more comfortable."

Hilda looked uncertainly at the rough garments. "And should we spread the wet ones on the bushes to dry?" She stopped, suddenly aware of what he was asking. "What about you—these are your clothes, not mine!"

"Please put them on, my lady. I'm not as cold as you are," insisted Caedmon. "I'll not have you ill."

"And you? Won't you be ill?"

"My clothes will dry as we walk. We'll put your wet clothing on the donkeys' backs; perhaps it will be dry by night."

Hilda started to point out the problem with his logic—if his clothes would dry, so would hers—when he suddenly walked away.

"I'll go along the path here—you change." Whistling softly to himself, he moved forward, eyes discreetly front. Hilda knew she was beaten and knew too that she wanted to be beaten; she was unbearably soaked. Quickly she removed her wet clothes and slipped Caedmon's tunic over her head. Then she started laughing; even as short as she was, the tunic only came slightly below her knees.

"Caedmon," she called. "I have nothing on my legs!"

Caedmon glanced back, and blushed at the sight of his mistress. Then, without turning around, he told her how to wrap her legs with the rough cloth then use leather thongs to secure the ends at her ankles and thighs. It took Hilda quite some time, but when she'd finished, she stared down at her legs and began to laugh once again.

"Oh, Caedmon," she giggled. "I look so very silly! Look at me!"

Caedmon turned around and saw before him a slight figure, seemingly part male, part female. It embarrassed him to look at her legs even though they were encased in the makeshift leggings, but he soon found himself laughing also.

Despite the laughter that morning, the day became more nightmarish than the previous one. Toward noon, they saw figures in the distance. Hilda, who hadn't heeded Olwinda and Alfgif's warning about the moor, decided that it would be best to pay attention to their warnings about strangers. "I thought travelers avoided the moor," she said to Caedmon. "Who could be out here?"

"Perhaps travelers who cut across, like we're doing," he replied, but his eyes didn't show confidence in his own words.

"Or they might be bandits; we have no way of knowing and I'm afraid to take a chance. We can hide beneath some of the heather," Hilda suggested.

"The donkeys can't be hidden under the brush," the anxious Caedmon replied. They're too large and wouldn't stay still. Unload them and set them free as if they were strays."

Hilda nodded and quickly stripped her drying clothing and the pouches off the donkeys and—although she didn't want to—removed their halters. After giving the donkeys a quick slap to make them move off, she and Caedmon crept low along the ground in the opposite direction and finally laid themselves down in a thick patch of heather which grew around a small dwarf pine.

The branches of the heather were sharp, but their discomfort soon increased when they discovered that small creatures and a lizard inhabited their shelter. The insects crawled under their tunics and began to bite. As small spots of blood appeared in patches on their legs and arms, Hilda began to think that perhaps it would be better to take their chances with the men.

However, just then she heard voices. She had never wished more that she could understand the language they spoke. Suddenly, one of them let out a whoop of discovery, and the other men joined in quickly. Hilda began to shake, fearing that they had been seen. The voices, however, began to move quickly away from where she and Caedmon were hidden. Lifting her head slightly to peer through the bushes, she saw the group pursuing their donkeys. Within moments, the donkeys were captured and a short time later, both men and donkeys were out of sight.

Once they were sure the men were gone, Caedmon and Hilda resumed their journey. Afraid to be caught, they pushed themselves across the moors, until fatigue caused them to fall asleep in their tracks. The following morning Hilda felt stiff and sore. Weaker than she should be, she realized that she could no longer ignore the fever

246

and chills afflicting her. One look at Caedmon's face confirmed what, on some level, she already knew. She was ill.

"I'm sorry, my friend," she whispered. "I can no longer walk—my legs betray me."

Caedmon patted Hilda's shoulder, then rose to leave. As she protested, he attempted to reassure her. "Don't worry. I'll be back soon; there must be some kind of shelter where you can rest." Then he left her where she was lying.

Within a few minutes, he came running back excitedly, "I've found a spot—it's not too far—you can make it there! Give me your arm and I'll help you."

Much to his dismay, Hilda only looked at him blankly, not seeming to know where she was or who he was. Her skin burned with fever. Partially carrying her, partially dragging her, Caedmon managed to move her towards a large rock which had an overhang that provided a small enclosed space. Inside, straw and pine needles had been pushed together to form a bed; Caedmon refused to consider who might have made that bed and when. Gratefully, he deposited Hilda on the straw and drew out what little remained of the strong drink Olwinda had provided for them. He managed to get a few sips down her throat and then forced her to swallow large gulps of water from his flask. He lay her back down and within minutes, she fell into a restless half-sleep, occasionally stirring and sometimes whispering: "John...John."

Exhausted and frightened, Caedmon meant to watch over his mistress, but soon he too fell asleep in the shadow of the rock only to be rudely awakened by a ragged woman, whose face was very close to his own.

"Who are you?" croaked the voice that went with the face. "What you doin' in my bed?" The creature shook him impatiently. "Answer! Answer!"

"Who...who...?" Caedmon sputtered, finding it difficult to speak against the fingers the woman pressed into his neck.

The voice hissed back. "Answer now or the spirits will take your voice away to the winds forever! What do you here?"

"I mean no harm. I'm seeking shelter. My, m…" he began to stutter, intimidated by the creature standing over him. "M-my sister took ill. And… and I needed a place for her to rest." Suddenly he realized that he had not heard a word from Hilda, and his fear for her overcame his fear of the angry woman before him. Jumping to his feet, he almost knocked his inquisitor over, but he couldn't escape her grasp. The wiry but strong hands that closed over his arm held him fast.

The hand that held him showed evidence of hard labor. The eyes, hawk-like under the furrowed brow, held his gaze insistently, and he found he could not look away. Wild hair fell in tangled masses from under a ragged cap which, like her other garments, was frayed from long use and exposure to the weather.

"Please," Caedmon pleaded, "Please, she's ill…." Hilda stirred restlessly and whimpered slightly. "Let me go, I have to tend to her!"

"First, tell me the truth. Your *sister* will be well enough if I choose her to be."

Caedmon was taken back by her emphasis on "sister." She clearly didn't believe him. Everyone else had accepted his lies; why didn't she? He had to hope she wasn't the enemy.

"We run from the red-haired soldiers! We hope the monastery overlooking the sea will give us refuge."

"Liar," she sneered. "Those red-haired beasts would have no cause to disturb two peasants. Your *sister*," again he heard the disbelieving tone, "has the unmarked hands of the rulers. Peasants don't have such pale skin and fine hair." Once again, the tone became imperious, "Who is she?"

"Please," Caedmon again began to plead, "Her story is not mine to tell, and she is desperately ill. If you want to know, let me go to her." His captor's fingers loosened their grip on his arm.

"Go to her, then, but I will have the truth!"

Caedmon quickly got to his feet and turned to bend over Hilda's prone body. The fever was still upon her, but she didn't seem as restless. He took out his flask and wet a cloth to wash her face. After a moment, the woman behind him began to talk in a far less aggressive tone.

"The monastery isn't strong as it once was," she replied shortly. "The invaders left it in ruins long ago, and those who survived have had little help in rebuilding it."

Caedmon thought he detected a hint of regret in her voice as it trailed off. After a moment, she spoke again.

"I help them when I can. They're good women." She chuckled to herself, "I once believed as they believe, but that was long ago, and we've come to terms."

"Does it still offer..." he started to ask, when she gave him an admonishing hiss.

"Quiet!"

Her warning brought to his attention the voices of men, many men. His interrogator disappeared over the rocks, leaving him even more fearful. It seemed a choice between falling into the hands of whoever was coming and being in the power of the wild woman. He decided they would be better off in the grasp of those bony fingers—and remained quiet.

The woman's voice rang out, laughing and chanting nonsense which hailed mysterious creatures and not the men at all.

"Sit, sit, victory women, fly to earth! Do not go wild into the woods! Be mindful of my good as each man is of food and homeland— sit, sit, victory women, fly to earth!"

The strange creature's voice rose and fell and gradually became harder and harder to pick out from the noises of the increasing wind as it too fell and rose. Caedmon could hear the angry voices of the men disappearing in the same direction, and so he dared to raise his head and peer cautiously over the top of the protecting stones. Far off, disappearing against the horizon, bobbed the figure of the moor-woman, taunting a troop of soldiers as she led them away from the shelter where Caedmon and Hilda had found safety. Obviously angry, their voices disappeared on the wind as they ran after the fleeing creature.

"She's leading them away from here," Caedmon said to himself in disbelief. He sat back on his heels, marveling at what had just happened so quickly that he almost doubted he had seen any creature here at all. He turned to Hilda, not knowing how he could help his mistress, only to find that she slept quietly, her cheeks no longer flushed, a slight smile on her lips. He resolved not to fall asleep again and sat himself as close as he dared to the body of his lady, waiting for the moor woman to return. She did not. As night fell, the sounds of the moors ebbed away, and gradually a full moon shown on them, so brightly as almost, but not quite, to extinguish the stars. Even a servant as faithful as Caedmon could not fight off the fatigue of the long journey, nor the unexplained contentment which crept through his aching body. It would not rain that night; there was shelter for his mistress. Pulling more hay up over Hilda's body, he lay down a decent distance from her, covering himself, too, as a protection against the growing cold.

He woke to the warming rays of dawn, sitting bolt upright as though someone had shouted in his ear. He looked about expecting to find the wild woman, but no one was nigh. Hilda slept as peacefully as before. The events of the previous night were dreamlike. Perhaps none of it had ever happened, he thought. Stretching, he roused himself to peek again over the protecting stones only to bump against a small bundle between himself and Hilda.

"Where did you come from?" Caedmon said softly to the strange little package wrapped in a crude basket woven of heather and covered with an old, but clean cloth.

With wonderment, he unwrapped the cloth to discover fresh fruit and bread as well as an inner package filled with cold meats and cheese. Surely, the woman had been a fairy or an angel sent to provide for them! Eagerly he seized the bread, for the very sight of it made his hunger painful. As he wolfed down the bread, guilt overtook him. He must not eat when his lady surely felt as hungry as he.

He turned back to her and found her looking at him with great merriment.

"You are hungry, aren't you, my gallant protector?"

"Oh, Hilda! I mean, M-M-My Lady," red-facedly he corrected himself. "I'm a very poor protector indeed!" With an excitement that left no time for her to ask a question, Caedmon related the events of the past day right up to the present moment. "And then I woke up, found this food and ate the bread without thinking. I was hungry." He paused, confused by the events he'd just described. "I'm a miserable, selfish creature."

Hilda laughed heartily. "A wonderful, unselfish servant— that's what you are, and I shall treasure you always, but I think you have had many bad dreams."

"Where did this food come from, if it was all a dream?" answered Caedmon. "Certainly we had already eaten what the good women provided for us—or more likely dropped it as we ran from our pursuers. But who cares now! Let's eat!"

Hilda sat up, brushed the hay from her hair and upper body, and stretched her arms up to the warmth of the sun. "Was I really so sick that I remember nothing about the last few days? Nothing except heat and bugs. Ugh! They bit me. Did they bite you too?"

Hilda's arms, which had been covered with red welts, were now smooth. "Did I dream about the bugs, too?" she asked. Before Caedmon could answer, something close by caught her attention. "Look, over there, in the corner of those two rocks, isn't that a pitcher of some sort?"

Caedmon's eyes followed her pointing finger and lit on a fair-sized brown pottery pitcher. With the same wonderment he had when he discovered the bundle of food, he reached out for the pitcher and found it full of water! Behind it was a small flagon closed with a plug. Removing the plug, he sniffed the contents. Mead! The wild woman with her magic spirits was providing them all they needed.

A bit stiff from sleeping in the cramped quarters under the rock, but cheered by the provisions they now possessed, Hilda and Caedmon set off toward the northeast once again. More than once, they thought they heard someone in the rustling underbrush behind them, but they never saw human or animal.

"A rabbit? Some small wild creatures? "Hilda ventured.

"Or our wild savior," Caedmon suggested; "the moor woman might be watching us still."

About midday, something in the wind evoked a sense of water and moisture, and far off in the distance slight grassy knolls appeared beyond the heather and gorse. Gradually the moors fell away, turning into grasslands sprinkled with squat little trees. Just as they left the moors, a voice singing praises of the wild birds and the purple heather came to them on the wind, making them feel safer than they had felt for days.

People of the River

Emerging onto the grass, they saw off in the distance a strip of water, the river Alfgif had spoken of. Their relief at having survived the moor and arriving at the river was short-lived. It was vast and deep. Standing on the shore, both looked in silent awe at the land opposite.

"We need a boat," whispered Hilda, having no idea where to find one. They looked up and down the river's edge, but sighted no means for crossing, and no village where they might find help.

"Let's walk up the river, against its flow—perhaps it's more shallow nearer the source," Caedmon suggested.

Hilda feared it would be quite some way before the river narrowed or became more shallow, but she saw no alternative. As they walked, she cheered up some because small rafts propelled by flat paddles began to appear. If the boat travelers noticed them at all, they gave them no attention. All seemed quite peaceful, but their imaginations didn't allow them to rest easy. Calling out to a passing boat might be dangerous since they didn't know who piloted it.

Finally, they sighted a cluster of small buildings. "Let us see what that might be," Hilda suggested. They were both too tired to continue much longer. And as they drew closer, Hilda became more and more convinced that they had happened upon a small abbey. Men and women in rust-colored habits and the familiar leather sandals moved about the grounds, some repairing fences, others prodding cattle and sheep to stay within the newly built fences.

"It's a settlement of some religious order," she assured Caedmon. "Perhaps we'll be safe there—although," she added, "revealing the whole truth about who we are and where we are going might not be wise. Let's rely once more on the story that we're remnants of our family, seeking distant relatives near Whitby."

A young man tending to a garden looked up inquiringly as Hilda and Caedmon approached. Once again, Caedmon did the talking. "Good day, my friend," he said easily. "We travel north to the coast to seek relatives. Might we find shelter for the night here—and perhaps a bit of food?"

"I'll find Abbess Claennis," the youngster replied. "She decides who may and who may not stay within Rosedale Abbey." Quite soon, he returned with a portly, sunny-faced woman, who observed the travelers closely, but without suspicion.

"What may we do for you, my children?" she asked.

Caedmon bowed respectfully. "We are looking for a place to rest on our journey, My Lady. My sister and I have no living family in the west," Caedmon gestured vaguely toward the setting sun. "We think we might find other family members on the coast near Whitby."

The Abbess regarded them curiously but with kindness.

"Your name, and your sister's name?" she inquired.

"Caedmon, My Lady," then he pointed to Hilda, who made a quick bow as well. "And this is my sister, Hilda. We only ask for food and shelter for tonight—and advice about crossing the river tomorrow."

"Come," responded the Abbess, seemingly satisfied with his answer. "One rule, however: refrain from speaking to us or with each other while on the grounds. Our order maintains complete silence as part of our worship, and we'll expect that you honor that practice."

Caedmon and Hilda nodded in consent.

Rosedale Abbey, small compared to the richness of Buxton and even to the grounds at Northwich, had a simple one-story priory, banked by a small cloister as well as a few outbuildings. The Abbess led them through the outer walls to a small room on the inside edge of the building. Pointing to two straw mats, she indicated that they should leave their bundles. Then she signaled for them to follow her, first to a basin where they could wash and then to the refectory, where they found food already laid on the table. Not quite sure how to thank her, they smiled and bowed gratefully. Returning the bow with a smile, she left them to their meal. While Caedmon had to catch himself periodically to keep from speaking, Hilda found it comfortable to sit silently for the rest of the evening. That night, much to the Abbess' surprise, Hilda attended the midnight Matins prayer hour and the three o'clock Laud service. Even more surprisingly, Hilda worshiped respectfully at both Prime and the nine o'clock service, Terce. After they had completed the meager morning meal, the Abbess led them to the river's edge where one of the young farmers from the abbey awaited alongside a small raft.

Hilda turned to the Abbess, drawing out the small pouch in which she held the jewels and decorated clasps she had wanted to give to Alfgif. Holding the pouch open, Hilda spoke quietly.

"Please," she offered, "Take what you'd like."

The Abbess shook her head, and pushed back the pouch, but Hilda, undeterred by the refusal, pulled out a small ivory cross whose intersecting arms were surrounded by a small circle. Taking the Abbess' hand, Hilda pressed the cross into it, folding her fingers over it. The Abbess looked at the cross with wonder, but then extended her hand as though to return it to Hilda, who raised both hands toward the Abbess, shaking her head no. She was, in fact, pleased to note that the Abbess was enchanted by the small cross. Bowing to her once more, Hilda turned to allow the boy to take her hand and guide her onto the raft where Caedmon sat. Waving to the Abbess, she settled in as the youngster used his pole to push off the shore and head across the river.

The boy used the river's flow to help him propel his small craft, and in less than a half hour, he had deposited them on the opposite shore. As he helped her off the raft, Hilda pressed a shiny coin into his hand and walked away quickly so he could not return it. The boy, however, looked at the gift delightedly, showing no indication of returning it.

"Thank you, miss," he said as he began the trip back.

Caedmon was nonplussed to hear Hilda laughing softly to herself. He turned to her questioningly. "Oh, Caedmon, I was just picturing our two mules on that raft with us! Perhaps it's just as well they were taken off by those men."

Again Hilda and Caedmon walked along the bank of the river for a time, occasionally passing carts drawn by oxen or farmers driving sheep along a clearly defined path. Their experiences at the abbey had convinced them that they no longer needed to hide. This was obviously a well-traveled road. No one confronted them, but simply nodded and continued on their way.

By late afternoon they had turned away from the river and headed north, following the small map given to them by the Abbess. Shortly after, they arrived at a deep escarpment that rose high above an endless expanse of water.

"Beautiful!" exclaimed Hilda.

Caedmon, stunned by the enormity of the sea, nodded in agreement as Hilda continued to gaze at the sight before her as in a trance. "Such a big boat one would need to get to that horizon. And yet, hundreds of the enemy arrived on these waves from that horizon."

Hilda shook her head, allowing the events of the past to arise briefly from her memory before she dismissed them. "We have a more practical problem now. How do we get down to the beach? It's so steep!"

Caedmon looked about for a solution. "Let's move along the edge here, and perhaps we can find a way down that's more friendly to our feet!"

They moved forward, and slowly the cliffs became a gentle slope, and it was safe to make their way down to the coast. As they stood on the beach, they spotted a group of five or six figures coming toward them. As the group neared, Hilda realized that they wore the black habits of nuns.

"We're safe, Caedmon. We're safe!" Hilda started forward, then paused. She suddenly saw herself as the nuns must see her, dressed as a peasant in a tunic and leggings. Nothing could be done about that now. So she waited until the nuns came closer, and then moved toward them.

"God be with you, sisters," Hilda said with a low bow.

"And with you," one of them replied, surprised at being greeted by such a pair.

"I seek the monastery at Whitby," Hilda announced. "Are you perhaps of that house?"

"We are indeed," the oldest of them replied sadly, "At least of the ruins our monastery was left in."

"So you no longer live there?" Hilda asked. The group surveyed her curiously.

"No, we still abide there. With the help of the nearby village, we have partially restored some of the buildings and the small chapel. Why do you seek Whitby?"

Hilda hesitated, unsure of how much to reveal.

"God has called me to his service," Hilda said quite simply. "I've heard of your monastery and thought it a good place to serve Him."

The nuns stared at the young woman, silent for the moment.

"If you will take me there, with my servant here, I will explain all to you." Hilda tried hard to contain the fear that they would turn her away.

The nuns, not quite sure how much to believe from this young girl dressed as a boy who referred to the young man with her as a servant. However, the pair seemed to offer no threat and, with the sureness that comes from certainty about their place in God's universe, they were accustomed to greeting those who had suffered turns of fortune. After a glance at the others, the woman who led the small group stepped forward and spoke.

"I am Abbess Fridewith; Whitby is under my charge. We're at least two hours from the abbey; if you wish, walk with us. I'll speak with you, child, but only at the journey's end. We've made a vow to complete our trip in silence."

Caedmon, although excited about the meeting, thought it strange that nuns valued silence so greatly, but he said nothing. He could not picture for himself a life of silence; if that was the way of the monastery, he might have to leave his mistress.

The now enlarged group continued along the coast in complete silence, broken only by the occasional tuneless whistling that Caedmon produced to avoid speaking. As the sun began to set turning the expanse of water darker and darker, Hilda could begin to discern the shell of what must once have been an extensive settlement. Ruined as it was, the small group of buildings showed signs of life. A few cows, even a couple of horses, grazed by the barn; pigs and chickens moved in the courtyard. A small garden banked the community, and a somewhat larger field, filled with the usual sheep, lay beyond the settlement. As she watched the inhabitants of the settlement, some of them in sacred garments, others in farmer's clothing, Hilda unexplainably felt a sense of peace. She was at home.

Chapter 8: Leova Loses One Love and Discovers Another (880)

Leova's wedding-night prediction proved accurate. Over the following months, the two young people learned to love not only the moments spent in their marriage bed each evening but also the pleasure of awaking next to each other. They quickly fell into a routine which allowed Leova to attend to the day's tasks at the hall and William to learn the business of Lothlar from Bertram and Jankin, whom Leova had insisted be transferred to Lothlar as reeve. Each afternoon, they took time to share with one another the tasks each had assumed responsibility for. Leova took her new husband to the medicine hut and talked with him of cures and preventatives, even sharing the small bit of healing magic she had learned from the forest women. She found him to be most respectful and willing to accept her strengths as a healer.

In turn, Leova joyfully let William teach her to read and write. The letters on the pages of the books he had brought from Buxton held secrets, she knew. And while they were perhaps not as practical as the secrets she learned from the forest women, they were nonetheless as fascinating as herb lore. And learning to read sustained her curiosity about a wider world, a curiosity she previously had no way of examining.

Just before the coming of spring, they sat in the small room William used for business, going over a page of his book of saints. "Do you know this name?" asked William, pointing to a series of letters beautifully executed on the page.

"Bede?" ventured Leova after carefully sounding out the letters as William had taught her.

"Excellent!" William exclaimed. "In the monastery we called him 'The Venerable Bede' because of his wisdom and learning. His name means 'life,' and his works bring life to those who read them."

"Really," Leova replied. "All names mean something, don't they, William? It's important to choose them carefully. Did you know," she said shyly, turning her face up to look at him, "that my name means 'loved'?"

"Yes," said William, smiling at her as he spoke, "And a more suitable name I've never known. Certainly everyone who meets you, loves you."

"Be serious," Leova laughed. "you've no one to compare—no other 'Leova' exists...it's something my mother made up and gave meaning to!"

"Not so," her husband retorted. "I've even seen your name written in manuscripts in the old language. In fact, a nun at the monastery who became interested in learning to read pointed it out."

"How curious. Why would she do so?" asked Leova.

"She and John—I mean Rolfe—were learning to read the aged texts together, and she pointed it out because it was her friend's name. She thought it quite thought-provoking that her friend's name means 'loved,' and her name means 'battle.'"

"So, that would mean her name was Hild or Hilde or Hilda? My own best friend's name is Hilda. I'd heard she was sent to a monastery." Her words trailed off as she saw the look on William's face. "What? Do you think this nun is my friend?"

"Perhaps," William stammered, unsure of how much to say, "She wasn't yet a nun, and in her own world was a princess. What does your Hilda look like?"

Leova quickly described both her friend's looks and demeanor, and the more she talked, the more sure William became that the young woman at Buxton was the friend his new wife sought. "Yes," he replied quietly, struck with the memory of the girl he had known, "she must have been your Hilda."

"What happened to her, William? Surely she didn't fit into a monastery very well—not the Hilda I knew!"

William laughed at the thought of Hilda's struggle with the routines and rules at Buxton and patiently recounted all he knew of her: how she had been bound by her dying mother's vow, how she had worked in the kitchen, baked bread, swept floors—even milked cows—and how more than anything, she loved learning of all types.

"She was always intrigued by the scriptorium, not only because it's where the books are stored but also because she loved every step of creating new books. After she'd completed her required tasks, she would often come and look over my shoulder as I copied manuscripts, asking about the pens, the ink, the process of treating the velum, everything. More than anything, she wanted to learn to read and to write. The Mother Abbess assigned my brother the task of teaching her Latin, but that wasn't enough for the two of them. They both wanted to learn to read in Englisc, our language, the one we use every day, the one we're using right now." He paused to laugh, "They had to teach themselves, or teach each other; no one else really knew more than a word or two. They compared a Latin text to an Englisc one...very clever, actually!"

"And is she still there?" Leova probed.

William hesitated. The story wasn't his to tell—and repeating the whispers of scandal was an unchristian act.

"No. No, she's not. During a raid on the monastery, the Abbess hid her in the monk's quarters—I saw her there. But the next day, she was gone—perhaps to another monastery." Leova sighed sadly, causing William to hurry on with his story. "I've heard nothing since, and she did not return when the monastery was reestablished." Surely there was truth in that, he thought, even if it wasn't all the truth.

For a long time, Leova sat silently, her head bowed, tears gathering in her eyes. With her blonde curls hanging over her shoulders, William could not help but think that she looked like the angels he had seen so often on manuscript pages.

At last she raised her head and looked directly into his eyes. "William, I am sure you speak of my dear friend because we had been told by a traveler that she had been pledged to a monastery by her mother. Please, help me find her, I need to know what happened to her even if I never see her again."

Her tears began to flow as William pulled her toward him, stroking her hair. "Yes, my love," he promised. "We'll find her—and perhaps you can send her a letter when you learn to write."

"Yes," Leova said firmly. "I would like that. If she can learn, surely I can, too. And it will be wonderful to have a way to reach out to her again. Let's get back to work, but before we explore the Venerable Bede, show me how to write 'Hilda.' No—teach me to write 'My most beloved Hilda.' It will be a good beginning for the letter!"

William carefully followed her instructions and wrote out the greeting to her friend, then watched with pleasure as she slowly copied and then sounded out the words.

"Would you like me to write your letter and let you copy it?" he asked.

"No!" she replied. "When I'm ready I'll write it so that it will remain a message between Hilda and me, private as our talks used to be."

He nodded. "Then I must get back to my own work. Will you work with me? It's the best way to learn."

She agreed, understanding that reading and writing were not accomplishments learned in a short time, but both were skills she ardently wished to master. For the next hour, they pored over a manuscript, their two heads and two hands touching at intervals, William reading aloud while pointing out characteristics she needed to both understand and appreciate. However, the Venerable Bede and his fellow saints couldn't hold her attention, and Leova frequently broke into the lessons, urging William to tell her more about her old friend. Eventually Leova had no new questions to ask about Hilda, but her curiosity turned to her new husband and his past.

"William, why did you enter the monastery? What inspired your desire to be a monk?" The questions caused him to pull back and grow tense. Anxiously, she asked, "Has your mother's insistence on our marriage robbed you of that chance?"

"My *mother*," said William, with more than a hint of distaste, "has done only one good thing for me in all my life—and that's have me marry you." He smiled at Leova to reassure her before going on. "But she didn't arrange our marriage to make me happy." He sighed, "Being a monk was never my choice. How could it be? I was quite young when the woman who calls herself my mother, simply took me to Buxton and handed me over to the gatekeeper. She didn't even come in."

"How could she be so cruel?" Leova asked. She couldn't

imagine a parent with so little concern for a child.

"Who knows," William sighed. "Allmana had never been affectionate, so abandoning me was in character, but I felt lost—my father was dead, my home, my brothers, everything I knew suddenly became beyond reach. I withdrew from all human contact, no longer trusting anyone; for over a year I spoke to the monks only when spoken to. Gradually I learned to trust the members of the monastery—they were—are—good people who were kind to me. Allmana was and is the opposite: she's evil."

He paused for a moment, obviously deciding whether or not to tell her more. Then he cautiously went on.

"My only comfort is that Allmana isn't really my mother."

"Not your mother?" Leova gasped.

"It's true," replied William, the pain clear in his voice. "I only found out a few years ago, and that knowledge gave me the leverage I needed to take my rightful place." He laughed harshly. "It seems that my father married Allmana when I was a baby. I never knew she wasn't my real mother, never even knew there was such a person other than her."

"How did you find out?"

"By listening and asking. Two years ago, I overheard one of the nuns, as she looked at me, say, 'He looks so much like his mother.'"

"Indignantly, I broke into her conversation, insisting that I *did not* look like Allmana—even though I barely remembered what she looked like—and was glad of that. 'No,' she explained, 'I mean your *real* mother. Before I took my vows, I lived as a servant at Stonehart, where I helped to deliver you of her.' Seeing the shock on my face made her try to backtrack, but I refused to quietly forget what she'd said. Seeing that I wouldn't leave off my questioning, she told me that the woman who gave birth to me, my mother, had died. Her name was Maria, and she came from one of the great families. The nun knew no more except that my father had remarried and brought his new wife, Allmana, back to Stonehart. The nun telling me all this left quickly after more than one confrontation with Allmana. 'I had long wished to study and take my vows and that's how I came to be here, and I saw the woman who abandoned you at our gates. It was Allmana,' was the conclusion to her story."

"How angry you must have been," Leova said.

"Frankly, I was overjoyed to learn the truth. She's mad, you know, as well as evil. I didn't want to inherit that legacy."

"And you've never learned more?"

I made efforts to trace my father's lineage, but had to admit defeat. There was no one who knew even as much as that nun had told me. Nor does anyone I've questioned know Allmana's heritage."

"Did you confront Allmana when you returned?"

"Yes, and that's why now she was so anxious to arrange our marriage. I was, of course, quite young when my father died, but it was his land and I was the legal heir. Her second husband came to her as a younger son of a large family, information that I received from Rolfe, and he had no land to contribute. Sometimes I think Allmana married him to cover up my father's lineage." William looked a bit uncomfortable as he continued, "That's why she initiated our marriage, to provide me with land in the hopes that I would not pursue my rights to what she claims, wrongly, is hers. And initiating our marriage is the only good thing she has ever done."

Leova leaned away from her husband, and laughed joyfully. "William, I must be honest, I am absolutely ecstatic that Allmana is not your mother! I could not bear the thought that any child of ours might have even a drop of her blood."

William dropped his head and laughed also, relieved that Leova felt as he did.

"Rest assured, he—or she—won't," he replied as he reached out affectionately and replaced a wayward curl that had fallen across Leova's cheek.

"That's certainly ironic, isn't it? My father arranges our marriage so that he will profit financially from the connection and save our lands. He sees her as a powerful force, but if the truth were known, your so-called mother," she smiled with pleasure, "lives on that land at your pleasure. She owns nothing."

"Not quite. I agreed not to take Stonehart Hall from her as

long as she turned over the control of the land to Ragen and me. So she still has a sense of control. I could have claimed it all, but that would have beggared Ragen and Rolfe, and I have no desire to harm my brothers. And even though we are not related by blood, I consider both of them my brothers. Both are good men. They don't know the truth—Allmana will confess the truth to no one and periodically continues to deny the truth to me. The secret can be kept between the two of us, my love." He marveled at how quickly those words of endearment came so naturally to him.

"Tell me more about your childhood," Leova demanded. "Did you feel a bond with your brothers? Certainly you would have known them as brothers."

Even as a very young boy, William confessed, he had felt nothing but hatred for Robert—who bullied the younger boys relentlessly, but he remained quite fond of Ragen and Rolfe. "I knew Rolfe best because we served at the monastery together, but Ragen came often to visit—probably to get away from Allmana—and I grew to love him as well." He paused, "They're good people. Ragen can be a bit strange and those who are cruel say that he isn't a 'true' man. But I find him simply a person curious about unusual things. Rolfe is simply the best of us."

"Perhaps," Leova laughed again and kissed him quickly but firmly on the lips. "I believe that my husband is the best, but I'm rather fond of you and that might influence my opinion."

Slowly, William and Leova learned to trust and depend upon each other for all their tasks. He discovered the quick mind in the body he cherished, one which would eagerly pursue the properties of herbs for healing as well as the complexities of learning to read. In turn, she learned that his early years at the monastery included being set to herd sheep and cattle. More amazingly, he had actually enjoyed the task. Working with Pagany and Bertram, they decided who was responsible for what task, and gradually the elder couple turned over responsibility to the younger one. As spring approached, the two often rode out to the fields together. William never issued tasks or orders before discussing them with Leova, and she granted him the same curtsey. Both gave orders and their servants and laborers knew that they served two masters, but two masters who were of one mind. That one of those masters was a woman never seemed to be a problem. The residents of Lothlar had long been accustomed to Pagany's wise leadership; and the years William had spent in the monastery serving the Abbess had taught him to accept women as leaders rather than fall back on old traditions that placed men in charge and made women subject to them.

Winter passed, spring set in, and the couple began the yearly tasks so important to ensuring that the estate and its occupants survived another year. One afternoon as Leova waited for William to examine some barrier markers which had been downed by the previous winter's heavy snowfall, Jankin approached her somewhat timidly. That he was reluctant to address her directly puzzled Leova since he had worked so easily with her in the past. Attempting to set him at ease, she pointed at William's careful inspection of the markers and joked, "Your master will take over your job if you're not careful, Jankin."

He smiled shyly. "Perhaps, my lady, but I'll still need to follow behind to carry his tools." Leova laughed and Jankin relaxed a bit. Then clearing his throat, he began to stammer slightly as he went on. "I—I—I've done something you may not approve of, mistress, but...."

"Rest easy, Jankin," Leova said, curious about his uneasiness. "You and I tend to think alike. I have always trusted your judgment."

"Do you," he asked carefully, "Remember the lady Wyomina?"

"How could I forget that poor woman and the life she must have led under Lady Allmana's roof?"

He nodded, and then rushed ahead, anxious to get the words out. "I've come to know Lady Wyomina's parents quite well and have great respect for the way they've handled misfortune: they've lost so much. And now Lady Allmana—despite the promises she made when their daughter married Lord Robert—has ordered them removed from the land their ancestors had possessed for generations. I—I..." he hesitated again. "I fear for their safety and so I, well, I...." He stopped and turned away from her.

"Go on," she encouraged him gently.

"I asked if they might like to settle themselves here, on Lothlar's land," he blurted out. "I know of a spot, a farmstead deserted after the head of the family died. They could settle there—if, of course, you approve. I should have asked you first. But they are there now." He dropped his head as though he expected a reprimand.

None came from his mistress. "Jankin, of course! If I'd known, I would have done the same. Where are they? I want to make them welcome."

"What will Lord William say?"

"He'll be as pleased as I am," Leova said with absolute confidence.

And indeed he was. When Leova explained Jankin's actions to William they had almost no time to wait for his reaction. "Marvelous. Just the right thing to do," he responded immediately. "Our patronage may in some way—some small way—help make up for Allmana's harm."

He smiled at his wife and his reeve. "Shall we go and see that they are well situated? Did you find them a good place, Jankin? We need to help them and make sure that their life will no longer be so hard."

The spot Jankin had found as a possible location for Wyomina's parents was lovely, a bower almost totally surrounded by thick bush-like trees which overhung the opening like a natural roof. A small shelter, much battered by weather and age, little more than a lean-to, occupied the center of the bower. A small woman emerged from the makeshift doorway, clothed in a dark gown tied with a rope and wearing handmade sandals; she looked almost like one of the itinerant monks who occasionally visited the hall. The older woman looked at the younger one anxiously but not submissively; she might be in reduced circumstances, but she was still as much a lady of the manor as Pagany or Leova.

Leova spoke quickly to assure her that she would receive the respect she was due. "Welcome, My Lady," she bowed slightly. "My husband and I freely offer you a place to live on our land, but..." she looked about at the bare surroundings, "I find myself most distressed by your situation!"

"We're not beggars," the proud voice of Wyomina's father, Ian, rang out as he came out of the lean-to. "We don't need charity. We've been pondering a return to the lands of our ancestors for some time. This," he gestured vaguely at the lean-to, "would be just a stop on the way."

"I offer no charity," Leova hastened to tell him, "merely a refuge from the elements."

Aware of how sensitive Ian must be about his losses, William approached the elderly couple with a warm smile and a respectful bow. "My Lady, My Lord, how may we address you?" he asked, and Leova suddenly realized that she didn't even know their names.

"Iona, My Lord, and my husband, Ian, once of the manor Eastvale, just north of your lands." Iona turned to Leova. "We're grateful, Lady, for your welcome."

William glanced over to the side of the bower and noticed some fine sheep penned behind the lean-to. He looked at Ian, "I assume these sheep are yours?"

Ian nodded hesitantly, his bravado gone. According to the law, if Ian had brought sheep from Allmana's lands, he could be accused of stealing them.

William had no desire to frighten the man, so he quickly clarified the reason he asked. "Stonehart and Lothlar share resources, and our shepherds are paid for the wool their sheep produce. If you choose to stay, your sheep will treated as part of the land and you will receive recompense for their care."

Ian relaxed visibly and replied gratefully, "Thank you for your generosity, Lord William, please forgive my shortness." He hesitated before continuing, "Given the fact that Lady Allmana turned us out of our manor, I wasn't sure where we could go."

"Of course, of course. Ian, my mother has done irreparable damage to your family. I cannot restore your daughter, but I can provide a home where you will be protected from the elements."

Ian started to protest, but William cut him off. "I know, this is just a stop on your way to the land of your people, but while you are here, you will not want. Jankin will see that the lean-to is refurbished. But now we insist that you be our guests at Lothlar. Tonight we will dine together—and perhaps you can tell me more about the people and land that will be your journey's end."

Iona, overcome by this sudden generosity, protested to Leova. "My Lady...we cannot...you need not...."

Leova hugged the woman gently and attempted to put her concerns aside. "My Lord William will be most offended if you do not accept his offer. Is that not right, William? Please stay. Let him make up, as little as he can, the harm Lady Allmana has done."

"It would be my honor to share my new home with you," William confirmed.

"We will then be pleased to accept your invitation," Ian replied.

But as Iona headed back toward the lean-to, she suddenly turned back, staring at William. "I knew your mother," she blurted out.

"You mean the Lady Allmana?" Leova asked, wondering what Iona meant, but immediately realizing that, of course, she knew the woman who had caused her family so much trouble.

"Not Lady Allmana, my dear, but Lady Maria, who was as sweet and kind as you are. She'd be proud to call Lord William her son."

Flustered, William could only nod before saying, "Perhaps you can tell me more about her...."

"It will be my pleasure," Iona smiled, "and though it may be small payment for your generosity, perhaps some knowledge of her can bring you happiness."

Later, as they rode toward home, Leova leaned over toward William and told him impetuously, "You're a wonderful person. I could be by your side forever!"

He laughed and looked at her with love and appreciation. "Think so?" he asked. Uncomfortable with praise and still a little disturbed by the allusion to his birth mother, William tried to lighten the mood. "You could be with me forever, but can you keep up with me on that nag of yours?"

"What?" Leova said, thrown off by the sudden change of topic.

"Can you keep up?" he repeated, snapping his horse's reins and beginning to race toward the dyke.

Leova grinned and yelled at his speeding back, "I'll keep up and pass you!" Then she, too, kicked her horse in the flank and started after him, determined to best him.

And as suddenly as it began, it ended. William's horse stumbled at the edge of the dyke, then fell, and in its desperate attempt to get up again, trod on its master before William could move away.

"Jankin," Leova screamed as loudly as she could. "Come quickly! Hurry!"

Leova dismounted and hurried toward William, trying to avoid the panicked horse as she sought to reach him. Jankin caught up with them and ran immediately to help. First he calmed the horse and led him away, returning to his fallen master whose injuries were obvious. Leova shook off her shock and knelt beside her husband, carefully examining his arms and body, looking for broken bones. She had no doubt that his left leg was broken, it was unnaturally bent and two bones protruded out of the flesh just below his knee. Jankin could see a gash on William's forehead, probably made by the sharp-edged rocks bordering the dyke, and blood flowed from his side where the hip was definitely crushed.

Jankin immediately put a supporting arm around Leova's waist and tried to draw her back from the injured man, but she fought him off. "Stop it, Jankin! He needs me to stop the bleeding, so he can be moved."

She took her meat knife and started to cut her cloak into strips, preparing to bind his head.

"But—"Jankin stuttered. "How can we move him?"

"Go back to Lothlar and bring some men with a cart; fill it with straw and get some covering. I'll need the top of a short bench and some cord to make a brace to hold his leg securely. We can't let the bone tear through his muscles any farther."

As Jankin mounted his horse, he heard his mistress plead softly with her husband, "William—can you hear me? William— wake up, please...." He didn't stay to see if Lord William answered her. There was no time to waste.

Leona realized that Iona was now at her side; she was grateful. Beads of sweat stood out on William's face, and he shivered as Leova wiped the blood from his forehead and, with the help of Iona, wrapped the gaping wound with the shreds of her gown. As soon as Jankin returned, accompanied by two of the farmers with a cart and a plank to serve as a brace for William's leg, Leova utilized all the skills she had learned as a healer. Then, as quickly as possible, William was moved inside the hall where he remained unresponsive.

"William, my love," Leova whispered again and again, hoping that he could hear her and respond. Finally, hours after the accident, his eyes opened slightly and he looked into her face.

"Leova?" he questioned. He tried to lift his head, but pain made him gasp, and he let it fall back against the pillow, once again unconscious. Leova could not remember when she had been so frightened.

"Mother!" she called, and Pagany, who had not left her daughter's side since William had been carried into the hall, leaned over and smoothed the hair back from his forehead. When the cart arrived at the hall, the older woman had prepared hot water, salves, and bandages in anticipation of his wounds. The two women had conferred quickly, and decided to place William on the small cot in the herb cottage, close to the medicines they would need to help him. Moving as quickly as they could, they undressed him, trying to be gentle, but realizing that in his unconscious state, he felt nothing. After bathing his wounds, Leova covered him with blankets. At this point, utterly exhausted, she looked helplessly at her mother. "What do we do next?" she asked.

"The bone must be reset and the skin around it sewn together. I can stop the bleeding, but the other injuries must heal on their own. The forest-women are coming. They'll know what to do."

Not long after, three women entered carrying baskets of herbs. The first of them looked at the wound in William's side and shuttered. "It's bad, bad," she said, "he bleeds beneath the skin as well as from the cuts—see how his flesh swells. He may not come back to us."

William awoke and called "Leova!" Then he cried out in pain.

"Please," she said to the women who surrounded her, "We can't give up!"

The old woman reached into her pouch and extracted a small vial. "Water," she uttered. Pagany quickly procured a drinking gourd filled with water. The old woman poured out most of it and emptied the vial into it. "This will ease his pain while I clean and set his leg—at least we can do something for that." Waving Leova and Pagany away, she gestured to her companions who came immediately to help her. Pagany had to pull Leova away with all her strength.

"Let them do what they need to do. Let me see to your needs."

"Mother, I must stay! He may need me."

"Right now he needs care that you aren't yet trained to provide, my child. Let the wise ones work. It's his only hope."

"Let me go!" Leova pulled away from her mother. "While they work, I will stand back, but once they have done all they can do, I'll reclaim my place." Pagany recognized the tone in her daughter's voice and knew it was useless to argue. She also knew what her daughter could not face, William's body had received death blows. He was dying.

After setting his leg and tending to other cuts, the wise women made him comfortable, giving him poppy juice to ease the pain and help him sleep. Leova sat at his side almost continuously, singing softly to him, telling him stories, reminding him of their happiness, telling him how much she loved him, trying to give him strength.

"I've started a new weaving project, my love, one you'll be most excited about. A blanket of finest wool, small and light, but patterned with flowers and birds. Can you guess what it's for? I was going to use it to surprise you—give it to you and watch you puzzle out why I'd make such a delicate coverlet. It's for swaddling! We'll have a child soon, a boy or girl to carry on our legacies, to...." She choked suddenly and wiped away tears she hadn't realized were

271

overflowing her eyes and coursing down her cheeks onto the little coverlet.

William opened his eyes and looked at her—eyes filled with love, but full, too, of death. He struggled to speak but for a moment it looked as though he lacked the strength to make himself heard.

"Don't fret," Leova whispered to him, her tears falling on the coverlets. "I know what you want to say. I know you love me. I will always know that."

He raised his head and tried again. "The baby...don't let Allmana claim the baby!"

Taken back, Leova grasped his hand even tighter. "No, no. She won't have the baby. I promise."

"Rolfe will help you and Regan, too. Flee if you must—she's evil. She'll hurt you!" William's voice rose with each word, until it attracted the attention of Pagany, who rushed forward to help Leova calm him. Together they pressed him down against the pillows, telling him to be at peace, to rest so that he could heal. And suddenly he lost the will to struggle and lay still.

"Love—Leova means love," he mumbled, then closed his eyes. Moments later he was dead. Leova rested her head on his breast, too exhausted for tears but not so weary to avoid the thoughts she had been repressing: the guilt she felt for William's death.

Pagany moved forward to help her daughter rise, but Leova refused to move. She remained silent and lost until Pagany once again attempted to move her away from William's body. As she allowed herself to be moved, Leova stopped and looked at those gathered around as though they were all ghosts. "It was—is—my fault," she whispered.

Her mother and others gently shook their heads and tried to reassure her, but she would not be comforted. "No," she said. "It was my fault! He's dead because of me—because I thought racing horses would be fun—because I allowed it when he was so inexperienced with horses! I was stupid, stupid, stupid, unthinking. I should have told him 'No!'"

Leova, unable to bear the thought that William would be laid to rest at Stonehart, insisted that the funeral be at Lothlar and that

William be buried in their sacred ground where she could tend to his grave. Quickly she ordered one of the young farmers to mount their fastest horse and carry the sad news to Stonehart. A few days later, with all details settled, they buried the young man who had been destined to be Lord of Lothlar and Stonehart. Although Allmana attended the funeral, the older woman said almost nothing to anyone, standing when the service demanded it, kneeling—but staring into space, not praying. When William was alive he meant nothing to her but a tool to stake her claim for land, and her response to his death proved that material interest. Throughout the service Regan remained silent and aloof from his mother.

As the priest finished his blessing, there was a stir at the doorway to the small chapel. Leova turned and took in a deep breath. Rolfe, much disheveled and road-weary, entered, went immediately to his brother's side, crossed himself, and knelt. Leova wept at the sight. She should have known, of course, that he would come if he could, but she had not known that she would react so forcefully. Bertram pulled his broken-hearted daughter toward him until her head rested on his shoulder. It was all he could do to restrain his own tears; he wished he could alleviate her pain but he knew he could not.

After the service, after the procession to the graveyard, after William lay in the ground, and the other mourners had left, Leova knelt alone next to the new grave. She could cry no longer; she was drained. Finally she turned from William's grave and walked across the fields of sheep and into the woods beyond. She did not think about where she was going, and so she was surprised to discover herself at the edge of the small grove where her mother had brought her the night before her wedding. In the center, as always, was a circle of stones. Slowly and quietly, she sat herself down on the same stone she had occupied such a short time ago. Closing her eyes, she was able to recreate that scene and its emotions: fear, anxiety, a bit of anger, wonder, even a bit of hope.

And somehow, William was there with her. Feeling his love, his goodness, relief flooded through her, her body relaxed, and she closed her eyes. A short time later, hearing sounds about her, she opened her eyes and found that the forest women had gathered at the edge of the clearing, their hands clasped and utterly silent. Pulling herself up, she looked around at them and slowly walked to their circle which parted to admit her. No words were spoken, but Leova could feel their power and their love for her. Embracing each of them lovingly, she took her leave and walked slowly back to the hall.

Her feelings of peace lasted until she drew near the door, when they were disrupted by the sound of heated voices: Allmana's, Ragen's, and Rolfe's.

"I will not," she heard Ragen say. "And you know why. So just let me live my life. Otherwise I'll leave. I'll marry no one—ever!"

She heard his retreating footsteps, and then the strong voice of the dictatorial woman rang out, "Then you, Rolfe, will do it!"

What on earth did she want him to do? And whom did she want Ragen to marry? Leova was far too miserable to consider these questions. All she wanted to do was go to her sleeping quarters and never wake up. As she moved away, she was alarmed to be approached by Allmana who leaned in close to her. "William claimed to be heir to my property, but I will never allow you that claim."

Leova's voice rose; "Away from me, evil woman."

Bertram immediately appeared at her side. "You," he said, with a steely-eyed stare at Allmana, "will leave my property now. All dealings henceforth will be with your sons."

Allmana snorted. "You think I want to be here? But you well know that I can claim all your land through my son William. Be grateful for the compromise we've made."

Bertram was about to reply, when Pagany approached. "Lady Allmana, I understand you wish to return to your hall. I've asked to have your horses brought to you. May you have a safe ride home," she added as she drew Bertram away.

"I will return," Allmana snarled as she moved away from them.

When Leova woke up the following morning, she found herself feeling a bit lightheaded. Before she could get up, her mother entered the room and clasped her in a gentle embrace. "Leova, I have been ill with worry. You've not eaten or slept regularly since William's accident. I want to help you build your strength, so you can become healthy and whole—you know it's important now."

"Important *now*?" Leova looked quizzically at her mother. "You know about the baby?"

"Of course," Pagany smiled. "I heard you speak of it to William—how happy it must have made him to know you were with child." Her mother turned away. "Gwynned can help you get dressed. I'll let the men know that you're up and about."

"The men?" Leova wondered whom she meant—Ragen and Rolfe? Her father?

Once dressed, Leova ventured a few steps out of her quarters and into the small garden she loved so much. "Nature doesn't seem to know William is dead," she thought. It was, as always, beautiful. The trees were in full leaf; the blue flowers which always grew up against the palisades were opening to the sun. A tall sunflower, much like the ones which she and Hilda had so loved, turned its face to the morning light. Two or three squirrels scampered from limb to limb almost as though they were playing a human game. As Leova watched, a small brown bird landed on a branch above her head with a twig in its beak.

"I'll sit here a moment," she said to Gwynned. "The men can wait." A small log had been carved out years ago for her and Hilda to use in their play. "Why am I thinking so much of Hilda?" she wondered. Hilda's leaving had marked the end of girlhood. She found herself to be a woman, a woman now a widow carrying a child. In less than three brief years, so much had changed. She felt far older than she should. Did Hilda feel the same strangeness that being a grown woman seemed to bring? Although she did not know the details of Hilda's recent life, she had heard bits and pieces of it; it didn't lack its own kind of travails.

Leova sat motionless for close to an hour, then stood up and started toward the hall door. In the great room she saw her mother and father in close consultation with Ragen and Rolfe. The sight filled her with confusion. Why had Ragen not returned home? Wasn't Rolfe supposed to be back at the monastery?

Her questions were shoved aside by an attack of dizziness, not the morning sickness she'd begun to experience, but the gnawing hunger that she was just beginning to feel. She swayed and stumbled just a bit, and quickly Rolfe rushed to her side to keep her from falling.

"I think I need to eat," she confessed. Everyone came alive at once. Rolfe led her to the table where Regan pulled out a chair. Pagany signaled to a serving girl. Feeling useless, Bertram patted Leova's back gently. Almost immediately a bowl of pottage appeared, and Leova became the focus of attention as she raised her spoon to eat. It was all too much. "Are you all just going to stand there and watch me eat?" she objected.

"We've eaten," her mother replied. "Don't load your stomach with too much—you've not eaten since William...."

Suddenly, Leova couldn't bear being the center of the conversation. She looked about the hall and addressed Ragen and Rolfe. "Why have you stayed?" she asked querulously. "Shouldn't you have returned with your mother to the hall, Ragen? Rolfe, why haven't you gone back to the monastery?"

Neither of the two answered immediately. Finally, with a shrug, Ragen said, "We were concerned about your health, Lady Leova, and...we had some business with your father."

"Business? William trusted me to see that the property and lands are properly tended to; my father need not make decisions for me!" she said defiantly.

Pagany interrupted, addressing the men around the table. "When she's had time to grieve, then we can talk about all this—it's too soon!"

"Pagany," said Bertram gravely, "we can't put it off for very long."

"Then, let's not put it off at all!" Leova demanded, turning toward the two young men. "Tell me what business keeps you here."

"Perhaps your lady mother is right. It would be better to wait," Rolfe responded, trying to calm her.

"No, I will not wait. Life's been hard enough recently; I need to know what will affect me—as obviously your 'business' will."

276

Leova's father motioned, and the two young men left the hall. Reluctantly, he took his daughter's hand in his. "My child, this business is as difficult for me to say as it will be for you to hear."

Leova felt a chill.

"Leova, now that William is dead, Allmana wishes another marriage—between you and Rolfe."

Leova was struck speechless. At last she managed to speak, spitting out her answer.

"What am I? A sheep? A goat? A servant on your land who can be bartered about! I won't have it! I accepted one marriage and grew to love and respect William—who has been dead for just a week. Can you not mourn him with some respect rather than try to sell his wife!" Her tone carried an authority her father and mother had never heard. "That evil woman's whims mean nothing to me! I will not marry again."

Leova stood and strode toward the door, though she felt herself close to stumbling. She braced herself against the lintel a moment, allowing Gwynned time to come to her side, and then, giving Ragen and Rolfe a contemptuous look, she left the hall.

She dropped down on the bed and, seizing a pillow, beat it hard with her fists. With every blow, she cursed Lady Allmana, her father, everyone involved in this latest scheme. Gwynned put her hands upon her mistress's shoulders and appealed to her.

"Please, my lady, don't go on so. It isn't good for the baby. Just calm yourself, please."

"No. I'll not be calm—being pregnant does not make me weak—I need my anger now!"

Shortly, Pagany appeared at the door and signaled to Gwynned to leave them. Leova watched her mother warily as she came to sit next to her. It was obvious that the older woman was trying to push back her own feelings.

"Leova, there are other reasons you should marry—you might as well know them all. Your father and I fear that unless you're married, Allmana will claim the child and our land."

Leova's anger dissolved. "What are you saying? What makes you think that?" she stammered. "William warned me—he wanted

277

me to make sure Allmana would never take our child. I didn't think she could—but now you say she can? I have been led to believe that this hall and all that belongs to it, plus Stonehart would be my property as my husband's widow. And," she paused, "How can Allmana know I'm pregnant? Help me, please."

"She doesn't, but when the child is born, she will know and could act at that time. And what's worse, since William, as we've now come to know, was indeed the true heir of Stonehart, any child of his will have that title also and may strengthen her claim to our lands. Allmana might even insist that the child live there rather than here. She may have no legal claim to do that, but the laws are ambiguous and we might need to bring in the king's counselors. The unpleasantness could remain unresolved for some time. And, unfortunately, it might well affect the baby's future."

Leova was too stunned to speak. Pagany could do nothing but hold her daughter tightly. She saw no way to avoid the new marriage.

Later that night, after hours of talk, followed by hours of formulating plans in her head and rejecting them, Leova couldn't sleep. Gwynned, who had no such problem, snored rather loudly on her pallet on the floor. Quickly but silently, Leova crept out of bed, threw a cloak around her shoulders, pushed the door open gently and stepped outside. It was a clear night; star patterns decorated the sky. The moon appeared broken into segments by the branches of a tree just outside the walls of the hall. Leova moved into the garden and sat down, hugging herself against the slight chill in the air.

Many scenarios played out in her mind. She would run away and take Jankin with her or run away and take no one with her. Wyomina's parents might take her in and help her when the baby came. Or, the forest women—she could live with them. Perhaps...she could seek out Hilda and the two of them would raise the baby together. "Foolish, foolish," she thought. Could she stay in the hall and vigorously refuse to be married off again? As a widow, she had more authority than she had had as an unmarried daughter. She would simply not do it.

Or, she *would* do it and marry Rolfe and live happily ever after. That idea brought a twinge of remorse; it seemed disloyal to William. However, it would appease Allmana and keep her from claiming the baby. In spite of herself, she revisited the idea. It might be a desirable outcome if he wanted to marry her. Did he really want to be a priest? Had he already taken vows? Could his mother force him to break them?

Her thoughts were interrupted by the sound of quiet footsteps. She looked up and saw Rolfe walking toward her. Quickly she realized, however, that he had not seen her. For fear of being detected, Leova almost stopped breathing. Something about the way he was moving, something about the way he was holding his shoulders and flexing his arms told her that he might well be going over his options, too. Just as Leova began to wish that she could just get back into her bedchamber without being heard or seen, something unseen crawled over her foot and slithered away. A hand to the mouth stifled her response a bit, but Rolfe heard. He turned and saw her watching him and seemed about to turn and run away. Instead, he stopped and looked at her for a long time after which he walked slowly toward her.

"You couldn't sleep either? Should we talk?" He smiled at her, and Leova moved as though to make room for him to sit.

"No," he stammered, "I'm more comfortable standing. After a moment, he began again in a stronger voice. "I can't imagine how you must be feeling; I know your love for my brother was life-affirming and all-encompassing. Don't feel obliged in any way to accede to our parents' plans. The custom for a woman to marry a brother of her deceased husband is ancient; it carries no weight for me. I'm prepared to defy my mother and return to the monastery if you want. You have only to say the word."

"He doesn't want to marry me," Leova thought, wondering why that realization caused her pain. She struggled to find honest words with which to respond. "Rolfe, I loved William with all my body and heart; I still do and always will. I felt—still feel—his strong love for me. He was so good and kind to me—and to others," she added. "And, in the end, I failed him; I bare responsibility for his death."

"No, Leova, no. Were William here, he would tell you so. Iona and Ian said it was his idea to race; you were doing what he wished to do. Please don't forget that."

"How can I forget that day, that awful day...?"

Rolfe looked at the tear-stained face so close to his own. "You won't forget the day. None of us will. I shall always grieve for him, and you shall always grieve for him. He came to love you very much; you know that. He wrote to me at the monastery and told me of his great happiness. Wherever he may now be, he would not want you to feel any blame."

Leova remained silent, after some time shaking her head as though ridding herself of demanding thoughts. After some quiet moments, she looked up, "He loved you as well, Rolfe. And Regan."

Shaking her head again as though she needed to clear her thoughts, she altered her demeanor. "Rolfe, truthfully, I'm angry with my mother and father; they think only of agreements about the land. I mean nothing to them." She turned away from him, wanting to strike out and hit something—anything—but hugging herself tightly, she repressed the feeling.

Rolfe made a step toward her, but when she turned back to him, he saw her face and immediately stepped back. "It's more than the land, Leova. They're thinking of you, and the child, too. Yes," he said, well aware of the fear his last remark had produced on Leova's face, "your mother told Regan and me of your pregnancy. My mother might well claim custody when the baby is born if we don't marry. Possibly demanding that you live at Stonehart. If a lord has a child, his widow is never the true heir."

"But William wasn't even her son," Leova retorted angrily. Immediately she realized that Rolfe didn't know.

"What are you saying? He was my brother."

"No. He wasn't." Quickly Leova told him William's history, filling in additional information she'd learned from Wyomina's parents.

Rolfe was silent for some time, pondering what she told him. Finally he sat down and spoke earnestly to her. "Leova, if that is so,

Allmana has no right to your child. She has no power over you! As a widow, you control all that belonged to William, especially his child. In truth, you can claim that Stonehart belongs to you also."

"Rolfe, you know this to be true?"

"Yes, yes I do. We had a similar case adjudicated at the monastery." He remained silent, as though lost in thought. "I wish William had told me—or had at least insisted that Allmana acknowledge the truth. My mother won't tell the truth, I fear, and she'll claim that the nun told William the story out of spite and hatred and that Ian and Iona want revenge. She'll keep trying—and...I can't stand by and see her hurt you. Marry me and be sure you're safe!"

"You'd marry me to protect me from your mother?" Leova feared his plan was based on his sense of duty and she wanted no more to do with "a sense of duty."

"Yes...; I mean, no. I owe too much to William and to Ragen and, like them, I care too much for you. We can't let you be hurt."

Leova sat silent for a moment, pondering on Rolfe's use of "we." Finally, she asked the question that had plagued her for some time. "Why you? How is it that our parents wanted me to marry you instead of Ragen? Wouldn't birth order determine who got 'the prize'?"

Rolfe smiled a little, thinking of Leova as "the prize." Then he became serious.

"Ragen will never marry because of his...his nature."

"Meaning?"

"Leova...you don't really need to know, do you?"

"Stop patronizing me. You can't make a statement and expect me to stop my questions! I'm not an infant. I'm a widow who knows how she stands in the world; Ragen can decide not to marry, but I must, despite my wishes." Her voice was deliberate, strong and desperate at the same time.

"I told you that I will support your decision, whatever it may be," Rolfe replied quietly.

"Rolfe, answer my question. What in Regan's 'nature' prevents him from marrying?"

The tone of authority in her voice left Rolfe no choice. "Leova, he prefers the company of men to that of women. My mother has probably known that for years; William and I came to understand it only a few years ago."

Leova's self-assurance left her momentarily. "You mean...he's, he's—I don't know the word for it: a sodomite?"

"Yes...but that's merely a word, a most unpleasant one too. Ragen is a good man, one loyal to his family and to those he loves."

Leova had no problem believing in Ragen's goodness. She wouldn't condemn him. The second, more important, question was harder. "Do you wish to return to the monastery? To take your vows and spend your life as God's man?" Leova saw the conflicting emotions engendered by her question, and unwilling to accept that he would sacrifice his calling to protect her, she did not wait for a reply. "You don't want to give up the life you love, and you're afraid you'll insult me by refusing marriage. Please, please know that I don't blame you. Go back to Buxton, let that be the end of it."

She moved as though to stand. Rolfe stopped her, drawing her to him carefully.

"No, Leova, no. That's not the end of it. It can't be the end of it. Listen, please." It took a few moments for him to collect his thoughts. "I've never had any intentions of taking vows, nor do I wish to be a priest. While I love the monastery—the quietness there, the study, the manuscripts—I don't want to preach, to read endlessly from the Bible, or to perform the sacraments." He sighed. "I sought the monastery largely to get away from my mother and the darkness that permeated her hall." Rolfe shivered a bit. "I admit that I could be—I think—quite happy to be at Buxton the rest of my life, but, in truth, you stirred up other feelings over six months ago." Guiltily, he did not tell her that loving another had first created in him the desire to leave monastic life. That revelation would serve no purpose. What he had begun with Hilda could never come to fruition. "Those feelings are still alive; I will not leave you if you would have me."

Leova sat silently, thinking carefully before she spoke. "Rolfe," she said, "If we planned something between the two of us and it proved to be a great mistake, could you go back to the monastery?"

"Yes, I could," he replied, returning her direct gaze, puzzled.

After some moments of silence, Leova whispered, almost inaudibly. "Do you know I'm pregnant?"

"Yes, and I rejoice in the child, but my mother will see the new life as another argument for claiming the land."

Leova, tired of trying to make sense of everything, began to reconsider some ways of escape: finding Hilda, just running away? Whatever she did, it was she who had to make the plan; it was she who had to carry it out. Determined not to be helpless, she faced her husband's brother squarely. "Rolfe, I'm not sure marriage is the answer, but I know I must do something. Will you help me run away?"

"Where would you go?" asked the confused young man.

"I'd look for an old friend of mine, one who serves at a monastery—possibly even at your monastery—one who would give me shelter and sanctuary. I'd accompany you to Buxton when you return. At least there I might be my own woman."

"If you retired to the monastery, you'd have to turn your child over to others to raise."

She paused, conscious of the flaw in her impulsive plan. "I couldn't do that."

Rolfe kneeled down before her, taking one of her small hands in his.

"Leova, take time to think. Know this: I don't feel forced to marry you. If you choose me, I will strive to make you happy, and William's child would be raised with the same love and care our own children would."

She looked down at him and gestured helplessly, not rejecting his offer nor accepting it. He rose, still holding her hand.

"Do not dismiss my proposal lightly. Consider it as a heartfelt offering," he said earnestly. "I'll await your answer and abide by it."

She allowed him to help her up. What she had felt for him months ago returned at a rush. She was glad it was too dark for him to see her face. He raised her hand to his lips, kissed it gently and then slowly lowered it, reluctant to let it go. "Now, perhaps, you should get some sleep, and so should I. We can talk more tomorrow."

Leova returned to her bed, but it was dawn before she slept, and even that short sleep was tortured rather than peaceful. As she dressed, she chose a dull gray tunic, covering it with a brown kirtle. "I'll wear no color for the next few months," she said when Gwynned urged her to select more colorful garments. "I wear this for William, whose death has taken color from my life."

Everyone watched as Leova moved to the table, carefully taking William's chair rather than the one she had used before his death. She avoided greeting anyone, and when Pagany started to approach her daughter, one look forced her back. At last Leova stood and in a strong voice made her position clear. "I'm mistress of Lothlar now that William is dead."

She looked at her mother and father, at Ragen and at Rolfe. "All problems come to me and all decisions will be made by me." Her eyes surveyed the room until she found the person she was looking for, the loyal Jankin. Looking pointedly at the servants, she announced, "I remind you all that I have appointed my servant, Jankin, as reeve. In the event he cannot consult with me about our lands, he will consult Lord Regan, who has my complete trust." The silence which greeted her words was palpable. Determined not to brook any disagreement, Leova refused to look at her parents or Ragen. She did, however, smile at Rolfe.

"Rolfe, would you please walk with me," she requested gently.

He nodded and rose, but when he approached and offered his arm, Leova ignored it, stepped off the dais, and—staring straight ahead—left the hall. Attempting in vain to control his puzzlement, Rolfe followed her out the gate and across the fields toward the woods.

They walked for a short time in the woods, until at last they stood on the edge of a small clearing near one of the ancient hill forts.

Leova settled herself against a tree, inviting Rolfe to sit beside her. She had not once looked back to see if he was following her. It was a test of sorts—much depended upon his willingness to follow as well as to lead.

"I'm not ready for marriage, Rolfe," she said, "and I'm not sure that you're as willing to leave the monastery as you claim. So I would like to propose a way out of our mutual predicament. You know that Wyomina's parents would like to seek peace in their homelands. They've told me that they plan to leave in a fortnight and travel into Cymru. I would like to begin the journey with them."

"You'll go alone?" Rolfe asked, fearing that she'd rejected him completely.

"No, no," Leova replied quickly, seeing his distress. "I need your good counsel and your protection. Will you go with me? I plan to go far enough away from Lothlar and Stonehart to avoid interference from our families. Jankin can go and help us get settled: he knows the land and will keep our whereabouts secret. Ian and Iona know the language. Regan will then be in complete charge of both Stonehart and Lothlar. I'm certain that you, like me, trust him completely." Rolfe nodded at these words and she continued. "After the baby is born, we'll decide whether or not to marry."

"I'll marry you now," Rolfe said, and it was obvious that his offer was heartfelt.

"No," she shook her head slowly. "Too much has happened. I need to grieve for William, sooth my anger for my parents, and bear my child."

"Are you saying we'd just go away? Not marry? Just go?"

"Yes. I ask only for some six or eight months before I make my decision about our future. Now I am not emotionally stable enough to make irrevocable plans. When I see my situation clearly, I will be able to choose whether to return here alone, go elsewhere, or marry you—if you still want me. Or, if not, you can return to the monastery without feeling an obligation to marry me."

Rolfe was silent for some time, but slowly he began to think out loud. "Surely you know, Leova, that a woman of your status would be greatly faulted for traveling with a man not her husband."

"I care not one whit for my reputation. I know who I am. You know also."

Again Rolfe was silent for some time, faced by a possibility

285

that would never have occurred to him. Then, looking steadily at the woman beside him, he answered her. "Yes, our parents would perhaps think we had married, probably because they would not believe that a woman such as you would run off with a man to whom she was not married. To save your and their reputation, they might even make others believe we were married. I suspect that any taint of shame might well keep them from searching for us. We could take time to get to know each other; you could have the baby...." He caught himself before he went further. "We can plan *together* from there."

Leova's smile showed her relief. "Good. We agree. Let's speak first to Iona and Ian; if they don't consent, we need to devise another plan."

The Escape

Less than a week later, Leova and Rolfe, Iona and Ian, and Jankin were miles away from Lothlar, having left in the middle of the night on the fastest horses in the stable. They had moved both west and south into the lands of Iona's and Ian's ancestors and relatives, who the elderly couple hoped would welcome them. Leova simply trusted to fate that they would find some spot in which to settle. She brought with her some of her jewelry and a bag of gold coins which she had taken from the estate's money chest. On this beautiful day, Leova felt freer than she had ever felt in her life. For the first time in all her years, no one had dictated to her. She had made the decisions necessary to produce a good life for herself and the child to come. She'd followed it through, keeping her parents and Allmana from interfering with what she knew was best.

In the letter addressed to their parents, Leova had once again underscored her intention to make her own decisions about her life, and reassured them that her absence would not be permanent. In precise terms, she made it clear that she and Rolfe would explore the wisdom of marrying, and that Regan—and Regan alone—would be the overseer of both Stonehart and Lothlar. She requested strongly that they not follow her.

By the end of a week, however, her sense of well-being had

faded. All of them were overtired, wearied by sleeping on hard, uneven ground, and watching their food supply dwindle. Leova began to tire easily, becoming exhausted by what once would have only made her seek a brief rest. She found herself longing for a place to settle and wait for the birth of the baby.

In the course of their travels, they had already skirted around several small settlements, agreeing that they were not yet far enough away from Lothlar to stop. On the eighth day, they saw a small clutch of huts, and Iona suggested to Leova that they stop for some information about possible places to settle in the countryside.

"We're among my people here—and I'm finding my old bones tired of travel." That wasn't exactly the truth, but Iona hoped she would be forgiven for the lie. She had begun to fear that Leova would never admit to her obvious fatigue and that her refusal to rest would prove dangerous to her health.

"Yes, I think it would be safe to do so," Leova replied, not fooled by the older woman's story, but ready to admit, at least to herself, that she was weary. That weariness seemed amplified by the beginnings of cold weather.

Iona and Ian agreed to keep Leova's identity a secret, and introduced her to the members of the small town as their ward, living with them since her parents died. Iona and Ian filled out the story with bits of truth, acknowledging that their own daughter's death made them even more fond of their ward, whose husband, Rolfe, acted as their surrogate son. Jankin passed as a lone traveler who had joined them for safety's sake.

At last they asked the most important question. Could they become part of the community, settle down in their midst?

The townspeople were sympathetic, but not helpful. They had little to share in the way of provisions, and would be unable to provide any but the roughest accommodations. In fact, they couldn't see how they could feed extra mouths, even if Rolfe and Ian helped with the work. Travel on, they urged. In towns farther along there might be a need for farmhands, they told the travelers. Leova suspected that they well knew the small party wasn't a band of workers.

That day and the next they passed through several other small gatherings of cottages and peasants with no promise of work or on-going lodging, though the people were more than generous with food and advice. On the third day, their luck changed. Iona and Ian returned from their conversation with the local farmers, with good news.

"There's an empty cottage here. A young man with a family wishes to move to his wife's people and would be willing to part with his rights to the cottage in return for some compensation— though no one has said just what he wants."

"I brought some coins and jewelry," Leova reminded them.

"How," Rolfe asked, "will we be able to explain owning such riches?"

"Perhaps," ventured Iona, "I can say that the coins were all Leova had left of her parents' heritage, that she had sold their cottage and hoped to use the coins for just this purpose?"

Once they had agreed on this strategy, Iona led them to a young man who listened intently. After some further consulting and final agreement, he led them to a small cottage. Leova started to groan in disappointment, but immediately suppressed her reaction. What choice did they have?

"Don't worry," Jankin whispered in her ear. "We can make this cottage larger."

Iona withdrew with her countryman and began a long interchange before she came back to report. "He's asked for a piece of your jewelry as well as a great number of coins. I'm not sure how he knew you had jewels; I didn't tell him when we started bartering."

"That's troubling,' Leova said. "How do you think he knew?"

"Probably guessed. We're obviously not poor. But I told him that you had only one piece—a gift from your mother. Choose which piece you will offer him and give the rest to Rolfe to hide. I don't want everyone knowing that you have more."

Leova thought about the pieces of jewelry. She cared little about their financial value, which didn't matter to her but which would mean a great deal to a villager. Yet the choice was not easy since each piece represented a moment of personal history, times which were important to her. Finally she opted to give Iona a little brooch which had indeed been a gift from her mother, who had pinned it to her shoulder when she was quite young. The brooch was but an inch across; however, the intertwined gold lacing and the enamel setting held by this lacing made it quite exquisite. Wearing it not only proved more than adequate for closing a young girl's outer tunic, but more importantly, she felt more grownup and beautiful with it on her shoulder. She kissed it briefly, remembering her mother, and handed it over to Iona with almost all her coins.

"Don't offer him all the coins at once," cautioned Rolfe.

"I've been making bargains longer than you've been alive," Iona laughed. "I know how to get the most from a seller."

Iona returned to the young man and the two of them began to haggle in earnest. At last, she opened her hand to display the brooch, and his eyes lit up. He clearly saw the quality of the piece. Seeing his reaction, Iona offered him only three of the coins, but eventually and reluctantly, after quite a bit more negotiating, she parted with two more, and he eagerly went to seek his wife to tell her about their good luck. Not only had he sold the house and land for an unexpected profit, Rolfe and Jankin had volunteered to help the young couple gather their belongings and stow them on a small cart.

"Only one more night outside or in a stable," Leova thought, her spirits lifting. "We'll have a home of sorts...not like Lothlar, but a solid roof over our heads."

The following morning, the man, his wife, and the cart were gone. Iona attacked the small cottage, ordering the others about as if they were her soldiers. The years of poverty brought on by Allmana's ruthlessness had taught her much about maintaining her family on nothing. She sent Rolfe and Jankin off to build tables and benches for the house, and then with Ian's help began cleaning the inside, first discarding the old rushes on the floor. As soon as she had them burning in a well-controlled bonfire in the yard, she sent Ian out to collect clean ones. Once he returned, she bound several of them together to create a broom with which she swept the floor clean before covering it with fresh, sweet-smelling layers of rushes. At last, when the cottage met her standards, she removed several pots from her saddlebag along with everything she needed to cook. By evening, they were all seated in front of a small fire while Iona's pots boiled away, emitting seductive flavors.

As they were fleeing and seeking safety and lodging, the small company had not really considered how they would survive as they remained on their own with no family holdings to provide stability and bargaining power. Once they had eaten their fill, however, Rolfe uncomfortably brought up the issue of sustaining themselves. Ian, who—like his wife—had been forced to live a life the younger couple had never known, answered confidently.

"We'll farm, but as freemen, a large portion of what we grow must be given to the local overlord; he'll visit five times a year to collect his rents."

"But we bought the cottage and land: why do we owe the overlord anything?" Leova asked.

"Think of it as a tax of sorts," Rolfe said. "The poor own nothing outright, just permission to rent the farms on which they work. In return the Lord becomes a protector against enemies if battle ensues. Surely you know this—you and William were overlords of two great estates."

Leova considered the business of the estate as she never had before. While she had taken full responsibility for the household, she had had little to do with the farms and had never questioned how the freemen and villains played into the wealth of those in the hall.

"I...didn't really know, but now I understand why my mother and father insisted that we take care to provide for the needy on our lands."

Ian interrupted, as much to ease Leova's sudden discomfort as to continue with his plans for their survival. "After we pay the duty, what's left is ours to sell. But to begin with, we need more than grain. Perhaps we can trade two of these horses for some farm animals—pigs, chickens, a cow."

Leova protested. "But we'll need those for our possible return!"

Ian looked at his wife, and then back to the young woman

he'd learned to love. "Iona and I would not return with you, My Lady. We...we feel more at home here among our countrymen and," he hesitated, "so many unpleasant memories hang onto Stonehart and Lothlar. Within a few years, we should be able to recompense you for the purchase of land and housing.

Leova waved her hand as though to say that was unnecessary. She was well aware that whatever pain she had left behind, it was matched by the pain of the elderly couple. "Then we'll trade the horses. Surely they're worth something."

The two horses turned out to be quite valuable, procuring for them two pigs—the female pregnant—and a cow with a young calf. They also ended up with several chickens, and a neighbor promised the use of a bull in return for the loan of a horse in plowing time. Leova had never in her life been so close to so much livestock. She had known they smelled, but hadn't realized how much odor she would have to become accustomed to.

Everyone had to work to keep food on the table and clothing on their backs. Nothing, it turned out, connected to her easy life at home, where servants delivered meat to the table and weavers provided cloth for pretty, impractical garments. As the days passed, Leova would have felt quite useless if it hadn't been for her skills as a healer. She searched in the forest for herbs and established a medicinal garden, adding to such supplies some potions she had brought from Lothlar. And soon she also supplied vegetables for cooking. Little by little they let it be known that she could provide potions for fever and powders for pain. The townspeople began to come to her for ointments to ward off infection and cures for sore throats. Although she would have gladly given her skills for free— and did on many occasions—her patients took care of her in return. Each encounter brought a gift to stand as payment: eggs, jams, feed for the livestock, a warm cloak. She hated being idle, however, and sought other ways to help her new family. When she discovered that Iona was quite skilled at weaving and was able to trade that skill for bed coverings, she set about bartering for a loom, carding tools, and wool. Soon she and Iona began to create cloth for their own needs as well as extra to sell.

The season changed and the nights became chilly. Jankin had departed after he had assisted the other two men in building two small additions to the cottage. Now they had a room for Leova and one for Iona and Ian. Rolfe continued to sleep on the straw before the fireplace. Jankin hadn't wanted to go, but finally agreed that he would be more useful as reeve to Lothlar than as a farm hand on their tiny plot of land. He promised, after much pleading, not to return once he'd taken his place at Lothlar. Rolfe and Ian feared he would be followed and their hiding place discovered by Allmana. He had protested, but eventually he acceded; he had no desire to endanger them, and he agreed that Allmana would find a way to take the child if she could.

Gradually the four remaining travelers became firm residents of western Cymru living comfortably if not leisurely, happy to be free from the threat of malicious plots to keep control of land. One evening after a long day's work, Leova noticed Rolfe rubbing his neck to relieve the strain of the day's labor. She spoke to him gently.

"This is so unfair to you. You work as one of your servants would: tending a garden, milking cows, herding sheep, cutting firewood, building rooms. Look at your hands!" She took one of them in her own two hands and traced its calluses. "Your hands never looked or felt like this before. You've helped enough—you should leave us and go back to the monastery. You should be among manuscripts, reading and copying, not digging and wrestling with stubborn livestock."

"Leova," Rolfe laughed easily, "living here isn't much different from living at the monastery. Life there was never easy." He started to tease her. "Of course I did not build rooms at Buxton because we did not need any, but I've stacked stones and thatched roofs when there was a need. Praise God that the need was rare: the good brothers would not have fared well in a place built by these clumsy hands!"

Seeing that she was not convinced, he turned serious. "My sweet Leova, in a way, the quiet here, the simplicity of day-to-day life, is much like living at Buxton: I do miss the manuscripts— studying them, copying them," he admitted. His voice sounded so wistful to Leova that she felt a twinge of jealousy, but the next moment he laughed, once again in a playful mood. "I have a chance here to do some things I'd never get to do at the monastery. Tomorrow, for example, I must slaughter a sheep," he grimaced unpleasantly, "a thoroughly disgusting task, but I think perhaps I can save a small piece of hide and prepare it as I learned to at the monastery. Eventually, I'll be able to write on it. And, perhaps, I can continue to teach you to read and write as William did." Rolfe paused, having a momentary pang of remembrance as he thought of his other love, Hilda, brought to him by the teaching of reading and writing.

"I would like that, Rolfe," Leova replied, somewhat comforted by his plans.

"And tomorrow, I shall take up an old pleasure, one I missed when I was at the monastery. Last week I spoke to a hunter who has volunteered to make a bow and a quiver of arrows for me. I promised him my first kill."

"Hunt? What will you hunt?" asked Leova.

"Squirrels and pheasants and other game birds, to begin with. Perhaps a deer after I've regained my skill."

Leova smiled awkwardly. "Then you intend to stay?"

"Yes," Rolfe replied quickly, "I do."

Without warning, Leova felt the baby move in her belly, and she gasped in surprise. Rolfe responded immediately. "What's wrong? Are you in pain?"

"No, no." she reassured him. "The life in my belly wants attention." Leova placed Rolfe's hand over her swelling stomach. "See, William's child is active. Can you feel that? It's truly a miracle, isn't it, Rolfe?"

Rolfe found it difficult to reply. He was forced to acknowledge, if only to himself, that he was jealous of his dead brother. Jealous of William who had conceived the child growing in Leova's belly. Jealous of the man who had touched, caressed, and possessed Leova's body.

He grimaced as he recalled the one time they'd talked about her love for William, over a month ago, when they had been

293

struggling to establish their home. That evening, after Iona and Ian had retired, Rolfe and Leova had sat alone before the waning fire.

"They seem happy, don't they?" Leova asked.

"Iona and Ian?"

"Yes, despite so much tragedy they have built a strong, enduring love for one another, the kind William and I never had a chance to create." Her voice faded off.

Rolfe rose to stir up the fire, sending small sparks up and out through the vent in the roof above them. He didn't dare look at her.

"You're young," he offered, "and may yet find their kind of love."

"Might I?" Leova responded looking at him carefully.

"Yes," replied Rolfe and turned to face her. He carefully cupped her chin in his hand. She gently took his hand in hers and removed it from her face, then after studying it silently, she raised it to her lips and planted a light kiss in his palm. He leaned forward, intending to kiss her cheek lightly, but before he could, she carefully folded his fingers and placed his hand so that it rested against his knee.

"Not yet," Leova whispered, "Not now. My body is...changing...and my spirit as well. It takes all my concentration just to make sense of what has happened in these last months, to forgive myself, forgive myself.... Maybe someday, later...later...." Leova's voiced trailed off, then she turned toward Rolfe, looking him full in the face. "Let's not speak of love again—at least not until I'm ready. Please?"

"Of course," Rolfe had replied, and locked away his feelings for her. Now, however, still recalling the feel of his hand in hers, Rolfe acknowledged fully that he wanted her as his wife—and that he would have to wait until the baby was born before he could even speak of it.

Buds and new seedlings had been appearing for some time before the night in which Leova awoke and knew that her time had come. She called out for Iona, and quickly all three of her companions were at the door. She didn't have to speak before they started to take action.

"I'll go for the midwife," Ian announced.

"Rolfe," Iona's insistent voice ordered. "Hold Lady Leova's hand." Feeling commanded, Rolfe took the small hand in his own, instantly surprised at the force with which she gripped his fingers.

Iona continued, "Squeezing her hand in yours will take her mind off the discomfort."

"I'd not describe what I feel as 'discomfort'," Leova said sarcastically. "It's pain!" The pain subsided momentarily, only to return with greater force. As she watched Iona prepare for the birth, bringing out the swaddling clothes she'd woven, setting water to boil, and stacking extra sheeting for the bed where she could reach it easily, Leova bit her lip, trying to restrain her desire to scream.

The older woman, suddenly aware of the strength of Leova's restraint, issued an order. "Scream."

"Scream loudly," echoed the midwife from the door. Coming to Leova, the midwife placed both her hands on Leova's stomach. "Tell me when the pains come, and I will help you push." Turning to Iona, she nodded approvingly as she noted the water and cloths and other supplies. "Bring in the birthing stool," she ordered Ian, and then keep the fire going—we need it warm in here."

"Now," Leova shouted, and immediately the midwife's strong hands grasped her stomach.

"That's right, let the child come as it will," she demanded. The two older women set up the birthing stool and had Rolfe help Leova to mount it. As soon as she was steady, he attempted to move away, but she once again grasped his hand and pleaded, "Stay here; I need you."

Rolfe wished he were elsewhere, but seeing the pain and fear in Leova's eyes, he could not move away. He nodded, and following the instructions from the midwife, began to rub her arms and sponge off her sweaty forehead as the hours went on. After a time, the pain became steady, rather than intermittent, and Leova's screams more strident. After several more tortured screams, the midwife turned to Iona. "Here, put your hands where mine are, and push hard when I tell you."

Then the midwife knelt before Leova and pulled her gown

over the young woman's knees. Leova leaned forward and grasped the midwife's shoulders, desperation in her eyes.

"Be patient, my dear," the old woman laughed. "You'll soon be a mother." Everyone in the room took a deep breath, and time stood still for a bit, as Leova pushed once more. But the tension was broken within several minutes by a different sound: a baby's cry—and by Leova's "Thank God!" as she collapsed against the high back of the birthing stool.

Rolfe looked down at the midwife as she held the baby. The woman, working quickly, picked up a knife, dipped it into a kettle and cut the cord that still connected it to its mother. Then she set about transforming the small body by cleaning away the pink and bloody residue. Small white arms and legs pumped up and down as the red-faced creature howled until Iona wrapped the small creature in the swaddling blanket Leova had told William about so many months ago. Rolfe could hear Leova's heavy breathing. He once again wiped away the sweat that poured from her face.

"The baby?" she whispered weakly. "Where is my baby?"

Smiling, the midwife took the little bundle from Iona and placed it against Leova's breasts. "You have a son," she beamed. "A strong healthy boy to carry on his father's name.

Rolfe and Leova looked at the tiny living bundle. "Wulfram. We'll name him, Wulfram." Leova pronounced the name carefully, making sure that the child, as well as all those who witnessed his birth, would know his name.

The next three months passed rapidly. Iona and Ian delighted in serving as Wulfram's grandparents, both of them doting on him to such an extent that Leova was convinced he would become the world's most spoiled little boy—not that she wasn't complicit in his spoiling. Leova relished motherhood, spending many hours rocking and nursing Wulfram, singing the same lullabies that Gwynned had sung to her and Hilda so many years ago.

Even Rolfe was surprised by his own reactions to Wulfram. After the ordeal of the baby's birth, he found that he embraced the child as his own, often having to remind himself that he was not the baby's father.

As the weather warmed, Iona and Ian began to talk about enlarging the garden space. It became more and more evident that they were considering settling in permanently. One morning in early July, they both tarried after breaking their fast and spoke hesitantly to Leova.

"We don't wish to leave you without help, but we've heard of a family that might be our kin," they said apologetically. "We thought we'd seek them out; the trip will only last a week or so."

"Yes, yes, please do go. We'll be fine." Seeing them look questioningly at each other, Leova laughed "I may not cook as well as you, Iona, but we'll not starve. Please, stay as long as you wish. Harvest would be when we most need help."

"We will plan to return before that time," Ian assured her.

"Then you must take the horses," Leova insisted. "Rolfe and I have no need of them and, in fact, their absence will make our chores a bit easier!"

"We'll travel more quickly and easily if we ride," Iona told her husband, who looked ready to refuse.

"Well, then," he grumbled, "We'll take the horses...just so we can return in time for harvest."

The following morning, Iona and Ian were off on their journey, and Rolfe and Leova had complete control of the small farm. "I hope they find some of their family. The loss of Wyomina sits hard on them. Discovering nieces and nephews, young people, may sooth their pain," Leova commented to Rolfe as she turned back into the cottage, responding to Wulfram's hungry wails.

"I'll be in the yard, making more arrows, he said. "It's a good time to go hunting, but I'll put it off until they return. I don't want you to be here alone with Wulfram."

Leova smiled at his concern, thankful that he cared so much for them. She lifted the baby out of the small crib Ian had built for Wulfram. He'd proudly placed it in the corner of Leova's sleeping quarters before the baby was born, and Leova took great delight in its careful construction. After feeding him, Leova put Wulfram back in the crib and stood gazing at him as he slept peacefully. He resembled William, she thought, but strangely, some of Rolfe's features were also in the bone structure of Wulfram's face. The residents of the small settlement had quite naturally assumed Rolfe was Wulfram's father, and he did nothing to disabuse them. He had laughed when one excited woman had gone on at length about how much the baby resembled him.

But Leova saw William in their baby: his smile, the color of his eyes and hair, his nose, the way his ears sat against his cheeks. As she stared at Wulfram, filled with her love for William, she felt her sense of guilt melting away, feeling permission to begin to accept her lack of responsibility for his death. Perhaps, perhaps...she could finally shed that blackness in her memory. Wulfram looked up at his mother and Leova saw William's forgiveness in their child's face.

When she returned to the fire, Rolfe was sitting before it. He offered her a cup of the mead he had helped a neighbor produce. Leova took it and tried to sip a bit even though she thought it bitter. Rolfe laughed at the face she made, and then the two sat and watched the fire as it waxed and waned. Never having been alone in the cottage before made them both feel a bit uncomfortable. Usually Iona bustled about, giving Ian orders and setting the place "to rights" as she called it. Without the conversation and company of the older couple, Leova and Rolfe became more and more aware of each other.

Leova had never been as happy as she was at that moment. Happier even, she admitted ruefully, than when she was a child with Hilda. Happier now than she had been with William. Did that make her a traitor of sorts, she wondered? The fire and the beer warmed her body and loosened her tongue.

"Rolfe," she murmured, not daring to look him in the face, "Do you still want me?"

A look of disbelief crossed Rolfe's face; he knew not what to say.

His silence engendered a frown on Leova's face. Leova looked down at her hands folded on her lap. "I know I'm no longer as pretty as I was, and I no longer have beautiful clothes and soft hands. In truth, I'm rather raggedy—just a peasant girl." She looked up at Rolfe, and suddenly he found that he could not tell whether she was serious or poking fun at herself or teasing him. He also realized that it mattered not what she was doing—he wanted her.

Taking a deep breath, Rolfe dared to ask, "Do you want me?"

"Yes, yes, I do, Rolfe," she spoke quickly, afraid to stop and think. "Very much. I haven't allowed myself to feel that until now, but—yes, yes."

Rolfe picked her up lightly and spun around in the center of the room, laughing aloud.

"Then it's off to my room," Leova pronounced, looking as pleased as any peasant wife in love with her husband.

Rolfe stopped still in mid whirl. "We'll wake the baby!"

"No, he'll sleep soundly—for at least three hours anyway."

"Then let's begin," Rolfe whispered. And so they did.

The Return

An obviously joyful Iona and Ian returned, as promised, just before harvest time. They'd had the good fortune to locate Ian's sister, three of her grandchildren, and several nieces. Leova watched them with pleasure as she listened to stories about people with strange names and connections that she couldn't get straight. That didn't matter; the reunion had lifted some of the cloud from their faces.

"We've decided to stay here," Iona told her, slapping her hands together happily. "I know you'll be returning to Lothlar before long; you have a mother there that you love and who'll want to help raise her grandson. Our life is here now. We'll remain and find a way to pay you for the cottage once you decide to leave." She stopped, realizing that she'd made too many assumptions. "That is, if that's still your plan."

"I have no plans, but you're right, we need to forge them soon. Rolfe and I..." she paused, her cheeks reddening. "Rolfe and I...will be sleeping together in my chambers from now on."

Iona hugged her mightily. "I'm happy for you. My blessings on your union." Suddenly, a bit of a roar and guffaw came from the open door. Ian stepped in, smiling his approval. "Well, it's about time!"

Iona patted Leova's shoulder to reassure her. "Don't worry yourself, my dear; the two of us have talked of it often. You belong to each other."

Two weeks after the major harvesting had been completed Rolfe asked Leova to walk with him. Leaving Wulfram in Iona's capable hands, Leova took Rolfe's arm, content to spend some time alone with the man she loved. Not long after they'd passed the newly turned fields, they paused at the edge of the forest. Rolfe kissed her gently and impulsively he asked, "Leova, do you wish to stay here? Go elsewhere? Return home? We need to decide what will happen now that Wulfram's arrived."

She bent her head and stared at the ground as she thought.

"Rolfe," she said at last, looking up, "I miss my mother, and now that I've seen how overjoyed Iona and Ian are to be reunited with their family, I realize that I can't deprive my own mother of the pleasure of a grandchild. Lothlar is, after all, my hall, and Wulfram has a role in its future—as well as in the future of Stonehart."

"I agree, but we need to decide how we present ourselves when we return. I want to marry you, and claim Wulfram as my heir."

"What's the need of that, Rolfe? Only my parents know that he isn't your son. And," she touched his cheek lightly, "I'm as married to you as anyone could possibly be. We need no church ceremony, no priest."

"You don't. I don't. However, I don't trust my mother. Were she ever to discover that we were not legally married, she might...." He paused, "I don't know what she might do: I can't think like her, but I know she will stop at nothing to regain control over our lands! Trust me, my love. On the way back, we need to locate a priest and satisfy the laws and conventions. Besides, we would not want to jeopardize Wulfram in any way. If you and I are married, he will have claim to William's land, my land, and your land, claims my mother will be unable to deny."

"Then we shall do it, but not because that will make us married in any way I consider important."

Turning her toward him, Rolfe laughed. "And what ways do

you consider important, my love? Perhaps we can figure that out under the tree over there."

Ian and Iona were proud to be witnesses at a simple marriage ceremony with a local priest officiating. Leova found herself a bit surprised by a wish that somehow the forest women could have been there to bless the union also. Inside her head she heard her mother's voice wishing the same wish.

By mid-September, Rolfe and Leova had completed preparations for the journey home. Worried about Iona and Ian, they installed one of the new-found nephews and his wife in the house, giving them a home in return for helping their aunt and uncle with the farm.

As they loaded the last of their provisions on the horses, Leova became convinced that the couple was far more upset about Wulfram's leaving than about anything else. They had become attached to him, surely as a substitute for the grandchild they would never have. After Leova had mounted her horse, she reached for the baby, whom Iona relinquished reluctantly.

"I know you'll miss him," she told the weeping woman. "We'll return with the baby whenever we can—and you must try to visit us also. It's only about a fortnight away if you travel steadily." Even as she said it, she knew the journey was one the couple would be unlikely to ever make. On impulse, she withdrew an armlet from the pouch at her side and placed it in Iona's hand. "Keep this in remembrance of me."

"No, my love," Iona protested. "I'll remember you without any trinkets at all. Keep that for your own pretty arm."

"I insist that you take it," Leova replied, "I want to know that you will always have something of mine. It's only fair. I take something of you with me...the love you have bestowed on Wulfram and me."

Iona continued to resist, but Leova gave her no choice. "Iona, keep it for a year. If you still don't want it after that, you can visit me and return it." Seeing the puzzled look on Iona's face, she laughed. "Of course, I won't accept it, but perhaps you'll come believing that I will." Tears welled up in Leova's eyes. She knew it was time to leave.

Rolfe was not finding the leave taking any easier than Leova did. He tried to keep his dignity by shaking Ian's hand firmly, but then the hand shake turned into a tight hug, first for the old man and then for Iona. During the past year, they had been parents to him in ways his own father and mother had never been.

"I'll never forget you. And mark my words, I'll come back to fetch you if you don't come to visit us!"

And then—with nothing more to say—they took to the road, as excited about the life ahead as they were sad to leave the old life behind.

Ten days later, Leova guided her horse onto the well-known lane, both happy and apprehensive at the sight of her family hall through the trees. That there seemed to be no outward sign of change was reassuring. Although she had greatly feared that her family's fortune might have continued on its downward trend, she was far more concerned with how her return might be greeted. She had, after all, left without saying goodbye.

As the travelers approached the hall, the sounds of activity behind the palisades were the usual sounds of the mid-afternoon. The main gate stood open, evidence that her family expected no danger from the outside. As they passed through the gate, Leova felt a sudden surge of joy at the sight of home. At first, no one paid any attention, but then Hannah appeared, walking slowly, absorbed in her own thoughts. As she neared the gate, she raised her head and found herself looking directly at Leova. For a moment, she stopped and stared, as unbelieving as a person who comes upon a ghost from the past. As Leova dismounted, Hannah dropped the just butchered chickens she had been carrying and threw her arms around her long lost mistress.

After a bone-cracking hug, the happy woman turned toward the hall, calling out the news. "She's home! She's home!" Hannah stopped a passing boy, "Little Sebbi! Rouse the household—get Gwynedd, tell my Lady Pagany and Lord Bertram! Don't forget Jankin. Tell them My Lady Leova's come home!"

As she turned back to her mistress, she noticed Rolfe and the small golden-haired baby he held. She looked quizzically at Leova and then at Rolfe and the child.

Leova laughed and answered her unspoken question, "Yes, Hannah, he's my son."

After that, the small world of the hall thundered with movement. Wulfram, frightened at the noise and the newness of location, began to howl. His mother took him from Rolfe, comforted him, and then held him up so the growing circle of servants and guards could see him. Gwynedd elbowed her way through the crowd and, with a cry of joy, embraced both Wulfram and Leova; the tears and sobs rising in her throat made her unable to speak. Leova felt the tears rise, too. Suddenly, the crowd quieted and Leova looked up to see her mother and father in the doorway of the hall. Handing Wulfram quickly to Rolfe, she ran to her parents and, even though they held out their arms to receive her, she dropped on her knees before them, her head bowed humbly.

"Mother, father—can you forgive the pain I've caused you?" Leova raised her head, her eyes pleading with her parents. "I want so to come home. To bring my child up in this place where you raised me."

Pagany raised her daughter slowly and cupping her chin in the palm of her hand, stared into her daughter's tearful eyes. "You have been missed. Come inside."

All formality disappeared as mother, father, and infant embraced. Beckoning for Rolfe and Wulfram to join them, Leova and her family started to withdraw into Lothlar, but just as they reached the doorway, Jankin appeared. Full of wonder at the sight of his young master and mistress, the young man ran to Leova's side and went down on one knee before her. Taking his hand, Leova pulled him upright and impulsively embraced him. As he backed off, blushing, she laughed as his discomfort.

"You're always here when I need you," was all she could think to say. "We will send for you soon."

Once inside the hall, Pagany and Bertram seated themselves on one of the benches. Leova winced as she noticed how much more slowly the two of them moved. Seating herself on a facing bench and beckoning Rolfe to sit beside her, she spoke quietly, "I have come back with your grandchild. Doesn't he look a bit like his father? He is a good child, healthy and happy."

"Let me hold him, child," said the older woman.

Rolfe placed the baby in her arms, and she presented him to Bertram. "Look at this wonder, my husband. What a gift!"

Leova, seeing the tears on her mother's face, started to speak, "Mother, I'm so sorry about leaving...."

"We'll talk of these matters later," Pagany cut her off abruptly. "I want to know other things now." She faced her daughter, looking deeply in her eyes. "How is it with the two of you?"

Pagany turned toward Rolfe, and Leova sensed the real question.

"Rolfe and I are married." Wordlessly, Bertram shook Rolfe's hand, his smile reflecting the relief he felt at securing the estate as well as the joy he felt at his daughter's marriage.

Pagany remained perplexed. "I don't understand," she said. "If you were going to marry, why run off?"

Seeing her daughter's face, Pagany realized that Leova had no intention of talking about the marriage or discussing the reasons for leaving home. She decided it was best to let the matter go. Now that her daughter had returned home, there would be time to solve the mystery. She asked no more questions.

Relieved, Leova asked the question she had repressed: "Where is Regan?"

"He is off to make his report to his mother about matters here, but enough talk; I see that you're all exhausted. Let's find a place for you to rest; your old room, I believe, will do nicely. The room next to it will be perfect for a nursery."

The following morning, Leova awoke from a much-needed sleep. Rolfe, who had slept beside her, was gone. Wulfram, she supposed, was still sleeping in the adjoining room. She stretched luxuriously. How odd to have all this room after a year in the cramped hut they'd shared with Iona and Ian.

As soon as she stirred, Gwynedd appeared at her side. "I'll see to your hair," she offered, but after Leova was settled before a mirror and Gwynedd struggled with the tangled locks, her long time nurse burst into tears. Leova turned to her loyal servant and held her tightly. When the sobs subsided, Leova tried to divert any questions her servant might have by asking the first of the many questions on her own mind. "Gwynedd, what's happened while I've been gone?"

Gwynedd hesitated. "Your father and mother are the ones to answer that question."

"Of course, of course, but you'll tell me everything, and they tend to hide matters they think I might not need to know."

Gwynedd chuckled. "You're probably right. Besides, Lord Rolfe has been in deep conversation with your father for over an hour; each has probably told the other everything of importance! He'll tell you later."

"Are you reluctant to tell me because the news is bad?" responded Leova.

"Oh, no. No...it could have been worse," Gently she started to share information. "Allmana claimed this land on the basis of your marriage to William—her right, she argued, because you were no longer here. Although your father protested at first, he finally realized there was nothing he could do and just retreated into himself." Gwynedd's voice dropped almost to a whisper. "I think your leaving was the last blow he could bear."

Leova pressed her palms against her chest, pushing hard to relieve the pain in her heart. How could she have thought her father didn't love her?

"Luckily," continued Gwynedd, "Allmana ordered Ragen to take charge, and he's not given to ordering people about. He simply let your mother and father stay in control while he made reports to his mother. Whether she pays attention to them, isn't clear," Gwynedd paused and didn't continue until Leova motioned her to go on. "We've begun to hear strange stories about Allmana. She's getting more peculiar—nothing she does is understandable."

Rolfe appeared, and Gwynedd immediately stopped talking.

After he embraced his wife and dismissed her old nurse, Rolfe sat down to talk. "You need to know what I've learned from your parents," he said, his voice full of concern. Quickly he confirmed and elaborated upon what Gwynedd had started to tell Leova.

"Your father and I have agreed not to send for Ragen yet. None of us want Allmana to know that I have returned much less that we're married, for fear of how she might react. Regan will know best when and how to deliver the news. Apparently, the old woman has taken to sleeping all day and prowling the hall and grounds at night. She often doesn't seem to know where she is, and she just as often insists that her dead husbands pursue her."

"Remember what Iona and Ian told us of their suspicions about the deaths of both of her husbands," Leova said. "Could the specters of her husbands rightfully haunt her?"

"Perhaps," replied Rolfe. "On the other hand, a guilty conscience might account for the ghosts she thinks follow her about. We'll wait for Ragen to tell us more, even though I'm not anxious to hear it!"

Ragen appeared two days later, and finding Rolfe and Leova married pleased him immensely. He hugged each of them together and separately again and again. Ragen also took an instant delight in Wulfram and spent many hours with Pagany and the boy. He would have made a good father, Leova thought. Not the least of Regan's joy was the prospect of turning the major responsibilities of Lothlar over to his brother and Leova. He took no pleasure in being a landowner. Together the brothers decided that Rolfe would accompany Ragen when he returned to Allmana's hall. Neither felt any need to hurry, but the following week, both acknowledged their strong obligation to travel to Stonehart. In another three days they returned. Rolfe was visibly distressed by what he had witnessed there. His mother had gone fully mad. Unkempt, confused, she ate little and slept almost all day every day. She treated Rolfe as though he had never been gone, and when he had told her of his marriage to Leova, she had snapped back, "I know that!" before turning from him and walking away as if the matter didn't concern her in the least.

At night she wandered the hall in her nightclothes, shrieking at apparitions unseen by others. As dawn arrived, she climbed into bed, often sleeping until the sun set. In the long run, Rolfe realized that there was little they could do for Allmana. Ragen had procured the services of a healer whose drugs and potions accomplished nothing, but who had agreed to take up residence in the hall and care for the raving woman.

"My mother has receded into a world where we cannot reach her," Rolfe said. "We can only hope that she causes less trouble in this state than she did in what we thought of as 'her right mind'."

Leova shared Regan's hopes, but when it came to Allmana, she found it impossible to think of her as harmless. "I worry about Wulfram. Do you think she could harm him?"

"No, dear sister-by-law," said Regan. "Her days of wreaking harm have come to an end. The fortunes of both Stonehart and Lothlar are in the hands of you and Rolfe, and both of you will protect the land and the people you love—and who love you."

They stood for a moment, three young people who now had immense responsibility, and then with a laugh, they went together to see Wulfram, the future Lord of Lothlar and Stonehart.

Chapter 9: Hilda Finds Her Calling (879-888)

The grounds of the monastery at Whitby had been extensively damaged, the original buildings destroyed. Stones from the wall and from what must have been a large refectory lay scattered about, smaller ones in piles, larger ones where they had fallen during the raid. Only a minor part of the community had been rebuilt, but the nuns had done their best to restore what they could. The church's doors had great axe gouges in them, but they hung true, their hinges restored, the great lock new and polished. Around the buildings flowers had been planted, and carefully tended shrubs lined walks from building to building.

"They've been faithful with their work," Hilda thought. "But more needs to be done—surely I can do service here."

Abbess Frideswith beckoned her to follow. "Come with me, my daughter. You must be properly clothed. Once you're attired decently, I'll hear your story." Turning toward Caedmon, she motioned him toward one of the small buildings, "Please, take some food."

An hour later, outfitted in a peasant's dress and cleansed of the dirt and dust of travel, Hilda sat down beside the elderly nun in the shaded cloister, prepared to tell her a great deal, but perhaps not everything.

"My story could be long, Abbess, but I'd rather tell you the sum of my trials and the hope I have for living within your community."

The Abbess nodded, her eyes never leaving Hilda's face.

"I am Hilda, daughter of Lord Ecgbert of Yorvik. Before my mother died, I was forced to promise her—and God—to enter the monastery at Buxton. Almost immediately, it became obvious that I wasn't suited for such a life—no excuse for what followed—I knew that I'd leave the monastery before taking vows." Hilda paused, wondering how much she needed to tell the Abbess.

"What brought you here, my child?" Abbess Frideswith asked.

"I'll just say this; I...I sinned. Sinned gravely enough that when I was forced to leave Buxton to escape enemies, I was told never to return. I'd rather the nature of my sin remain between God and me—if that's acceptable...?"

"It's not my place to judge you. I merely have to understand why you've come to us seeking help."

Hilda looked carefully at the elderly woman, trying to determine her reaction, but seeing nothing in the woman's face but kindness, she hurried on to complete the speech she'd been planning for days.

"After leaving Buxton, I spent time at my father's hall, Highhear, and a realization began to awaken in me that God had called me to His service. Strangely enough, despite my initial anger at my mother, I came to know that she had forced me in the direction that I might well have chosen of my own free will had I known that path existed. Now no one else will make my pledge for me; I would do so voluntarily and with all my heart, renouncing the world outside the monastery. I would serve wherever and however God wishes. I hope it can be here with you, but I would go where He wills. "

Abbess Frideswith seemed to be turning over Hilda's words in her mind, remaining silent until Hilda began to fear her petition would be rejected. Finally, picking up the young woman's hand and holding it gently, the Abbess spoke.

"The world seems quite small sometimes—and sometimes quite vast," she said. "Years have passed since I had contact with the community at Buxton; however, I do know of your father, your mother—and *you*, my daughter—as we all know of the families who have protected our homes from the invaders. Your sin has not been revealed to me, and I can't confirm that God has forgiven you. Only your confessor can intercede for you with God."

Hilda nodded, relieved that this woman willingly refused to pass judgment on her. Abbess Frideswith had not finished, however. "Your desire to take vows and leave the world must be tested. This test will involve hardship but that burden will be lightened with community. Even a princess such as yourself must learn to serve others. Everyone at Whitby shares work as well as bread."

Hilda felt the tears well up. "I'm humbly grateful to you, and I'll happily strive to perform any trial you set for me." She hesitated, then plunged ahead. "May I make one last request as a princess?" The Abbess nodded slightly. "My servant, Caedmon, has braved much to help me reach you. God would not want me to abandon him. Is there a place for him at Whitby? He's a good man and a hard worker. He'd serve you well: I have released him from all obligations to me."

"He'll be quite welcome, my daughter—we always have need of good, hard-working men," the Abbess said with a laugh and a smile. "Let's go to meet your new sisters; I know they'll be happy to greet you, but they will not push you to answer questions about your life if you desire to remain silent." She paused for a moment before rising, but then continued with a hint of wonder. "You bear the name of our founder; perhaps you know that. Maybe God sends you as some kind of messenger to us." The Abbess put a gentle but strong hand on Hilda's head. "Bless you, my daughter, in this your spiritual journey."

Hilda and Caedmon settled gratefully into the routines of the abbey, enjoying its peace and security as well as the daily rhythms of the monastery. As the Abbess had said, the nuns accepted Hilda without hesitation. And the mostly elderly men and women servants delighted in having a young strong lad in their midst, not only to ease their burdens but also because many of their own sons and daughters had disappeared during the intermittent onslaughts of the Vikings.

Unlike the monastery at Buxton, Hilda was not assigned to any easy task like minding the scriptorium. Work began early in the morning: tending livestock, gathering eggs, and milking cows. The baking of bread had to be done each morning, and the stews for the mid-day meal set to simmer over the hearth. Throughout the day, there were fields to be cleared, gardens to be tended, and a multitude of garments prepared from the busy looms had to be washed and folded for those who would wear them. The community retired not long after sunset, exhausted both from the tasks which fed and clothed them daily and also by the work which had to be done in order to prepare them for the harsh winter months.

While the work done by the nuns at Whitby proved more severe than that at Buxton, the prayers that came every three hours remained the same, their comforting moments breaking up the demanding tasks of the day, but unfortunately also interrupting the much needed sleep of the night. Often these devotions were without the services of a priest, who, Abbess Frideswith explained, could only come at rare intervals. Each season, one or two priests would make the journey down from the northern or western houses, traveling between the many monasteries which had fallen into disrepair and ruin. Hilda was shocked to discover that the Abbess herself administered the bread and the wine to the women in her charge because priests came to Whitby so intermittently.

"The bishop knows, my daughter, that it is better to have an abbess oversee communion than to forego it for lack of a priest," Frideswith said without any hint of defensiveness. "When I was young, we sisters lived in chastity alongside a community of monks. Then a priest resided on the grounds and ministered to our needs. That all changed many years ago. Now we are only women monastics. My own duties are limited. I do not and cannot hear confession. We confess directly to our God during the long months when no priest is available. When a priest comes, we make full confession so that he can assign penance, and we can be forgiven and made truly clean for communion."

Gladly accepting Abbess Frideswith's reasoning, Hilda smiled to herself, thinking of what her own mother would have thought of such a practice. But soon the limitations of the Abbess' authority became obvious. At Prime, several weeks after her arrival, Hilda sensed a slight stirring in the collected group of sisters and then an unaccustomed low murmuring. A stern glance from Abbess Frideswith stilled the momentary disquiet, but within seconds the Abbess left her seat at the front of the small church and moved swiftly down the aisle through the main doors. Shortly after, she reappeared, accompanied by an elderly priest who nodded benevolently at the kneeling women. An air of expectancy became

311

palpable in the small chapel. The prayers continued but now several male voices joined in the ritual "amen." Hilda, unable to restrain herself, turned to peer toward the rear where she could see the bowed heads of three priests. Happily, she resumed her prayers, believing that, finally, she would be able to take her vows. At the end of the service, when responses were no longer needed, Hilda lingered at her prayers, giving herself a few more moments with the peace that came in the church. Although she had heard the sisters leave, she was surprised to find herself all alone in the chapel. She rose hastily, knowing that chores awaited her, but as she turned to go down the aisle, she saw the figure of the elderly priest at the doorway. He seemed to be awaiting her.

"Sister Hilda, I'm Father Jerome—your confessor and guide for the next few days as we discuss your wish to make your vows. Shall we walk together for a while?" Hilda joined him at the doorway, ready to talk and even more ready to listen.

Father Jerome had served the abbey as a young priest before the time of destruction, and he willingly shared his memories with the young woman. As they strolled among the fallen stones, he pointed out the wall that paralleled the coastline and the bay, and the general outlines of a much larger church extending beyond the walls of the present small chapel. Over a low wall, they could see the cemetery where many stones lay broken. "Some of your princely ancestors may be buried there," Jerome told her as he guided her by the cemetery and then past the remnants of a group of small buildings set far from the main building.

"The kitchen stood here, and there a smithy. We stand in the nuns' quarters; weaving and sewing were their main activities as they are today, especially through the winter months. And here," he added, almost as an afterthought, "are the walls which once enclosed the scriptorium."

He bent over, arising with a rusty stylus between his fingers as though presenting proof of his memory. The small instrument caused Hilda to recall her own pleasant days in the scriptorium at Buxton, but immediately that pleasant memory faded as she remembered what followed. Jerome noted the change in the young woman's countenance. "Tell me, my daughter," he said gently, "Why have you chosen to take vows—what brought you to this place?"

"Father Jerome, I have confessed my sins to God and I believe—or hope—He has forgiven me, but I understand that I must confess to you also before we can talk about taking vows. I would not presume to know the church's requirements for my atonement."

"Yes, that is so," he concurred. "Let's attend to your confession before we speak of your place at Whitby."

The small chapel resonated with the business of God. The bare feet of a kneeling sister protruded from the hanging tapestry of the small confessional on one of the inner walls. At the front of the church, another priest prepared to baptize an infant whose mother was one of the young servants who served the abbey. Mother and father and godparents smiled with pride at the new life being given into God's hands, but as Hilda listened to the ritual that would guarantee the infant a place in God's kingdom, she could feel the tears coming. Had her child been baptized? Would God receive her baby into His blessings, into His heaven? Did the babe still live? Despite her resolve to put the past behind her, she let out a deep sob, causing the group assembled before the small altar to turn toward her. The priest paused momentarily, and she could see the infant in his arms as his raised hand made the sign of the cross with the baptismal water.

Leaving Father Jerome behind, Hilda fled, not wanting to bring her sadness to the happy group. She emerged into the sunlight, impelled to get away from the looks, from the memories. She ran along the path that led beyond the old walls of the monastery. Miserable, she dropped down on an uprooted headstone of the disrupted cemetery. Some maternal grief, long stored away, welled up inside her and inhabited her whole body. As her sobs subsided, more from fatigue than anything else, she felt a gentle hand on her head and turned to see the kindly face of Abbess Frideswith.

"My child, my child," were her only words. Hearing these words, Hilda sat up and allowed the older woman to engulf her. In the arms of the Abbess, she continued to weep, only slightly aware of the tender hand that stroked her hair. Her sobs slowly subsided, then faded away altogether. Abbess Frideswith continued to stroke the disheveled locks of the young princess and waited for her to speak.

"Oh, Abbess," came the choked sound of her voice, "I fear I am not worthy to be one of you. The worldly loss which I suffered is so great that I find I'm unable to reconcile or accept it. I did not know until just now how greatly it affected me. I am not worthy to be one of you, not worthy to receive God's forgiveness."

"That, my child, is not your decision or mine. Who told you that your sin was too great for even God to forgive?"

"Bishop Ceolwulf condemned me for sinning in the eyes of God. Abbess Edyth and her sister Abbess Moira declared that I had disgraced my family and their abbeys.   Both sent me away because I was unworthy to be in a monastery. " Hilda shuddered, remembering Abbess Moira's parting words: "You have brought disgrace to my monastery, to my sister's monastery."

"Time passes. Perhaps today neither abbess nor Bishop Ceolwulf would make such judgments. Ask Father Jerome to transmit the words of God to you. I believe you will not be found unworthy. He will not condemn you."

Silence united the two women. Hilda, comforted by the older woman's compassion and forgiveness, gradually became peaceful. She was now willing to accept whatever fate lay before her. If she were deemed unworthy to enter the order as a nun, she would stay on nonetheless and contribute as she could. If she were deemed worthy, she would serve God in any way He opened for her.

The Abbess patted her shoulder soothingly. "Rise, my child, let us return to Father Jerome. I'm sure he is ready to hear your confession."

It was a troubled Father Jerome who emerged from his side of the confessional some time later. Hilda's sin did not surprise him. In truth, more than one holy establishment had been tainted by prolonged sins between nuns and priests, many of which, he was sure, were never confessed to any priest. Most of the double monasteries, an arrangement more prevalent in the north than in the south of the country, had never reopened after their destruction by the red-haired ones. Saint Cuthbert himself had condemned the practice of allowing men and women to inhabit the same monastery. Bodily hungers, he had warned, are indeed the weapons of the devil.

Jerome concurred, but, surely, he thought, such hungers are the blessings of God upon those who have sworn fealty to one another in the worldly fashion. This young princess had indeed suffered much from early childhood, from her parents' abandonment, from her banishment from two monasteries, and from her treks through punishing wastelands.

She had known only a few years of peace off in the west, and had succumbed to sin only once. Her child had undoubtedly been spirited off somewhere, and she would very likely never set eyes upon it. However, her contrition was undeniably genuine, and he believed her ready to renounce the world. Her penance, which would begin at the start of the next day, would consist of nine months of solitude in which she would entertain no words with anyone.

He had promised to return at the end of that time and talk to her once again about her commitment, though he was fairly certain Hilda would be unwavering. Something in her quiet acceptance of the penance assured him that she welcomed and would profit from it, that her resolve would only be strengthened through meditation and contemplation.

Penance

Abbess Frideswith assigned Hilda to one of the small cell-like rooms that stretched out from the refectory toward the hillside so that she could begin her seclusion. Designed originally as private cells for prayer and contemplation, these rooms, at least half of which were still in ruins, were perfectly suited for Hilda's penance. This suitability had two sources: first, the spare and dark interior provided no relief from the spiritual task before her, and secondly, the room closely resembled the small room where she had given birth to her child. In that small space, there was nothing to interfere with her contemplation of her sin and her calling. The stone walls held only a crucifix which hung over the narrow cot with its straw mattress. The only other furnishing in the small cell was a loom for weaving. The monastery had to be self-supporting, and so no one, perhaps least of all a penitent, could be excused from working. Weaving could be done in silence; many of the women had learned to recite prayers to the rhythm of the shuttle as they produced cloth. Twice a day, food would be left at the door, but since she was doing penance, the meal would be little more than the simplest of sustenance.

For the next nine months, Hilda would pray and work, leaving her room only for regular prayers in the chapel and for two brief walks every day. Knowing that her atonement required that she keep silent, speaking only with her God rather than with any human soul, Hilda sought out Caedmon that evening to inform him about her upcoming confinement. She was accustomed to seeking him out almost every day, sometimes just to greet him, sometimes to reflect with him about what the situation might be at home in Ecgbert's hall. Her father often occupied her thoughts, causing her to wonder if she would ever again be welcomed into the hall—or even if she wanted to be. Had he looked for her? Was everyone safe? She could not dwell upon the pain that she must have caused him and her old companion, Ethel. At times when her pain was the sharpest, she longed to feel her nurse's sheltering arms, to once again be soothed as she had been for her trivial childhood miseries. This last evening before her confinement, she sat with Caedmon and gazed back toward the moors that they had crossed together some weeks before. Caedmon spoke of his life as it had once been, of his family, his brother and his many sisters. He missed them, but in his voice Hilda heard something that led her to examine his expression closely.

"Tell me, Caedmon, am I right—you sound almost happy that you're here and not back at my father's hall?" Caedmon's face reddened and he nodded. "Good. I have worried about you and felt much guilt because you left so much behind to follow me. Yet, I would never have arrived here without you...." Her voice trailed off.

"My Lady, you need not worry about me," Caedmon hastened to assure her. "I'm most happy here." He ducked his head shyly. "I met a young woman who tends the hives and oversees the making of honey and mead. Her name is Alanya." Caedmon blushed again. "She teaches me how to handle the bees."

"I see," responded Hilda, smiling as she understood what the rest of the story must be. "And perhaps, I think, she teaches more than what is directly taught."

Caedmon nodded, his smile beaming. He continued thoughtfully, "Alanya and I have discovered a strange thing. She learned her craft from her mother, once the abbey's beekeeper, before the red-haired ones attacked."

"And have her mother and father given their blessing to your union?" Hilda asked.

"She has no one to approve or disapprove other than the nuns here at the abbey. During the attack of the enemy from the sea, her mother was greatly abused by the red-haired ones. She was beautiful and resistant, so they took great pleasure in defiling her. After the enemy left, much changed."

He paused. "Alanya does not know her father, he could be any of the men who...." Somehow Caedmon could not name the deed. He shook his head sadly and looked at Hilda. "Alanya is a good woman, even though she may be a child of brutality."

Hilda nodded. She could not condemn any child born outside marriage. "I have no doubt that both she and her mother are good people. What has happened to the mother? Why is she no longer here with her daughter?"

"Unhappily, Alanya's mother lost her faith; she could not understand why God would have permitted her to be so misused. Shortly after that, she began to behave strangely, and it often seemed that her spirit wandered far away from her body. Certainly her detachment from those around her grew. Eventually, even her daughter meant nothing to her. She'd leave Alanya to be cared for by others and slip outside the abbey walls. No one knew where she went. When Alanya was fifteen, her mother disappeared altogether. Occasionally, travelers report seeing her roaming the moors. She lives off the land, creating trouble for any red-haired man who attempts to cross the moors unprotected."

"And do you believe it was Alanya's mother who saved our lives back in the moors?"

"Yes," replied Caedmon. "Certainly it must have been. Alanya wishes to go seek the wild woman we encountered, to see if she is her mother. But first...." Caedmon reddened once more, "We plan to marry when the priest returns next month. Someday I will return to my family with a wife and perhaps with several young ones."

Hilda spoke solemnly to this man who had grown to maturity during their journey. "I shall be sorry to miss your wedding ceremony, but I will be with you in spirit. May I meet your Alanya before my penance begins?"

Caedmon was on his feet quickly. He returned just as quickly, guiding a fair-haired young woman by the hand. Hilda first took her hand and then, almost spontaneously, drew her close in a warm hug embrace. "I think I have done a good deed for both of you by providing the cause for Caedmon's being here. Once my penance has been served, we will meet again. I predict that the two of you will get along quite well. You, Alanya, will have a husband who is strong, courageous, and loyal, a young man whose wits are as strong as his arms and legs."

Hilda could see in Alanya's face a degree of assertiveness and self-confidence that guaranteed intelligence and strength in the woman. "And if I'm not mistaken," she added, "Caedmon has found in you a mate of equal, maybe even stronger, character."

"Thank you, Princess Hilda," Alanya responded, lowering her head.

Hilda faced the two of them and said firmly, "No, do not address me as a princess, either of you. That role I left behind when I chose to stay here and serve God."

Pressing their hands warmly between her own, Hilda looked at them sincerely. "I am happy for you. May you each be a blessing to the other forever."

With those words, Hilda turned and made her way back to the chapel. This night would be devoted to prayer, prayers for them and for the strength she would need to live the life she had chosen.

She woke several hours later at the sound of the midnight bell announcing Matins or the Office of Vigils, the first prayers of the new day whose purpose was to prepare monastics, men and women, for that day. This was the beginning of daily prayers, eight prayer ceremonies of the day devoted to praise of God. As she sat in chapel, isolated from the others as her penance dictated, Hilda tried to listen carefully to each word Abbess Frideswith spoke, but her mind wandered back over the last two years. Guiltily, she pulled herself back to the present and listened attentively to the familiar words of the liturgy, more than ever aware of how hard it would be to give her full attention to God.

Returning to her small space, she lay awake for hours staring toward the thatched roof as she envisaged the next nine months. At three o'clock she rose again to attend Lauds, praising once again the coming day, but still she could not sleep when she returned to her bed. Only as the world lightened with the approaching dawn did Hilda's eyes began to close in sleep. Moments later, it seemed, the bell rang for Prime, the first prayers of daylight. Once again, she sat alone in the chapel and listened to the words of the liturgy. After she returned to her little cell, Hilda knelt in prayer, her mind almost emptied of everything in order to be receptive to other messages.

After some unmeasured length of time, she heard a rustle at the door and turned to discover that food had been left there for her. After eating, she began weaving. The need to control her shuttle made it difficult to pray at first, but soon it moved swiftly back and forth as the words fell from her lips. Such work was always scheduled for the "little hours" of the prayer cycle. These daylight prayers, shorter than early morning and evening hours, allowed time for weaving and other tasks, but, too, a break for the weavers to stretch and rest their arms. All carefully orchestrated, Hilda thought to herself, to remind us of the attention due to a loving God. After the mid-afternoon prayers, she ate again and spent the rest of the evening on her knees in her cell. Only the calls for the evening services, Vespers and Compline, which were dedicated to thanksgiving for the blessings of the day just past, interrupted her personal acts of contrition, in which she confessed her sins and asked for God's forgiveness.

Thus the first of her days of silence and atonement passed in public and private prayer. The hours had gone by more quickly than she ever imagined, and the next days elapsed in exactly the same manner and at exactly the same pace. As she fell into the routine of prayer and work, Hilda began to wonder what purpose the penance served. It seemed too easy to fulfill her obligation to repent her sins.

"Perhaps," she thought, "the intent is to demonstrate my perseverance and determination to Father Jerome." Soon, however, Hilda's fervor began to cool and boredom replaced zeal. Her thirty-minute daily walks helped to calm her physical restlessness, but one morning, as she sat on one of the overturned headstones in the graveyard overlooking Whitby Bay, Hilda felt a greater restlessness, one that had little to do with the cramps in her arms and legs.

"Am I going to be able to tolerate—much less embrace—this regime?" she asked herself, making certain that she kept the question mute. Not liking the answer that was coming to her lips, Hilda roused herself and began to look more closely at the headstone on which she had been sitting. She could make out some letters in Englisc, the language she had learned to read at Buxton, but their incompleteness robbed them of meaning. Her curiosity whetted, she began to examine the other stones attentively. Almost all of them lay on their sides, cracked in several places. In her mind, she began to reassemble some of the pieces and reconstruct what each of them had etched into their surfaces. She became so absorbed in her mind-game that she neglected to return as she was required and was surprised to hear the bell for the next set of prayers. Guiltily, she hurried to the chapel and began mutely to castigate herself for not adhering strictly to the rules established for her penance. She vowed never again to lose track of time.

When she returned to her cell and finished her meager meal, she knelt once again on the small cot and stared at the crucifix above her head.

320

"Who am I? What and who do I truly want to be?" The questions formed in her mind, but she heard no answer.

Born a princess, she had inherited a role she never questioned when she lived in Leova's hall. All those years, as she looked back on them, emerged as a form of paradise. She and Leova had grown to love one another more than sisters ever could. It was a world where everyone had treated her with respect and deference. What would her life be like now, if she had remained there? Surely she would have married; she could hardly have lived with Leova's parents forever.

Yes, she would have married and made her new residence in the hall of her new husband, sworn fealty to that husband's family, become a part of it, and continued the husband's bloodline. Perhaps they might even have chosen to live at Highhear. She would have had to marry someone of the noble families, probably from a family whose lands were close by or even connected to her father's acres, probably one of the two young men her father had invited to Highhear for just that reason. She and her husband would have joined two properties and two bloodlines, and her father would have achieved his goals. A bit guiltily she thought again of the two young men who had come to court her. Surprisingly, she discovered that her guilt was tinged with anger. What choice had she in marriage? Her groom's family would have to own extensive property and exert considerable control over other land in their region. What kind of a person would she have become in such a regal setting?

More memories and questions about the life that was lost to her arose: vague, fearful, repetitious, and yet somehow exciting images, mostly focused on her arrival at Lothlar. She remembered falling off her horse and the eyes of the man in black who had tried unsuccessfully to carry her off. Deadly hatred had shone from those eyes that looked at her so fiercely. The memory triggered another, the image of Berghorf's face years later when she asked him to identify that warrior with evil in his eyes. The images faded quickly, replaced by more difficult ones, and she returned to contemplating what God might intend for her. The years at Lothlar brought fond memories, but the years since? Perhaps she would have been better off not living them. Was there a purpose in those sad events?

As the days passed, creeping by in their slow progress, Hilda's mandated silence forced her to travel ever more deeply inside her memories and to reflect more on words that had been said and deeds which had been done in the days before she made her choice to take vows. She found herself trying to understand God's purpose and trying to determine what role she had played in bringing herself to this battered abbey so far from all she had ever known. She acknowledged that since leaving Leova and her family, she had been escaping—escaping from the monastery, escaping from her father and his plans, escaping from the world. Even her one tryst with John now seemed an attempt to run away from the life being forced on her. Yet this memory, of all the memories, made her long for the outside world. God, however, had closed that door for her. Now she prepared for a life of prayer and service instead of a life in the world, with a family. Is this what He required of her? And is it truly what she desired—or mostly an escape from the ordered world of a princess where others always seemed to be in charge of her life.

Gradually the weather cooled, and the winds coming off the water carried a penetrating chill. One morning, Hilda discovered a warm cloak and an extra blanket at her door when she went to fetch her food. As she picked up the sorely needed articles, she caught a movement from behind a nearby stone. When she looked up, the smiling Caedmon waved happily at her before turning and running away. Hilda smiled to herself: she thought God would forgive this small infraction of her penance—at least she hoped so. She had spent the night cold and unhappy. Caedmon's present lifted her spirits: he always seemed to have an inexplicable awareness of her needs.

Some days went quickly; others were eternal. She relived the past, alternatively rejoicing in it and regretting it. She spent many days in contemplation of the future. As her atonement wore on, she would wake some days in a state of serenity and peace; other days found her anxious and self-accusatory. One morning she awoke to discover a light coat of snow on everything about her. The whole world, except for the ocean, appeared to her as one unbroken, undifferentiated mass, punctuated by risings and fallings as though something dwelt just below the surface. Her life was like that: something was always just below the surface, something she could not quite uncover or even identify. But it was there, waiting.

As the year drew toward Advent, Hilda found herself almost numb. She had jettisoned all her emotions and become an empty vessel waiting to be filled. The serenity she had experienced back in the small chapel at her father's hall when she had felt the saints looking down on her with forgiveness and understanding, eluded her. All she could uncover was emptiness. What would be her worth to anyone, to the monastery, to God, to anything or anyone, feeling as she did?

Just before the Eve of Christ's birth, Hilda felt as though she could no longer bear the little cell and her own feelings of unworthiness and emptiness. After Prime, she did not return to her cell, but instead walked despondently toward the limits of the monastery from which she turned to look out over the sea. It was still and dark. The sky was impenetrable except for a few small spears of light that seemed to offer a lens into somewhere else, a somewhere else which eluded her. She had a sudden desire to escape the confines of the monastery, to feel once more the freedom she had gloried in at other moments of her life. Almost defiantly, she stepped past the monastery limits and into the outer graveyard. Shivering, she pulled her cloak about her and sat down on a nearby stone, too melancholy to make good another escape. As it grew lighter, she could see far up and down the coast. The white foam of the waves outlined the edge of the shore. As she looked, the foam began to give off a pinkish glow that slowly turned a deeper and deeper orange, almost red. The shore was outlined with fire. Hilda caught her breath.

The sun appeared over the ocean's edge, throwing out bright golden orange beams from its red center. Hilda could hardly look up without being blinded. Some of the rocks on the shore and the wispy clouds above her picked up the color. It was as though the whole world was illuminated by the glow that originated in the foam.

"A new day," she said aloud—hearing her voice for the first time in months. "This is a new day, so bright I cannot look at it, but I can see its reflection everywhere." Something stirred in her, a feeling of awe and reverence, of potential and possibility, of joy. As she stood up, the cloak fell from around her shoulders, wrapping itself around the stones on which she sat. The warmth from within herself made her unaware of the cold air about her.

"God has given me a life to live. He considers me worthy to serve him!" Hilda wanted to scream the words, but they never left her lips. They took root in her mind and heart.

"I must get back to my cell and complete my penance," Hilda thought and turned to collect her cloak. As she removed it from the stone, the letters she saw carved there captured her attention. They reflected the fierce red of the rising sun. Brushing away some of the accumulated dirt and twigs and gravel, she caught her breath. The letters formed her own name. Quickly she brushed off the rest and read the worn inscription:

Abbatissina Hild nata DCXIV.
Hic corpus iacet, cum deo animus.
Mater episcoporum, dilecta omnibus.

Some force had brought her to Abbess Hild's resting place. Surely this was a sign. The message she thought she heard when the sun rose had been confirmed. Her long dead predecessor reached out to her from across the centuries, reassuring her, confirming her decision.

Gratefully. Hilda answered the call to Lauds and hurried to the small chapel. As she approached it, she saw a small group of figures, one of whom pointed in her direction. She drew closer, recognizing the two priests with Abbess Frideswith. Before she could greet them, they moved into the small chapel, where Father Jerome stepped up to the altar and began to read the liturgy of the day.

"Why?" Hilda wondered briefly, "had he returned before the elapse of the nine months?" Probably on some errand not related to her, she concluded. But even curiosity could not displace her new sense of commitment to her chosen course. She engaged herself in prayer with far greater earnestness than had been her wont in the prior few weeks. Once the day's office and prayers had concluded, Hilda sat for some extra time in the chapel before leaving. Abbess Frideswith met her at the door.

"Father Jerome has come with a guest to talk to you on an urgent matter. The Father has released you temporarily from your vows of silence; I assured him that you have adhered to them without fault since his departure. They await you in the guesthouse."

The priest with Father Jerome was Bishop Ceolwulf. Hilda shuttered, remembering his last cruel words. "You have sinned greatly." The happiness of her morning revelations faded momentarily. Was this another test of her determination? She faltered only briefly, however. With her newfound commitment, she raised her head and looked at him directly, bowing slightly.

"Princess Hilda," Father Jerome began. "Here is Bishop Ceolwulf, come with me to bring sad news for you. Your father is dead. As his heir, you must now make decisions about his lands and people."

Hilda remained silent despite the powerful impact the news made on her.

"Bishop Ceolwulf will serve as witness to your pronouncements."

Hilda remained silent.

Finally Father Jerome prompted her a bit more gently. "Princess Hilda, God wills that you be temporarily released from your vow of silence. Speak without fear."

"I no longer answer to that name, Father." Hilda replied. "I have committed myself to the work of God on this earth, and I will not turn back from that path. Please instruct me in light of that commitment."

"May I remind you, Princess Hilda," he emphasized the title carefully in an authoritarian voice, "that you have yet to take your final vows."

"As far as the world and its concerns are, that does not matter, Father Jerome; I have made my personal commitment." Hilda replied, turning to look at him directly. "Please do not address me as princess again. If you consider me unfit for vows, I will remain here and serve God as a lay person. And so, I repeat: you must needs instruct me in light of my commitment."

There was no mistaking the authority of Hilda's voice, modulated to be respectful but not insubordinate. "Tell me, please, how was it with my father?"

"Unfortunately, dear Princess, he did not die in battle as he might have wished. A great pestilence has broken out in your lands, killing many. He fought the disease, but succumbed to its power."

The Bishop moved toward her and took her hand in an attempt to console her. "But his last words were of you. He urged me to seek you out and bring you back to your inheritance. For a long period of time, he did search for you and authorized others to do so also, finally conceding that he could not find you and, furthermore, that you did not want to be found. Only within the past few months, did I learn of your presence here. In the end, he forgave you for disobeying him; his dearest wish would have been to see you once more before he died. I regret for both of you that such a meeting was not to be."

Hilda remained quiet and still for some time. "I have no earthly family now," she then whispered. "Both my father and mother are dead; my cousin Berghorf was killed; my child can never be restored to me. My spiritual family in this monastery replaces that earthly one; these holy women and those who serve us stand for those who are dead. I shall give my lands to the church."

Ceolwulf's response was immediate. "That would be unwise, My Princess. Your father's lands are vast and he holds them—that is, he held them—as a lord in service to King Alfred, whose strong army perhaps will prove the match of the invaders. If you will not take your place, it would be well to allow me to petition King Alfred to appoint a regent for your lands."

Hearing the scorn in his voice, Hilda felt she needed to respond, "Bishop Ceolwulf, the last time we met you told me that I had defiled both my family and my church. How is it that now you do not wish me to bless either my church or the memory of my family by making this bequest?" A slight edge of defiance and sarcasm had crept into Hilda's voice. She wondered why she had once been in such awe of this man.

"Father Jerome tells me you have atoned for your sin and are in the process of cleansing your body and soul in preparation to take your vows. I do not ask you to turn from that path; you can take your vows and still follow the advice I have given you." Ceolwulf's voice softened somewhat, but he did not acknowledge any softening of his condemnation.

"I will consider this matter during the course of the evening and give you my answer tomorrow," Hilda said and then, without waiting for a reply, she wrapped her cloak around her once more and left the two priests to stare at one another.

Hilda again contemplated the ways in which her exterior matched the new fallen snow. The snow covered all irregularities but could never destroy them. Her calm covered the fact that she was, in truth, distraught. Her father was dead; she had not been there to comfort him. It was ironic; she had been with her mother before she died, and her mother had never loved her as her father had. And, yet, her mother, in fact, was responsible for her presence here. Hilda was convinced of that. She was equally convinced that her mother had loved good deeds far more than she had loved any human being.

Hilda followed the path to the small chapel and entered quietly, glad to find it empty. The glazed windows allowed in a defused light that dispersed to adumbrate the altar ever so vaguely. The jeweled communion cups and the greatly worn psalter from which the priest read the day's lesson caught the light of the candles on either end of the chapel. Hilda found herself wondering how the cups and the manuscript had survived the depredations of the red-haired ones.

Slowly she approached the altar and reached out to the manuscript on the altar, placing her hand lightly on the opened text. The pages were slightly crinkled as though they had been waterlogged at some point. The worn leather binding was beginning to fall apart. Brother William could have repaired this treasure, was her immediate thought. The page of the psalter which met her glance appeared to have been the victim of moths in addition to water, but Hilda could still make out the words: *et veritas liberabit vos.*

"Yes, of course," Hilda said, "*and the truth shall make you free.*" The text ratified her epiphany at dawn. The bell for prayer began to ring once more, and she returned to her seat. The other sisters began to slip quietly in for the next round of their daily prayers. Bishop Ceolwulf led them in the liturgy, but his eyes carefully avoided Hilda.

Immediately after the conclusion of the readings, Hilda sought out Caedmon. He had become a valued counselor, one she trusted. He and his new wife were tending the hives, but put aside their labors when they saw her approach. "Caedmon, Alanya: Father Jerome has temporarily released me from my vow of silence. I need to ask you a most important question." The group of three settled themselves on stones that had been arranged, seemingly, for such talks. After some length of time in discussion, Hilda rose and embraced the young woman and the somewhat embarrassed young man and returned to her small quarters.

The following morning after Prime, Hilda went directly to Father Jerome and requested an audience with him and Bishop Ceolwulf. She also asked that Abbess Frideswith join them. Seeing their discomfort, she immediately announced her decision. "I have reflected upon both what my mother and father wished for me and what I wish for myself. I have not been unaware of my sins and the need for atonement; that is my task and duty now. Once that time has passed, I plan, of my own free will, to remain here at Whitby and serve my God either as a nun or in whatever other way might be open to me. Although I would wish to give all my lands to the church, I understand Bishop Ceolwulf's concerns and the problems that would confront my people if they suddenly had to face the possibility that they might be unseated from their land."

The two men and the Abbess nodded in agreement, but said nothing, waiting for Hilda to continue.

"This settlement, I hope, meets most of these conflicting concerns." Her voice became stronger as she outlined the details of her plan. "Father Jerome and Bishop Ceolwulf, please consult with the emissaries of the great King Alfred to select an overseer for my lands. Someone who knows the property must be its caretaker. My servant Caedmon, and his new wife, will accompany you. Make clear to the authorities that he is to be appointed reeve and given the charge of supervising those who work the land. They have both agreed to undertake this responsibility; please make that a condition of my request."

If they had wished to protest, they did not. Her voice indicated that she would brook no disagreement. Never before had she been so much a princess as now when she was divesting herself of that role. She continued: "I wish to give two hundred hides of my land to Bolton Abbey, a small priory just beyond the western end of the Highhear property, along with an appropriate portion of my goods. My mother took me there a couple of times when I was very young. When I last saw it, over a year ago, it had been partially destroyed, but there were monks and priests there. Perhaps it could be rebuilt. Those farmers who work those hides now may decide whether to become a part of the monastery or move to another part of my lands where they will be welcome. Caedmon will oversee the reorganization. I will remain here and await Father Jerome's decision about my vows." There was no mistaking the resolve in Hilda's voice. Father Jerome and Abbess Frideswith had never seen this side of Hilda before and were somewhat in awe of it, but Bishop Ceolwulf was acquainted with the young woman's strength of will. He spoke immediately.

"You act wisely. We will carry out your wishes; both your mother and father would approve." He rose and took her hand. "I will advise Father Jerome to act favorably on your petition—*Sister Hilda*."

He smiled to emphasize his acceptance of her new role. "Will you accompany us?"

"No, my father has been buried; he has no need of my presence. I will pray for his soul when I return to my cell and my vows of silence."

Two months after her decision, Father Jerome once again appeared at the door of the small chapel. Only a slight movement of Hilda's shoulders and a slow intake of breath revealed her eagerness to hear his news. After the conclusion of the prayers, she waited until the others filed out of the small chapel. Father Jerome came and sat down beside the hopeful young woman. Taking her hand gently, he signaled to her that she should join him in the confessional. When Hilda emerged shortly from her side of the confessional, there were tears on her cheeks. Father Jerome had given his blessing. She could take her vows.

The Religious Life (880)

The epidemic which felled Ecgbert arrived at Whitby in full force shortly after Hilda took her vows. For months the sisters struggled with the pestilence. Unable to secure the help of the medical men who were overworked and in short supply as a result of their own vulnerability to the malady, all the women could do was isolate any one of their community who showed symptoms of the disease. The sisters found themselves fighting additional enemies as well. A number of their community fell back on the customs of their ancestors in their despair and in their disappointment with what they began to call "the new gods." Hilda was not as outraged as the other sisters. Her youthful remembrance of Leova's mother kept her mindful of the old ways and tempered her condemnation of those who embraced them. Leova's mother was a good woman as were her forest companions; these folk at Whitby were desperate and needed to be guided back to the church gently, rather than abandoned spiritually.

Eventually, despite all the efforts of the dedicated women, nuns and others, the number of the community began to diminish. Those who remained well found no time to sleep as they tried to alleviate pain, wash bedding, prepare food and potions. Some days went by that Hilda could not even remember. Hardly any men were left to dig the graves, and Abbess Frideswith found herself playing priest by default since no priest remained to administer the last rites. As she went about her sad business, Frideswith was comforted by her knowledge that God would understand her actions. Having a woman perform last rites was preferable to allowing the innocent to die without a blessing.

The plague began to lose its force, and one morning the weary Hilda realized that almost two weeks had passed without any new patients. But before she could rejoice, Abbess Frideswith fell ill. Hilda insisted on being her nurse twenty-four hours a day, but as Frideswith's pain increased, Hilda despaired at her inability to ease it. One day, as she sat next to her patient, her tired head resting against the edge of the bed, Hilda heard a movement at the door. Looking up, she saw a strange woman, one she did not recall ever having seen on the grounds. "I'm Ælfwynn. I bring a potion. It cannot cure her, only relieve her pain." The woman handled a small vial to Hilda and disappeared. Hilda sat and looked at the vial for a minute or two, confused by the sudden arrival and departure of the stranger.

Shaking her head in puzzlement, she looked out the door, but saw no one. "Should I trust this woman? Who is she?" Hilda muttered. Then she heard noises from Frideswith's bed and turned to find her Abbess struggling not to cry out. Frideswith would never allow pain to get the better of her, but the struggle against it was becoming more difficult every day. Hilda looked at the vial in her hand; it called to mind the herb-women at Lothlar who had been able to relieve the pain of many. Surely it couldn't hurt to use it. It did not seem just that Frideswith should suffer longer than she already had. Hilda turned to a small table where there was a spoon and a cup and carefully emptied the contents of the vial into the cup. Dipping out a small amount with the spoon, she spoke to Frideswith gently. "I have some new medicine for you; it may help with the pain, my dear sister."

Frideswith, beyond protesting any offered treatment, dutifully opened her lips to receive the potion. Fearing that she might give the sick woman too much, Hilda administered only one spoonful. Then she sat down beside her superior to be ready if she were needed. She took Frideswith's hand in hers and stroked it gently. Frideswith's blue eyes opened and became intent on her. "You're a blessing to me and to the church, my child. You must take my place when I am gone: no one else is as qualified as you to be the leader here." Hilda had not the heart to remind her that there was barely anyone left to lead. She merely nodded in agreement as the Abbess struggled to speak more. "Search your own spirit to discover how best you may further the work of the church. Think of it—we will have peace someday, and you will be able to carry God's word to the newcomers who are greatly in need of it." Hilda marveled at Frideswith's forgiving heart, for she knew that the red-haired ones had slain many in her family. "I'll rest now, child," her voice fell away as she drifted into the first peaceful sleep she had had since the ordeal began. Hilda whispered thanks to the stranger who had provided peace to the Abbess and she too soon fell asleep, seated at her superior's side.

When she awoke, she jumped up quickly. She must have missed evening prayers; it had been days, weeks, since she had slept so soundly. Guiltily, she turned to look at Frideswith and was comforted to see that she was still sleeping soundly. And, for the first time in days, Hilda realized she was hungry.

She emerged from the doorway, taking a deep breath of the evening air, and walked down to the infirmary. Several beds were still in use, and two of the sisters moved back and forth between their patients. They did not seem to need any help, so Hilda proceeded to the refectory which at first appeared to be empty. On the table some bread had been left out for those who could not attend regular meals; Hilda ate eagerly. When her hunger had eased some, she realized that a woman was sitting quietly in the far corner, the woman who had brought the potion. She rose and greeted her.

"Thank you for the medicine. Abbess Frideswith is sleeping peacefully."

The woman smiled.

"You said your name is Ælfwynn as if I should know you, but I've never seen you before."

332

"I am the beekeeper."

"Then," Hilda blurted out, "you're Alanya's mother. You saved Caedmon and me in the moors!"

"Yes. And now Caedmon has married my daughter and taken her away to your land," she said without rancor. "But I am certain they have a good living there; they have you to thank for our family's good fortune."

"But I owe you and Caedmon more than any human could ever repay." Hilda smiled. "Like him, you seem to appear whenever I am in dire need of help I cannot find elsewhere."

"There's soup in that pot," Ælfwynn pointed toward the hearth, ignoring her reference to the past. Gratefully, Hilda found herself a bowl and poured out some of the soup which she ate greedily.

"There's cheese also and more bread," Ælfwynn said. Once again, Hilda felt well taken care of. Ælfwynn watched the young nun eat. "Why would a young, healthy, rich, beautiful woman like you want to be a nun?" Ælfwynn asked with obvious puzzlement. "You could probably do and be anything you want. Why a nun?"

Hilda wasn't stumped by her question: she had asked herself the same one during the last year. She turned the tables on her inquisitor.

"Why would you, a woman with a young daughter and a good living as a beekeeper, want to live in the moors like a wild person?"

The two women stared at each other in mutual bewilderment for several minutes before both of them broke into laughter, each laughing at herself more than at the other.

"Well, perhaps my choice is as incomprehensible to you as yours is to me," Hilda told Ælfwynn. "Maybe we can just leave it at that. Answer me this one thing, however. Why did you return now and what did you give me for Abbess Frideswith?"

"That's two questions," Ælfwynn answered, "but I'll give you one answer. I came back because I have medicines that can help. Abbess Frideswith was always good to me. I am glad to be able to help her. And perhaps, just perhaps, I am weary of living in the moors and look to again live with walls around me as I grow older.

Perhaps I'll take one more journey across the moors and go join my daughter and her husband. She's your age, and it's nigh time she became a mother herself."

"That will indeed be a rewarding trip for you and for Caedmon and your daughter. Your help has been a blessing here, a miracle, but the pestilence has spent itself. I ask only that you leave some of your potions for Abbess Frideswith."

"Your Abbess will not live much longer, I fear. I will leave you with enough to ease her final days. And then I will go."

"Why now?" Hilda asked.

"I've guarded these lands for years so that our people could cross safely. The moors are mine; the red-haired ones know that and, despite the fact that they chase me back and forth, they cannot catch me. I hate them for what they did to me and to my mother and sisters...." Her voice broke off. "That's in the past. I've come to terms with their deeds, and," her voice suddenly turned sharp and bitter, "they've been rewarded amply."

"Take provisions for yourself and whatever else you need. Our little group has been so depleted that we have excess. Give your daughter and Caedmon my blessing. I miss them both daily."

When Hilda returned to the Abbess, she was pleased to see that she continued to rest quietly. Shortly after, the Abbess opened her eyes. "My daughter, you have eased my death. For that I am grateful, but I'm ready to meet God and his saints. Do you think you can reach Father Jerome? I wish to have his absolution on my death bed."

"I will send for him, mother." Hilda smiled as she realized how easily the word "mother" came to her for Frideswith. How much she wished her own mother had cared about what she wanted in the same way Abbess Frideswith did. Within the week, Father Jerome appeared. Soon after he had finished the funeral mass for Abbess Frideswith and two of the serving women, he asked Hilda to come to his makeshift quarters.

"Hilda, my child, it's time for you to move on. I know of a settlement to the north, the abbey at Rosedale, where some fifteen or twenty sisters reside."

334

"Rosedale," Hilda whispered, containing her surprise. "Caedmon and I stopped there for a night on our way here. Abbess Claennis was most gracious to us. Strange, that I should now return as abbess."

Father Jerome smiled at the brightened face before him. "Abbess Claennis passed to her reward months ago. Now, there is no abbess there; it would be an ideal place for you to begin your larger duties for God. The abbey was founded by nuns and priests from Whitby many years ago as a double monastery. There are still a few monks there who may or may not move on—but they would not object to your appointment as abbess. You came into my mind immediately when I was last there because I discovered a cache of manuscripts—apparently from Yorvik. Some of the monks were able to flee with the manuscripts when the enemy overpowered the city. I know of your love of reading and your devotion to both Latin and Englisc; you would be an excellent caretaker there for both God's word and His servants."

Hilda contained her eagerness at the thought of the manuscripts. "What about the few sisters who are left here, Father?"

"They'll travel with you, both lay and consecrated. Rosedale needs all of you. We can only pray that someday Whitby can be returned to its former stature."

On the evening before her departure, Hilda sought out the humble headstone that marked her predecessor Hild's grave. Who was that predecessor? She knew very little of what had happened in the 200 years between their two lives, but she had developed an avid desire to find out. Father Jerome could not tell her: the only stories he had heard were vague tales of her virtues. He had once heard a monk in one of the northern monasteries reading from a manuscript which told stories about Whitby and Abbess Hild, but he had been young and the reader poor at his job, so he remembered little of the reading.

"I have been told that many important churchmen were educated here," Jerome reported. "Who they were or what they were important for, however, I do not know. I have also learned of a cowherd here who wrote divine poetry in our own language, but I can't attest to the truth of that report."

"If only dumb stones could talk," she said to herself as she gazed on that fading tombstone. Her time at Whitby had not weakened her nascent love of knowledge nor her passion and desire to search for that elusive commodity in words on parchment. John had brought that love and passion to life, but Hilda stopped herself from following that link or dwelling on one part of that passion. She focused her thoughts instead on their shared passion for deciphering the written word, those of the church and those in Englisc.

That love of words made her feel very much attached to the Hild whose gravestone she now left behind.

Rosedale Abbey (882)

The young cleric from Buxton Abbey found the Abbess of Rosedale lost in contemplation of the open manuscript before her. He hesitated to address her and watched for a minute or two as the slender fingers meticulously entered marks above the Latin text on the vellum. The young monk was able to decipher the Latin, but he could not puzzle out the language of the Abbess' additions.

Soon Hilda felt herself being watched and turned to meet the intense eyes of the young monk.

"Forgive me, sister, for interrupting you. I am Brother Olaf, and I have a message from Abbess Edyth of Buxton." Hilda stifled the instinctive rush of emotion she always felt when she heard that name. It had been almost five years since she had been shamefully banished under cover of night, but although time may heal, it erases pain slowly.

"One minute, Brother," Hilda said softly as she turned back to her manuscript to complete the series of notations. The delay gave her time to compose her thoughts as much as it allowed her to finish her work on the vellum. It certainly seemed to the young messenger that the Abbess rose from her stool with great reluctance, but he was not surprised because he had heard how assiduously she examined the old works.

"Come, you must be weary and hungry after your trip; when you have been refreshed, we can hear your message." Hilda led the young man out of the scriptorium and along the path through the garden. She smiled at the middle-aged woman on her knees before a small patch of herbs. "Still nursing the Whitby chives?" Without rising, the gardener nodded her head. Olaf sensed the rapport between the two. Following his guide around the cloister, he was delighted with the aromas coming from the kitchen.

"Anna," Hilda called to the woman chopping vegetables, "I bring you a weary traveler. Please find him drink and food, direct one of the youngsters to care for his mule, and then show him to quarters where he can rest a bit." Turning to the monk, she said, "You are called Olaf?"

"Brother Olaf, if you please," he answered. Hilda studied his facial features more closely than she previously had.

"Olaf," she said, considering the implications, the name of a red-haired one? "The church is making progress in its conversions!" she thought.

She smiled as she turned to go, "Anna will see to it that you are fed."

The cook nodded and wiped her hands on her apron before going to find a cup for the visitor. "And did you come a long distance today?"

"Ay, and yesterday and the day before that also." The weary Olaf seemed to melt onto the stool, but he was determined to keep up a pleasant and polite conversation.

"Where'd you come from?" she asked, unable to fathom traveling such a distance. The trip from Whitby to Rosedale comprised her entire knowledge of distance and geography. She had been born on a farm close to the former and very likely would end her days exactly where she now was. She placed a plate before him and he fell to, eating with great gusto.

"Abbess Edyth at Buxton sent me with a request to Abbess Hilda," he replied but without slowing his eating at all. Anna returned to her task, stopping only to offer some of her labor to Olaf, who accepted it greedily—young carrots and various greens were rare in his world, and he loved them, perhaps a little more than his religious calling would approve. The two settled comfortably into an easy conversation about the nurture and use of herbs, about the weather, about the food in the monastery. Olaf felt the tension and fatigue seeping out of his body until he was in near danger of falling asleep as he chewed.

"You need to lie down a bit," observed Anna. "There's yet an hour before vespers—rest 'til then. Your message will wait."

Olaf allowed himself to be led into the dormer where Anna pointed him to a mattress of straw on the floor. He was asleep almost immediately and woke only at the sound of feet passing before the open doorway. Sitting up, he realized it must be vespers, and drew on his sandals which appeared much cleaner and fresher than they had before he slept.

"Thank you, Anna," he whispered to himself.

He left the guest house and joined a silent group of monks, following them into the small chapel. He seated himself to the rear, nodding at a number of the monks and nuns who regarded him quizzically, but then turned their attention to the service. This was not the place to question the messenger. Olaf, on the other hand, listened to the reading with half of his attention, while the other half studied the group around him. The same assortment of lay and consecrated communicants matched those of his own monastery. There was something comforting about that, the knowledge that in monasteries throughout the landscape, brothers and sisters, nuns and priests, lay and holy were engaged in the same ritual. To him, that represented peace, a world of security and safety. It made him feel in control of his life.

The service over, Hilda signaled the recent arrival to join her as she walked out into the field where the sheep grazed. Settling herself on a flat stone, she waved Olaf to another close by.

"Now, young man, what is your message for me? Is the news from Abbess Edyth and her companions good?"

"The Abbess sent me to tell you of an aged monk who arrived at the monastery more than a month ago."

Hilda could only wonder what such a person might have to do with her.

"He came accompanied by a servant who departed almost

338

immediately, simply announcing that he had delivered his charge there because he was ill. The servant called him Father Jerome, but we never learned where they had come from. The monk, although his health improved at first, soon failed and died. Before God granted him the peaceful sleep that comes with death, he kept repeating your name and gesturing with his hands as though writing in the air. He spoke more, but we could never understand anything else he said. After a proper burial, someone remembered the sack the servant had brought. Inside we found three manuscripts as well as his few personal belongings. One manuscript is in Latin, but the other two appear to be in what looks like Englisc—to me," he added. "Once our Abbess saw them, she believed that she understood his message: he wanted you to know of the manuscripts because of your interest in old writings."

Hilda thought about Father Jerome. Her old mentor had consecrated her, heard her confessions, and brought her to Rosedale, but he had left shortly thereafter and never returned. Whenever traveling priests or monks or even merchants or noblemen or women arrived at the monastery, Hilda had sought information about Jerome, but, as with other friends and family from years past, she never heard a word about his life since he had heard her vows

"And did Abbess Edyth send the manuscripts with you?"

"No, she did not, but she requests that you come to Buxton and look at them."

This was not the first time Abbess Edyth had invited Hilda to return to Buxton. Three years earlier she had sent a message inviting her to a gathering of abbesses. To the general invitation sent around the countryside, she had added a personal note expressing her wish that Hilda could find it in her heart to come. The decision not to go had generated much anguish for Hilda. As an abbess, she knew she should go. As a woman, she had no desire to return to scenes she could only remember with pain. She sensed that Edyth was making some attempt at reconciliation, and Hilda wished she could accede, but she could not. Perhaps Edyth had done the proper thing, banishing her from Buxton and helping to decide what would become of the child, her child, but it had not been humane. Hilda's

God, the one who guided her life, would not have approved. About that, Hilda had no doubt.

As it turned out, Hilda would not have been able to go to that meeting. Before she could refuse the invitation, her own abbey suffered a devastating fire. She had to stay to supervise the rebuilding. Nonetheless, Hilda was left with worrisome guilt about her decision. She confessed it as a sin, as an indulgence of private feelings of betrayal. Now, here again, was another invitation to visit Buxton. Again, Edyth might well be seeking reconciliation. Once more, Hilda felt the anguish and the pain of making a decision.

"Brother Olaf, I'll give you an answer tomorrow. Meanwhile, I believe the community is now gathered in the refectory. As you discovered earlier, our provisions are simple but delicious, and I would be pleased if you would join the meal. I intend to walk yet a bit."

Hilda wandered into the scriptorium and turned the leaf of the manuscript she had been reading and glossing when Olaf arrived. Edyth was tempting her with manuscripts. Even Father Jerome tempted her from the grave with manuscripts. Obviously there was work to be done, and she was one of the few who could complete the task.

"What right have I to put my personal pain above my responsibilities as an abbess?" Hilda spoke aloud as though she expected an answer from one wiser than she. "Perhaps," she continued to muse, "I should seek my answer elsewhere."

The chapel was darkening as Hilda knelt to pray. The return to Buxton would bring personal pain. The four years between her forced and hurried departure and the present peace she felt had dulled the sorrow and guilt which had originated at that lovely old monastery. John had become a memory both fond and hurtful. She had no idea what had become of him or whether or not he remained at Buxton or some abbey like it. He could have left the order, married, had children—more children, she reminded herself—but there was no means of discovering his whereabouts. If John had returned to Buxton, she might see him. Despite the many years, she wasn't sure she was emotionally prepared for that. Just talking to him again would bring conflict. She doubted that he knew about the baby, and she didn't want to be faced with the prospect of having to tell him—or the guilt if she decided not to tell him.

That black spot in her soul had almost closed off, but it opened again, opened up at the thought of returning. Had the child died? If not where might it be? A boy? A girl? It was both disquieting and stimulating to think there might be a child of hers somewhere in this land—a child who would now be four years old. Had the child been given to a kind and loving mother and father? Who could answer these questions? Did she even want the answers? Was it justifiable to avoid Buxton? Some part of her recognized that it was time to lay these fears to rest.

Hilda continued to sit quietly in the chapel lost in her own thoughts, but gradually, knowing that she had tasks to perform and souls to minister to, she left the peace of the sanctuary and stepped into the courtyard. What greeted her took her breath away: a brightness in the sky at the horizon, far brighter than a star, but not as bright as the full moon. The bright spot left a slight trail behind it which faded into the distance. Several members of the community stood in the courtyard, completely awed at the sight.

"What is it, Mother Abbess?" one of the young novitiates asked.

"A comet, my child," Hilda answered. "They do not appear often, but they stay in the sky for quite a few days. One of God's wonders and gifts...and," Hilda thought, "the answer to my dilemma, a sign to me that I can and ought to bring light to at least some of my former life."

A Visit to the Past

Two days later, Hilda and Brother Olaf set off on mules for Buxton accompanied by two young and burly sons of local farmers. Hilda felt the trip was as much a pilgrimage as a visit. The years had brought immense change. There was no longer a spirit lady on the moors, except whatever spirit had been left behind by a former bee-keeper who had gone off to join her daughter and Caedmon. There were no red-haired ones to hide from—the great king from the south, Alfred, had pushed the warriors north and east toward the shores on which they had first landed. Others, tired of constant strife, had stayed on and made a home in the land they had once invaded. Even the size of the moors seemed to have shrunk in the years since Hilda's last trip.

Because no dangers threatened the small group as they moved along the clearly defined path, Hilda passed the time by questioning Olaf about his own history. She learned that he had been left at the monastery by someone, perhaps his mother or so he thought, when he was quite young—perhaps three or four. The name Anlaf had been scratched into the dirt before the gate, but the good sisters had altered it to Olaf.

"Do you ever wonder why you have such a name?" Hilda asked. "Your coloring suggests that you are a descendant of the invaders whom we call Northmen. They call themselves Vikings."

Olaf was silent for a bit. "Yes, Abbess," he finally replied. "I have thought about that, though I do not speak of it. I remember words I must have heard and spoken before being left at the monastery; no one there taught them to me. The nuns only spoke Englisc and some Latin, and at first I was sad and lonely because I couldn't understand anyone. As a boy I wanted only to find my family and desperately hoped they would reappear one day and take me home."

He shook his head sadly, remembering the boy he once was, then he continued more optimistically. "Gradually I have learned to love the life of the monastery. I hope one day to take my vows."

Hilda heard the determination of the voice and knew that he'd achieve his goal. How ironic, an offspring of the pagans becoming a priest of their enemies. His placement in the abbey sparked her curiosity.

Remembering Ceolwulf's history too, Hilda wondered out loud, "Why would parents leave a child in such a way?"

Olaf owned to many fantasies on that score: he was a prince and needed protection, he was found wandering alone somewhere, he was a bastard child.

"More than likely," he said ruefully, "my parents were just too

342

poor to feed another child."

He fell silent for several minutes then spoke quietly and solemnly. "The truth may well be that my mother fell victim to the invaders and that my father came and went too quickly to even know of my existence—and perhaps would not care if he did know." Hilda felt his sadness, the reverse of her own. Did her child make up fantasies to explain its parentage? Was the child even aware of not living with a biological mother? That would probably be a blessing. Hilda smiled as she reminded herself that neither of her two genuine mothers, Pagany and Abbess Frideswith, had been a biological mother. She fell silent, feeling a strange bond with this young man at her side.

After two nights of sleep, courtesy of farmers along the road, Hilda began to recognize features of the landscape and acknowledged to herself that the road beyond the moors might well pass close to the hall of her birth, the hall of her mother's and father's deaths, the hall she had fled so long ago. She had decided upon her arrival at Rosedale never to visit the home where she had actually spent very few happy years and garnered mainly memories of death and unfulfilled hopes. Luckily, Olaf was unaware of her background and of her prior attachments to the land they now passed through. It was not a history he needed to know.

Although she and Olaf had chatted almost incessantly across the moors, as they grew nearer to Buxton, Hilda fell silent, remembering when she had ridden alone along parts of this road, eagerly looking forward to her return to Hearhigh. She had been so excited, so curious about what life might be in that home she had left as a small child.

"Perhaps," she reflected to herself, "it was best that I did not know what the future would bring."

Aware of the increasing silence of his companion, Olaf, too, fell into introspection. They passed the remainder of that day and the morning of the next in almost complete silence. About noon, Olaf announced that they were within three hours of the monastery.

"Perhaps we should rest and have something to eat before we start on our last leg," he suggested. Mutely, Hilda agreed.

After a brief rest, during which she ate little, Hilda turned to Olaf. "Olaf, I can't explain my reasons, but I'd like to travel alone for the remainder of the trip. The past and present are much confused for me, and I am in need of solitude—to think about God's reason for calling me back to Buxton."

Olaf listened and although he would have liked to have an explanation, he knew that it was not his right to ask for one. Hilda saw his struggle and, smiling quietly at him, gave a partial answer to the questions she knew he would have.

"What I will tell you is that I left Buxton virtually alone in body and spirit quite a few years ago. I would like to return alone; you will not take offense?"

Olaf could hardly deny the Abbess her unusual request. "Of course, Abbess Hilda. But if I'm to be comfortable, I feel we must keep you in sight."

"Yes, Olaf, of course, you three are, in a sense, my guardians."

She smiled her thanks to him and set off resolutely alone but at peace. She had, of course, not told all the story. She had left—more exactly, been exiled—under cover of early morning darkness with Caedmon and Ethel as her companions, her tresses shorn and her gender disguised by a monk's tunic. She also could not help remembering being exiled from a second abbey with only Ethel and a taciturn farmer as a companion. It was as though an ouster from an abbey had life-altering force. What would be the outcome of a return to one of those abbeys?

Lost in thought, Hilda suddenly became aware of voices calling to one another, and as she came around a bend in the road, she saw a group of young, muscular men loading stones onto a small cart. They peered at her in some amazement: a nun, but unlike any nun they'd seen before. Several locks of black curls had escaped Hilda's wimple, her cheeks were flushed with exertion, and her eyes sparkled as though in anticipation of some adventure.

Intrigued by what they were doing, Hilda stopped to study their work. All told, there were almost thirty men at work. Some of them jointly carried large stones along a path which led into a small grove of trees. Others sorted stones, piling the largest ones along the

344

road and putting the smaller ones into an oxen cart. Driven by curiosity, Hilda lifted the skirt of her habit slightly and walked into the low underbrush to look farther into the grove. As she had suspected, after seeing the product of their labors, the clearing held ruins similar to those she had stopped at many years ago on her return to Highhear. On that visit, she had decided that she had stumbled across a ruined abbey; she was not sure about this seeming ruin: was it the same one? A different one? Her reasoning then had been based on the single piece of vellum she had found and the fact that some of the stones had engraved but crumbled markings. She smiled as she remembered too the rune stone she had carried away from the site.

"Are you in need of anything, sister," one of the men asked, looking at her questioningly. "Surely you do not travel these roads alone?" Hilda recognized the language, but not the accent. Pondering on that, she almost forgot to answer.

She smiled, pointing to Olaf who raised his hand in recognition. She then turned back to gaze at the scattered rocks. "Oh, no, it's just that I wandered through a similar site years ago and saw a stone with some letters on it. I just wondered if such stones might be here also. Then I could not read them; now I can."

"Englisc," she heard one of the workers whisper to another.

Pretending that the word was meant for her, Hilda answered, "Yes, I'm Englisc, born and raised for much of my life a two-day journey from here. And you, I am thinking, are not Englisc?"

The man who seemed to be the leader of the group laughed. "Well, Sister, I'm really not sure. I too was born and raised not far from here, but my father is not Englisc. This is my homeland, so maybe I am. It feels that way."

The men laughed together, all agreeing that their heritage wasn't as clear as it could be, but then remembered who their questioner was and became sheepishly silent. To clear the air, their leader changed the subject.

"If you want to look about for your letters, I'm sure we wouldn't mind."

"Thank you, kindly," Hilda replied as she began to pick her

way carefully among the stacks of rocks. If she was aware of male stares at the shapely ankle revealed as she moved about, she did not react.

"What will you be doing with the stones?" Hilda asked.

"Lord Ragnar is building himself a new hall—these stones will form part of the foundation."

"And who might Lord Ragnar be," inquired Hilda politely.

"The overlord of all the lands beyond those markers," the man responded, pointing to the west.

"But the abbey to which I travel is there," Hilda replied with some puzzlement.

"Yes, his land includes the abbey, but he has allowed those who live there to control that part of his estate."

Stifling a protest, Hilda listened to the men's proud claim that Lord Ragnar controlled all the land, apparently from the edge of her own ancestral estate, to beyond the abbey to which she traveled. This may well have been her cousin Berghorf's land. Her father had inherited it after Berghorf's death and she, in turn, had inherited it from her father. Perhaps Lord Ragnar had been awarded some part of the land for his service to some Viking lord and was honoring the bequest she had made: that part of the land be set aside for the abbey. On the other hand, she concluded, it would not be wise to ask these men about that. It could wait until she arrived at Buxton. Strange, she commented to herself, that she felt no sense of loss. Shaking her head, she continued her search for engraved stones, marveling all the while that the stones of this ruined abbey were being used to build the houses of the invaders who probably had destroyed it, the same enemy who had tormented her father for much of his life.

At last, unable to locate any small stones with letters, Hilda decided to continue her journey. She stopped first to examine the large stones piled along the edge of the road. "However will you transport these huge pieces to your building site?" she asked another of the men.

He smiled at her earnestness and curiosity. "We will construct a road of logs, hitch thongs on the rocks, and pull them along," he explained.

"That will take a great deal of time," Hilda commented.

"Building a great hall takes much time. My father knows that."

"You're Lord Ragnar's son?" Hilda asked.

"Indeed, sister, I am. That was my older brother you were talking to in the grove. There were three of us. My twin brother...." He paused. "Well, he no longer lives."

Hilda crossed herself. "My sympathies to you and blessings to him."

"Truth is, I never knew him, as he was gone from us when I was only three or four. It's my father who cannot forget."

"I am Sister Hilda, and what is your name, my son?"

He smiled at the thought of being a son to this young woman—surely she was not much older than he. "I am called Redwald. My older brother is Rodman, and my twin brother was Rothwulf."

While they spoke, Hilda continued to look closely at each of the stones along the road, though she remained puzzled as he listed family names which seemed more Englisc to her than Viking. Suddenly, all thoughts of heritage were stripped from her mind.

"There, look!" Hilda said excitedly, "Just like the one I saw so many years ago." And there indeed was her stone or its twin: a small cross etched in on the left side, a cross with a circle encompassing the intersection of its two parts. Seating herself before the stone, she began cleaning off the letters with a tree sprig. What emerged, Redwald could see, was something that pleased her enormously. He knew almost nothing about nuns and priests and their religion, but he acknowledged, ruefully, obviously these nuns and priests had human emotions and could be talked to and listened to just like others.

Hilda traced the engraving with her finger, seeking to etch into her memory the letters before her." The date she could decipher as 657, but the name had deteriorated. It looked like...Hunville...perhaps, and the inscription, like ones common to Christian gravestones, ended with the words *per crucim cristi*, "through the cross of Christ...."

A cloud passed over the sun, causing Hilda to take a good look at its position in the sky. She had tarried long enough and was aware that Olaf, whom she could see in the distance, appeared quite impatient wandering in circles so as to keep his distance. Rising from the ground and brushing off her habit, Hilda turned to the young man and thanked him for his courtesy. "I must go to the abbey. I hope that one day you will visit there. Meanwhile, I wish you and your family well with your new hall. It is a good use for these sacred stones." Hilda realized that she had just blessed the efforts of an invader. "Perhaps they are no longer invaders," she thought, "and perhaps we should no longer think of them as enemies."

Resuming her journey, Hilda quickened her pace until she was able to see just at the horizon, the tower of a diminutive church. Gradually evolving out of the distance, the other buildings of the abbey became visible. Surprised at how pleased she felt to see the grounds, she decided that she had been right to come. The warm feelings continued as she saw the stile she had climbed over when she had escaped into the fields to be alone; the rush of emotion became almost unbearable when she recognized the tree and even the branch on which she had spent a contemplative afternoon. The pain was not far behind, for it was while on that perch she had been introduced to the coming together of male and female, and under it that she experienced her own passionate contact with John. She shivered, but whether from fear, longing, or sorrow she did not know. Could she still climb that tree?

Hilda shook her head. Such an adventure would be a sinful indulgence, guaranteed only to bring to mind what should be forgotten. Nonetheless, she could hardly hold back the desire to spend at least some moments there even if she did not climb out on the branch. It was almost as though the habited nun she'd become was being tugged along on the arm of the eighteen-year-old romantic she had once been. Somehow she felt herself living her life backward, sights and sounds pulling her back from the present to the past.

Her entrance onto the abbey grounds caused no stir of recognition at all. The novices in the field looked up, but continued their work. One of the young shepherds smiled and nodded. Hilda smiled in return. Probably all nuns looked much the same to him. The setting sun indicated to her that it was almost time for vespers, and though she had eaten almost nothing the whole day, she longed only to enter the chapel and sit in obscurity. She slipped in and found a dark corner into which she settled gratefully. Soon enough she would have to meet the community and interact with it. Olaf settled himself apart from her, honoring her wish to remain alone. Sitting in the quiet space, Hilda ruminated on her past, remembering when, with John's guidance, she had first read Pope Gregory's analysis of the active life and the contemplative life. At that time, Hilda had had no question that she preferred the active life. However, as the years flowed on, she now recognized, she had become more and more attached to the contemplative one.

Reading manuscripts had become a form of contemplation for her, a time when she pulled into herself and felt strongly the presence of God, of some inner spirit which nourished and was nourished by the words on the page. Abbess Fridewith had introduced her to glossing, the writing of translations within a text, for she had indeed learned to read Latin before she had learned to read her own language. This work, too, became contemplative as she reflected on how changing a word from one language to another subtly altered meaning. Another of the monks had begun to instruct her in the elaborate task of illustration, another source of meditation. There were times when she was sure she would be quite happy if she could spend the rest of her life studying the old manuscripts and helping to produce new ones. In moments of doubt, she could not help but wonder how much of her love of books and manuscripts was the product of who her teacher had been. Had she transmuted her love for John into a love for the manuscripts? What was the connection between a love of God and his works and a love of people or of a person and what they do?

As they filed in to take their seats in the chapel, several of the members of the community, male and female, looked idly at first and then with the more intense gaze of recognition at the nun lost in thought in the semi-dark corner. Hilda had not changed much in appearance in the years since she had left. Those who had been there at that time knew the history even though Abbess Edyth had tried to keep secret the reasons for her departure. Secrets were almost never kept in an abbey where people shared so much of their inner and outer lives. True to form, however, whatever their reactions were to Hilda's return, they did not speak directly to either her or to Abbess Edyth, though after chapel there would be whispering enough.

Hilda's worst fear was that John would be the next one to come into the door of the chapel. At the thought, she felt the blood rise in her cheeks. He presented no temptation for her, but she did not know exactly how she might react if she were to see him. Too much and too little had passed between them. Once the service started, however, her mind returned to its former dilemma: what was the connection for her between an active and a contemplative life? Her mother had been more a doer than a thinker. Hilda never had any desire to clip the nails of a dead saint; the thought was as repulsive to her as it had been when she first learned of it. She certainly enjoyed gardening and tending to the ill, but such tasks would never satisfy her in the same way the manuscript study did. God, she thought, intended more for her, or he would not have given her such a passion for reading and writing.

Abbess Edyth had not been aware of Hilda's presence when she entered the chapel, but she had sensed enough of something in the air to seek its source. And in so doing, her eyes lit on the figure in the corner. Once the services were over, she went directly to Hilda and, taking her hand in her own, guided the visitor out into the open.

"Let us, at long last, talk," she said.

Seated on a low inner wall of the cloister, Hilda listened as Edyth spoke of Father Jerome's death, the manuscripts he carried, and her own belief that his dying wish was for Hilda to undertake a study of them.

"I feel bound to those wishes," the Abbess confessed, but

Hilda heard the reluctance in her voice.

"You have never forgiven me, have you Abbess?" Hilda asked, determined not to leave the unspoken as continuously unspoken. "You blame me for bringing disgrace to your abbey through, as you would call it, fornication, with one of the brothers. Since that brother is no longer here, I assume you banished him also. I have suffered every day of my life for what you called sin. Perhaps I was not quite ready to devote myself to God during those years, but later Father Jerome saw that need in me. He conveyed to me God's forgiveness and directed my penance. I feel —God's forgiveness." Hilda hesitated briefly, "I had hoped that you would forgive me also." The tone and authority of the former Pryncesse Hilda crept into the voice of the determined nun who had become an abbess.

"Hilda, you know that I did what I...."

Hilda interrupted her. "I've done my penance. It is sufficient." Hilda wished she was as sure of the feelings which lay behind her words as her tone implied.

Abbess Edyth heard only the sureness, not the doubts, and determined to let the past go. Nodding her agreement, she patted Hilda's hand and brought them both into the present.

"Come, I'll take you to see the manuscripts."

As Hilda followed Abbess Edyth into the scriptorium, memories flooded back to her with such strength that she halted for a moment and stood silently by the reading desk nearest the door, glad the Abbess could not see her reaction. Before her was the spot where she had always found Brother William bent over one of his beloved manuscripts, Brother John standing next to him. She shook her head and came back to the present: it was not likely she would ever see either of them here again.

"He brought three manuscripts," Edyth announced, pointing toward one of the shelves on the back wall. "I will leave you to them."

Hilda smiled slightly, murmured a soft "Thank you," and waited for Abbess Edyth to leave the room. No doubt they would never be easy with each other, but at least they could work in the same monastery. She turned to her task, aware of the curious eyes of several of the monks who had briefly interrupted their activities when she and Abbess Edyth had entered the hushed confines of the scriptorium.

Olaf had told her that one of the manuscripts was in Latin and the other two in the vernacular. Hilda determined that she would devote her time to the ones in Englisc first, since the Latin text was more likely to be a religious tract of some kind, and there was no shortage of manuscripts of that kind. She lifted the first manuscript from the shelf and placed it on one of the reading desks. It was in fairly good condition despite the fact that the spine was fraying and the leather binding was worn from what had obviously been much handling. The parchment on the inside was also in fair shape, but the folios were beginning to dry out and flake a bit on the edges. She resisted the temptation to begin reading at once and laid the book aside. She needed to know the total of what she was facing before she began any significant work.

She pulled the second manuscript onto the desk. This was the Latin codex. Glancing only briefly at it, Hilda put that aside also and pulled down the third of Jerome's treasures. In far worse shape than either of the other two, this book appeared to have lost both individual pages and whole folios. In some cases, pieces of the vellum appeared to have worn away naturally, but in other instances, pages of the manuscript had been torn out. Looking more carefully, she determined that the manuscript pages had seen much rewriting. The writing had been erased over and over again, almost illegible in large blotches on many of the folios. There was even an indication of searing, probably from a mild fire.

"What a loss," Hilda said to herself. The condition of this manuscript and its age, however, drew her to it. She decided that this was where her work would begin.

Several hours later Hilda heard the bells announcing Compline. It seemed as though only minutes had gone by. Slowly returning to the reality around her, Hilda gently picked up the treasure in front of her and returned it to its shelf. She would have preferred to stay and continue her reading, but she knew where her duty lay and, brushing the dust and particles of the manuscript from her habit, she hurried into the small chapel. She heard almost none of the service; her mind could not let go of the stories from the manuscript. It held tales she had heard Father Jerome and Bishop Ceolwulf tell many, many years ago. Had Father Jerome possessed the manuscript then, or had he come across it later? She had seen a number of manuscripts in the spoken language, in the Englisc of her people, but these had been, almost without exception, translations from the Latin Bible, sermons, or religious poetry. Never had she read any of the old stories, which she knew only through hearing them.

The liturgy seemed to go on forever. She hoped God would forgive the sin of inattention. All she knew was that she longed for the service to be over quickly so that she could return to the scriptorium. When it finally ended, she avoided Abbess Edyth's stern and quizzical gaze and hurried out of the chapel. Hilda suspected the Abbess wanted her to tell her something more about the manuscript, but she had no intentions of giving the Abbess control of the work. She would never understand, Hilda was sure, the interest in old tales or in the language in which they were told. It would be best to be very sparing in the information provided to Abbess Edyth.

Despite her desire to return to the scriptorium, Hilda found that she could not. Abbess Edyth had planned a special entertainment to welcome her guest, and there was no way to avoid it. The entertainment consisted mainly of a young novice chanting melodiously many of the psalms, accompanying himself on a beautiful lyre. Hilda, despite her small annoyance, found herself thoroughly engaged.

The following morning after services, she was finally able to return to the scriptorium and resume her examination of the manuscripts. As penance for letting the manuscript occupy her attention more than the prayers she owed to God, she reluctantly ignored the manuscript which had held her attention the previous day and drew down the Latin manuscript. The penance proved a poor punishment, however. The manuscript turned out to be far more interesting than she had expected because it contained a medicinal section, some pieces on Latin grammar, and several travel commentaries. As she replaced it on the shelf, she made a note to give it a more detailed reading at a later date. She then turned her attention to the other vernacular manuscript. In it she recognized translations from Genesis, Exodus, and several other excerpts from the Old and New Testaments. These translations, however, in contrast to others she had read, were rhythmic and resonated with the language of the old stories and songs. For some time she found herself quite caught up in the new version of the Israelites flight from Egypt and through the Red Sea. Here was something new, new to her at least: an alteration from prose to poetry. Immediately Hilda sensed the value of this retelling of the biblical stories—surely such lively text, the rhythmic sounds of the old language, would appeal to those steeped in old stories. She couldn't work on everything at once, she allowed, so this manuscript, too, she lay aside for further perusal another day.

Returning to what interested her most, the oldest tattered manuscript, Hilda became so absorbed that she missed the remaining offices of the day, never even feeling hunger or thirst until she heard the call to Vespers. Abbess Edyth would surely decide she was incapable of avoiding sin, Hilda thought to herself, almost with delight. Then she checked herself quickly. She sinned more with such childish thoughts than she did with neglect of services. Feeling only somewhat contrite, she slipped into the chapel quietly and relished the peace which evensong always brought to her.

After the silence of the last meal of the day, Hilda sought out Abbess Edyth. "May I speak with you, Sister Abbess?" she asked as deferentially as she could.

"Of course, my child," the Abbess replied, with a slight emphasis on the word "child."

"I have examined all three of Father Jerome's manuscripts, and all three are worthy of continued study. However, I must return to my own abbey. I would like your permission to take them with me so that I might devote more time to them without neglecting my responsibilities."

Abbess Edyth drew herself up, prepared for battle. "I cannot

354

allow it. The manuscripts were brought to us and here is where they'll stay."

"He did not necessarily come to you by choice, sister," Hilda argued. "He was left here by a man who did not even stay long enough to see if he recovered from his illness! You called me here because you determined it was his wish that they come to me. It was my name he uttered as he died."

"He wanted you to see them, Sister Hilda," Abbess Edyth declared, "And I have given you access to them, granting his wish. You may study them as often as you like, but here they will remain."

"I cannot stay here long as I have my responsibilities at Rosedale," Hilda replied regretfully.

"Yes, I know," Abbess Edyth said flatly.

"That, then, is final? The manuscripts will stay here and I can examine them only by remaining here or returning later?" Abbess Edyth nodded, and Hilda, fighting to control her anger, bowed her head briefly and left the room.

As Hilda lay in the rough bed that night, the anger turned to tears. Years ago Abbess Edyth had desecrated her love for John, now she was denying her again, denying her another love. Hilda clenched her fists in desperation; it didn't make sense that the Abbess was so intent on keeping her from what she loved. With great difficulty she suppressed evil thoughts and slept little that night, but she knew what she must do.

After Prime, Hilda returned to the scriptorium and sought out the young man who had escorted her from Rosedale. Finding him seated before one of the desks carefully copying a manuscript, Hilda sat quietly beside him at the next desk.

"Brother Olaf, I must return to my own abbey." As he started to speak, she stopped him. "I need no escort other than the two young men who came here with us. I'm quite capable of finding my own way back. And I can certainly rely on those who sheltered and fed us on the way here. I would, however, ask a great favor."

"And what is that, Sister?" Olaf inquired.

"I've looked at the three manuscripts Father Jerome left for me—they're quite valuable. Worth far more study than I have been able to give them. Unhappily, I cannot stay and Abbess Edyth will not allow me to take them back with me." Hilda tried very hard to keep the note of disapproval from her voice, but she wasn't quite sure she was succeeding.

"Will you keep an eye on them for me? Make certain they're protected? The oldest is in quite poor condition, and the temptation will be to restore it. Make sure that any mending does not further obliterate the text—not even one mark." Olaf sensed the quiet desperation in Hilda's voice: he shared her concern about the state of the manuscripts.

"Yes, Abbess Hilda, I will care for them, I hope, as you would yourself." He had become quite attached to Hilda during their brief journey, recognizing in himself the same love of the old writings. He respected that shared love enough to fully carry out her wishes.

"Thank you. I can leave confident that when the day comes and I can once again study them, I will not find them altered or destroyed, their pages scraped and rebound to make newer manuscripts."

A Change for Good (882-888)

As the progress of events would have it, Hilda could not make the trip back to Buxton for several years. As a bold administrator, she never failed to seek advantages for her abbey wherever she might find them, even approaching a number of former invaders now settled down as farmers. She acquired additional livestock and even some return of lands which had belonged to the abbey before the invasions. Although some of the local landowners were suspicious of her aims, most came to respect the young abbess who acknowledged openly that she had once been a princess but no longer desired to be entangled in the affairs of the world. She simply wished to provide a place for meditation and peace for those under her care. Hilda's dealings with the landowners were rendered more amenable as a result of her willingness to supply herbs and ointments to everyone who sought them. She had prolonged the life of one of their most famous leaders and aided their wives in childbirth. Several of the young men, including those she had met on her trip to Buxton to see Jerome's treasures, offered their services to the abbey after a particularly devastating storm destroyed several of its buildings.

All in all, life in the abbey satisfied Hilda. She enjoyed being in charge and giving orders—even though she often chastised herself in the confessional for not being properly humble. Her best hours still remained those she spent in her scriptorium repairing and copying her beloved manuscripts. Whenever she came across some piece in one of them that she had never seen before, it was as though she had discovered a chest of jewels. The other nuns and monks could usually discern when such discoveries occurred since their Abbess could be heard to sing under her breath as she went about her work.

Six years later, just as Hilda emerged from the scriptorium to head toward the small chapel for evensong, she was pleasantly surprised to see Brother Olaf arrive, accompanied by two elderly church prelates whose clothing marked their authority. Hilda quickly brushed off the flakes of parchment which inevitably adhered to her habit and hurried to greet them.

"Brother Olaf, I do believe! What a pleasure to see you once more. And your companions?"

"Abbess Hilda, may I present Archdeacon Eadred and Bishop Eduard. We have been sent by Archbishop Wulfstan of Yorvik to deliver an important message."

"Welcome," Hilda responded, bowing slightly and bestowing a light kiss to the ring the Bishop extended to her. She had had previous correspondence with both of the men she now met face to face, and they had always opposed the changes that she wished to make in the monastery and the care of the people who depended upon it. Something within her revolted against ceremonial obeisance to these men; she vowed to show no unearned subservience to their position nor deference to their wishes.

"We begin evensong," she announced. "Please join us." Without waiting for an answer Hilda started toward the chapel.

Olaf hurried after her, whispering, "Abbess Hilda, I have taken care of your manuscripts, all of them, since you saw them. No one has even looked at them or asked to look at them."

"Bless you," was Hilda's quick reply. She looked back, aware that the two prelates seemed reluctant to accompany them, but hurried on, glad she had given them no choice. In truth, they would have been derelict had they avoided an event in the church's daily calendar, no matter the importance of whatever message they carried.

After the service, she joined the two messengers from the Archbishop who were waiting for her outside. As was the custom, she extended the abbey's hospitality. "Gentlemen, will you take some food and drink and rest a bit before we talk?"

"I think not," replied the Bishop sternly. "Our message is of great import, and we wish to deliver it immediately. Tomorrow we all must be on our way early."

Hilda noted the reference to "all" but made no comment. She led the two men across the path leading to the refectory and into a small area around which stones had been placed at intervals. Seating herself on one of the smaller stones, she invited the two men to select a seat for themselves. With fairly obvious displeasure at the possibility of soiling their vestments, the two seated themselves.

"As you know, Abbess Hilda," Bishop Eduard began, obviously irritated that she had been told he had a message and yet had postponed the hearing of it, "we have for you an urgent message from Archbishop Wulfstan of Yorvik. With your permission we will break the Bishop's seal and read its contents to you."

She stopped him before he could break the seal. "Brother, please, it's unnecessary for you to read it to me." She wasn't quite sure she had kept the sarcasm of her tone muted.

The archdeacon handed her a roll of parchment clasped with the impressive seal of the Archbishop. Hilda stopped a moment to admire the quality of the vellum; she wished she had access to such quality. She knew that her slowness in breaking the seal and unrolling the parchment was giving no pleasure to the two seated with her, and resolved to reprimand herself later for the pleasure that was giving her, particularly since they had spoken as though she were not capable of reading the message herself.

Carefully unrolling the parchment so as not to harm it in any way, Hilda smoothed it out with her hand and began to read the carefully crafted message it contained. Some element of surprise, immediately repressed, might have been visible on her face to anyone who knew her well. But she had learned to control her expressions.

"Gentlemen, this message contains a sadness, an honor, and a surprise. I was unaware that the Archbishop had any knowledge or awareness at all of my interest in manuscripts."

She really wanted to say something much more caustic. "So, gentlemen, if you knew I was being asked to be the abbess of a particular monastery simply because it was the repository of a significant collection of manuscripts, why did you suggest that I could not read?" But, Hilda's diplomacy had been increasing through the years, and she repressed the words; it was not so easy to repress her anger.

"Your fame has traveled, Abbess Hilda," responded the Archdeacon, but despite the compliment, there was little warmth in his voice. "The Archbishop would be most pleased if you were to leave immediately and take up your responsibilities at Buxton. He does not wish the establishment there to be without an abbess for any length of time. Abbess Edyth herself recommended that you succeed her."

Those words shocked Hilda so that, even with her years of training herself, she was unable to block her spontaneous astonishment. "Abbess Edyth asked that I succeed her?!"

"Yes, Sister Hilda.... Is that so strange?"

"Abbess Edyth had never been fond of me: I would not have expected her to point to me as her successor, to single me out for this honor." Hilda's voice manifested puzzlement. She could only rue the unkind thoughts that Edyth's name had often evoked. More fodder for confession, no doubt.

Hilda rose in indication that the conversation was over and dismissed the two more like a princess than an abbess. "Please leave me now, gentlemen. I have much to ponder before I consent to this change."

Archdeacon Eadred, anger causing his voice to rise slightly, clearly was outraged by her reception to the Archbishop's edict.

"Abbess, may I remind you that you have no choice? This is the Archbishop's request, of course, but his requests are in fact orders. He expects you to leave immediately."

"God," said Hilda, as she looked at the two men directly, "always wishes us to consider changes in our lives carefully. He will determine the course of my life. I go to pray. Even the meanest of lay brothers has the right to decide his fate." Signaling one of the nuns passing by, she turned the tending of the two messengers to her care and walked firmly away from them and toward the chapel.

The next morning after Prime, Hilda approached the two rather disgruntled looking prelates who, with the help of two young assistants, were preparing themselves and their horses for departure. Brother Olaf had been ordered to stay behind, and so he stood quietly on the sidelines, enjoying the discomfort the two prelates were experiencing. With only the simplest of greeting, she handed the bishop a sealed document.

"My answer is here. Please deliver it to the Archbishop."

The angry Bishop glanced at the document and looked her in the eye.

"And what are we to tell him?"

"You need say nothing. I have explained my decision and outlined my future plans in the message. God be with you both as you return to your duties."

With those words, Hilda bowed curtly and strode away to attend to the morning chores she always assigned to herself in the herb garden.

"I'm inherently evil," she thought, but she smiled to herself, knowing that the two irate churchmen could not discharge their anger at her. She was quite sure that they would have much to say to the Archbishop when they returned. Nonetheless, she refused to give them the pleasure of knowing that she had acceded to the Archbishop's "request."

Hilda knew the Archbishop by reputation and by his dealings with Rosedale and its community, so she had little doubt that he intended her to leave—immediately. His message did not insist upon it, and she knew he would understand the need to see that her house was in order before she went elsewhere. In her message, she recommended that Sister Estrella, whom Eadred and Eduard would no doubt consider too young, assume the duties of abbess. Hilda had faith in her intelligence, devotion, and mercy. She had the potential to be a good abbess, and the other nuns already admired and deferred to her in many ways.

"Once again," she thought, "I return to Buxton. God keeps bringing me back, so he must have some task for me that can only be accomplished there."

Chapter 10: Leova and Hilda Together Once Again (892)

Stooping slightly to avoid hitting her head, Leova stepped through the low door and out of the thatched cottage. She'd been attending the wife of a tenant farmer who had been unable to nurse her newborn babe. The young woman didn't seem quite sure what to do and, since as a child she'd lost her own mother, she had no one to advise her. Jankin who now supervised, under Rolfe's direction, much of the manor, had informed his mistress of the young woman's need. During the last ten years, Leova had slowly taken over the healing tasks of Lothlar and its people just as Rolfe had relieved Bertram as the lord of the manor. Although at first she had feared offending her mother, Leova cautiously began to take over more and more of the business of the hall. It became an arrangement that satisfied both generations. Bertram returned to his confident self in the company of such a thriving world; Pagany lost the worried frown that she had worn when her daughter returned to the estate. With the aid of Jankin, Rolfe soon had managed the lands into quite profitable ones where crops and livestock flourished as did the farmers who tended to both.

As she stretched and looked out over the fields, she saw Jankin riding toward her and, as he neared, she could tell he was grinning happily. "My lady, come see. Iona and Ian have come to visit."

"What wonderful news, Jankin! Are they at the hall?"

"No, they've stopped to rest just over the hill by Bryna's place." Leova mounted her horse and rode with Jankin over a slight rise into an area that reflected the attentive care of Bryna and her sons. Standing in front of the well-kept large cottage, obviously watching for someone, stood Ian and Iona.

"My Lady!" the older couple called, one voice overlapping the other.

Leova climbed down from her horse and happily embraced first one then the other of the couple. "What brings you here?" she asked.

"We began to long for our old sites and, not getting any

younger, we decided we needed to visit our old land and companions," Ian answered with a shrug of his shoulders, as though he did not know, even for himself, why they had returned. "We've turned our place there over to the niece and nephew for a bit."

The reunion, begun with a series of hugs, continued with questions about their life to the west; and once they had answered them, the old couple had questions about Rolfe and Wulfram.

"Rolfe is well," Leova said. "Being in charge seems to have agreed with him. And Wulfram is the kind of son all parents wish for. He even cares for his brothers and sisters albeit with a little teasing."

"Brothers and sisters?" Iona repeated.

"How many?" said her husband.

Leova blushed, though she couldn't have said why. "Two girls, Riana and Rosaleen, and two boys, Berghorf and Bryan."

The older couple laughed. "Four children in eleven years! We knew you and Rolfe were a good healthy pair; we told you so!"

Leova blushed a bit more, but her smile acknowledged that Ian and Iona had been right. Then Iona placed a careful hand on Leova's arm and leaned forward to speak quietly. "We wish to learn more of Regan and the affairs of Stonehart—but later for that please." Leova nodded in agreement. Straightening up, Iona continued: "Bryna, the woman of this cottage, has invited us to rest. Come sit with us. Jankin can find Rolfe."

"Oh, no," replied Leova immediately. "Come to the hall with me—we'll find lodgings for you there."

"Lady Leova," responded Iona hesitantly, "She has gone to fix us refreshment. We cannot walk away."

"Of course," Leova replied, remembering the kindness of the farmers who had tended to them when they had fled the hall and land so long ago. "It would be an honor to stay," she continued as she sat down next to Iona just outside the cottage door.

They barely had time to be seated when a young girl appeared carefully balancing cups and a large pottery pitcher on the short wooden stool she used as a tray. A woman, who appeared to be over sixty, followed the child, carrying warm bread; she bowed and backed away, obviously intending to return to the cottage. "Bryna," Leova called after the woman, "please stay. I remember clearly when you arrived, but I have not seen you since you moved into this cottage. Rolfe tells me that your sons have become our most skillful watchers and hunters. We are indebted to you and them. I do hope it goes well with you and these sons and your daughter."

"Yes, my lady," Bryna answered, "you and your people, especially Jankin, have made us quite welcome. We are grateful because, as you know, the enemy forced us from our home in the east." Having spoken, Bryna again began to turn away.

"No, no," Leova beckoned to her, "stay with us, share this bread you have so kindly provided to strangers."

"I would not want to disturb you, my lady," said Bryna. I know you must have much to talk of since, as I understand, you parted when your son was but a baby."

"That's true." Leova smiled, "but you are welcome to join us." She turned then at the sound of approaching horses bearing her husband and son. The couple rose to greet Rolfe, whose enthusiastic embrace lifted them off their feet, making them all laugh. When she caught her breath, Iona turned to look at the boy she had once held as a baby.

"My, so this is Wulfram," was all Iona could say. The boy had grown into a strapping lad, faired-haired like his mother's family but with the high cheekbones and bushy eyebrows that had marked his father's face.

"Wulfram," Leona said. "Iona and Ian have come to visit— perhaps to stay! They were there when you were born and took care of you when you were a baby. You might say that they were your first grandparents!"

Wulfram shuffled from one foot to the other, slightly embarrassed since he wanted to impress the young girl standing just behind the bench on which his mother sat. "I'm most pleased to meet you," he said hesitantly. "My mother and father have told me much about you." Then he produced a lovely, warm smile and said with a slight laugh. "I wish I could remember that time, but I don't."

He looked at Leova for approval, and she smiled with

maternal pride at her son's ability to be genuine and polite with the same words. And she also smiled at his sly glance at the young girl behind her.

The formalities finished, Wulfram sat at his mother's feet and appeared to listen as the adults happily shared the events of their lives since they last saw one another. It was obvious that he was only vaguely interested in the conversation. His attention was focused on the young girl who had moved away from the visitors and returned to her chores, but had not strayed so far that she was unable to hear the conversation. She dragged a large burlap sack behind her into which she was dropping small tree branches, leaves, and other debris. She then carefully raked the yard, adding the stray pebbles and stones to the bag. Wulfram guessed that she was deliberately lengthening her task in order to stay in hearing range. At last, though, she moved to pick up the bag, but before she could lift it to her shoulder, Wulfram jumped to his feet, calling out "Wait, I'll help you."

The look she gave him made it obvious that she didn't want or need his help. However, before she could speak, he'd hoisted the bag and stood smiling at her nervously.

"Where shall I take it?" It made no sense for her to protest.

"Follow me," she mumbled irritably, and he did.

"I'm Wulfram," he said as he followed her.

"I know who you are," she replied shortly. "I've seen you out riding and hunting with your father."

"What's your name?" Wulfram asked, determined to engage her.

"Elene–it's really Helene, but my brothers—I have five of them, all older than me—call me Elene, so that's what I call myself now."

At that moment, his mother called. "Wulfram, it's time for all of us to go back to the hall."

With reluctance, Wulfram turned to go, and then turned back. "Would you like to ride with us some day?"

Elene laughed. "I've never been on a horse. Girls like me don't know how to ride."

"Then I shall teach you," said Wulfram triumphantly as he turned to join the group moving toward the hall. "Maybe tomorrow!"

As Wulfram rejoined his parents and their old friends he felt a sense of anticipation. There were very few boys and girls close to his age on the estate, and mostly they avoided him because he was their Lord's son. Wulfram's brothers and sisters were, in his mind, all babies, and he often yearned for a companion. Now he'd found one. The fact that Elene wasn't a boy only added to the pleasure.

We wanted to visit," Ian said, as he walked alongside Rolfe back toward the hall, "but we still fear Lady Allmana. I'm not sure that she's satisfied with just taking our land. Ian thinks she'd like us dead, too."

Rolfe and Leova exchanged a quick look. "You need not worry." Rolfe said. "My mother is dead some seven years now. And long before she died, she'd lapsed into madness."

"Madness? Wasn't she already mad enough!" snorted Ian.

Leova smiled ruefully. "This madness was the kind that the old so often fall prey to. Gradually she lost the ability to think through simple everyday problems. Stephen, no longer able to control her, left without a word, and Lady Allmana decided that he'd been killed, and that she would be killed also."

"As she grew more confused," Rolfe continued, "my mother locked herself in her room, refusing to open the door to anyone but Regan, but even he couldn't persuade her to eat. She feared poison. You might say she died of her own fears—she starved herself into such weakness that we couldn't revive her."

"I hope she descended into hell—both in body and soul," Iona declared with passion. A guilty look at Rolfe followed quickly. He pretended not to have heard the condemning words.

"You may be forgiven for your thoughts, my dear," said Ian. "Not only did she steal our daughter and our lands, her treatment of Wyomina caused the child to go mad; evil lurks about those walls and eventually it invades everyone who stays there."

"Not Rolfe, not Regan, and not William," Leova answered. "William was banished as a boy, and that banishment probably saved his soul. Rolfe also left fairly young to go to the monastery. And Regan, well, Regan's different. Perhaps that was his salvation. It was only Robert who was truly his mother's son; he paid for that with his life. And now Regan is in charge of the lands and he has kept them prosperous. I'm sure he'd be overjoyed, as we would all be, to return your land to you and see you settled."

"No," Iona said in a whisper, "We are grateful for your generous offer, but there is much sorrow there that we would not want to revisit."

Leova knew not to tarry on what had to be a painful history for the old couple. "Enough. We do not have to deal with whatever happened at Stonehart. We have land here we can exchange for your land at Stonehart; our house is blessed. Please say you will accept the offer and stay with us, even if only temporarily."

Much to Leova's and Rolfe's pleasure, Ian and Iona, increasingly aware of the distances between them and their scattered family in Cymru, decided to remain at Lothlar, and Leova commissioned Jankin to provide a dwelling for them close to the hall, within immediate access to its protection should that ever be necessary. Additionally, Rolfe and Jankin were able to allot them nearby farmland. Once the cottage was complete, Leova proudly turned it over to her guests, insisting that it belonged to them in exchange for the land they once held at Stonehart and for how long or how briefly they wished to stay. Rolfe was equally insistent, partially because he had become much attached to both of them during the years when they had lived together, and partially because he wanted to recompense them in some way for the evil his mother had brought down upon them.

Pagany was equally pleased, for she had missed her own people, and Ian and Iona reminded her of the culture into which she had been born. The emptiness she had often felt after becoming the mistress of Lothlar had been eased on occasion by trips back to her homeland, but these had become fewer and fewer. The women of the forest had comforted her. However, that group shrunk ever smaller as generation after generation became accustomed to the "new" religion. Once Ian and Iona had settled in, the three of them often spent hours together reminiscing about the old ways, delighting in using the Cymric language, a pleasure Pagany had not known for years.

Wulfram loved nothing better than to sit quietly and listen; he found the old ways strangely enchanting and the old language delightfully musical. Increasingly, when she had fulfilled her work chores, Elena sat with him; she seemed equally enthralled. Gradually, the two began to understand their elders, who would stop from time to time to translate phrases for them, warmed by their interest.

One day as they were so occupied, a lone donkey approached ridden by a monk. At their friendly wave, the monk guided his donkey toward them and dismounted slowly, as if he were elderly, brushing away the dust that attested to his long journey.

"Good people, I have come a long way. May I rest here?"

Iona immediately rose to prepare drink and food for the new arrival, who, upon closer perusal, was far younger than his sore muscles made him appear.

"Father, how are you called?"

"Brother Olaf," he made a little half bow, "of Buxton Abbey. My Abbess sent me with a message to the brothers at the monastery at Shrewsbury, but I seem to have lost my way. I would be most grateful for a place to rest, some conversation, and advice from someone who might put me back on the right path."

Wulfram spoke quickly and unexpectedly. "You shall come to the hall with me. My mother and father are the Lord and Lady of this land. They can direct you or will know who can."

Brother Olaf smiled gratefully at the young boy and eagerly consumed the food and drink placed before him. Pagany, Ian, and Iona thought it best not to resume their conversation about the old customs. None of them had any quarrel with the new religion—they simply preferred their ancestral ways—but many of the new religious community found these old ways threatening and offensive. Better remain silent than offend the monk. When Brother Olaf had refreshed himself, he seemed none too eager to make his way to the hall, relishing the opportunity to continue at rest.

Wulfram, ever curious, began to question him about his life as a brother at a monastery. "What do you do at the abbey? Can you read and write?"

Brother Olaf was somewhat amused. "My, young man, you get right to the point...."

But before he could begin, Elene interrupted.

"Are there any women there? Do they have the same duties as the monks?"

At this point Brother Olaf laughed, not sure who or what to answer first. "Let me start with the young master's question. I work in the scriptorium, copying, creating, and sometimes mending, manuscripts. Abbess Hilda, my mentor, taught me the art of bookbinding and also how to read in both Latin and English. In fact, it was she who sent me to seek out the brothers at Shrewsbury because she had heard they had a manuscript she wanted to copy."

Upon hearing the name "Hilda," Pagany conjured up the memory of the lively girl who had seemed so much like a daughter. She knew that Hilda's mother had placed her in a monastery years ago. Pagany chuckled at the idea that her Hilda and Olaf's Hilda might be the same person, but even as she did so, she knew it was not impossible. The old religion had taught her that life often creates the inexplicable. Lost in thought, Pagany did not hear the question addressed to her by the young brother.

Wulfram repeated the question quietly, placing his arm gently on Pagany's hand. "Olaf wants to know if you could suggest anyone who might guide him to his destination."

"Oh, please forgive me. Whenever I hear the name 'Hilda,' I remember my daughter's companion of many years ago. Such a lively, bright young girl. She was a princess who returned to her ancestral lands at Hearhigh. We have often wondered what happened to her."

"My Abbess was once a princess also!" Olaf exclaimed.

Pagany drew in her breath and held it a moment, but she stopped herself before she could ask the questions that rose to her lips. "You must come with us. We'll talk at the hall when you're fully rested. My daughter and her husband will want to hear what you have to say and," she added, "there's no need for you to repeat any story you'd tell us now." She touched his arm gently and leaned in to whisper in his ear. "Save the story of your Abbess for the last. I'd like to give them a surprise!" She turned to Wulfram: "Please guide Olaf to the hall so he can rest and we'll all talk later."

After a short rest and dinner, Olaf became the center of everyone's questions. Rolfe, recalling his own days at Buxton, smiled at the young man. "Tell me, how do you serve the monastery?"

"I'm in charge of the manuscripts."

"What a strange coincidence. My brother William had that task when we were both there." He paused for a moment, taking a deep breath. "I wonder if any of the people I knew still serve there? Does Abbess Edyth still govern?"

"No, she died several years ago. Abbess Hilda, a lovely, devout, and learned woman leads us now." Rolfe's gaze became more intense, but he quickly closed his eyes as though refusing intrusive images.

Leova seemed to be resisting jumping from her seat. "Do continue; tell us more about this Abbess!"

""Most of her time is spent in prayer," Olaf continued, "she devotes the rest to old manuscripts: copying them, illustrating them, working on deciphering those which are in a ruinous state."

"Now, young man," Pagany asserted, "Tell us about this woman. I doubt this pious abbess is our Hilda, who was a wild thing more likely to climb on the roof than sit still and embroider a piece of tapestry. Still," she hesitated, "this world is not always predictable." She turned to Leova, who had suddenly become quiet. "Stop staring at the young man, Leova. If you have a question, ask it!"

"And what is her character like, this Abbess Hilda of yours?" Leova questioned. Rolfe looked quickly at his wife and then turned as though he were searching for something unseen.

"Abbess Hilda can be wild too—at least for a nun." Brother Olaf hurried on to make sure no one thought he was disrespectful to his Abbess, "I once saw her jump on a horse bareback in order to quiet it, and another time, when it was hot, she pulled off her wimple and her hair fell around her shoulders in ringlets—her head should be shaven and it's not! In the evening, after prayers, she often sits out in the fields and sings while she plays a beautiful little lute."

Pagany smiled to herself, Brother Olaf may not have known it, but he was deeply in love with his Abbess.

Leova could be silent no more. "Our Hilda must be your Hilda also! We've found her after so many years, my wonderful friend. Rolfe, we must go to Buxton. We'll leave tomorrow!"

Rolfe, who had grown more erect and somewhat stiff as Brother Olaf described his Abbess, did not seem to hear her. He had retreated into the past, remembering his Hilda, a Hilda whom neither Olaf nor Leova knew. Leova had once questioned him about the Hilda of whom William had spoken. Rolfe seemed not to know much of her background and confirmed William's statement that the woman had not returned to the abbey after the raid and, in fact, no one knew what had happened to her. Now, it was possible that this Hilda was back at that abbey. Leova could not contain her joy. "Rolfe, Rolfe, listen to me. We must make plans. This woman is my Hilda!"

"Plans?" Rolfe asked, coming out of his daze.

"Yes, yes, yes! We must go immediately; I've waited years and years, dreamed of the time when I would once again see Hilda. We can make preparations now and leave tomorrow."

Rolfe knew at once that Leova's determination to journey to Buxton would be impossible to derail, but he shuttered inwardly at the thought of the trip. He shared his wife's hopes that she'd found her friend, but the thought of seeing the woman he had once loved frightened him. What if she had not forgiven him for seeming to have abandoned her? He'd left by night without saying goodbye after seeking her in vain and without knowing for sure that she had escaped. He had attempted to lessen his guilt by returning to the monastery and seeking information—fruitlessly as it turned out. Perhaps he could meet Abbess Hilda before Leova saw her. If she was the one he'd known, he hoped they would have some chance to talk before Leova appeared. He knew it would be best if he went ahead, saw her first without Leova. He hatched a brief plan to make a trip of his own.

"I know you want to leave immediately, but we do need to enable the messenger to finish his journey. It would be best if I were to accompany him down to Shrewsbury—so he will not get lost again." He hesitated, seeing the look on Leova's face. "Regan can go with you if you really want to leave at the end of the week," he offered.

"No, everything on the estate can be put in order immediately—Jankin can care for people, sheep, and crops. And we can ask that one of Bryna's sons accompany this young monk. I do so want you to meet Hilda—if it is indeed my Hilda."

He shook his head. No matter what he said, he'd only be able to delay the trip for several days. Leova was undeterred about going and about his going with her. His days with Hilda were the only secret he had never shared with another and he feared the outcome of this visit.

Two mornings later, the trip began. Leova hurried the small troop along, cutting rest periods short, traveling into the dark, and rising early in the morning. Finally the monastery appeared in the distance; Leova urged them to increase their pace. At the end, she broke away from the others, galloping at full speed into the monastery yard, much to the dismay of monks, chickens, pigs, and sheep who were, each in their own way, performing their daily routines. With a bewildered look on his face, one of the older monks approached Leova apprehensively while he looked also at the others who were approaching the yard more slowly.

"My Lady, may I be of service?"

"I wish to see Abbess Hilda," she demanded. "It's important." Leova took a deep breath and calmed herself as she began to see herself from the monk's point of view. He must think me quite mad, she thought. "Is she here?" she asked in a more subdued voice.

"Yes, My Lady, but Abbess Hilda spends the late afternoon in the scriptorium and is not to be disturbed." By this time, Rolfe and the others had joined Leova. Sensing no harm, the monk became gracious. "Please rest your horses and take some refreshment. Our quarters are simple, but comfortable, and should serve your people well."

Leova slipped confidently off her horse and extended her hand to the monk, attempting to regain some dignity. "I'm sorry for my rash behavior. I am Leova of Lothlar, and this is Lord Rolfe. We have come to see Abbess Hilda. Could you send her word?"

"I'm sorry, My Lady. I am not permitted to draw Abbess Hilda from her duties. She can see you after Nones, perhaps, when we're given a free period."

Leova experienced a sudden drain of energy, recognizing that she would simply have to wait until the Abbess completed her daily routine, but she couldn't rest. For the next two hours she wandered restlessly about the monastery, marveling at the craftsmanship of its builders, the artistry of the carved figures on stone arches, the serene beauty of inner courtyards, and fantasizing about life within the walls. She noticed groups of nuns who seemed to be studying pages passed out by one of them; other nuns walked purposely from one building to the next, surely on some important errand. She did not think it was a life she would find appealing even though she recognized the attractions of the quiet sense of contentment—even in the animals! Somewhere during the tour, Rolfe disappeared; she assumed he must be resting.

But Rolfe was not resting. He moved as close as he could to the scriptorium, wanting to catch a glimpse of Hilda before Leova did. If it was his Hilda, she would surely recognize him. Rolfe's heart ached. He had kept nothing from his wife in all their years together except this one thing. He had been sure it would never need to be confronted, for he could not conceive in any manner that Leova's childhood friend and the Hilda he had known could be the same person. Now he knew he was wrong, and if Leova recognized that Rolfe had never acknowledged any connection with a woman of that name, she would have every right to be angry with him–perhaps to not even forgive him. Certainly she would wonder why he had not spoken of a woman with that name.

Lost in thought, he did not notice the young monk approaching him until he almost ran into him. Startled, he stepped back. The monk looked at him questioningly, and Rolfe suddenly saw a way to gain access to Hilda before Leova did. "Brother, I was once an acolyte in this monastery, but our collection of manuscripts at that time was much smaller than the one I see now. Would it be acceptable for me to look closer?"

"Certainly," the young man replied, pleased to show off the monastery's treasures. As he stepped inside the door of the scriptorium, memories took over his thoughts and Rolfe again was, for a few moments, Brother John. The sense of solitude and contemplation was as palpable to him as it had been years ago. Looking around, he saw no female figures, only several monks who were fully absorbed in their copying activities. One of the monks lined manuscript pages and another carefully rubbed blank sheepskins, preparing them for ink. Still another bent intently over a folio, carefully outlining decorative letters with gold. The scene almost made him jealous; he found that much in the life of a monastery still appealed to him.

Then he noticed the bent figure, isolated in a corner cubicle— the wimple gave away the gender. Wanting to avoid startling her, he stepped back into the shadows so she would not see him if she looked up. He stood quietly against the wall for what seemed an eternity. Finally, the woman brushed off the manuscript she had been studying and carefully folded and closed it. She stood up, shaking off the pieces of manuscript skin which had fallen on her habit. Surveying the entire scriptorium before she slowly moved toward the door, she turned in his direction. Rolfe drew a sharp breath and pressed himself farther into the dark. The eyes, the cheeks, the resolute chin, could not be disguised by a wimple. Bracing himself against the wall for fear his knees would not support him, he struggled with his emotions and the need to act. She had not seen him, but he couldn't remain standing there: he had to talk to her and quickly. Composing himself as well as he could, he quietly approached one of the young monks.

"Brother, I need your help. I would speak privately with Abbess Hilda. Could you ask her to meet me at the well? It's quite urgent! Please!"

The young boy looked at Rolfe quizzically, but seemed to sense his desperation. Quickly he stood and ran after Abbess Hilda while Rolfe hurried toward the well, grateful that no one else appeared there and knowing that it was fairly well hidden in a small cubicle. When the monk caught up with the Abbess, he pointed toward Rolfe; she nodded her head and turned to move toward him.

"You wish to see me?" Hilda asked. Her voice had not changed.

"Yes, Abbess Hilda—do you remember me, Brother John?"

"Brother John," she whispered, almost as though she were talking to herself, placing her hand against her breast and for a moment looking as though she might faint. Rolfe reached out to lend her support, but she quickly brushed his hand away and supported herself against the wall of the well.

The two stared at each other, but it was the Abbess who was able to control herself, having had years of practice. Her control, however, was only outward; inwardly she struggled with a confusion of emotions and remained silent for some time.

"Come, let us walk across the field," Hilda said quietly, recognizing her own need to quiet inner struggles by moving about.

Rolfe, relieved that they would be walking away from prying eyes, hoped his wife was nowhere near. Wordlessly, he followed. Hilda, too, remained silent until they had crossed the field and entered a small grove of trees just behind the refectory. Then she turned to him: "Let us sit on the log there," almost as though she were attempting to delay talk.

"What has brought you back here?" Hilda asked, emphasizing the word "here."

"My wife," he blurted out without thinking. His carefully worked out plan: what to say, how to say it, deserted him. Hilda turned and looked at him again as directly as she had done when first recognizing him.

"Your wife?"

"Yes, my wife."

Again controlling all outward signs of emotion, Hilda replied calmly "And what would bring your wife here?"

"She comes to see you."

"Why?"

"My wife is," Rolfe took a deep breath, clenching his fists, "my wife is your old friend Leova." Rolfe had decided that it was simply best to just get the worst out.

"Leova?"

"Yes, and I am called now by my family name Rolfe; 'Brother John' ceased to be long ago."

For several minutes she remained silent as though meditating on the name change. Finally, she smiled at him and spoke, "Indeed that is so." Rolfe felt himself relaxing somewhat, but the sudden proximity of the woman he had once loved wouldn't allow his fear to subside. "Let us sit for a bit longer," she continued, "I wish to hear, but only briefly, about the years since you left here; then we need to seek out Leova."

Rolfe stumbled almost incoherently through the years since he had last seen the woman he had once loved. Although he avoided speaking about their closeness and the afternoon they had spent locked together, he suspected that the past was still vivid in both their minds and hearts. Even remembering that love, his eyes more often than not avoided hers, not from shame, but from the pain of remembering.

With her hands in her lap, alternately joined as if in prayer and twisting as though in pain, Hilda listened. When he finished his halting narrative, Hilda sat quietly for some time before telling him her story. The telling of it was made easier by the lack of recrimination and emotion that would have made them both miserable. Her guilt about the child had never been put to rest since she did not know its fate, but she had long ago come to terms with keeping her pregnancy and the child a secret. So while she told him of her flight from Buxton and about her vows at Whitby, she omitted the most traumatic part of her history.

"It would be best," she acknowledged silently to herself "to omit any telling of a child's existence—since I'm not even sure if the child still exists."

For a long while, they sat quietly, turning each other's story silently this way and that in their thoughts, each processing the past. Finally, interrupting the silence, Hilda asked, "And what does my dear Leova— your wife —know of us?"

"She knows of my stay in the monastery," Rolfe explained, "why I was there and why I had to leave. She knows nothing of the connection between the two of us. Perhaps that's best?"

Hilda shook her head to indicate that she was as unsure as he about the next step. "I need some time to reflect and ask God for guidance. I'll go to the chapel now. Then I'll happily seek out your wife, my old friend who is, and always has been, so often in my thoughts."

As she rose, she touched his shoulder lightly and strode toward the chapel, Rolfe could do nothing but admire the calmness of the woman she had become. For some time he watched as she disappeared into the abbey, aware of an ache in his heart that he thought had been buried long ago. Then, rousing himself from his reverie, he resolved to seek out Leova.

Hilda found herself wishing to fly into the chapel, not wanting to encounter or speak to anyone. Once inside, she sought the dark corner where she had once sat so many years ago. Now her emotions could not be restrained and the tears came, her body shaking with her attempts to suppress her reactions.

As he returned to the main yard of the monastery, Rolfe could see Leova in conversation with one of the monks. Seeing him, Leova beckoned him to approach. "I'm getting quite impatient, Rolfe. This young man says that the Abbess has gone to pray and will meet us in a half hour or so in the chapter house. I'll have to bear the wait."

Leova sighed and looked up at her husband. He smiled, loving always the face before him, made more beautiful by the flush of excitement on her cheeks and the look of anticipation in her almost transparent blue eyes—so different from the dark curls and the green-flecked eyes of the other. Almost immediately, he felt guilty.

Leova, always attuned to his moods, became concerned. "What is it?" she asked.

"No, no, it's just your excitement and my fear that it all might be...well, a disappointment." He smiled ruefully and then attempted to match her good, if impatient, spirit. "Never mind, we'll know soon enough. Did you rest at all?"

"No, no, I'm too, well, just too...." Words failed her.

"Then let us walk about a bit," he said. Taking her arm and looping it over his, Rolfe guided her toward the fields away from the scriptorium and the chapel. "Why," he wondered out loud, "does nature go on looking much the same, following its own ways and seasons, while the human world trips and bumbles about, sometimes smoothly, but more often not?"

"You're quite solemn," Leova responded, concerned about her husband's mood.

"Yes, I was thinking how little control we have over the beauty and the destructiveness of the natural world. Perhaps that's God's way of reminding humans of their own transience."

"So true, but so unhappy a thought," Leova cajoled her husband, attempting to raise his spirits.

As they walked together arm and arm, Rolfe tried to be more at ease, tried to repress his own anxiety about what the next hour would hold. "We had best go back and find the chapter house."

As Rolfe and Leova approached the chapter house, they could see the Abbess waiting. She raised her hand as they approached and began walking toward them, keeping her eyes on Leova and seeming to dismiss Rolfe altogether. As the two women approached one another, the emotions on their faces went from excitement to wonder, to apprehension, to delight. Each finally broke her careful walk and rushed to embrace the other. Rolfe stood aside, watching them as the tears and laughter mingled.

At first, the two spoke almost in unison, each asking the questions that had been unanswerable for so many years. After the first excitement began to calm, Leova remembered Rolfe.

"Hilda, this is my husband, Rolfe," she said proudly, taking Rolfe by the arm. Hilda looked up, smiled, and took the hesitant hand Rolfe extended to her.

"You are a most fortunate man in your wife," she said, hugging her friend as she acknowledged the introduction.

Rolfe relaxed a bit, as Hilda continued to speak to him as if he were a stranger.

"We will have some time to talk perhaps later. Now I'd like Leova to myself."

Rolfe nodded and backed away. "Yes, yes, of course, I understand."

In reality he had no way of understanding; his future happiness was in Hilda's power and he did not know if the woman who spoke to him now had the heart and compassion of the girl he had once loved. He knew he was at her mercy. But he also knew how much he was to blame for keeping his secret.

The two women moved outside the chapter house and began to stroll, arm in arm, toward the fields where Hilda and Rolfe had just been. Rolfe watched them as they moved away together, their faces eagerly turned toward one another. He was happy for them— at least for the moment.

Rolfe did not see his wife again until he met her in the refectory for dinner. He noticed no change in her attitude toward him; happiness and fulfillment infused her face as she moved toward him. He was glad for her—glad for himself, also—which only fed his guilt.

Dinner in the refectory was governed by silence except for the monk who read the story of Jonah's escape from the whale. Rolfe listened with an eerie sense of companionship with Jonah. During the final moments of the meal, the monk read from a manuscript in Englisc the adventures of a young warrior and hero named Ingeld. Rolfe was surprised by the monk's ability to read in Englisc; much had obviously changed since he had left these grounds. He smiled to himself. Others must have trod the same path as he and Hilda once had, moving from step to step to decode their own language. Monks and traveling priests had always told the Bible stories to farmers and peasants, but now those who were educated could actually read the words to them. That was good, Rolfe thought to himself. And, at the same time, he wondered if he would be able to read those words as well as they. The life he had not led had its attractions, he knew. He did wonder, however, what the inhabitants of the monastery thought Ingeld had to do with Christ.

At the end of the meal, Abbess Hilda approached her guests

and took each by the arm and guided them out into the starlit yard. "I have prepared quarters for you in the guest house." Looking up at Rolfe, she added, "Leova has promised to stay a few days so we can get reacquainted. I do hope you can both stay."

Unsure of his own wishes, Rolfe remained silent. But the following morning, having reflected on the possibilities, he approached the Abbess. "Hilda...I, mean, Abbess, perhaps it would be best if I were to leave. Leova can stay and then come back with the servants. I take it that you have decided to remain silent about our history?"

"Yes. Nothing is to be gained by revealing the past, though I...," she did not finish her sentence.

"I agree. I ask once again for your forgiveness, and once again, I thank you for keeping our prior connection secret. You've made me feel as though the connection has been truly broken, that in some ways, it no longer exists. That's obviously...," he too left his sentence unfinished.

Hilda nodded quietly. There might still be a connection—a very real child—somewhere, but Rolfe did not need to know that. She acknowledged, with accompanying guilt, that she had more to keep secret than Rolfe did. But she resolved to enjoy her long-lost friend's company for as long as she could—and hope that it would not be so cruelly disrupted again.

That evening, before leaving the scriptorium, Hilda reached into the bag at her waist and removed the eternal knot Brother John had given her so long ago and placed it carefully at the end of the poetic biblical account of Genesis. And then she whispered "Goodbye" as she closed the ancient manuscript.

Chapter 11: Hilda Confronts Rules and Her own Identity (901)

Hilda smiled graciously at the two high ranking clerics who had announced themselves to her earlier, indicating that they came from the archbishopic at Yorvik and wished to speak with her in private. "Please seat yourself; I have a message to deliver to one of the sisters and will return shortly."

The younger of the two clerics seemed about to protest, but the other laid his hand on his companion's arm. "We will await your quick return."

Hilda left her small cubicle and its two inhabitants and hurried off toward the herbalist's garden. She did, in truth, have no message to deliver to a sister, but wanted a few minutes to collect her thoughts and calm herself. She had not liked the tone of voice in which the cleric had uttered "in private." Quickly, she devised a request she could give the herbalist, but was relieved the sister was not there.

She returned to her cubicle and settled herself. "Now, please let me hear your message."

"We have some concern about the turn matters have taken here since your ascension to the position of Abbess and need to speak with you about these concerns." Hilda remained silent.

"First and perhaps least important, we have heard that the sisters here, including you, do not shave their heads, but allow the hair to grow. As you know, this is against the dictates of St. Paul as written in the book of Corinthians."

Hilda could only wonder at the source of such information about the sisters in this particular abbey. She was even tempted to remove her head covering and let them see her long hair, but resisted the temptation. "Sirs, it was my understanding that the head should be shaved at the time a woman officially enters our order as a nun, but that thereafter it needed only to be kept short."

"That is not the Archbishop's understanding; we do hope you will attend to this matter."

Hilda forced a smile, but said nothing, resolving to re-examine the dictate at its source. After a long uncomfortable silence, the younger of the two clerics announced "There is another issue, perhaps more important."

"Please," Hilda spoke quietly, "continue."

"Since your arrival here, we know you have established a school in which you teach novitiates, nuns, monks, and even lay people how to read both Latin and English. In keeping with this practice, you now have several nuns whose duties are limited almost entirely to work in the scriptorium. All this must be questioned as to its necessity."

Hilda knew she was becoming angry and needed to calm herself before replying. Finally, she broke the silence. "Brothers, it was my assumption that the late Abbess Edyth specially suggested that I succeed her because of my interest in, and skills with, the old manuscripts."

"Yes, that his certainly true," one of the clerics answered. "But it was not presumed that you would extend that interest to so many others. There are multiple tasks associated with a large monastery such as this and these tasks require the labor of many monks and nuns. Isolating so many of them into the scriptorium leaves other tasks with fewer to complete them. That is our first concern. Our second concern is to question the necessity for so many to learn to read and write in our language and the then necessity for you to spend so much time as a teacher, time which surely lessens your work in the scriptorium."

"And what is it you suggest I now do," Hilda asked as quietly as she was able.

"Please devise a list of all religious and non-religious in your community indicating the task or tasks to which each is assigned."

"That will take some time," Hilda replied.

"We will return soon to look at the list and make recommendations; we hope also we will hear no more about the rules regarding hair."

"Then I will now wish you farewell and a safe road back to your destination."

After the two clerics had left, Hilda sat for some time facing the two seats where they had sat.

"Gentlemen who told you about the nuns' hair here? I do hope there have been no male clerics about who have been able to report such information. Should that not concern you more than the condition of nuns' hair? And who is it who has conveyed information about assignments here? Is there a spy? Someone who desires my removal? Someone who is envious?" These, of course, were the questions Hilda had wanted to ask. One thing seemed quite sure to her: there had to be some in the abbey who liked neither her nor the changes she had made since her arrival and were conveying that information to the church hierarchy in Yorvik.

In the years since Hilda had assumed the role of abbess, she had quickly established herself as an exacting administrator, but strove also to be a kind administrator. The establishment itself was almost five times as large as her prior abbey, both in terms of people and possessions. During her first year, Hilda had tirelessly re-acquainted herself with every person, every corner, every garden, every animal, every possession of the abbey. During her survey, she had been shocked to discover among items that surely had belonged to Abbess Edyth, the letter she had written so long ago to Leova. As the years had passed, she was forced to realize it had probably never been delivered. Now she could be sure. Had Abbess Edythe somehow known of it and confiscated it? And, if so, why would she keep it? As she felt her anger to that woman stirred up, she calmed herself. It mattered not now, she knew, and stowed the crumpled up missive with the stone and manuscript scrap she had found also long ago and kept for reasons that eluded her.

It was during this time of re-acquaintance with the whole of Buxton, that the idea of the school had developed. She had enlisted the aid of Brother Olaf in making a written inventory of all that the abbey owned, which meant that she had to educate him beyond what he had learned in the scriptorium. He was an eager student, but dissatisfied with the limits of his knowledge. No sooner had they begun the inventory than he asked to be taught more—he wanted to illustrate as well as read the manuscripts under his care.

Together they tried to account for all the abbey's possessions: the acreage of each farm and the size of the cattle herds and the chicken flocks, estimated production of wheat fields and vegetable gardens, the equipment in the refectory and herbarium and, finally, all the manuscripts, each listed in its language group. Hilda often had worked into the morning hours, sleeping only when she could no longer think logically about the matters before her. The old habit of working through chapel had to be abandoned. She had to set an example for those under her care, and that meant keeping those hours of prayer sacred. Once the inventory was complete and the monastery running to her satisfaction, however, Hilda finally had time to turn to her beloved manuscripts. Her love for them was so great that she could only marvel that Archbishop Wulfstan thought he must "order" her to take this most desirable post, and that he actually felt he had to remind her of her holy duty to attend to them. She had begun by helping Olaf first to read Latin and then to read Englisc; she quickly discovered that she was almost as devoted to teaching as she was to reading the manuscripts. Others asked to be taught, which led her to start up the small school to which she invited everyone at the abbey—men and women, religious and lay— who wanted to learn to read.

It was at this time that the original disagreements with the Archbishop and the other officials of the church commenced. During the campaign of letters that made their way back and forth from Yorvik to Buxton, Hilda continued teaching with increased determination. Three times a week, a group of almost thirty students gathered to learn from their Abbess. In her correspondence Hilda had stressed what was most important for her: the value of reading for everyone and not just for a chosen few. She had not been unaware that there were those at the abbey who opposed her plans; any number of times she passed a group of monks or nuns who turned away from her and ceased their conversations as she approached.

More than once, Hilda had stopped and tried, usually unsuccessfully, to engage them in further conversation. On one such occasion, she realized that Sister Olelana was in the group; she was one of the assistant herbalists. "Sister," she said addressing herself to the herbalist, "I understand you have identified a new use for a plant. That must have been most satisfying to you and most appreciated by the others here." It was apparent that the others in the group did not know of this achievement; and they began congratulating Olelana who smiled at the attention, but not at Hilda. Hilda, in fact, knew that Sister Olelana had disagreed with Abbess Edyth years ago about Hilda's appointment. Hilda surmised also that she knew of her shameful banishment years ago from the abbey and may well have passed those suspicions on to others. Hilda had discovered many years ago that gossip was one of the favorite activities in abbeys and monasteries.

Hilda thought, however, that she had eased the Archbishop's criticism; he had reluctantly conceded to her work with the school, only ordering her to be certain that all tasks had sufficient persons assigned and that classes not interfere with services and holy days. Eventually the Archbishop had written a letter addressed to all those at Buxton, mandating that Hilda read the letter to members of the abbey. In it, the Archbishop expressed his concerns about the potential dysfunction that might befall an abbey as a result of too many hours set aside for learning. He concluded his letter by encouraging any who might not want to continue with the education or the work in the scriptorium to speak to the Abbess. Anyone who did so, he concluded, would have his support. Two students had relinquished the class; neither, however, expressed a desire to spend less time in the scriptorium. But, apparently, the issue had been raised again. By whom? Hilda could only wonder. Probably by the same person who had reported that her hair was too long. Hilda resolved to bring the matter of the hair into the conversation at the next chapter meeting. Before that, she thought sadly, she had best shorten her own hair. And she knew, too, that she would have to ask one of the nuns or monks to create an inventory of the task assignments. She smiled to herself as she recognized that that person would probably need to be one of the students in her class.

At the next chapter meeting after the two visiting clerics had left, Hilda reported their concerns to all. When she mentioned the hair, there was some tittering among the group and each looked surreptitiously at other colleagues as though wondering who might be offenders. And she did hear one female voice stating loud enough for all to hear: "How do they know?" Hilda ignored those words, announcing as contritely as she could that she was an offender and that since the clerics' departure, she had cut her hair. "If this particular criticism applies to any one of you, I expect you to do as I have done."

Hilda had examined the words of St. Paul in Corinthians and did not conclude that he ordered women's heads to be shaved; what was important was that women's heads should be covered. But Hilda did not want to create controversy over hair; certainly it was far less important than her work with the school. She had no intention of lessening her attention to the school she had created. After several months, she identified three students, including Olaf, who had learned so quickly that they were advancing far beyond their peers. Putting Olaf in charge, she assigned to these three the task of making an inventory of the assignment of each person at the abbey, the inventory the visiting clerics were requiring. For these three also, she began to hold a class in Englisc so that they might read their own language from the manuscripts that Hilda treasured the most. Occasionally, she feared that her devotion to these manuscripts might be a form of heresy—the contents of the manuscripts were not always religious in nature—but she did not fear heresy enough to make any genuine effort to cleanse herself of the love of the secular. God, she was convinced, valued all languages, and her three students were as thrilled as she had once been to be able to read and write the very words they spoke.

The only dark spot in the project was that the memories of her earliest contacts with this learning refused to lie quiescent. Pointing out a particular word might suddenly revive a moment she had spent with John. Watching her pupils struggle together to learn put her in mind of her own awakening—not only of knowledge, but of love. At first she had worried that some of her students might also fall prey to that piece of the passion that had led to such pain for her, but soon it became obvious that only a few were as enraptured by the experience of reading as she had been, and that careful oversight on her part would preclude them from becoming as entangled as she and John had become. As always, the specter of Brother John haunted her, but she knew him to be happily married to Leova; he was Rolfe now in another life, and Brother John took on the status of a symbol as the catalyst for her own intellectual awakening, almost (but not totally, she had to admit) separated from the man married to her friend. A flesh and blood Brother John, she had to remind herself more often than pleased her, no longer existed.

What occupied her thoughts often, however, was the question of what God intended for her or even what she intended for herself. She knew without question that the life she was currently living was one the younger Hilda would never have chosen for herself. Her initial resistance to it was, consequently, to be expected. She could not forget that she had not been lovingly brought to this very abbey, but forced to it by a promise that she had not genuinely made, but had been forced to make. "Ironic, is it not," she often reflected to herself, "here I am at the very spot my mother insisted that I be. Perhaps her gift of me to the church enabled total forgiveness for her sin–whatever it might have been." And, certainly, at one point, she acknowledged to herself, the choice had become hers, partially engendered perhaps by the desire to not be what her mother had been, but partially, too, by her desire not to allow her father to control her life by choosing her husband. Undoubtedly, it was such fatherly control that had increased her incentive, many years ago, to transcribe the ancient story of Juliana. Juliana's refusal had led to her death. Hilda smiled to herself. She, at least, was still alive.

The matter that engaged these thoughts the most, however, remained her concern about what role she most desired in the world of religion. Often she realized she would rather spend her time on manuscripts: reading, copying, illustrating, than on matters relating to the functioning of the abbey itself. In truth, she had to acknowledge, she preferred the scriptorium to the chapel, a preference she would never reveal: it would probably be considered blasphemous. She feared, however, that if she were to ask to be relieved as the Abbess of Buxton, she might well be sent elsewhere far away from the manuscripts that were her major love. Such a result might well drive her away from the church.

Conversions

A month later as she closed up one of her precious manuscripts, she saw Olaf approaching with two young monks. "Abbess," Olaf said, "Brothers Eric and Sebastian, with just a little help from me, have finished the list of assignments of all who serve here." He handed it to her. "Please let us know if there is more to do on this task"

"Olaf, I suspect I'll find this complete. I look forward to going over it and thank you all for your quick completion of the list."

Leaving the three men behind, Hilda, continuing to allow herself this one indulgence, walked slowly up to her beloved spot underneath the climbing tree and examined the list. So sure was she that it would be complete and satisfactory that she glanced at it quickly and then folded up the sheets, resolving to examine it closely after the evening meal. She leaned back against the tree and fell into a light sleep only to be awakened by the touch of a small hand. She looked up into the face of a little girl with golden curls who was staring at her intently. "Are you alive," said a high-pitched whispered voice.

Hilda took the child's hand, laughing. "I am quite alive, just taking a nap. Do you take naps when you're tired and need a rest?"

"Oh, yes," came the reply as the child sat down next to her, smoothing out her skirt and curling her feet up. "But why do you come here to rest?"

"What a good question you're asking. I call this tree my 'climbing tree' because once many years ago before I was a nun and wore these clothes, maybe I wasn't much older than you, I climbed up this tree and thought it was fun to look down on the world from that branch up there." Hilda pointed up to a thick branch somewhat above her head. "Do you think you would like to climb the tree?"

"Oh, yes, I want to, very much, but," her voice floundered. "I think I'm too short."

"Would you like me to help you?"

"Oh, would you, please, that would be such fun."

Hilda picked up the little girl and held her up to the point

388

where she could grasp one of the lower limbs and pull herself up to it by almost walking up the trunk of the tree, Hilda still holding her. When she reached her destination, the branch Hilda had pointed to, she pulled herself along it toward the end, one leg dangling on each side. "What do you see from up there?" Hilda called to her.

"Oh, I can see the roofs that I've never seen before and all the people and animals look like toys. It's pretty and I love it up here."

"And so did I," thought Hilda to herself.

After a few minutes, the little girl looked down at Hilda. "How am I going to get down now?"

"Let me see if I can remember how I did it," Hilda replied. "I think you'll have to scoot backwards a bit and when you get closer to the ground, lean against the trunk and see if you can put both legs on the same side of the branch, hold on carefully while you're doing this and then slip down and I'll catch you."

The little girl inched herself along the branch, almost lying down so she could hold on with both hands and arms. Finally, when she was lower, she embraced the branch tightly and swung one leg over. In the process, she fell from the branch and into Hilda's arms. Laughing Hilda sat her on the ground.

"Oh, let's do it again," the young girl said excitedly.

"Maybe some other day. You better go find your mother; she may be worried about you."

"Yes, Sister," she responded, but then hugged Hilda as tightly as she could and kissed her on the cheek. "Thank you, oh thank you!"

As Hilda watched the child run down the hillside, she could only wonder. Was her child like this child? Was she or he happy and settled somewhere with a loving family? The hug stayed with her as she too descended the hill.

Some weeks later, at the close of classes on one of her routine days, she saw Brother Olaf waiting for her with a somewhat eager expression in his eyes. Hilda sighed—there would be business to tend to. She would rather walk out into the surrounding grove of trees, remove her wimple, and feel the fresh air and the smell of just greening shrubs and trees. As much as she loved her manuscripts and the work in the scriptorium, she continued to need the refreshment of nature as well as the solitude and silence of a world uninhabited by humans. She shook her head and spoke to him.

"Yes, Olaf?"

"Visitors have arrived and they wish to speak to you."

"And they are...?"

"Lord Ragnar and his two sons."

Hilda smiled as she remembered her meeting several years ago with the two young men who had been carting stones from the old monastery to their father's hall. Since that time she had come to know more about Lord Ragnar, lord of all the lands to the east of the monastery, but she had yet to meet him. The peace between that enemy and those she thought of as her people was only newly established. She had reason to trust him, however. More than one of the farmers at the abbey had told her that the monastery owed its protection during the most recent lengthy outbreak of war to Lord Ragnar, who had asserted that the abbey was on his land and therefore not subject to the destruction other monasteries had been plagued with. Nor had he sent any of his sons or people to fight. Like many of the once-foreign invaders, he had settled permanently. And the battles now raged mainly to the south.

As Hilda entered the small cubicle where she usually conducted the business of the abbey, three tall men stood and bowed slightly toward her.

"Gentlemen, perhaps we can walk outside and conduct our business in the open air?"

They nodded in agreement, obviously uncomfortable in the small space. As they walked out, the two younger men dropped behind while their father matched his footsteps to Hilda's. He turned toward her a bit awkwardly.

"I have come, Lady Abbess, to ask for your advice and help."

"Gladly, Lord Ragnar. You protected the abbey during the uprisings, even though you had no responsibility to do so. We are grateful to you for the peace, and for making it possible for us to continue our lives here."

"I do not like war," Ragnar stated bluntly. "I wish for peace,

Sister. However, my request for advice has nothing to do with war, peace, or ownership of the abbey lands. I seek personal counsel."

Hilda hid her surprise, a strategy she was becoming increasing skilled at. "Yes? How may I be of service?"

"I wish to marry. And my chosen bride is one of your people and religion who wishes us to marry through your customs. And..." Lord Ragnar paused just slightly, "she desires that I accept your religion."

Hilda thought for a moment of the conditions governing Christian marriage: they might present difficulty for Ragnar, particularly the dictum that the church does not condone marriage of any whose former wife or husband might still be alive. Marriage was meant to be an eternal commitment. "First, Lord Ragnar, I must ask you some questions about your desire to marry. I assume that these, your sons, are the product of a marriage. Where is their mother? Are you widowed?"

"Sister," he answered quietly, "my wife, the mother of my sons, disappeared many, many years ago with one of my twin sons, at the height of the warfare here, when my boys were little more than babes. Perhaps they were carried off by an enemy or even killed. That was twenty years ago. I long ago gave up hope of ever finding her. Perhaps she is dead. Perhaps now she does not wish to be found. I don't know, and will never know, I suspect. My concern is with the present. I wish to marry another woman, one who is good and who returns my affection. She tells me that I cannot marry her unless some resolution is made of my previous marriage, some resolution confirmed by the church. How do I go about that, sister? And, additionally, she asks that I convert to her faith—your faith," he added quickly.

Hilda studied the face of the man before her. He had the coloring and physical appearance of the red-haired ones, her people's enemies for so long. He had most assuredly demonstrated trustworthiness in his behavior during the war. He was an enemy no longer, just a man who needed her help.

"Lord Ragnar, I understand your dilemma, and I will endeavor to help you resolve this problem. Let's start by letting me talk to your sons." She turned to the two young men walking discreetly behind them. "I regret it, but I've forgotten your names."

"I am Rodman and my brother here is Redwald."

Hilda nodded in remembrance. "We met some time ago when you were dismantling the old monastery to the east. Do you remember?"

"Yes, Abbess," the young man replied. "You were much attracted to a stone with strange carvings on it; we removed it to our hall. Perhaps one day you will come to see it?"

Hilda nodded at the invitation with little intention of indulging that interest of hers. "Do you know why your father has come here?"

Both nodded.

"And do you approve of his request? After all, your mother will be replaced."

Redwald answered, "Our mother disappeared, taking my twin brother Rothulf with her; Rodman and I were so young that we can scarcely remember her, and for many years, I was angry. But I've come to realize that she may have been abducted or even murdered, that she could not come back, even if she may have wished to. But regardless of how I feel, she is gone."

His brother took up the conversation, "Our father is a good man. He's lived many years without a wife, and the woman he has chosen is good and will bring him joy. We'd like to see him happy."

Hilda turned back to Lord Ragnar. "Your sons, as you undoubtedly know, confirm your statement that their mother has been absent for many years. We can safely conclude that she is dead. If you embrace the Christian faith, there will be no impediment to your marriage as far as I understand the church's laws on marriage, but the Bishop will have to issue a dispensation stipulating the death of your first wife. That will take some time, but in the interval you may come—with your sons if they wish—to learn more of our faith and, I hope, eventually dedicate yourself to it. Please, when you next come, bring your intended bride to the abbey. I'd like to speak to her as well."

"Perhaps, Lord Ragnar suggested, "you might honor us with

your presence at my hall?"

Hilda smiled, excited by the prospect of a trip. But then she hesitated, remembering the many tasks that had to be attended to at the abbey. Reluctantly, she dismissed the idea. "Someday, perhaps. For now, it would be best if she were to come here where I might speak to her in private. "We must, in particular, consider her wish that you accept our religion and your motivation for doing so."

Lord Ragnar smiled and nodded. "It shall be as you ask. Some other day, perhaps, you will visit at my hall."

Several days later, Lord Ragnar once again appeared at the monastery accompanied by a smiling woman who appeared to be about forty-years-old. Before Lord Ragnar could introduce her, she approached Hilda and announced,

"I am Ydesa." Hilda found herself drawn to the woman immediately.

"Welcome to Buxton, Ydesa," Hilda responded. "Let's walk together; I have many questions of you."

They left Lord Ragnar in Hilda's cubicle and disappeared among the trees paralleling the walls of the monastery. They were gone for some time, but when they returned, both were smiling.

"Lord Ragnar," Hilda announced, "Ydesa has convinced me that she wishes to marry you, but has also convinced me that the strength of her belief demands that she marry only someone who also adheres to her religion."

Lord Ragnar bowed just slightly to the Abbess and took the hand of his intended bride. "Many thanks, Abbess Hilda. I will make arrangements for my own conversion, but my sons will need to make their own decisions."

"Yes, of course," Hilda replied. She turned to his companion, "Ydesa, if you wish, you are welcome not only to visit us but also to pursue your desire to learn to read."

Lord Ragnar appeared somewhat surprised by his intended wife's desire, but showed no sign of disapproval. As the two returned to their waiting mounts, Hilda could see them talking eagerly, enjoying the pleasure of merely being side by side. She could only smile at the dissimilarity in paths: she had turned to

Christianity to avoid marriage; Ragnar turned to Christianity to achieve marriage.

In the following weeks, Hilda arranged regular visits so that Lord Ragnar and his two tall offspring could discuss Christianity and its beliefs. Lord Ragnar proved particularly observant, curious, and probing about the religion, questioning many of the basic beliefs that Hilda herself had never questioned very deeply. She came to the religion through the manuscripts, believing in the power of words on parchment to order the world and make it safe—but not just the words of the scripture itself. Somehow for her it was the reader's ability to decipher and analyze any text that provided power, regardless of the language of the text.

Ragnar did not hide his frustration with some of the basic principles of the Christian faith. "Abbess Hilda," Lord Ragnar said, deferential as always but unwilling to accept the scriptures without confronting the questions that arose for him, "I do not understand the importance of a *virgin* birth. Never has a woman been both a virgin and a mother. Why should it be so important that your Jesus be born of a virgin? And I understand that the church is now solidifying the dictate that priests, your fellow nuns, and monks remain celibate. What is so desirable about virginity to your church?"

"Virginity," Hilda began, "indicates a complete devotion, body and soul, to God. We do not think it sufficient to mouth beliefs and swear to prescribed behavior; words and vows must be matched by action. Abstinence from all sexual activity, coupled with other bodily temperance, such as eating and drinking moderately, working up to one's physical abilities, and attending scheduled services every day, are signs of devotion and faith. Originally the rules were less rigid, but, over time, church leaders began to understand that celibacy offers unique values."

Lord Ragnar thought for a few moments and smiled before he asked the next question. "Isn't being celibate breaking the laws of nature that were created by God himself?"

"Ah," said Hilda, enjoying the debate. "The church does not advocate chastity for all believers—only for those who have dedicated their lives to worship and service. Mary, mother of Christ, symbolizes that devotion. True, a virgin birth is against those laws of nature of which you speak; we all know that. As Christians, we accept the paradox of a virgin giving birth. It's a matter of faith. Some things can never be fully understood. Is that not true of many aspects of life?"

Hilda doubted that she had explained this matter to the satisfaction of Lord Ragnar. She wasn't even certain she could explain it to her own satisfaction. Perhaps, she thought ruefully, it might be wise for her to focus a bit more on the significance—both ideal and real—of the words she uttered every day as part of the liturgy.

On another occasion, she seized the opportunity to learn herself, asking for a story from Ragnar's religion.

"In our old religion," he began, "we have a chief god by name of Odin. He, like your god of the old writings, often warred against other gods, but he was ever victorious. Our people believe him to be all-powerful with magical abilities, like your god's magical ability to create his own son out of a virgin," he smiled at her, remembering their previous conversation. "And Odin always takes those who die in his service to Valhalla, where they stay until the world ends and then is recreated."

Hilda listened carefully and asked questions of her own. Then she offered her opinion on Ragnar's gods. "The stories of your gods and your heroes fill hearts with bravery, but there is no sense of personal and emotional connections. Their lives offer valid ways to see the world and the moral and ethical issues we have to face in war, but these gods and heroes don't seem representative of a deep belief in an overriding and all-inclusive system. They're quite human in their ways of coming to terms with the world, but you haven't said anything that leads me to believe there is, within your religion, any emphasis on how we should treat our fellow humans, especially those who are need. Our Jesus sees the world differently."

While Hilda and Lord Ragnar passed many an afternoon discussing a wide variety of religious beliefs, Brother Olaf tended to the education of Rodman and Redwald. Olaf was particularly pleased by this assignment because of his own heritage; the destructive power the invading warriors had unleashed on so many of the religious places haunted him and made him ashamed. Consequently, he endeavored to bring others of his people to the church. He felt particularly drawn to these two young men who were his own age. They, in turn, enjoyed both the learning and the company of the young monk, especially since he had an eager ear for the stories of their own religion.

"We have," Redwald explained one day to Olaf, "a figure much like your Jesus—Baldor, the son of our highest god, Odin. A sorceress made him invulnerable to all weapons, and all the creatures and plants of the earth swore not to harm him, except mistletoe which was not sworn since it was considered too small to do any harm. His enemy Loki, however, discovered this weakness through guile and manipulated Baldor's own brother, who was blind, to pierce Baldor with mistletoe. Balder died but, because of his virtuous nature, went to a special heaven that we call Asgard. I see similarities to your story of Jesus' betrayal by his close companion, Judas."

"Tell me more about this Loki," Olaf asked, eager to find points where the old and the new religions mirrored one another.

"He's the god of mischief and his chief delight is in playing tricks on others. While some of the tricks are harmless, many are not. Certainly the death of Baldor disturbed the whole world, making it imperfect, and ensuring that it would eventually decay. Loki was punished well, however. He ended up bound to rocks in chains while a poisonous snake dripped venom on his face!"

"In our religion," Olaf responded, deep into the storytelling, "Satan, a fallen angel, would be more like Loki than Judas. He is the chief enemy of God, and plots to make all humans fall into sin. He, too, was punished—thrown out of heaven and bound in the burning fires of hell for all eternity—but unlike Loki, he can work his evil even from his prison."

During this period of instruction and story exchange, Ydesa accompanied the men and spent time in the scriptorium turning over pages of the old manuscripts. She marveled at their beauty and at the evidence of the monastery's tireless devotion to preserving words. A quick and intelligent learner, it took her only a short time to begin to learn to read, and an even shorter time to question what she read.

One day Ragnar arrived at the monastery followed by a peasant driving an oxen cart. "Tell the Abbess I have a special gift for her," he said to the acolyte who met him, then settled down on a bench to await the Abbess. When she appeared, he rose and with a smile announced respectfully, "Abbess Hilda, I have brought you a gift that I think will please you."

In the cart was the stone she had seen so many years ago. Now, incomplete as it was, she saw that what she had thought of as decorative marks were the remains of a Latin inscription: *Verta...vorne...ceram...oss....*

"Ragnar," she began breathlessly, "You think right! This is a rare gift, one I shall treasure both for myself and for the abbey."

"My sons told me that you would find joy in it," Ragnar said, happy that his sons had such insight into what would please the Abbess. "What, may I ask, is its importance?"

Hilda paused a moment as she decided how to explain her excitement. "When I was a young girl, returning to my own hall and to my father just before my mother died, I passed by that ancient monastery, which was a ruin even then. I wandered through the ruins and noticed this stone with its strange markings, obviously produced by human hands. I could not read it then, but with some effort, I will be able to do so now, despite the fact that much of the lettering has been destroyed." She paused to catch her breath. "For me, this stone represents continuity—both personal and doctrinal. My life and my faith have changed greatly since the day I first saw it! But, more important, this rock and its words testify to the continuing strength of the religion even when it appears to have been destroyed. I will need to consult with others and decide where and how to best display it." She stopped and looked at him full in the face. "I—we at the abbey—thank you for this generous gift and for the thought that engendered it."

Ragnar had not finished with his surprises. "Abbess, I knew

you would be happy with this gift, but I give it not only to honor you, but as a sign that I am ready to accept your God as my own. Your faith, like the rock of Peter, has made the difference for me. This rock will ever stand for your influence and your love of God."

Hilda allowed herself to take his hand, "Lord Ragnar, you are most welcome to our fellowship. I hope that after your confirmation, you will return here often to worship. I have profited from our discussions. You have forced me to look ever closer to the precepts of my religion and perhaps even to understand them better as a result."

"As have I, Lady. What has attracted me most to your religion has been its concepts of life and eternity. I have come to picture our world as a big hall in winter. A swallow comes in one door and flies out another. It's impossible to know what happens before the bird enters or what will happen to it after it leaves. All we can know of life is what occurs during our own time in the hall. What happens before birth or after death is closed to us: your religion gives us knowledge and hope for the latter. It is that system you have so often described to me; I have come to consider it superior to the religion I have served up to this time as it gives me the sense that I and all others are part of some larger world, both here on earth and elsewhere.

Hilda smiled, happy with the explanation he offered. She supposed it might be the reasoning of many who had come into the church over the past years, especially the descendants of the red-haired ones.

Within a month, a priest arrived carrying a dispensation from the Archbishop of Yorvik allowing Lord Ragnar to remarry. This same priest presided at his baptism, confession, and first communion. Hilda participated at all these sacraments, praying that all her people's enemies might follow this path. And, that her people would welcome the newcomers with warmth and joy.

A Wedding

On Lord Ragnar's wedding date, Hilda greeted him and his bride with fond congratulations. Ragnar took her hand as she extended it to him. "Abbess," he said expansively, "On this my wedding date, I wish to make a donation to your monastery of the twenty hides of land which adjoin your lands to the north. I include with that the livestock grazing on the land. Those who inhabit it may choose to remain on it; those who do not so wish will be allotted land elsewhere."

Hilda could hide neither her surprise nor her gratitude. "On behalf of our community here, I accept your gift!" she replied. Not wishing to appear that she was more interested in the land than the occasion that brought them together, however, she changed the subject. Turning to the people who had come for the wedding, she invited them into the chapel. "Let us now share the joy of their marriage with Ragnar and Ydesa." And that is what the small group did.

After the ceremony was completed, the small group filed out of the chapel and into the surrounding open air. As the happy couple mounted their horses, Ragnar leaned down for one last word with Hilda. "We plan a celebratory feast at my hall in two days' time. Please honor us with your presence. Without your guidance and assistance, our marriage might never have taken place."

She started to refuse, but Ydesa anticipated her answer and tried to forestall it by making her own request. "Please do say you will come; your community can spare you for a day. And your presence would add additional blessings to our marriage. We owe you much we can never replay. Also we'd like you to bring Olaf with you. He's having quite an effect on Ragnar's sons."

Hilda paused for a moment only, and then gave in to the temptation. "Yes, we shall be glad to join your festive evening." As she accepted the invitation, Hilda smiled as she remembered the festivities she had witnessed at Lothlar with Leova. She looked forward to witnessing that sort of pleasure again. Although she knew she could not participate as she once had, she sensed in herself a buried wish to be a part of that world again, if only briefly.

Once the wedding party had disappeared on the road leading to Lord Ragnar's hall, Hilda sought Olaf. "What good news we have, my son. We go to Lord Ragnar's hall to celebrate his marriage, and perhaps to convert his sons. More importantly, the good man has donated twenty hides of his land to the abbey. During our trip, I'd like you to arrange with his sons to mark off that land and then draw up a charter to record the transfer of the land. Will this suit you?"

The invitation suited Olaf very well. He was pleased to have a chance to spend more time with Lord Ragnar's sons. They had not yet indicated a desire to convert, but Olaf felt that they would within a not too distant time. The chance to work with them filled him with pleasure. Perhaps it was his awareness of a shared background that made this pleasure so intense. Olaf thought so.

Two days later Hilda and Olaf set off down the road toward Ragnar's hall accompanied by two hefty sons of one of the abbey's farmers who did not disguise their excitement at the chance to venture beyond their usual confines. Within the past several years, Hilda had not ventured more than a mile from the abbey. She found herself enjoying the trip, no longer haunted by her past. Although they would pass close to Highhear, she still had no desire to go there. On the other hand, she found that she would very much like to travel to Lothlar and see Leova whose frequent letters were always more than welcome. She must make that visit one day, she concluded and then, almost simultaneously, wondered if that were not too self-indulgent. Unlike her visit to Ragnar's hall, such a journey would serve no purpose other than giving her pleasure. But, she reminded herself, the trip to Ragnar's hall had tempted her too with pleasures she had once known.

Upon their arrival at Lord Ragnar's hall, they were warmly greeted by their host and his wife. "You will want to freshen up a bit and rest from your travel," Ydesa observed. "I will take you to your quarters."

Hilda's quarters turned out to be quite similar to those she had shared with Leova at Lothlar. Immediately after Ydesa left her, one of the servants arrived with a basin of fresh water which gave off sweet flowery scents. Hilda sat down on the small but comfortable sleeping pallet and removed her wimple. As the black curls, grown out once again, fell to Hilda's shoulders, the servant made a brief exclamation, which she tried to stifle. Hilda laughed.

"Yes, I know. Most people think that nuns have no hair. And, truthfully, I do need to cut it; completely shaving it off is not required, but...."

The young girl looked confused.

"You, my dear," Hilda continued, "follow the old gods, and I expect they would demand no such sacrifice from a woman."

"Yes, mum," replied the servant deferentially, "our religion would not deprive a woman, or a man of..." she stopped, apparently not wanting to offend a guest by criticizing her religion.

Hilda laughed again. "Don't worry child, your response is to be expected. I understand it."

The girl, turning her eyes away as though determined not to speak again, offered the basin of water and a soft cloth for washing. She stood still, but observant, as Hilda bathed her face and hands, then removed her leather sandals and sighed with pleasure as she soaked her feet in the still sweet-smelling water. At last Hilda looked up, realizing that the girl couldn't withdraw until given leave to go.

"I thank you. I feel quite refreshed, but I would like to rest a bit—unless, that is, something is planned for now?"

"No, mum, you will have at least two hours before the feast begins. I'll return to waken you."

As the servant picked up the bath articles and turned toward the door, Hilda called after her: "How shall I address you?"

"My name is Alfa, mum." With her back now to Hilda, the servant did not see the look on Hilda's face.

"Good heavens," Hilda exclaimed. "That was my mother's name! What a strange coincidence! My father's hall, Hearhigh, was about a day and a half from here. Do you know of it?"

It was now Alfa's turn to be surprised: though Hilda thought she saw some emotion other than surprise on the young girl's face, a sudden piercing look, immediately disguised.

"Indeed, mum, I have—and I have even traveled there once with Lord Ragnar when he had some dealings with the Lord there. I do not remember his name."

"And I do not know it at all," answered Hilda. "It's been many,

401

many years since I left there. And my father is long dead."

Alfa bowed and left the room, and Hilda wondered if Ragnar and his family knew of her relationship to Highhear. After she thought about it briefly, she decided that they had no need to know—and she hoped the young girl would not speak of it either.

After a brief rest, Hilda submitted to her desire to know her surroundings better. Donning her wimple and straightening her habit, she ventured forth into the enclosed yard where she was greeted by the combined smells of food and flowers. A sense of joy and contentment seemed to permeate the air and shape the mood of all those she saw.

When the time arrived for the wedding banquet, Hilda was seated in a place of honor next to the new bride, and Olaf found himself seated next to the two brothers who, in turn, were seated next to their father. Course after course appeared before her, most of which Hilda simply could not partake. Her body had become accustomed to fairly abstemious eating habits, she explained to Ydesa. The richness of the feast would have caused her great discomfort. Her hostess nodded with understanding and saw to it that simpler fare was placed before her. As the meal progressed, several singers performed in addition to jugglers and mimes: one had a trained dog who became a crowd favorite. Finally, Lord Ragnar himself took the small harp from one of the singers and struck it sharply thereby announcing that he would contribute to the festivities with stories. This potential quieted the festive gathering.

As Lord Ragnar began his recitation, Hilda listened attentively. She was delighted to realize that his story might well be the same one Brother Ceolwulf had recited so many years ago: a tale of a Viking hero who had slain monsters after traveling to a foreign country. Ydesa noticed Hilda's growing engagement with the recitation.

"Sister Hilda," she whispered once Ragnar had put down the harp, "you seem entranced by my husband's story."

"Yes," Hilda replied, "As a girl, I heard the same story recited by one of the elders of my own religion. Is that not strange? At that time it seemed to have meaning in terms of our faith, but this recitation—I can't pinpoint it—makes me rethink that conclusion."

"Let's ask Ragnar about the story," responded Ydesa.

Putting down the small harp, Lord Ragnar was delighted to talk about the tale. "We found an old manuscript in the ruins of the hall that served as the foundation for this one. One of our scholars read it to me—it was in my language—and I enjoyed it so much that I had parts of it translated into the language of my adopted land, and memorized those parts so that I could recite them for occasions such as this one." He paused, ever the gracious host. "I have long known, Abbess Hilda, that you love manuscripts, but I never thought to show you this one since it is in neither Latin nor Englisc. Would you like to see it tomorrow?"

"I thank you, My Lord, it will be a pleasure to see it." Hilda's excitement caused her to forget her earlier decision not to reveal her relationship to Highhear. "This visit has provided a wealth of discoveries. I learned earlier that the servant who has been so good to me, Alfa, has my mother's name. She tells me that you have dealings with the Lord of Hearhigh. Do you know the people there?"

"Yes, I've had dealings with Caedmon, the reeve there, and with Lord Heardred, originally awarded the property by your now deceased Cynge Alfred. Lord Heardred, one of my countrymen, told me that the family of the former lord's wife once controlled all the lands hereabout, even that on which this hall now stands. They had wrested it from another family, who still claims ownership, declaring its loss a fraud, theft, or deception of some kind." Lord Ragnar failed to notice the startled look on the Abbess' face. He continued, "Apparently this Lady of Hearhigh had wanted to turn the land over to your monastery, but her family resisted, and one branch of the Hearhigh family continued to live here until their hall was destroyed in the wars. My family was awarded the land by our Cynge and, as you know, my sons and I had the hall rebuilt."

Hilda forgot her surroundings as she struggled with this new information. Her mother's religious zeal had its roots in some great sin she felt she had committed. Was it possible that she had justified some kind of illegal seizure of another family's land? Justifying the act by attempting to designate it for religious purposes? Hilda had no doubt that her mother would have done so; after all, she had consigned her own daughter to eternal service in the church without ever consulting her. Hilda also realized that Lord Ragnar's hall must be situated where her cousin Berghorf's holdings had been. She was the guest of a descendent of the warriors who had killed her beloved cousin! "The Hearhigh family has not quite died out—not yet," Hilda thought to herself—not that it mattered since she had no intention of making any claims on the land.

Ragnar paused in his narrative, then brought the strands of the story together. "We leveled the old hall to the ground, and when we did so we found a metal box adorned with figures of fantastic beasts and birds. Inside it was the manuscript that you will find most interesting."

Hilda was brought back to attention by Lord Ragnar's voice.

"My Lady Abbess? What makes you withdraw? Have I disturbed you in some way?"

"No, no," she replied. "Please excuse my rudeness—I was caught up in the complexities of our people's history. So much has changed since I was a young girl. At a more appropriate time, I'd like to talk again about what you have just told me."

Lord Ragnar began to speak, but realized, along with his guest, that such matters were best left for a quieter time and place. With great difficulty Hilda directed her attention back to the festivities, but she was grateful when her hostess touched her lightly on the arm and invited her to attend the evening services in the chapel. Once she had completed her prayers, Hilda begged fatigue and went off to her small outbuilding to sleep. Her sleep proved uneasy, filled alternately with pieces of the puzzle that was her family: old engraved stones, secret doorways, a voice repeating "Promise me, promise me," dragons, snippets of pagan songs and the Christian liturgy.

She awoke early, distressed but unsure why, and quickly dressed so that she could make her way to the chapel. She very much hoped to find the priest there, for she felt a strong need to confess—though she wasn't exactly sure what she needed to confess. As she entered the darkened chapel where a single candle illuminated the figure of Mary in her blue robe, she was pleased to see the priest who had officiated at the nuptials. She knew at once that she needed to tell him of her family, her hatred of her mother, her periods of forced penance for a bodily sin, and her sudden desire to abandon everything and concentrate on the mysterious new manuscript.

"Father," she said humbly, "I should like to confess."

Some time later Hilda emerged from the confessional, signs of tears on her cheeks, her eyes focused on the ground. The confessor had proved a thorough, but not very sympathetic listener. "Not see the manuscript for a year! What kind of penance is that?" Hilda again felt tears rising. She knew that she had begun to value the work of scholarship over that of worship, and the secular manuscripts over the Latin, but she did not think that depriving her of those secular books would serve any useful purpose. She stopped short in her tirade, recognizing that the priest was right: she had become so absorbed in her work that she had forgotten her primary duty was to the words of God, not to the words on the manuscript pages. In defining the terms of her penance, the priest allowed that she might look at the manuscript the following day, but then must put it aside for the required time. She recognized that viewing it this one time would be likely to make her penance even more difficult. Wiping her cheeks with the sleeve of her gown, she returned to her small room and forced herself to prepare mentally and emotionally for the required penance placed upon her in the confessional. Exhausted, however, she fell asleep immediately.

A few hours later, she heard movement in the room and rose to see Alfa leaving a new basin of water. Surprisingly restored by her rest, she felt more at peace and better able to recognize the appropriateness of the penance. She needed to spend more time with the Latin texts, interpretations, and liturgy. Quite a few manuscripts in the scriptorium had never been opened because she turned so often to the texts in Englisc. The penance would return her to contemplation of the words of God and the fathers of the church.

There was yet another trial for her, however. After the early morning meal and a second round of prayers, Hilda and Olaf prepared themselves and their horses for the return trip. Ydesa insisted upon sending food and gifts that Hilda felt it would be impolite to refuse, and just as they were leaving, Lord Ragnar appeared with a curious metal box. He opened it with care and drew out of it an obviously very old and much used manuscript. Carrying it over to Hilda, he handed the treasure to her. For her, it was as though someone had awarded her eternal life. However, she set a determined look and carefully replaced the treasure into its metal box. "Thank you, Ragnar, for allowing me to see this precious item."

"Abbess Hilda," he replied, I desire that you take it to the abbey with my thanks for your support." When Hilda hesitated, Ragnar insisted. "Olaf can strap it onto his horse."

Olaf, always anxious to please his Abbess, agreed. He, too, wanted a look at that manuscript.

Once they had returned to their own abbey, however, Olaf was surprised when Hilda insisted that the metal box was to be put in a safe place and remain unopened for a full year. Olaf stifled his disappointment and did not ask for Hilda's reasons; he knew that he had no right to know. And he knew also that no entreaty would alter her decision.

Familiar Refugees

During the following year, Hilda's thoughts turned on occasion to the metal box and its contents, but she obediently kept to the Latin manuscripts she had overlooked, though she confessed, but only to herself, that quite a few of these manuscripts were not directly religious. Perhaps, she thought ruefully to herself, her penance was not as difficult as the priest might have wished. With pleasure she read manuscripts of her people's history, treatises on plants and flowers, visits to exotic peoples and lands. One manuscript was written in a language completely indecipherable— but it reminded her of some of the parchment writings she had seen at Lothlar, parchments treasured by Pagany even though she was unable to read them. Hilda was able to recognize the name Cuchulain and vaguely recalled Pagany pointing to his name on one of the rocks where the *auncient woones* met in the forest, and telling stories of his heroic deeds. More manuscripts in more languages occupied the shelves: some written in letters which resembled neither Latin, Englisc nor the language of Pagany's people. As she explored them, she had to acknowledge that she would never be able to truly know the contents of some of her treasures.

One summer afternoon, while she sat musing before one such manuscript, Olaf appeared carrying Lord Ragnar's metal box. "Pardon me, Abbess Hilda," he ventured shyly, "but the year has passed since we received this box." Hilda laughed at him. Obviously he wanted to open it, but he could not without her permission.

She smiled at him. "It's time perhaps. Good of you to remind me. I'd like to open it as much as you."

Clearing a spot on one of the flat tables in the scriptorium, Olaf handled the box as gently as though it were a wounded bird. Although two of the metal latches were difficult to pry open, Olaf soon exposed the contents of the box: an obviously ancient manuscript enclosed in a leather binding whose decorations had long faded away. Carefully Hilda lifted the manuscript from the box and brushed off the accumulated dust. As she turned the leather binding over, more dust rose from the decaying first leaves of parchment. Nonetheless, on that first leaf, Hilda discerned the faint figure of a mythical beast with huge arms and even larger claws.

"This must once have been a magnificent drawing," Hilda said to Olaf, who nodded his head in agreement. This first page had become detached, and the next few pages seemed to be missing entirely. Hilda upended the manuscript so she could look to see how intact the remaining folios were. "The manuscript appears to be in two parts," she declared, pointing to a spot where a disjunction was evident. Carefully she turned to that spot and found that, again, some leaves were missing. The works in the manuscript would never be complete. As Lord Ragnar had warned her, the writing was in his language, not hers. Nonetheless, the letters were similar to the letters of her own language. Hilda thought she could even make out some of the words.

"Olaf," she said to her adoring pupil, "We both need to learn the language of Ragnar's people. I think I see here the names of the same people I have heard in our songs of praise."

Olaf responded quietly but enthusiastically, "While at Ragnar's hall I made the acquaintance of Alfa, the young woman who was assigned to you. She learned the language of this manuscript as a small child. Perhaps she could help us in some way to decipher the texts? Shall I send for her?"

Hilda was silent for a moment as she turned over the leaves of the old manuscript, brushing away pieces of dried parchment as she did so. Finally she closed the binding and gently laid the treasure back in its box. She was not yet ready to give in to her desire to return to secular manuscripts. It could wait.

"Not yet, Olaf," she said resolutely, "But see to it that the binding gets oiled to delay further cracking of it. I'm not quite ready to examine it; we'll continue to set it aside for yet a while." Seeing the stricken look on his face, she gave him a reason to hope. "Be patient. One day Alfa will come here and help us read its contents."

As Hilda pulled herself away from the magnetic attraction of the old manuscript, she became aware of a flurry of voices and horses at the abbey gate. Looking across from the scriptorium, she was surprised to see a fair size group of women and children, carts and horses. As she strode toward the assemblage, she caught her breath. Surely that was Caedmon. She picked up her pace and soon knew her assumption was correct.

"Caedmon," she asked breathlessly, "whatever brings you and this troop here to Buxton. Is there trouble at Highhear?" Even as she asked, she knew the answer.

"My Lady," Caedmon smiled to see her, but immediately his expression turned to sadness. "Yes, we have had to flee; fortunately we were warned and were able to gather all and leave safely. But I fear the enemy has taken over Highhear and, knowing not where to go, we came here and hoped for your help. So far as we can tell, we have not been pursued. Apparently the enemy wanted only to take over the property and chase us off. My lord, Lord Heardred, also fled, but he went farther south. Those who warned us were puzzled, however, as the approaching enemy did not seem to be composed of the red-haired ones. But, whoever they were, we barely had time to gather ourselves and leave."

Looking around at all those gathered, with fear on her face, Hilda turned back to Caedmon. "Ethel, Ethel, is she here?" At the sound of her name, Ethel appeared from out of the gathered people. Hilda ran toward her with arms outspread. "Oh my, oh my," was all she could say as she enclosed Ethel's body in a tight hug and then pulled her off and gazed at her beloved nurse. "Thank God, you're safe too!"

With Ethel's arm still enclosed in her own, Hilda turned back to Caedmon. "Of course, you did right; we will provide for you." Hilda beckoned to Olaf and directed him to see that food was prepared and rooms made ready for the whole group. She then noticed both Alanya and her mother fussing with a sizable number of small children. Quickly she approached them and embraced both warmly. "You and all your people are more than welcome here. She smiled then at the children who seemed both intrigued and bewildered by her clothing. "And these, Alanya?"

"My grandchildren," Aelfwynn proudly announced.

"My goodness," was all Hilda could think to say as she counted and surveyed the young ones—five in total—ranging, she would guess, from two years to twelve years.

By nightfall, all had settled in. The youngest of the children were sleeping and the oldest were having difficulty stayed awake. Hilda, Caedmon, Alanya, and Aelfwynn sat on the rough logs in the abbey yard and laughed and smiled as they all told of their lives since they had last seen each other.

The following morning after prayers, Hilda pulled Caedmon aside. "I have a suggestion for you that you are welcome to reject. We here at the abbey would be happy to have you stay, but I do think that you might be better occupied at Lothlar. There you will be able to resume the life that more readily resembles the one you left. If that does not seem acceptable to you after you discuss it with your family, you will stay here. But if that does seem a good course, I will send a messenger to Lothlar to determine if Leova and her people can fit you into their world.

Caedmon was silent for some time; Hilda could see that he was turning the idea over and over in his mind. Finally, he answered, "I am grateful to you for your help, but I will need to present all of this to my wife and her mother. I will do that as quickly as possible."

Hilda was somewhat surprised by his quick return as he signaled to her from the door of the scriptorium. "My Lady, we agree that, if Leova assents, we will travel there." Within the week, Hilda's messenger had returned with greetings from both Leova and Rolfe and a gracious, warm invitation to Caedmon and his family.

Five days later, Hilda lingered sadly at the abbey gate, watching Caedmon and his family as they moved away toward Lothlar. She knew it was the best solution for them, but knew also that she had delighted in their presence at Buxton.

Chapter 12: Leova Faces War (902-906)

Leova leaned against the lintel on the hall gate and smiled as she watched the children playing in the grassy area leading up to the hall. Elene and Wulfram watched over them from one of the fallen logs. Leova smiled as Rolfe rode up, holding the reins of a second horse; beckoning to Wulfram to join him, he called to Leova that they needed to survey the latest plantings. Elene roused herself too and watched as the two men rode away and then, signaling to Leova, she turned and disappeared into the trees. The children's play continued, uninfluenced by the ways of the adults watching them. Leova's two youngest, Riana and Bryan, were among the liveliest of the group, made up of the offspring of the farmers and hall servants of Lothlar. Hearing the happy cries and laughter reminded Leova of the times she and Hilda had, so many years ago, laughed and played on the same green underfoot.

But, suddenly she was drawn from her joy by memories of the night before when Pagany had crept into the chamber where she and Rolfe were sleeping. The old woman had been watching the skies at night along with the ever-dwindling circle of *the auncient woones* in the sacred clearing in the woods. For months they had claimed to see signs of impending conflict in the movement of clouds and the sounds of the forest animals. And for the past three nights, a bright torch had appeared in the sky, dragging its tail slowly across the heavens; then last night a shadow had moved slowly across the face of the moon and just as slowly moved away.

"No good can come from such portents," Pagany had whispered as she made her way to Leova's sleeping chamber. She shook her daughter awake. "Wake up, my child. We must gather ourselves. Evil comes."

"Mother, sshh," Leova had whispered, soothing Pagany's agitation even as she brought herself up from sleep. Gazing apprehensively at her sleeping husband, Leova had eased herself out of the bed. Then, taking Pagany's arm, she had guided her to a small anteroom which gave out onto the yard. Her mother's appearance had alarmed her. The older woman's grey hair fell loosely about her

411

face and shoulders; her light cloak barely covered the thin nightdress she wore.

"Mother," she had said gently, "You shouldn't be wandering about like this. Come, I'll take you to your bur so you can lie down."

"No, no. Listen to me!" Pagany had pleaded. "I've seen dire warnings. In the woods and now in the sky...the sky...in the skies." Her voice faded away wearily.

Even though she was quite exasperated to find that Pagany had dragged herself out into the cool night air and damp woods, Leova couldn't bring herself to chide the exhausted woman. "Mother, you can't stay well if you insist upon roaming about in the night air."

"No...no...that doesn't matter!" Pagany had said urgently. "Our people will need to be sheltered within our walls; there must be a warning signal to tell them when to come! We need food for a siege—and armor and weapons!" She paused, her mind racing to another possibility, "Maybe we should all go west to my people. We'll be safe there!"

Leova had been concerned not with lights in the sky or prophecies but with the effect these fears were having on her mother's health. She had attempted to calm the distraught woman. "Yes, mother, I'll see to everything, but you must go to your bed and rest. I'll need your help later, and you can't give it if you're exhausted."

Leova's words had the desired effect, and Pagany's anxiety had lessened. With a bit more coaxing, she had even let herself be led back to bed. The anxious daughter sat watch until her mother slipped into sleep, but even then she had not moved, but sat gazing into that beloved aging face, its wrinkles and yellowing spots marking a long life. It hadn't been, and still was not, clear if Pagany's current alarm was a memory from the difficult past or if some very real danger was coming to Lothlar. She had, in the past, Leova knew, been aware of what had not yet happened, but eventually did happen.

Now, as Leova turned away from the pleasure of watching children in their happy play, she could only wonder at the source of

412

her mother's foresight, if indeed it was foresight or just the worries of an aging mind. It had been almost eight years since Viking fear had invaded the hall. At that time, the enemy had been advancing to the west of them, moving toward the southern coast of Cymru, apparently—or so it was reported to them in fragmented messages. Later messengers also told them that their enemy's march was a hard forced one since they had exhausted most of their food supply and appeared to desire only to get to the coast and back in their boats. The residents of Lothlar did not feel threatened.

Not long after, however, they had received news that a Viking fortification had been constructed just south of them at Bridgnorth. Those at Lothlar hoped to once again avoid battle, but an emissary of King Edward had come to them and calling Rolfe, in fealty to the king, to go with a contingent of fighting men to the site where a major battle between the Englisc forces and the Vikings was underway. Leova and others at Lothlar had watched anxiously as the men rode off, realizing that they had to bury their fears and begin to prepare themselves for a possible quick departure toward the west. Bryna's sons appeared at intervals to bring news of the battle. However, it was only two months after their departure when resounding horse hoofs brought them to the gate where they called out with joy as they recognized their own returning warriors. The news they brought was, and continued to be for the next few years, a source of comfort: Edward and his men had routed the invaders and predicted that this would be the last battle. But there was sadness also as three of those who had departed did not return. Rolfe assured their families, as he handed them the warriors' armor, that they had been admirably brave in battle and had taken the lives of many before receiving their own death blows. He assured them also that they had been given a proper burial.

Peace allowed them to return to their comfortable ways. Hannah and her cohorts argued in the kitchen over which pot to use for which soup, which jars were now unusable and which were still usable, and which herbs needed to be carefully meted out. Pagany felt safe to join the *auncient woones* in the forest at their sacred sites and to scavenge with them in the grasses to reap what they needed to flavor food and create potions for the sick and injured. Leova could sit for long hours with her oldest daughter Rosaleen and the other women to create new hangings for the hall and for the cottages of those who needed them. She also went back to the parchments a visiting priest had left for Rolfe to use as he tutored his wife, pleased to discover a quick learner who was mostly determined to stay in touch with Hilda through fairly long written messages. One of the priests had even been able to remain for some time and became for her a secondary teacher. Leova was content.

Now, however, Pagany was re-creating the fears of former years.

Two days later, as though to confirm those predictions, the first rumblings of renewed invasions reached Lothlar by means of a messenger dispatched by Hilda, who sent an urgent request for help. Her family lands had been ravished; the hall burned down. The reeve in charge, Caedmon, had fled with his family and sought refuge at Buxton. Hilda asked her old friends to take them in. Rolfe and Leova immediately sent an escort to bring the homeless family safely to Lothlar. Caedmon, his wife, Alanya, mother-in-law, Aelfwynn, and five children, as well as a small group of servants, arrived at Lothlar a week later. To Leova the newly arrived group represented Hilda's family, and while she had had no hesitation in her offer of aid, she had not expected quite so many family members. Hilda had decided to keep Ethel, her former nurse, with her at the monastery as she appeared to need a long rest. Caedmon, once he arrived at Lothlar, had somewhat settled Leova's worries about her childhood friend. "That monastery," Caedmon informed her, "is off the Vikings' path as they appear to be heading west toward Chester. "And," he continued aware of the concern in Leova's demeanor, "it abuts the land of a Lord Ragnar who, with Hilda's guidance, has converted in order to marry a woman of the Christian faith. He refuses to join in the fighting and his lands and Buxton Abbey remain untouched. Hilda," he added in order to allay Leova's fears, "is quite safe there."

The group of refugees had no intention, however, of being a burden. Caedmon, a kindred spirit to Jankin, immediately made himself useful. His wife, Alanya, quickly undertook a number of the household tasks while Aelfwynn retired to the kitchen—where the old healer and beekeeper caused more than one stir with Hannah who had ruled many years without fear of contradiction. One evening as the sounds of crashing pans reverberated into the weaving area, Leova knew she had to intervene. When she arrived in the cooking shed, Aelfwynn, and Hannah were glaring at each other with hands on hips. Several pans lay scattered on the floor. The two women looked at her guiltily. Leova could hardly suppress a smile as she suggested to them that they all go outside and resolve whatever was causing so much displeasure. As they passed through the doorway, Leova noticed Alanya, who had apparently heard the crashing sounds also. She signaled her to join them. Looking like contrite children, the two antagonists settled themselves uneasily on the log seats. Alanya joined them. "Now, tell me" Leova began, "how we can all live together without crashing pans."

After a long silence, Hannah was the first to speak. "The kitchen has always been mine and everything there has its place, but she," pointing to her antagonist, "puts things in the wrong places and sometimes I can't find what I need without wasting much time. Even Alanya comes in and adds to the disorder!"

Neither of the women denied what she said. And finally Aelfwynn spoke up softly but with force, "I have been beekeeping for many years and I know how to prepare all kinds of food."

Alanya, encouraged by her mother's words, added her own: "And I have been caring for others and fulfilling household tasks since I was a small child."

Leova remained quiet for a time. "Here's what I think; I hope you'll agree. Aelfwynn, I know of your skill with the bees and your quiet attendance to those who are ill. We do have some bee hives that have been untended for years. We would all certainly love to have more honey than we've been able to harvest. And, Hannah, I do hope you will ask one or both of these women to help you when there is need. Perhaps, there may even be days when you would like to rest. Alanya, I have heard much about your ways with those who are ill or wounded. That is one of my main tasks here and, with my mother's aging, I could use some help."

The three women looked carefully at each other and then nodded. "Good," said Leova, "let's start with this plan immediately. Hannah, you can return to the kitchen; Alanya and I will go out to the herb cottage and see if Pagany is there. And, Aelfwynn, I'll ask one of the servants to guide you to the once-thriving bee hives."

As Leova rose, she noticed Rolfe standing at the doorway into the cooking shed. He walked over to her and whispered as he put his arm around her shoulder, "Now I know whom to call on when the farmers begin to argue over some cow or piece of land." Leova smiled and took Alanya's hand.

Rolfe and Caedmon and Jankin had to work around similar problems as they sought places for the newcomers to settle. Additionally, as fairly as they could, they assigned the few farmers who had come with the group from Highhear to work with Lothlar farmers. Grumblings were heard, but mainly the farmers were pleased to have additional help.

Even in the midst of the continued anxiety brought on by the newcomers' flight from the enemy who'd plundered their home, there was happiness; once again children from Highhear and children from Lothlar became companions, and the hall rang, inside and out, with unknowing youthful voices and games from dawn to dusk. But, ever aware of impending danger, when night fell, the gates were closed and bolted with heavy timbers.

Barely three weeks later, before they had settled into a routine, Leova awoke to pounding on the palisade gates. She knew immediately that the enemy was near if not already upon them. To confirm her fears, the voice of a nearby tenant rang out on the other side.

"Lord Rolfe! The enemy comes! We must fight or leave!" Within minutes the residents of the hall began to assemble, and the air rang with fearful questions. Rolfe called for quiet and then began to issue orders. Two of the men he used as stalkers when hunting were told to open the gates and seek out Bryna's sons who served as constant watchers even in times of peace. "We'll arm ourselves and bring everyone into the inner walls of the hall until we get a message from you."

Although it was still dark, Rolfe assigned each of his men to bring in a certain number of farmers and tenants—he wanted to make certain that no one would be left unprotected, but he gave orders that everyone should bring only their families and whatever food they could gather quickly.

Several hours later, all the people from the farms had gathered in the hall. One of the stewards had guided the women and children to the far end of the great room, while the men drew together at the opposite end, closest to the door. Many held a bow and quiver of arrows, others had crude wooden shields and long daggers. Rolfe walked among them, checking their weapons and answering their questions as best he could. Leova went into the kitchen with Hannah and Aelfwynn to begin packing whatever food they might need if they were forced to flee.

For five hours, they waited for news from the scouts. The restlessness grew and adult voices often rang out in attempts to quiet the children who mostly just continued with their usual games. Leova tried to keep everyone busy by asking them to help with collecting food, medicines, warm clothing, and even some kitchen utensils. Most of those waiting had little experience with doing nothing and their restlessness increased as the hours passed. One of the farmers came with his wife to ask Rolfe if they could go out and collect some of their chickens to take with them if escape became necessary. Rolfe reluctantly denied the request and the farmer began to mutter that they were all wasting time simple sitting about. Others shared his feelings. The atmosphere in the hall became uncomfortable; even the children seemed to sense the difference.

Finally the scouts returned; their faces held no hope that the warnings had all been a mistake. "We've seen the enemy," the first man reported as he nervously shifted from foot to foot. "The watchers told us that the invaders have been moving toward us, burning everything they come to." He looked anxiously at Rolfe, "They brought us to a slight rise on one of the hill forts from which we could see for miles. The enemy is camped; the encampment covers miles and miles. Soon, undoubtedly they will recommence their trek in this direction. We can't stand against them."

Wulfram blurted out, "We'll stay behind our walls and keep them off!"

When no one agreed with the young man, he fell silent, ashamed to have spoken before his father. Rolfe, however, ignored the outburst and turned to the distressed scout, "Go on man, tell us all that you have learned."

"The pattern is the same. Bryna's sons told us that each time the enemy approaches a walled hall, they simply throw burning brands over the stockades. No defense can counter that. Those who rush out die; those who stay within burn alive. Nothing can save them. They destroy simple farmer huts in the same fashion and then round up all the cattle and other livestock."

"No one can escape?" asked Rolfe.

"The men are slain, but the women and children are simply shoved aside unless they protest. If they dare to speak out, they, too, are killed. We circled around, trying to get a sense of how many warriors and foot soldiers there are...." The scout shook his head wearily. "The troops stretch as far as the eye can see—perhaps 10,000 men—coming this way!"

Frightened and angry voices rose up as the crowd received the news, but Rolfe thought for only a minute before he silenced them. "Let's waste no more time in talking. It's obvious that we have no choice but to leave. Not only will that save the lives of our families, it may give us advantages in the future. If no one remains here, they might not burn the hall and farmhouses, but use them for themselves. If that happens, then everything will always be here for us to recapture."

"Where will we go?" Wulfram asked.

"West and south—to Cymru where Pagany and Iona's people dwell—I think we'll be safe there, as the enemy had to desert that area some time ago and have, from all reports, not returned." Rolfe replied. "But we must move quickly." He turned again to his messenger. "How much time do you think we have?"

"The troops move slowly. There are so many of them and their progress is slowed by their greedy plundering. They stop to torch everything in their path after they've confiscated all the food,

418

armor, and livestock. We'll have a day to escape them, perhaps more if we leave just after dawn. We might have longer if they stay encamped."

"Let's set to it, then," Rolfe ordered, "we'll send the women and children ahead with a few of the wagons and then follow with the remaining wagons as soon as we can. For now let's not think of fighting. War will come soon enough. But we must send a message to Stonehart for my brother Regan and those who dwell there. They must leave also."

"Lord Rolfe," one of scouts was quick to reply, "Bryna's youngest son has already traveled to warn them and to lay out a probable escape route. He hopes they will at some point join us."

"That relieves my mind greatly," Rolfe replied. "Now, let's prepare." He immediately put everyone to work. He sent Jankin and Caedmon and the servants out of the hall to saddle up horses and harness mules to carts. Leova began to pull out baskets and bags so the servants could load up the food, clothes, and warm blankets they had already assembled. Wulfram, aided by several of the farmers, began loading bundles onto several carts now lined up by the gate.

Bertram and Pagany, attended by Gwynedd, Ian and Iona, went from family to family to prepare the old and infirm to travel. It was not easy to persuade the grandfathers and grandmothers to separate from their families; only the constant assurance that they would be reunited in a short time convinced them, if still reluctant, to climb aboard the carts and settle down for the journey. Berghorf, Leova's second son, helped assemble boys too young to fight and girls mature enough to care for the older generation's needs. "Please keep an eye on your younger brother and sister," Leova whispered to Berghorf, for she could see that they already had tears in their eyes. Two strong men would also accompany this lead group. She then looked up at the large group and, in a voice she hoped covered her fears, addressed all of them: "Iona and Ian and Pagany will lead you—they know the western route well. We'll join you as soon as all else has been collected. You do us service, you know," she smiled. "The path you make will guide us. May God and the spirits of our

419

people go with you."

After the elderly, the tearful children, and their protectors had started up the path and onto the road toward the western woods and hills, Leova returned to help Hannah, Bryna, Aelfwynn, and the household servants finish packing what they'd need for the journey. Along with whatever food had been stored, the women collected pots and jars of all sizes, plus pokers and other implements that might be necessary for cooking over an open fire. Leova helped in the kitchen and then returned to the central hall to oversee the loading of the second contingent of carts and wagons and to check on available horses and mules. For a moment she rested gazing at the tumult in the hall, but suddenly turning wildly from side to side she screamed "Where's Riana; she was just here; help me find her!" She began darting around the room frantically calling and calling her youngest daughter's name.

"Mother," came Wulfram's quiet voice, "Riana's right here on the floor with one of her toys." He pointed to his baby sister sitting quietly talking to one of her dolls, telling the doll that they had to move from the hall.

Rolfe, having heard his wife's uncharacteristic screaming, appeared at her side. She collapsed against him and began to sob. "Why, Rolfe, why? Why? Do we really need to leave all of this and drag everyone through the country? Can we not stay and defend ourselves? I can't bear leaving, taking everyone away, my mother, my father, all the others." She was shaking as she spoke.

Seeing Pagany approaching, Rolfe beckoned to her, whispering, "Mother, have you something to calm her? She's being bedeviled by all that's necessary." As Pagany headed toward the herb hut, Rolfe forced Leova to sit and held her hand gently as she put her head on his shoulder. Others in the hall continued with their tasks as though they were not aware of the scene. Soon Pagany returned, holding some small branches of a dried herb. She held these under Leova's nose and told her to breathe deeply. Leova followed her mother's advice and, in a short time, calmed down.

"Rolfe," she whispered softly, "I'm not serving everyone well by reacting like this. Please go finish up your tasks; I am recovering."

Rolfe squeezed her hand gently, nodded at Pagany who remained at Leova's side, and returned to finishing up the loading of more carts. In a short time, Leova shook off her mother's hand and walked with determination toward the women who were carrying loads from the cooking shed. Without saying a word, she took some of the goods from them and carried it to one of the carts. Then, at the last moment she pulled down the small tapestry that hung in her bur, the one she and Hilda had made so long ago, and had it loaded on a wagon. It wouldn't slow them down, she reasoned, and they'd need protection once the cold set in. Her jewelry, she reasoned, could purchase favors should they need them, so she tied all she possessed in a small purse and hid it deep within the piles of blankets and clothes.

Finally, she visited the small building used to house medicines and herbs. To her surprise, everything she wanted to take had already been placed in baskets: bottles of elixir, carefully sealed and labeled packets of herbs, the bandages she always had ready, and jars of ointment to treat sore joints and keep infection from wounds. On top of one basket lay a small figure woven from straw, the emblem of the *auncient woones.*

"Mother," she mused. "I should have known you'd not leave such important matters in my hands."

"The *auncient woones* and Alanya have helped much," Pagany replied.

"Perhaps the *auncient woones* should come with us," Leova suggested.

"I have asked them, but I knew, even while asking, they would not come. They do not fear the fighting men. In truth, the fighting men are probably a bit wary of assaulting them. The old beliefs die hard; the women are protected by them."

"Please then, mother, thank them. And please tell them that whatever we have had to leave behind, they are welcome to use."

Leaving Pagany with a hug and a light kiss, Leova stepped into the courtyard, looking around anxiously for Rolfe or Wulfram. It took a few minutes, but at last she spotted Wulfram who was helping a family load their meager belongings on to one of the hall's mules.

With pride, she watched her son comfort the children who hovered fearfully by their parents. "All will be well," he said, hugging a small girl who clutched her doll fiercely.

"How is it progressing" Leova asked her son as she embraced him.

"As well as it can, mother," he replied somewhat sadly.

The look on his face revealed painful worries. They had always been close, and long ago she had learned to read his face.

"There's more, perhaps that worries you?" she asked.

He pushed his hair back from his eyes, revealing the trouble that filled his heart. "Elene's gone. She's with her brothers in the forest...what if...."

Leova stopped him. "If Elene were one of the other girls in our community, I'd be aghast, but she's not like the other girls." She saw him start to protest, but she didn't let him speak. "You said she's with her brothers?"

Wulfram nodded, his mouth shut tightly with fear.

"Then she will probably be as safe as she would be with us. Probably safer!"

"But I want to..." he stopped and hung his head.

Leova put her hands on his shoulders. "Yes. I know. You care for her much more deeply than you've ever said and you want to protect her. But there's nothing you can do now. Trust that you'll be together again." She lifted his chin and looked in his eyes. "Go back to what you're doing. Help those who depend upon you."

He nodded, too full of emotion to speak, and turned back to the frightened folks who needed his help. As she watched her son go back to loading wagons and organizing families for the long trip, Rolfe came up behind her and gave her a quick hug. "How is he?" he asked, watching Wulfram resume his tasks.

"Worried about Elene," Leova replied and turned to look at her husband. "When we are once again at peace, we need to talk to them about their relationship. They are of an age to marry."

Rolfe nodded. "Until then, Wulfram will have to prove his worth in ways that he should not be asked to do at his young age. Do you think he'll be up to it? Are we giving him too much responsibility?"

"He'll be fine. I wish his maturity could be tested in a different way, one that wouldn't endanger his life. But the invaders have made that impossible. Watch out for him. Please."

"Of course," Rolfe answered, wrapping his arms about her and holding her close. "I'll keep him as close as possible when the fighting starts...and..." he stopped speaking for lack of words.

"And care for yourself, also, my love," Leova whispered. "I would not want to live without you."

He gave her one more tight hug and then held her out at arms' length, looking gravely into her eyes. "You, too, take care. Our journey will not be an easy one—much harder, I'd guess than the year we spent living with Ian and Iona before Wulfram was born. It grieves me that so much falls on your shoulders. But do remember that we will be close behind you."

Leova wanted to stay at his side, but she knew that option was closed. She drew him toward her quickly. Then they both turned away, back to the tasks at hand.

After Leova had departed with the second wave of the community, Rolfe addressed the men and boys who were of fighting age. "Our job will be to protect our families. If the army catches up with us, we'll fight. But know this, any fight would lead to death. He paused, waiting for his own emotions to calm down, then finished what he had to say. "We'll leave the gate open so there will be no reason for these marauders to destroy our home." He shook his head sadly, "They'll slaughter our livestock to feed themselves and set fire to the fields; we cannot prevent that—nothing we can do to forestall that! Now let's join our families. My heart tells me we will return one day to this, our home."

Rolfe signaled Jankin, Wulfram, and Caedmon, who led the men out of the gate, most on foot, but some on horses or mules. As Rolfe watched, the men moved out slowly, their features grim but determined. When the last of the troop was beyond the gates, Rolfe followed. Once outside the barricades, now open to friend and enemy, he looked back sadly into the deserted hall, then rode on.

The Journey

The journey to Pagany's homeland proved to be days and nights of pain and fatigue. Most of the mothers and older daughters walked beside the pack animals, carrying small children and seeing to the needs of those who fell sick or developed the inevitable problems of forced marching: foot sores, aching backs, muscles pushed far beyond their limits. For hours Leova would carry a baby or small child who could not keep up the pace and who needed cajoling to keep away tears. Older farmers, used to herding sheep and harvesting fields, watched the older children and more than once slowed the pace of the group. Once Rolfe and the men of fighting age caught up with those who had departed earlier, they dismounted at times and let the mothers hold babies on the horses' backs. Everyone helped, Lord and lowly alike.

These hardships didn't cancel out the normal events of their lives. A longtime servant, one who had tended the stables for most of his adult life, suddenly dropped to his feet holding his chest and died within minutes. A pregnant woman, carrying her first child, announced that her time had come, and with the assistance of Leova and the other women gave birth to a healthy boy. In each case, the convoy stopped and although they feared the enemy would catch up with them, they took the time to make a proper burial and to make sure that both the baby and the mother could move on with them.

The men at the rearguard of the group turned often to look back, fearful of what they might see. Thus it was that one, hearing and then seeing a lone horseman, called to his leader, "A rider approaches!" the anxiety in his voice causing it to quaver a bit.

Rolfe quickly turned his horse to stare at the approaching rider; then broke into a cry of joy: "Be calm! That's one of Regan's housemen." Quickly Rolfe galloped to him. When the two returned together, Rolfe announced that those fleeing Stonehart were coming up behind. "Let us rest a bit and wait for our friends and relations." Many sighs of relief could be heard as all, young and old, armed and unarmed, male and female, settled themselves on the grounds looking toward the arriving group. When they joined up shortly after, a joyous atmosphere took over—if only momentarily. Most of the men and women from Lothlar knew Regan quite well, but also knew many of the farmers and their families.

When Regan appeared, he brought news from Bryna's sons who had joined his group for a short while. They had reported that the enemy had remained at both Lothlar and Stonehart for several days and were thus not too close behind. They also reported that neither hall had been destroyed. A sigh of relief rose from the collected group. But soon Rolfe and Regan, although reluctant to interrupt the mood, insisted that they must move on, knowing it would be foolish not to take advantage of the distance between them and the enemy. Soon the group, now enlarged quite a bit, began their trek again.

Two weeks into the trip, clouds gathered and soon they found themselves walking in heavy rain. That night they slept on damp ground next to smoldering fires made of wet branches. "Thanks be, it's summer," Rolfe joked half-heartedly as they tried to cook an evening meal. "At least we don't need heavy cloaks and our clothes will dry out as we walk."

A few people laughed, but most saw no humor in their journey. Ian voiced their feelings, "That's true, Lord Rolfe. But no one has ever been made comfortable simply by knowing that things could be worse." His wit amused them, and for a moment spirits lifted.

Decorum changed also. Everyone began to feel dirty and longed for clean clothes as well as for a place to wear them that was less demanding than a narrow road through increasingly wild countryside. While the men moved fairly freely, the women struggled with their skirts, which tore on brambles and grew heavy with mud. After a long morning of tripping over the hem of her kirtle, Leova at last hitched up her skirt and secured it with her sash, so she could move faster. Some of the other women pulled the backs of their dresses through their legs and bound them about their waists, creating rude forms of pants. The sight of their strange garb made everyone laugh, but the adjustment worked so well that no one objected to what might be considered, in other circumstances, immodesty.

Thankfully, they seemed to be far ahead of the marauders, and as yet there was no sign of pursuit. The distressed Wulfram, worried that there was no sign of either Elene or her brothers, hoped they followed in the woods. He realized that they served the travelers best by staying behind as monitors of the enemy's movements, thus precluding any sudden attack. Nonetheless, he feared for them.

After a fortnight, the landscape began to change, becoming more mountainous, more austere. "See that great mountain range?" Pagany said triumphantly, pointing to the west, "*Y Mynyddoedd Duon*—the Black Mountains!" She smiled at Iona happily, "They've protected our people for as long as time. No one will dare seek us among the rocks and the forests."

The group pushed on with renewed energy, hoping their flight would soon end. Their numbers had now almost doubled as they moved westward, joined by folks from the small villages, all of whom wanted the protection of a large group and a destination where they could be safe. Small landholders and the farmers who served them brought their womenfolk and children, and everyone was willing to contribute to the goods and supplies that the residents of Lothlar had gathered. Fortunately, some had horses, armor, and weapons to contribute as well. Rolfe hoped use of force would not be necessary, but he feared it would be.

Just as they approached the river that bordered their final resting place, an armored soldier rode up from behind, accompanied by two also armed men. Moving his horse carefully around the crowd, he asked urgently for their leader. Rolfe, signaling to Regan to join him, rode forward, positioning himself between the soldier and the people. "I am Rolfe, Lord of Lothlar and Stonehart with my blood-brother Regan, and these people are our tenants and neighbors and—he allowed himself to smile slightly—strangers who have joined us on our way. We've been forced to flee before a large host of our enemy."

The strange soldier looked approvingly at the proud man before him. "Well met, Lord Rolfe. I am Landstone, emissary of King

Edward who battles with our common enemy."

"How far off is Edward? And what is his strength? The enemy we flee has a force of perhaps as many as 10,000 men." Landstone's face showed immediate concern. To look at him was to know that King Edward was unaware of the enemy's numbers.

"No, the troupes we have encountered number considerably less—it appears that we have underestimated our enemy's power— how far away are those you have escaped?"

"At most a week's journey. We left Lothlar almost two weeks ago and my scouts see no indication that we're being closely followed."

"Good, I'll return and give this message to our King, who will find your news disturbing, but most useful and therefore welcome. Prepare yourself to join him with all those in your group who can do battle. He is traveling up from the southwest; we know the Vikings are to the east of us; most of them have come up from London. But we have received news that the enemy has also landed on the west shore of Cymru and may be pushing this way too. One of my men will stay with you now and lead you and all your able men to King Edward as soon as you can arrange to leave the group. We will meet again soon, Lord Rolfe, Lord Regan. God be with you and your people." With those words, Landstone turned and headed back to the southeast, leaving the citizens of Lothlar and the people they'd collected to continue west.

After he was gone, Rolfe sought out Leova. "I'm almost glad to join the fight," Rolfe said. "This retreat weighs upon me heavily."

"We had no choice," his wife replied, but the words did little to comfort him. His anger had increased as he traveled away from his home and as he witnessed the hardship the flight had cost those he loved.

"Yes, but now I do have a choice. Once we get you and the defenseless ones into the mountains, I'll lead the men to meet with the king."

"You'll abandon us?"

"I trust you to set up a settlement of our people near Pagany's home. The folks of Crymu will help you—and you are not without resources. Remember, you learned much about maintaining a home and running a farm when we hid out from Allmana all those years ago." He smiled affectionately at Leova, who returned his smile, knowing that he needed her encouragement. "Now, let's see our people delivered to the protection of these mountains."

Pagany and Iona estimated they were no more than a day's journey away from the town of Talgarth. Crossing the river would be difficult, but not impossible; from there they could push into the mountains to Pincelli, Pagany's birthplace. There, where the rocks and dense vegetation would limit fighting, they would settle. The women and elders heaved a sigh of relief, knowing that they would soon be out of danger, but the prospect of the men's joining Edward's army met with less than a unanimous reaction. The men expressed eagerness to fight alongside a King; their women were less than enthusiastic about the on-coming battle. Many a wife asked her man and older sons to forego the battle.

Looking anxiously at his wife, Rolfe decided to act swiftly. "I had not intended to separate from you so soon, but I must keep the men's zeal alive. Their women make them hesitant."

Leova said nothing although she desperately wanted to talk Rolfe out of fighting.

Swiftly he gave his last orders to the large group: women would rest for a short time before continuing, and the men would prepare for the on-coming combat before moving back toward the east to meet the King. Rolfe requested that one of Bryna's sons, along with a small contingent of fighting men, stay behind to warn of any danger. Within three hours, the goodbyes had been said. The women, their protectors and older male guides, the children, and the animals waded across the river where it was most shallow and disappeared within the forest; the remaining men hoisted their weapons and began to travel along the road which a short time ago had brought the King's messenger to them. Only the disturbed ground gave evidence that a whole village of people had been there.

The Worst of War

Five months into the stay at Pincelli, just as harvesting began, Pagany once again took to waking in the night, trembling with horror at a dream that repeatedly visited her. "One of them is hurt!" she'd tell Leova, ignoring her daughter's attempts to calm her. "One of them—Rolfe or Wulfram—has fallen in battle. We must do something to save him!"

Pagany's dream was vague, the man who fell, unidentifiable. Leova tried desperately to calm her mother, to stop her dreadful prophecies, but two things haunted her also: her gentle mother merely spoke aloud the fears that others carried, and Pagany had been right about the coming of the enemy. As a result, on the day that Garulf, Golmund, and Elene arrived, dragging a rough sledge upon which lay an unconscious man, her only question was whether it was her husband or her son who lay so still.

"It's Wulfram," shouted Elene. "Come, help him."

Leova and Pagany rushed to the young man's side, each in turn touching the pale forehead to check for fever and feeling for the pulse of life in the limp hands. Elene, aware of their distress and unspoken questions, quickly attempted to reassure the two women and the small crowd who had gathered.

"Don't be afraid. At present, Wulfram only sleeps. We gave him poppy juice to ease his pain and between that and the journey, he has given way to his exhaustion."

"What happened?" Leova whispered, afraid of what she'd hear. "Tell me as we bring him in."

Elene nodded to her brothers; and, as they moved their burden into the small cottage, she told those who gathered what she knew. "He has a head wound, a nasty gash from a sword in his thigh, and a broken leg. We brought him to you because he wasn't safe so close to the battle." She paused. "And because we weren't sure how to keep the cut from infection. We set the leg and packed the wound with moss and herbs," she hesitated, suddenly vulnerable, "He should recover, shouldn't he?"

"Much depends upon what's been done since he suffered the

wound. How long has it been since he was attacked?" Pagany asked. "Did he lay on the battlefield a long while, or was the wound treated early on?"

Garulf continued his sister's narrative. "It's been a week since Wulfram was lured into the forest and fell into a pit meant to trap our troupes.   The fall broke his leg, but when the enemy came for him, he still fought back. We got to him just as the soldier who set up the trap struck him with a cudgel. The spear he plunged into Wulfram's thigh hadn't kept the boy down." Garulf paused as if the action was more than he could comprehend, then spoke with anger. "We killed the coward."

Elene broke in. "Luckily we were able to get Wulfram out of the pit and farther away from battle. Each time we moved him we feared we were adding to his wounds, but at last we got him to safety and began to work on setting his leg and cleaning the laceration. The moss and herbs needed to care for the wound were easy to find, but he grew weaker with each day, and I thought it best to bring him to you. Even though the journey was hard, on the field he would die; here life awaits him." The determination in her voice did not mask her fear.

Leova worked to calm herself, knowing that her son's life depended upon the care she and her mother with help from Alanya and Aelfwynn, would give him. Blows to the head were dangerous as were broken bones, but the most alarming injury was the cut. If they didn't staunch it, Wulfram could lose his leg, or his life.

Garulf placed a comforting hand on Pagany's shoulder. The young man paused, "He conducted himself more than honorably, My Lady. You may be assured of that: many of our enemy no longer threaten us as a result of his bravery."

Leova nodded, too stricken to reply. His bravery on the battlefield didn't ease her fears. She knew that fighting an enemy took one kind of courage; the fight for his health would take another kind.

It immediately became obvious that Wulfram did not sleep easily. Gentle efforts to wake him failed, and the words he mumbled as well as the cries that came suddenly unbidden from his mouth, let

Pagany know that he was reliving battle. Sometimes, however, he grew calm, spoke Elene's name, calling to her until she came to the bedside and whispered soft and low. Pagany watched the interaction: she did not miss the evidence that Elene's worried face and gentle kisses showed more than a comrade's concern.

Late one afternoon, just as the sun was setting, Leova heard her son gasp and watched from across the room as he struggled to move into a sitting position. Before he could speak or she could reach his side, Bryna, who had been preparing to change his bandages, addressed him in her matter-of-fact way. "You've rejoined us at last," she said. And with little regard for his confusion, she went on as if it were an ordinary day. "Good, good. Let's get some food into you."

Wulfram recognized Bryna but not his surroundings and, in a panic, struggled to get up. "What place is this? How have I come to be here?"

"No, no," Bryna tried to calm him. "Don't try to get up just yet—you're too weak."

Ignoring her, Wulfram made a great effort and stood upright, but no sooner had he risen than he swayed forward and began to fall. Pagany and Elene rushed to help Bryna place Wulfram, who had already slipped back into unconsciousness, back on his bed.

"Why will these men not listen?" Bryna scolded, more frightened than angry, "Now look what he's done. The wound's bleeding again!"

"We'll fix it again," Leova said. "At least we know he's coming back to us." She brushed the hair from his forehead lovingly as he once again opened his eyes and stared at her in confusion and disbelief. "It's so good to see you open your eyes," she told him.

Wulfram reached out to Leova, who took his hand and held it tightly.

"Mother..." he started, still unable to understand what had happened to him.

"Where am I?"

"Safe in Cymru, in your grandmother's village," said Leova.

Wulfram's face registered his shock, "Pencilli's over a week away from the battle! How did I get here?"

"Garulf and Golmund brought you to us."

"And Elene? Where is Elene?" he questioned, looking to his mother anxiously. "Here," she answered, drawing the girl around to his bedside, fully aware of the joy and relief that lit up the faces of the two young people.

Wulfram relaxed as he felt Elene's hand on his arm. But several minutes later, Elene felt his arm tense up once more. "What of my father? Is he here also?"

"No, not here," Bryna answered quietly, "but Garulf and Golmund have assured me that your father is unharmed and safe with the King."

"And your other sons?" Wulfram asked.

"Gardorf and Garhild remain in the shadows, always aware of the enemy's movements and locations, reporting their observations every day to the King. Garamond carries messages from the King to those in battle."

Leova brushed back her son's hair, smiling at him as peacefully as she could. "You need now, my son, to rest and recover. I have brought you a special tonic that Aelfwynn has prepared. It will help you sleep." Wulfram was about to protest, but Leova put the small jar up to his lips and nodded to him. Giving up his resistance, Wulfram did as she requested; soon he was asleep.

Watching her son recover created a constant conflict of emotions for Leova. On one hand, each day brought another step toward healing—he grew strong enough to sit up in bed, then to walk with the aid of crutches, and finally to walk unaided except for the gentle strength of Elene to support him. As he regained his health, his nightmares ceased and his normally sunny disposition returned. He still had the haunted look of men who fight in battle, who see other men die. On the other hand, she knew that when he regained his health, he would return to the battleground where she could no longer be sure he would be safe.

While Leova and John had other children, other sons, Wulfram was all that remained of Leova's love for William, and the thought of losing him brought on old heartaches and insecurities.

Looking at Wulfram as he sat by his grandfather, she thought of William's ways, of his calm manner of adapting to change. Bertram, however, seemed unable to adjust to his current condition. He longed to join the battle, feeling less a man for his inability to stand beside his King. He complained bitterly about what he named his "uselessness."

"I've become a burden rather than a leader of my people!" he fretted. "I'm the leader of an army of women, children, and old men, hiding in the mountains instead of serving my King. I wish at least I had men to tell me of the war—young men!"

Leova regretted that the old man got his wish—learning from his wounded grandson. As Wulfram told the old man stories from the war, she remembered the gentle William, using words and kindness to ease her fears of a forced marriage. Wulfram had inherited from his father what Pagany called "the touch," which wasn't a physical thing at all, but a way of soothing frightened souls and reassuring them that there was hope even in the worst of situations.

"Perhaps I should see if he wants to be a healer," Leova thought. "He might prefer caring for the sick more than overseeing the estates he will inherit." She knew that the estates her family had owned and governed might be lost forever to the enemy, that being a lord might not be in his future, nor being a lady in her own future. And furthermore, until the war was over, no one could make plans for a future that didn't involve fighting and—too frequently—dying.

She could see that Wulfram himself was conflicted. As he began to explore his surroundings, and speak with others who were recovering from their wounds, a great restlessness would come over him. Wulfram was not the only seriously wounded member of the exiled group. Others had come before him and more after him. Once recovered, they all insisted on returning to the battlefield. Although they compared notes on the status of the battle and the potential for future attacks and defenses, none of them truly understood the situation—they were too far away to have first-hand knowledge of the progress of the war. One by one, other men recovered and were sent back to the King's encampment, and as he grew strong, Wulfram became impatient, wanting to join his father and the King's men. Like Bertram, the young man had come to feel useless, a burden rather than a source of help.

"Mother," he pressed almost daily, "When can I return to the front? The King has need of good warriors and my father needs strong compatriots as he faces the enemy."

Leova realized it would be only a short time before he made his way back east to join the forces there. With or without her permission, his need to be of service outweighed her need to have him safe. Only the fact that Elene would stay away from battle if Wulfram remained in Cymru kept the young man in Pencilli—but eventually even that would not be enough. Furthermore, Leova told herself, Elene too would not stay far from the battlefield. Her brothers were fighting and if they needed her or Wulfram decided to join them, she would go also.

Young Love

When at last Wulfram announced he would leave, Leova sought out Elene. "Can you not stop him," she asked the young woman. "I can't bear to think of him wounded again."

"No," Elene replied. "It's something he feels he must do, regardless of the danger. Others are dying and wounded, as he well knows. He pushes himself to be brave."

"Will you stay with your mother?"

"No. My place is with Wulfram. I've always been at his side, even though he seldom knew it. That is why we could get him to you so quickly. I...my brothers and I...were watching."

Elene turned away from Leova and began to prepare some bread, fruit and a flagon of water for Wulfram's journey. Her face was stern with resolve. "We will be with him again. I cannot, will not, let him go back alone."

"Will you tell him that you're joining him?" asked Leova.

"No, and I beg you not to tell him either," Elene looked Leova in the eye. "If he knows I am present, he will make mistakes. He'll try to protect me and end up falling victim to an enemy soldier."

"Do you love my son?" Leova leaned close in to hear Elene's

434

answer.

"With all my heart," was the answer.

While Leova could not be happy with the prospect of Wulfram's departure, the fact that Elene and her brothers would follow eased her anxiety somewhat. But now she had a new worry. Did her son know the extent of Elene's love? Would he respect such devotion? That night, his last night, she waited until most of the family went to bed and then asked him to join her for a last walk. As they stood under the stars, she decided to be direct; there was no time for gentle probing.

"As much as I will miss you, my son, Elene will miss you and worry about you equally. Do you know that?"

"Elene is one of the strongest and most capable human beings I know. Leaving her is one of the hardest things I've done." He dropped his eyes and sighed deeply. "I love her, mother. I want to marry her when all of this is over."

"Forgive me, but I must ask," Leova said gently. "Are you sure you're not just grateful because she saved your life? Or maybe because she was your only playmate when you were both younger?"

"No. My love for her has gone far beyond what I felt when we were children. I just didn't know until this war brought on hardships how strong that love is."

"Then," Leova said with quiet determination, "you shall marry—it's just a matter of when."

"You'll not object to her...background? Father will approve?"

Leova laughed. "I suppose that if times were calm, your grandfather would want you to marry a woman with estates to bring to ours. Certainly that's why he insisted I marry your father. However, we have no lands anymore; the enemy has taken them. You and Elene are on the same footing—no more the lord and the peasant, just two people."

He laughed, too, at the wonder of it all. "We can make our vows to each other? Will that suffice for now?" When his mother nodded, he threw his arms around her and lifted her off the ground in his joy.

"Wait, wait! I suggest you ask her mother for her hand first, then check with her brothers for their approval.

Smiling Wulfram strode off to find Bryna. After searching through most of the village, he found her sitting with the village women pounding seasonings into bread dough. "Please," he bent over and whispered, "I must talk to you before I return to battle."

Bryna looked up at the young man, a questioning look on her face as she rose and walked some distance away. "I don't quite know..." Wulfram began in a halting voice, and then pulled himself up and said forcefully, "I wish to ask you for Elene's hand in marriage. I love her and will always love her; she has sworn her love to me also."

Bryna was silent only momentarily. "This comes as no surprise to me. I have long known of your love for each other. My only concern is that she is a peasant and you are a lord's son. But I'm sure you will be faithful to her and she faithful to you. You have my blessing, but please speak to my sons also."

As if by some grand design, the next day Garamond and Golmund appeared, bearing with them news of the battle. They found Wulfram and Elene sitting in the shade of a large oak tree, deep in conversation. The brothers weren't happy to see the two sitting so close—their hands clasped, their eyes intent on each other.

"Hey, young Lord!" called out Garamond. "What business do you have with our sister that allows you to compromise her reputation?"

If they had expected the pair to jump apart or look guilty, they were disappointed. Instead both members of the couple smiled at each other and stood to welcome the newcomers.

"Brothers!" Elene exclaimed happily. "It's so good to see you! Have you brought news of the war? Are my other brothers here?"

Disarmed by her greeting, they relaxed a bit, but after embracing her, they turned their unhappy faces toward Wulfram. It was clear they did not approve of what they were seeing.

Wulfram, fully aware of their disapproval, glanced at Elene, touched her cheek lightly, then turned and spoke to her brothers. "I'd like to speak to the two of you. Alone, Elene. Just the men of your family and me."

Although Elene started to protest, she simply nodded and backed away smiling. He waited until he could hear her retreating through the leaves, then cleared his throat and—standing as straight as he could—addressed the impatient men.

"Elene and I plan to make our betrothal vows to one another and hope for your approval. We wish to marry. Your mother has already given us her blessing."

"You can't expect us to believe this!" Golmund said bluntly. "You are heir to the very land we toil on. Men like you don't marry peasant women whose origins are unknown, but they have been known to make promises they have no intention of keeping."

Before Wulfram could reply, a voice spoke out from the woods behind them. "For shame," Leova said sharply. "Have you not known our family long enough to know we do not take advantage of those who work on our land? And serve, as you and your brother do, as protectors and warriors when required?"

"Pardon, mistress," Garamond said, bowing to acknowledge her presence. "We have only one sister, and we must protect her."

"Did they not play together as children? Does he not treat you and yours as brothers of the heart?"

"We were children then, unworldly and unaware...."

"And a few years have changed you so much? The war has turned my son into a villain?"

Wulfram, anxious to resolve his own problems, gently tried to silence his mother. "They know that mother. But still they would worry about any man who wanted to marry their sister." He looked at the two brothers. "She is precious to you, as precious as she is to me. I know why you must object, but I trust you to listen to us, and give us your approval."

Garamond shook his head gravely. "You are still our liege Lord. And we are still peasants. We serve you and your house."

Leova laughed, "Perhaps that was once true, but notice please where we are and who serves whom in this refuge we share."

Wulfram once again broke in. "I love your sister—which is not something rank can prevent or control. With me, she will never come to harm. As my mother says, I've not much to offer now; our family lands are gone. What will happen if we regain those lands? Your sister will be Lady of my house. If we never regain those lands...."

Wulfram paused for a moment, unhappy at that thought, then smiled at his mother and Elene's brothers. "I will be a good husband and provide for her. Your mother has already given us her approval but we seek, and believe we must have, your approval also. As soon as we can, we will find a priest to bless our union, but we consider the vows we have made to one another as binding as the words of any priest."

"My son's words reflect my thoughts, Leova said. "I happily welcome your family to join our family. Will you honor us with your consent?"

The two men looked at each other and nodded. Garamond, the elder of the two, was the first to speak. "Thank you, My Lady. Wulfram, you have our approval. But should you ever desert her... harm her in any way...." Garamond left his sentence unfinished.

"Have no fear," Wulfram protested. "I've loved Elene for a very long time and will love her even longer."

"A strange world this," Golmund said as he strode off to locate his sister. When he returned with her, both were smiling.

That night, after the evening meal was done and the young people had gone to sit under the moon and talk about their hopes and fears, Leova—along with Bryna, Iona, Ian, Pagany, and Bertram—sat outside the cottage and talked of change. Even Bertram, who held on to tradition, had to admit that his world had disappeared and was not likely to return. "We are not what we were," he said sadly.

"True," answered Pagany, "but we are something new and quite interesting. Neither humble nor rich, lord nor peasant. I think I might like this life, however."

"Like it!" Bertram snapped. "We've lost all that made us who—and what—we were!"

"Have you lost our daughter? Do you still have me to see to it that you're fed and cared for? Do your grandchildren live?"

"I know, I know. We are rich in love and people. I miss my

land, however—and I'm not sure my son-in-law and all my grandsons still live. We have Wulfram, but others could be lost in the war...how can we know?" his voice faded away and Leova could see that her father would not be easily comforted.

"Father, you speak as if all is lost. It won't be impossible to regain our land if King Edward drives out the enemy. And if we do, even if Lothlar has been burned to the ground, we can return and rebuild. Our people remain faithful. Some, not all, but some will want to return to the land they left behind. Young men will need work after the fighting is done, and they will look to you and Rolfe for guidance."

Pagany, who had been silent, looked at her daughter. "And to you and Bryna and Aelfwynn to teach the young women how to care for their families...how to birth babies and bury the old."

"Perhaps, perhaps," Leova responded. "I found myself wondering lately whether Wulfram might want to learn the craft of healing. He and Elene could do much good together."

"Healing is not work for a man!" Bertram snorted. "He will need to manage the farms."

"As you said, he might not have any lands to farm...besides Elene probably can tend to cattle and raise grain better than Wulfram," Leova smiled to herself. "A wife should help her husband by giving the kind of aid she can!"

The conversation erupted into a flurry of excited exclamations.

"Husband?" cried Pagany.

"Wife?" questioned Bertram. "They are joined?"

"I knew it," said Pagany. "Any fool who has watched those two for the past month would recognize they loved each other."

Leova laughed at the excitement and confusion she had created. "Yes, they made vows to each other some weeks ago, and after talking to Bryna, Garamond, Golmund, and me, this very day they pledged to wed as soon as they can."

"It's not proper," Bertram grumbled. "They're not properly matched."

"Hush, old man," Pagany chided him. "Are you telling me that if I had not brought land and other property to you, you would never have married me?" Bertram had no answer. Pagany gave him a piercing look. "Why shouldn't the boy marry such a fine girl? We're all practically family as it is."

"I look at it this way," Leova said, "now we have something to look forward to, something good rather than something to fear. We need to start planning their wedding at once! We'll hold the ceremony after our return to Lothlar—and we will return. We must."

"Just so," Pagany said. "It's fitting for them to wed where they met."

Suddenly Leova started to cry. "I just wish I knew how Hilda fared. If she has survived the war, I want her to share my joy. So much has happened to us since we last parted. I've been away from Lothlar for what feels like eternity. And where has she been all this time? Once, as children, we planned to meet at each other's wedding, but that never happened. We'll make up for that with Wulfram's and Elene's celebration. It will be a grand reunion!"

War's End

The next four years crawled from season to season for all those clustered around the little Welsh hill towns. News from the battles trickled in rarely; anxieties thus never faded away. Occasionally, a wounded man would return with reports, but often he would know only what occurred in the same area where he was fighting. Occasionally, too, reports of the death of a son or husband would travel back. The community did what it could to soothe the pangs, anger, and regrets of those who suffered such losses. As time passed, the refugees from Lothlar and Stonehart settled into the routines of the community. There were even two marriages between the settlers and the newcomers—small opportunities for some happiness before the men returned to the battlefield. Only rarely did the family hear news of Rolfe, Wulfram, or Bryna's children.

One morning as Leova stood gazing from one of the hilltops, she saw a flurry of dust below her, raised by three horsemen coming

440

toward her at great speed. As they came closer, she realized that she was looking at three of Bryna's sons. She turned and hurried back to the village arriving there just as the horsemen did.

"It's over! It's over! The war is over, over, over!" the men shouted gleefully as they dismounted from their horses. In what seemed like seconds, the entire community surrounded them, asking questions, seeking information on their fighting men, wanting to know if their side had won.

Bertram's voice rang out over the crowd. "Let us be quiet and let them speak." And soon there was near silence. The news they received was met with sighs of relief. King Edward had been victorious, even against his traitorous brother who had joined the enemy; the fighting men would be arriving in a few short days, and perhaps they could all soon begin the long trek back to their own lands and halls, ready to rebuild if necessary.

Chapter 13: Friends Reunited (906)

Hilda sat in the scriptorium with her small group of students as they struggled with some of the words and strange rhythmic contortions of written *Englisc*. One of the young students beckoned to her, "Sister, what can I make of this?" She pointed to a group of letters on the manuscript.

"*Beaggifa*," said Hilda. "Think of the two words you see there. That will help you."

The young woman thought a moment, but suddenly her face lit up with wonder, "Sister, I see them both—'ring' and 'giver'—but what does 'ring-giver' mean?"

"In times past, and perhaps still now, rulers passed out gold arm bands to each warrior who supported him in war; he became a 'ring-giver.' Perhaps you have seen old warriors with gold circlets twisted about their upper arms?"

"No, Sister, but now I understand the significance of this new term! A 'ring-giver' is a ruler, or king, or battle leader."

Hilda smiled and continued to walk around the room, giving words of encouragement to some, asking others about words or requesting that they read for her. At last the time was up, and she dismissed the little group. Leaving Olaf to see to the storage of manuscripts, pencils, and scrap parchment the students used for notes, she started to her office only to discover a messenger laughing and talking to the women in the kitchen. They'd given him a large flagon of newly prepared cider, and he was entertaining them with his adventures on the road. Her entrance interrupted him in mid-story, and the kitchen servants hurriedly deserted him and went back to their work. Like a little child caught being naughty, the young man stood nervously at the hearth before he regained enough composure to put down his flagon and bow respectfully. Hilda, smiling to herself, put him at ease.

"Where have you come from? And what message to you carry to us?"

"My Lady Leova sends you greetings from Lothlar, Abbess Hilda," he said, struggling to pull a folded piece of parchment out of

442

his traveling pocket.

Removing the twine which bound the obviously worn and re-used parchment, Hilda read her friend's handwriting with pleasure. She and Leova now exchanged letters occasionally; Hilda could even see some of her prior message underneath Leova's words. She smiled at the image of the superimposed words, remembering the two girls who long ago could not have dreamed of reading and writing. It was also apparent that this piece of parchment had been scraped again and again and had reached the end of its message-bearing life. She would need to find another piece for her reply.

Olaf appeared at her side noiselessly; he had heard the messenger's greeting. "Abbess, is all well with your friend?" he questioned.

"Yes, Olaf. Her son is marrying and she invites me to attend the wedding. It would be a most pleasant trip," she added almost wistfully.

"Surely, you will go?"

"My responsibility is here," she said shaking her head regretfully.

Olaf cleared his throat uncomfortably. "But, Abbess...you have not seen her since all of them returned from the war, and you never met her family. Wouldn't you consider...."

"Olaf," Hilda cut him off sharply. As you well know, "Buxton demands much of all of us, much that I willingly give."

Olaf felt a slight bit of chastisement in Hilda's words; under any circumstances, however, he knew better than to make any further attempt to change Hilda's mind. He nodded and returned to his own duties. That evening, however, Hilda found it difficult to keep her mind focused on her immediate surroundings. She found herself distracted by memories of her childhood at Lothlar, by the remembrance of the special connection she had with Leova. These memories, unfortunately, were too often pushed out by the memory of Brother John, whom now she must, she knew, think of only as Leova's husband, Rolfe. Distracted by the movement and noise around her, Hilda knew she needed a peaceful spot where she could wrestle with and resolve her thoughts, but she yearned for the stillness of the woods, not the peace of the sanctuary. After the evening meal, she walked into the grove of trees that had always been a spot of comfort for her and sought a place to be quiet and ponder.

Not for the first time, she asked herself if she resented Rolfe's and Leova's life together. Was she actually disappointed that John had found another love and forgotten the love he had for her? Did she, on some level, want to be the lady of a great hall surrounded with many children and a loving husband? "It would not matter if I desire such a life. That love," she told herself firmly, "is gone, over. We've made other choices, and I'm as happy for Rolfe and Leova as I am content in my own world."

"But why then," she asked herself, "struggle with useless comparisons? And why be so quick to turn down the invitation?" In attempting to sort through her reactions, she realized that she did not want to see John again. Was it because she still harbored feelings that went against her vows? She sighed at the thought. To hold strong feelings—perhaps even weak feelings—for the John who no longer existed would be a dire weakness. Perhaps those confusing feelings needed to be confronted and put to rest. Hilda remembered the words of the confessor at Lord Ragnar's hall.

"It takes no strength to avoid the world's challenges. Test your commitments by taking on the challenges the world gives you, Abbess Hilda! And one of those challenges," the confessor had continued in a softer voice, "is to examine our own consciences."

It took several hours of prayer and meditation for Hilda to come to an answer, but when at last she walked back inside the walls of the monastery, she sought out Leova's messenger.

"Tell your mistress that I shall be most pleased to attend the wedding of her son and his betrothed."

"Most happily, Abbess. It will bring My Lady great joy." He continued, "She said that she would send an escort for you."

"That's not necessary. I no longer fear anyone here; our former enemies are now our countrymen. I'll take a few companions with me, Brother Olaf, and one or two of the younger monks to provide help in our travels." She suddenly brightened with an idea.

I'll especially bring my childhood nurse, Ethel, who so often speaks of wanting to meet your Lady. She has been here since the destruction of Highhear and would, I am certain, be delighted by a change."

The messenger looked at her, concern on his face. "Perhaps you are right to feel safe; however I urge you to include in your group two or three young strong farmers who undoubtedly will be pleased to take the trip. Our former enemies may now be our compatriots, but ruffian gangs are still about."

"Perhaps, you are right," Hilda acknowledged.

The Journey Back

Six weeks later, a small entourage set out on the two-day journey to Lothlar. The air, brisk with just a touch of fall, lifted their spirits as much as the many trees that had already donned leaves of gold and red and orange. Hilda found her spirits soaring. Soon she would see her friend and be back in the place where she had known only joy, love, and happiness. Confronting her weakness gave way to the understanding that it was right for her to go, right for her to share in her friend's joy. She had been derived of the sense of family for too long.

The first night they stopped at a large farm cottage. The farmer and his wife and children, although within a day's ride of Buxton, had never been quite so close to a real nun or monks, and they were obviously a bit perplexed about how to treat them. And Hilda, despite her familiarity with Lord Ragnar and his family, continued to marvel at the normalcy of marriage between former enemies, her people and the red-headed invaders. After the evening meal, Hilda asked the small children if they'd like to hear some old stories. The youngsters, encouraged by their parents, sat down before Hilda, not knowing what to expect from this mysterious woman in strange clothing.

Hilda took a particular pleasure in reciting the old stories, the ones she read from the aging parchments at Buxton and the stories she had heard from the mouths of itinerant singers who took lodging occasionally at the monastery. It was perhaps well that her confessors were unaware of her recitation of these whenever she found it difficult to sleep. As she spoke before the children, she seemed almost to drift into the world of dragons and cattle thieves and marauding monsters.

> *Came from the moors, under cover of darkness*
> *Grendel trodding, he bore God's anger.*
> *This wicked ravager intended to entrap*
> *Some one of mankind in the high hall.*

That's scary," one of the young ones called out, looking about ready to cry. Hilda knelt down and looked into the child's face. "It's only a story, a story that makes us think about how good our real world is in comparison to this made-up world. The ogres only live in that made-up world; they're not real." Even as she said these words, she wished she could truly believe their meaning. "And, listen now, because our hero—his name is Beowulf—will soon get rid of this monster." Slowly she spun out the tale, acting out each battle, each encounter with Grendel until, at last, he met his fate.

> *Then he who before had troubled*
> *So many of the hearts of men*
> *Enacted crimes—he was hostile to God—*
> *He discovered that his body could not resist.*
> *But Beowulf, the mighty kin of Hygelac,*
> *Had him in his hand ....*
> *Beowulf was granted glory in battle*
> *Grendel, mortally wounded, wished to flee far hence*
> *Go under a marshy trail, seek a joyless home;*
> *He knew well that his life had come to an end.*

Her audience was enchanted; child and adult alike called for more when she finished. Late that night, when everyone slept, Hilda marveled at how happy telling a simple story made her. And as the entourage prepared to leave in the morning, Hilda grinned as she heard one of the young boys whisper to his mother, "The lady wears black instead of white, but even so, she must be an angel."

446

They had not been on the road long, however, when the skies grew dark. A strong wind began to flail at the leaves on the tops of the tall trees, and the heavy branches swayed menacingly, conjuring up the poetic words of the prior evening. Angry clouds hurtled swiftly through the sunless skies, soon replaced by still angrier gray and black masses.

"The air wants to push us backwards, back from whence we came," Olaf shouted over the noise of the wind. "We need to find shelter and find it immediately."

He sent one of the monks and one of the young farmers to scout ahead for any structure that might offer protection from the impending storm, but soon large drops of rain hit against the tops of the trees, finally breaking through the dense foliage and pelting the people beneath.

A shout from down the road roused their spirits somewhat, though they were already soaked with rain. The young men had found an abandoned barn with its roof still largely intact and, amazingly enough, containing a large mound of fairly fresh hay. The group pushed forward and in a few minutes gratefully gathered itself under the crumbling thatch, glad to be out of the gale. While the men took care of settling the horses on one side of the barn, Hilda tried to watch over her companions on the other. As she looked around the large room, she became particularly concerned for Ethel, but when approached, the old woman scoffed, reminding her former charge that she was no stranger to such hardships.

"Tend to yourself, my Hilda," the old woman scolded. "My clothes will dry long before yours!"

Everyone grumbled about being wet; Hilda herself felt damp down to her skin. A nun's clothing, possibly one of the most annoying requirements of her vocation, was bothersome enough in good weather, but wet, it became unbearable.

"Sister," suggested the always solicitous Olaf. "If you slide under the hay a bit, it might help your clothing dry—at least it will warm you."

Hilda smiled and thanked him for his wise suggestion, settling Ethel and herself together in a corner of the barn. After a very short time, she fell into a deep sleep, but a sleep torn by visions of other times, when she had not been Sister Hilda and Rolfe had gone by the name of John. Olaf, distressed to hear the mumbled words and sounds created by his Abbess's dreams, hoped the rest of the party slept more soundly than he did.

"An abbess should have naught but dreams of heaven," he thought. "It doesn't sound as though my abbess's dream takes place in heaven!"

The following morning the storm had abated very little, and no one suggested that they leave their cover and resume travel. Their predicament did little to improve tempers, but Hilda fretted more than the others. She had never been skilled at being idle and, trapped as they were, there proved to be little she could do once she had seen to it that the others had been fed and made as comfortable as they could be. As the hours passed, the storm seemed to build up rather than abate, ebbing only toward evening, when a red glow first permeated and then flooded the western sky. The rain stopped altogether by sundown, and Olaf ventured to suggest a plan to his restless Abbess that he knew she would not find pleasant.

"My Lady, I think it best we stay here for the night. If we resume our travel now, we will not be able to go far before it is too dark to see, and it might storm again, leaving us without even this lowly shelter."

Hilda reluctantly agreed, once again trying to make everyone as comfortable as possible. She pulled away some of the wettest straw and found somewhat drier sheaves as replacement. She suggested to the young monks and farmers that they might do so also and would thereby gain some relief from the dampness of their clothing. Some in the company expressed hunger; Hilda remembered the food their hosts had insisted they take and offered it, more than a bit soggy, to one and all. Finally, most of the group including her, fell into restless sleep, never fully asleep, but not fully awake, either— with the exception of the young farmers who fell asleep almost before they lay down. At some point in the night, Hilda thought that she heard horses and men's voices pass by, but she fell back into sleep, not awake enough to believe that what she heard was real. In the early morning, she awoke suddenly with a feeling that something was very, very wrong. Only one farmer remained in the barn with her, Ethel, and the sister who attended her. With relief, she saw that Ethel still slept quietly in their corner. Moving as quietly as she could so as not to awaken either of the women, she approached their lone protector, who stood by the door looking anxiously down the road.

"Where are the other men?" Hilda demanded, but was immediately silenced by the finger the farmer put to his own lips, not answering, but pointing off in the distance.

A vague dread seeped into Hilda's bones. Why had she turned down Leova's offer of an escort so quickly?

After some time, a distraught Olaf appeared. "My Lady, I...I've most dreadful news...!" he managed to say, then broke down weeping. Hilda forced him to sit down and used all her strength to focus his attention.

"What's dreadful, my son? Tell me." When he didn't answer, she shook him hard and spoke in her most commanding voice. "Olaf! Tell me immediately!"

Olaf had never before flinched from conflict, but now he had to fight his fear in order to answer his mistress's question. "I heard noises in the night and looked out to see a small troop of men ride by. Swaying back and forth, drunk as lords, they sang—and laughed!—at two, maybe three, prisoners bound hands and feet. They pulled them along by halters—like animals!"

He stopped, lost in the horror of such treatment until Hilda commanded him to continue. "I took the boys and followed, but as we passed a thick stand of trees, we were assaulted by two who had fallen behind. Our men struggled in vain; I was able to slip away and dared not go back to rescue them!" he exclaimed. "I felt I had to return and warn you." He broke down and appeared on the verge of tears, but then regained his composure.

"As I ran, one of them called to me. 'Tell your princess she holds the key to rescuing your boys!' How strange they should know of you!"

Startled, Hilda stepped back from Olaf. Thinking quickly she said, "Take me to them, Olaf."

"No, we need to get help!"

"I'm a nun. They dare not harm me. Take me to them—now!"

Hilda strode out the door, trying to suppress her fears; the situation required her to be composed and use logic. But logic didn't seem to apply. How did these men know she traveled this road, stopped for shelter at this barn? More importantly, why did they call her 'princess' rather than 'abbess'?

Despite his reluctance, Olaf knew he would be unable to deter Hilda's intent. Leaving the farmer and the young nun behind with instructions to stay with Ethel, they quietly crept through the trees, moving slowly so as to make little noise. It took no effort to track the roistering group—the men continued to be loud, bellowing out songs and scraps of epithets difficult to comprehend.

Soon the roisterers became visible just as the pair turned off the dirt road at a small grove.

"They're so drunk," Hilda whispered to Olaf, "they'll never hear us."

Peering through thick foliage, Hilda and Olaf were able to count seven prisoners, five males and two females, all lashed to trees, their faces not visible. The men were putting together what seemed to be a scaffolding of branches and rope. Olaf and Hilda, now concerned about their decision to follow rather than go for help, crouched hidden, their horror growing as one of the men growled, "Why do we want these sad specimens of women and boys, Agenor? What use are they?"

The largest and roughest of the boisterous troupe stood up and, waving through the air the flagon from which he drank, shouted for quiet.

"I'll tell you what I want and why I want it! You look at me and think you see an old bandit, whose power rests in his ability to make others fear for their lives. You need to know that I have right and truth on my side. Who you really see before you is Lord Agenor of Yorvik, once a powerful landowner! And that's who I'll be again after tonight."

450

One of the soldiers snickered and laughed out loud, only to receive a blow to the side of his head. That quieted him and commanded the attention of the rest of the crew. Sure of his men's full attention, he continued his story.

"I lost my land and my family because of a so-called noble religious woman." He spewed out the last three words as if they were poison. "She convinced the other lords that my father had no genuine title to his land. As avaricious as she, they happily agreed with her and resolved to split the land—my family lands—among themselves. My father resisted and was killed for his trouble. My younger brother died, and my mother and sisters were carried off. Luckily, I wasn't at home at the time." he sneered. "My father had wanted me to appreciate the people who would serve me, so he had shunted me off to live with a farmer. I was to return once I reached manhood." He stopped to drink from his flask, as though gathering memories laced with anger.

"Six years old, I was, when it happened, but I vowed revenge and have sought for it ever since. The woman who instigated all that terror and hardship died before I could kill her—that was a vengeance I sorely missed. But once I nearly had her daughter in my hands!" His eyes became bright as he relived the past, and he grew so involved in his own story that he seemed to be in that far off time. "I discovered that evil woman's husband was going to take their precious daughter across country to foster her and keep her safe from the enemy. I alerted some of the enemy whom I had befriended for my own purposes, and they assigned soldiers to search and capture them. We chased after the girl and her father across the countryside, but just before I caught up with them, they managed to make the safety of Lord Bertram's gates, the very gates to which the princess and her group travel now."

His voice rose both in anger and regret. "Just out of reach, it seemed they were. But still I rode on—right through the gates themselves and into the courtyard! I had cornered the Lord who was carrying his daughter, but as I grabbed for her the child fell from her father's saddle and was rescued by another..." he snorted with disgust, "child...before I could take her.... I had to flee empty-handed. That scene imprinted itself on my memory." His words trailed off and he sat down heavily as though he were exhausted by his own story. But, soon re-animated, he shouted as though to the world in defiance: "Now I have my second chance—again on the road to Lothlar. We shall not fail!"

Listening, Hilda had to turn away and cover her mouth as she was gasping for air. "This man, this man, he's the one who...." She was unable to finish her thought, but stifled her breath and turned back toward the scene before her, framed by the leaves of a small tree.

The speaker's men sat still for a moment and when he didn't continue someone finally asked, "If the woman died and you lost the daughter, whom have we have captured?"

"She's the woman who became foster mother to the daughter I almost captured. After that final encounter, she and her husband guarded them so closely that I had to put off my revenge. But I never gave up hope that I would one day have it! And that is today, now!" he exclaimed.

One of his men found the courage to question him. "She and her friends have done nothing, why should they die?"

"They merit death, the pagans! We found her with one of her witch friends out there in the woods conjuring up evil spirits. They deserve to be dead for their blasphemies, but I plan to see that they suffer first—heretics and pagans! And besides," he laughed, "They're bait. The daughter is once again close enough to catch. She'll come to rescue these two boys," he gestured toward the two male prisoners, "and find her sweet foster mother as well."

He approached one of the bound figures and grabbed her by the hair, obviously pleased when she cried out. It was Pagany.

"Ha, we would strip you naked except the sight of your old body would be too disgusting. The others will have better bodies to stare at—and more than stare at. Soon we'll have your precious foster daughter, Princess Hilda." He uttered a raucous laugh; his companions joined in. A soft protest came from outside the circle. Agenor reached out and grabbed the protester, dragging her from the shadows, then pushing her so that she stumbled.

452

"Here you see my own daughter—who should have been princess in my hall instead of a servant in the hall of our enemy! Why do you object, you fool?"

Olaf drew in his breath—Agenor's daughter was Alfa, Lord Ragnar's servant. He watched as Agenor pushed her toward the prisoners.

"Be useful, prove yourself my daughter, Alfa! I named you after that evil woman because one day you will take her place as lady of the hall. Now, don't delay! Bring the good Lady Pagany to me."

Whatever doubts the girl had disappeared in her obvious haste to appease her father. Alfa untied the elderly woman and dragged her toward her father. Grabbing Pagany viciously by the upper arm, he shook her violently.

Hilda could no longer remain silent. She whispered to Olaf, ordering him to seek help, and then stood up and moved from her hiding place, making her way through the trees, walking purposefully toward Agenor.

"Stop," she commanded, "You want me for your revenge, not her. Let her and the others go! Now!"

Surprised, the drunken man loosened his grip on his captive and turned toward Hilda. "So, you appear, Princess Hilda. My revenge will be complete!"

"I am no longer Princess Hilda of Highhear. That child disappeared long ago. I am now Abbess Hilda of Buxton and I have no claim to your land or any other. Killing or torturing me will not bring back your land to you—if indeed it was once your land; surely you know that. Release Lady Pagany and I will take her place."

"Don't listen to her," Pagany began to shout. "Take me."

Hilda moved swiftly to Pagany's side, embracing her and talking gently to sooth her. "Pagany, this punishment is not meant for you. He seeks to hurt the mother I hardly knew, not you, the mother of my heart. You must leave this place and take the others with you." Hilda turned toward the captor. "Untie those two also and let them go. I'll stay."

Agenor's temper suddenly exploded. "You don't give me orders," he shouted. They'll stay where they are!"

Hilda cursed herself for thinking that a confrontation with this man would free anyone. However, knowing that showing fear would cause him to act even more irrationally, she sat herself down on a nearby stump, turned to him and, in a conciliatory tone, asked, "Tell me what my mother did so that I may understand the revenge you seek. I was but a child and know nothing of her crimes against you." Hilda was quite sure the story would be the same one she had just overheard again from Agenor but she hoped to bid for time until Olaf could find help.

Alfa laughed mirthlessly. "You can't stall so easily. He told the story already. You were hiding close by, surely you heard it!"

Olaf emerged from his hiding place. "Alfa, your beauty and subservience obviously hides treachery and evil."

Everyone was taken aback by the young monk's unexpected appearance. "Ah, Brother Olaf," Alfa taunted. "The cowardly, unmanly brother from the monastery, the one I attempted to seduce! Welcome! You, too, can join our prisoners and taste my father's revenge."

"Alfa! Enough!" her father interrupted, "I want Princess Hilda to hear the story from me—no matter if she hears it twice." Agenor turned toward Hilda who looked at Olaf in dismay. Why had he had not gone for help? Collecting herself quickly, she settled herself on a nearby fallen log, gathering her robe around herself meekly, looking for all the world as if she had no knowledge of any threat. One thing the religion has installed in her was the gift of erasing emotional reactions from her face and body.

Her attitude, as she had hoped, unsettled Agenor, but he continued to speak. "Your mother invented previous owners of our land and accused my father of killing and burying them in unmarked graves. Then she said my father had supported his claims by saying that they had given him the land before leaving to join a religious community. My father would never have joined a religion community!"

Hilda composed herself again meekly, making it appear as though she and Agenor were conversing on some intellectual subject. "Was there any proof of what my mother said? Or any

454

proof that these supposed landowners had, as your father said, gone to a religious community?"

"My father was not a liar! He spoke truth!"

Hilda shook her head and looked as if she were puzzling out a great mystery. "My mother was a pious woman, much devoted to her religion. Why," she said, almost as though she were speaking to herself, "why would such a good Christian make such an awful accusation if it wasn't true?"

"She made it because she was evil and avaricious and wanted my father's land," Agenor screamed in frustration.

"But you said that then the land was divided up and shared with others."

"I didn't say that! She got most of it! And you know what she did? She built a monastery to her God on the lands where our hall once stood!"

"You mean the abbey where I serve, Buxton Abbey, stands on what you consider to be your land? My mother often took me there when I was a child. She told me that the land was blessed, and God himself commanded her to build a monastery there. Are you claiming she made up the story to justify taking your inheritance?" Hilda paused and looked Agenor directly in the eyes. "Surely she could not be that devious...yet something haunted her when she died. To attempt to gain God's favor by stealing the property of others would have been a grave sin."

"Your mother sinned. She destroyed my family, and now I will destroy hers."

Hilda faced him fully and tried to be rational, though her heart was pounding the inside of her chest. "There's no one but me to destroy. It seems an unworthy act to kill a nun to avenge a wrong; the sin of murder will far outweigh my mother's sin. I would think," she added, attempting not to sound as though she were the authority in this exchange of words. "Furthermore, my death will not bring you land. Others, under the King's patronage, live at Highhear. And," she looked pointedly at Alfa, "a Viking family now lives in the hall rebuilt on the ruins of the hall you claim belonged to you."

"No more words," he growled, far too obsessed to listen to

any argument except his own. "I swore and I will act!" He turned to his men, giving orders. "Start with these two little pagans and then Pagany—even her name gives her away. Then we'll go to Olaf and the young monks. Defile all of them as you well know how! Princess, I'll give you a grand show here before you die!"

Hilda, fearful that she would only anger him further, bit her tongue, stopping herself from pointing out the irony of this man's turn to destruction. He considered himself a Christian, pretending to kill women like Pagany for being pagans and heretics, but, in truth, killing them solely because they knew the object of his revenge. Agenor, as interested in humiliating his victims as he was in killing them, turned to another tactic. He walked around Hilda, pulled off her wimple roughly and fingered the fabric of her habit.

"Wonder what's hidden under that nun's clothing? We'll find that out too, and when we're finished, I plan to string you all up on these gallows we've built."

Hilda opened her mouth to speak but was silenced when Agenor struck her across the face.

"I said no more words from you!" he shouted. Under his spell, his drunken companions untied the two female prisoners Agenor had pointed to, but as they dragged them toward their leader, the women began to chant in unison. Hilda recognized the song—she had heard it long ago when Pagany had taken her and Leova to the ceremonies of the *auncient woones*. Pagany, as she had then, sank into a deep trance, barely breathing. The song began to fill the air, echoing in the clearing, growing louder and louder, as though it were an emanation from nature itself. Soon everyone realized that the loudest chanting came from beyond the clearing, not from the two women they held captive. Hilda searched the forest and finally made out shadowy figures approaching through the foliage—how many she could not tell.

The closer the strangers came, the louder the chant grew until it seemed no other sound could penetrate it. Their captor and his henchmen seemed frozen–as though time had stopped. How long everything remained still, Hilda could not be sure, but as the women advanced into the clearing, Agenor broke the spell, his voice ringing out and bringing his men back to consciousness. "Grab them! Use your clubs! Are you spineless? They're only women!"

The men, perhaps dazed by drink and mesmerized by the chant, stood frozen in place. In his rage, Agenor kicked two of them violently, shocking them into movement. "And you," he shouted as he threw Hilda harshly to the ground. "Your family wanted my property! Eat its dirt!" Roused from their torpor, his men seized their clubs and started toward the women, but before they could reach them, the circle of women parted in two places and two tall husky men rushed from behind the tree trunks, uttering war chants and carrying clubs of their own.

Agenor's men retreated toward their leader, who reacted unexpectedly.

"My sons!" Agenor shouted joyfully, turning to his victims and then back to the young men. "My sons, Garamond and Garulf. Come to help me take my revenge!" He beamed happily at the two men and attempted to embrace them. "You at last understand why I scoured the countryside looking for this woman. You've come in time to assist me! Welcome, welcome. And here, praise be, come my other sons," he shouted as Golmund, Garhild, and Gardorf strode into the clearing.

None of the five acknowledged their father nor allowed him to touch them. Garamond looked at the situation for a moment, then, ignoring his father, addressed the nearest captors, "You. Unhand these women at once."

Instead of complying, the man stepped toward him aggressively, only to move backwards again quickly as he saw the challenge in Garamond's eyes. Sweeping the man aside, Garamond bowed down to raise Pagany, her companion, and Hilda to their feet. Agenor seized this moment to raise his club, and rush toward his son. "If you did not come to help me, then you must die too!" But before he reached his son, a lithe figure swung from the lower branch of a tree and with the blow of one bare foot, struck him directly in the face. Agenor fell in slow motion to the ground.

"Little sister," laughed Garamond, "you are a jungle cat. Let's get this ogre tied up; the county reeve can deal with him."

457

In relief, Hilda turned away from the scene around the fire and hurried to her surrogate mother. "Pagany...Pagany! Can you hear me?" she implored. Elene also ran to Pagany's side.

"We didn't know she was here!" she said.

Hilda raised Pagany from the ground and cradled the old woman's head in her lap. Slowly Pagany's eyes opened and she stared directly into Hilda's eyes. "I knew my gods would save us all."

The plunderers, realizing that they were no match for the power of Agenor's sons and the woman who fought with them, and perhaps also fearful of the ancient words of the chants, began to disappear, melting like ghosts into the woods. Alfa, joined them, moving stealthily toward the edge of the clearing.

"Alfa!" Olaf called out. "Don't dare to escape."

Ignoring his words, Alfa began to run. In what seemed like magical movement, the circle of women closed silently around her, making it impossible for her to move. As Olaf approached, his anger was evident.

"You used what I told you in confidence! Your father couldn't have known that Abbess Hilda was taking this trip to Lothlar unless you told him after I had told you when you last brought gifts from Lord Ragnar to Buxton Abbey." He turned to his companions. "What shall we do with her? Turn her over to the reeve with her father?"

"I suggest," interjected Hilda, trying to calm her assistant down, "that the reeve be asked to be lenient with her and strive to assign her to duties in a place where she may reflect on her actions; it's not too late for her to create a life unsullied by the revenge which devoured her father."

Alfa made no response, but Garamond, uncomfortably aware that the girl was his half-sister, seized the idea, "I will suggest that to the reeve. You're a forgiving woman, Abbess Hilda."

She merely smiled at him gravely, remembering the barely suppressed words of Alfa as she had spoken of her mother so many years before. She then turned to help the forest women tend to the prisoner's bruises and abrasions. Olaf watched as the brothers led Agenor and Alfa away, unable to completely reconcile himself to his mistress's act of forgiveness. At last, however, he unclenched his fists, and turned to be of help. Almost immediately he encountered the young woman who provided the final blow needed to rescue the captives. The act had been so unusual and so unexpected, that he didn't quite know how to thank her, so he merely bowed quickly and spouted out what was on his mind.

"I thank you for your bravery! And I marvel at your method of defeating such a strong man. A woman's powerful foot! Who would have thought it possible?"

"Not many, I'd guess," she laughed and started to tease this man who was so obviously ill at ease. "Perhaps its power comes from this strange symbol tattooed on my arch! Have you ever seen anything like it?" And she turned and held up her foot so that he could see the symbol more clearly.

Surprised at the comment and her actions, the flustered Olaf somewhat hesitantly examined the foot extended in his direction. "How strange! Though I've surely never seen it on a foot, the symbol looks very like the drawings in some of the manuscripts at our monastery."

Olaf reached out to trace the figure, but drew back in embarrassment when they were interrupted by Hilda. "I heard your brother call you Elene. Are you the bride whose wedding we have traveled to attend?" The girl put down her foot, and turning to her questioner with a slight bow, nodded happily. "Any other bride would be baking bread and pies and sewing little blue flowers on her wedding dress!" Hilda could not resist saying. "Clearly you are a different kind of bride."

"Garamond came up behind them laughing at Hilda's confusion. "My sister is not a typical bride!"

Hilda joined his laughter, "And for that, I'm exceedingly grateful!" She looked again at the young woman, "How did you happen to come upon us."

"My brothers and I were out hunting for game for the wedding feast when we heard the chanting of the forest women. It caused us to lose our quarry, I fear." Elene sighed ruefully.

"Both the deer and I will bless their song." Hilda smiled again. "Might I, too, see the image on your foot? Might it be a mark of protection made by the forest women when you were born?"

"Who knows? I've never been told anything about it—it has always just...*been* there. For years I thought it was a birthmark that I was born with." Once again Elene turned her back and bent her left foot up so that Hilda could see the sole. Hilda stared at the small incision in amazement; she did not hesitate to trace it with her fingers.

"That seems unlikely. Olaf's quite right. This is what is known as an eternity knot. It appears on many of the manuscripts at our monastery," Hilda replied, confounded by the puzzle but uncomfortably aware of the eternity knot she had once carried with her at all times. "It is called an eternity knot because it has no ending nor no beginning; it must have been put there for a reason."

"Perhaps," Elene shrugged her shoulders; the mark had long since ceased to interest her, "but that reason remains hidden. No one I've shown the mark to knows anything about it." Their conversation was stopped by noises near the road. Agenor and the remaining members of his band, were protesting loudly about the ropes that bound their arms.

"You didn't think such ropes so difficult when you tied them around mere women and boys," Garamond said harshly. "Be quiet, or I'll fashion halters as you did and fasten them around your despicable necks." He called Hilda and Olaf over to tell them the plans. "I've arranged for two of my younger brothers to round up the outlaws' horses. You've had enough hardship this day; you and Elene can ride the rest of the way to Lothlar on these villain's horses. But it's close to nightfall; we will help you find a place to rest and sleep. By tomorrow noon we'll all be at Lothlar." He then turned to his sister, laughing as he spoke in a teasing voice, "You really do need to start preparing to be a bride!"

"You help those who cheated me! I don't deserve to be treated this way." Agenor shouted at him.

Garamond turned to look at the man who was his father. "You've devoted your life to revenge. You abused and abandoned my mother and me and my brothers just to chase after this chimera. The punishment allotted to you, whatever it may be, will be well deserved. None of us—none—shall mourn your loss! Whatever happened, that history remains in the past and we live for today and tomorrow. I won't waste my life as you have wasted yours!"

Suddenly recalling the chain of events, Hilda turned toward Olaf, "We need to collect together those we left in our well-soaked barn and bring at least one horse for Ethel."

"Indeed," Olaf replied as he started back down the road.

Hours later, Garamond's words to his father continued to haunt Hilda. "History remains in the past and we live in the now," Hilda repeated to herself, over and over. The night's events, learning the story behind her mother's great sin, and seeing what evil obsession can breed, freed her from the past. She recalled her own words in reference to Alfa: "It's not too late for her to create a life unsullied by the revenge which devoured her father. Nor is it too late," she whispered to herself," for her to have a life unsullied by the past." Forgiveness was there for her; she felt it strongly: forgiveness for herself, for her mother, and for Brother John.

A Conversation

The remainder of their journey was uneventful, but another night spent in an abandoned house along their path gave Hilda a chance to come to know Elene better. After a small meal, the two women seated themselves in what was once a barn, with their backs against bales of hay.

"Can you tell me anything more about your father? I would understand how he came to be so twisted."

"He's not my father," Elene said firmly. Having spoken, she paused and said much less confidently, "I'm sorry, but I don't know how to address you. Should I call you Sister Hilda? Or Abbess Hilda?"

Hilda laughed. "What I tell you is far less traditional than usual, but we've been through much in the last two days. You may call me just "Hilda," if you wish. "I'm neither your sister nor your spiritual advisor; I hope we can be friends."

"And I am honored to be your friend, But...but," Elene stammered a bit, "I want to address you properly and not embarrass my family, including my new family."

Hilda smiled, "You won't, Elene. You won't. When we're with others you should call me Abbess Hilda, or Mother Abbess." They sat for a moment, enjoying the quiet and then Hilda, realizing that they couldn't be seen by the others pulled off her wimple and shook out her long dark curls.

Elene gasped. "You have hair!"

Hilda laughed. "Yes, I do. Like you, I sometimes break what others think of as rules. I did have to shave my head more than once and only once did I do it voluntarily; I vowed it would never happen again." She sighed slightly as she remembered the past. "When I took my vows of obedience as a nun, I shaved my hair." She looked ruefully at the wimple in her hands. "But when it started to grow back, I realized that no one knew the state of my hair when it was covered with this thing. Why deprive myself of every pleasure. I'm sure it's the least of my sins! I can't believe God cares all that much about hair!"

They both laughed merrily, each enjoying the fun of being with someone else who wouldn't be ruled by useless rules and requirements. Elene looked at Hilda with curiosity. "Are you indeed a princess?"

Hilda decided that perhaps she could recount some of her history to this young woman who reminded her so much of herself as a girl—swinging out of trees and defying conventions. Settling back against the wall, she began. "I was indeed a princess, and not a proper one at all...."

Elene listened raptly as Hilda recounted her history from the time she arrived at Lothlar at the age of six until her first arrival at Buxton. She talked of her mother's death, her unwilling commitment to the monastery, her intense love of language and of the manuscripts, the pleasure she experienced when learning to read. However, she omitted any mention of Brother John. "What would that gain?" she thought, and fell silent.

Elene, waited a few seconds and then asked gently, "Why did you leave the monastery that first time, Mother Abbess? Had you come to love it? Did you want to stay? You seem so sad when

462

speaking of it; does that part of the story bring you pain?"

"Yes, my observant audience, it does," Hilda replied, patting Elene's hand fondly. "Before being forced to leave that monastery by my father's enemies, I had begun to feel a new kind of life and possibility. The sudden deprivation of the manuscripts, the order, and the chance to learn, made me aware of just how much I had a growing love of it. Nonetheless, we had to flee. My childhood nurse, Ethel, and my friend, Caedmon, set off with me and for days we worked our way toward another, safer abbey." She recalled creeping into the night with amazement. How could they have been so brave and so foolish at the same time!

"Is your Caedmon the same as our Caedmon?"

"Yes, he came to you when my ancestral hall was destroyed. I had appointed him as reeve there, my final action as the princess of that hall. Now I'm not sure who claims that property, but it does not matter since I am the last of my father's line."

"But when we ran from Buxton, the three of us, my head was shaved. I was supposed to be disguised as a monk, but I doubt we fooled many people. Not your mother, for instance."

Elene looked at her strangely. "My mother? How did she get into your story?!"

"As unlikely as it now seems, I think we spent one evening with your family. I'm not sure it really happened—it was long ago—but surely few women have had five such brothers as yours!"

"No," Elene grinned. "It's not likely. I certainly will ask my mother if she remembers the three of you, but now I do recall she once said she had known Caedmon before he arrived at Lothlar. There really was no reason for her to tell me when and where she had known him."

"Have you always lived near Lothlar?" Hilda asked as she continued to build a story of Elene's life.

"No. We moved there from the moors almost ten years ago—because of the enemy. We could have returned, but we elected not to do. I'm glad—I met my future husband at Lothlar." Elene colored a bit. "I'll be anxious to see if my mother recognizes you. But you haven't finished your story! What happened next?"

463

Hilda abbreviated the remainder of her life's story—leaving out the birth of her child, of course, and shortening other unpleasant memories until they reached this time, this place. Then she returned to her original question. "Now, about you. If Agenor is not your father, who is?"

"I don't know, Mother Abbess; I do not know who either of my parents are." Elene took a deep breath, "My earliest memories are not pleasant."

Hilda interrupted, "Please, you do not need to cause yourself pain."

"No, perhaps," Elene continued, "I'd like to tell you;" she hesitated only briefly and then continued. "I recall living on a farm with a man and a woman I certainly thought were my mother and father. I had an older brother who tormented me all the time and a younger sister whom I adored. But...but...." Elene took a deep breath. "That little sister was the only one who was nice to me. We loved each other. But then, one day...." She again hesitated, but suddenly rushed on. "Then one day, we were in the woods looking for good fuel for our fire, and my brother tried to take my clothes off. I fought him and, in desperation, bit his arm—hard! He ran away screaming to his mother who believed him and would not listen to me. That night they made me sleep in the barn with the cows.

"Once I knew they were all asleep, I searched for whatever food I could find and stole away into the trees. The paths there were familiar to me and I got fairly far before I found a spot where I could rest. When I woke up, I could hear them calling for me, but I found a space between some rocks and stayed there for a long time. When their voices faded, I continued on the path much farther than I had ever gone. At the end of two days, I think it was, I was so hungry I couldn't move and just found a smooth patch of weeds and lay down. The next thing I knew I was being picked up by a person I had never seen, a big boy. I screamed and screamed and he put me down, but I was too exhausted to run."

"Next I knew I was surrounded by five young men who kept questioning me. I had made up my mind to say nothing." Elene smiled a bit, "they decided that I couldn't talk, and one of them said he'd go get his mother. I didn't move and the other four just sat down and laughed and joked about hunting and every so often looked at me as though I were some strange beast. It wasn't long before a woman came, sat down next to me, and put her arms around me. I remember crying and crying and she didn't ask me anything. After I ran out of tears, she said she was going to take me home, and she did. That's how I got a real mother and real brothers."

"And that real mother is Bryna, I'm sure," Hilda replied.

"Yes, I have lived with them ever since; she and her five sons have become my family."

Hilda continued her questioning: "With such a father, how did they come to be such fine men—not men like their father?"

"Agenor only rarely came, but the family feared and disliked him. He...he hit my mother and my brothers until they grew large enough to stop him. They've always protected mother and me."

She had been looking down as she talked about Agenor, but at this point she turned to Hilda and spoke to her with an intensity that the older woman had not seen before. "They helped me become the woman I am. Since they wanted me to be safe, they taught me how to take care of myself in the woods. I would not be dependent on a man to 'take care of me.' Good fortune came to me again because Wulfram, my future husband, continued my education, teaching me to ride and even to fight in armor—though I must admit that at first I was a comic joke!" She paused, and went on more somberly, "I'm truly not his equal, but his family and mine have blessed our marriage." "She hesitated for a moment, "and—at least at first—I felt unworthy to be his wife and tried, not very successfully, to conquer my feelings for him."

The tired Elene leaned her head against Hilda's shoulder. The older woman smiled and stroked the young girl's hair, "Being noble has little to do with birth. Nobility is not inherited—it's developed as one grows and matures—when she interacts with the world about her. Your nobility shines through whatever you do!"

The two sat still and silent until Hilda realized that Elene had fallen sound asleep, her head resting on Hilda's shoulder. Then Hilda let herself sleep, too—and it was a more peaceful sleep than she had

had for many a night.

The Wedding

The wedding brought about a reunion that war and distance had delayed for ten years. And more than a reunion of the two friends took place. Hilda re-met and embraced Bryna, who, to Elene and her sons' delight, remembered taking in Hilda and Ethel during the flight from Buxton.

"You burned our bread, I recall. Knew almost at once that you were no scrawny monk! Always wondered what happened to you and those with you!" Bryna stopped and looked at those around her. "How," laughing as she spoke, "can it be that we come together all these years later? Life does have a way of surprising, does it not?"

Hilda laughed. "God does work in mysterious ways, I guess. Perhaps He wanted to make sure you knew how grateful we were for your help in that awful time. But it's even more amazing that that great troop of boys whose bread I burned became our champions so many years later! You must be truly proud of them—and of your daughter! I much admire young Elene. Your family has done well by her. And that 'young man' who was with us was indeed Caedmon."

Bryna looked puzzled and then laughed, almost as though she were laughing at herself. "There was something about Caedmon that struck me, but with the passage of so many years...and he, if he recognized me, had his reasons for not speaking of it. I respected him for that." Her voice faded off, but then Hilda saw her face brighten. "Look," Bryna pointed to an arriving couple, accompanied by an older woman. "There's Caedmon now. More friends, more answers about the past!" Hilda looked up to see the smiling face of Caedmon, his wife, and mother-in-law.

"I had so hoped to see you again, my good friends," she said, embracing each of them with affection. "We have survived much to bring us to this day. How fortunate we all are!"

A long deferred introduction took place also. Hilda had the great pleasure of bringing Leova and her own childhood nurse, Ethel, together—and in turn, Leova introduced Ethel to Gwynned, who had tended the girls at Lothlar. After proper greetings and affectionate

466

hugs, Gwynned took Ethel by the arm and led her off to a bench outside the hall. Relieved from duties by their age and their former mistresses' affection, they exchanged one story after another, laughing at some memories and commiserating about the hard times that each had with their "little girls."

Leova and Hilda, wanting a little time together, were thwarted by the need for preparations. The family had decided not to put off the wedding since guests were already on the road, and Leova, having satisfied herself that everyone was safe, needed to switch her energies to the upcoming festivities. However, they were able to sit apart for a short time, allowing Leova to question Hilda more closely about what had happened. Hilda retold the story, until satisfied at last, Leova stood up and put an end to the conversation. "We'll talk again later; I don't even have the words to say how overjoyed I am that you're here again at last. And to think that your intervention led to the saving of my mother's life!" Leova took a few steps and then turned back again to give Hilda another warm hug. "We'll talk more after all this madness is over! Now I have to see to roasts and bread and linens for the table!" As she watched Leova return to her tasks, Hilda continued to feel the warmth of that embrace. There was little body contact at the abbey and certainly almost no hugging.

On the day of the wedding, the guests assembled in the open area in front of the small chapel where Elene and Wulfram would exchange vows. Benches had been set in place for the older guests and Gwynedd and Ethel were settled in them gratefully in a place of honor next to Hilda. Caedmon, his wife and mother-in-law were seated just behind them, making room for Olaf, who placed himself almost directly behind his beloved Abbess. Jankin and his family sat alongside Olaf, and Ion and Iona had places of honor at the other side of Hilda. As soon as those seated were settled, Elene, with her arm folded into Bryna's arm, started on her path to the stairs that led to the chapel where Wulfram, Leova and Rolfe awaited. Her five brothers, protective as ever, followed, visibly happy for the union of the bride and groom.

Elene's soft blue gown moved gracefully as she walked, and

the small purple, yellow, and white flowers that surrounded the hem, bodice, and sleeves only added to the loveliness of this woman who could fight with warriors and still be worthy of becoming the mistress of a great house. The circlet of flowers and leaves that Pagany and her forest friends had designed rested on Elene's hair, emphasizing the charm of her eyes and the smile on her lips.

The guests murmured and whispered to one another happily while the families gathered, commenting on everything from the clothing the bride and groom wore to the height and obvious prowess of Elene's brothers. Hilda slowly became aware that Olaf was whispering to Caedmon, telling him about Elene's prowess in the woods, complete with a graphic description of the way she had put down a formidably sized enemy with her bare foot.

"She claims that strange emblem on her foot—which Abbess Hilda identified as an eternity knot like the ones in our manuscripts —endows it with magical power," Olaf jested.

Caedmon, suddenly attentive," asked, "She has an eternity knot tattooed on her foot?"

Next to him, Hilda's old nurse, Ethel, also stiffened into attention.

Ethel, turned to look directly at Olaf. "She has an eternity knot on her foot?"

Olaf, surprised by Ethel's stare, answered in a whisper, "Yes, she has an emblem on the bottom of her foot that looks like some of the designs in the manuscripts at Buxton."

At that moment, the wedding party reached the chapel door and Wulfram's and Elene's families stepped back a bit. The young couple turned to face one another, clasping hands, prepared to recite the traditional vows.

"Please, Olaf, you have to tell me now! Is it an eternity knot?" Ethel's voice became louder.

Olaf, his finger on his lips to signal silence to Ethel, nodded toward the couple on the stairs. "Wait until they have finished their vows. Then I'll tell you about it."

"No. Now!" Ethel replied, her voice rising so suddenly that everyone turned to locate the source of the disturbance. Garamond glared at her, but Ethel by now had turned to look at Olaf intently. Confused and embarrassed, Olaf hurriedly traced the design with his finger on the inside of Caedmon's palm. In unison, Ethel and Caedmon cried out, "Stop the marriage!"

Elene and Wulfram, their families and all those present turned to look at the two. Swiftly Ethel stood up and moved alongside Caedmon to the front of the assembly. Garamond's voice rang out above the pregnant silence as he glared at the approaching couple. "Why do you speak? Why call halt to such a long awaited event?"

Caedmon looked at Ethel for confirmation and then replied in a quiet but firm voice, "God have mercy, I fear that they are brother and sister!" Stillness reigned for a moment as everyone took in his words. Then wedding party and guests alike began to call for an explanation.

Elene shook as she faced the two people who were threatening to destroy her happiness. "Explain! Are you saying that Wulfram's father is my father too? Or do you mean that Leova is my mother? Surely that cannot be." She appeared to stagger a bit, and Wulfram clutched her hand to steady her.

Ethel replied quietly, "Rolfe, once known as Brother John, is your father." At these words, Hilda stifled a gasp and stared fixedly, appearing to hold her breath as Ethel continued. "You were born as a result of his stay in the monastery at Buxton. He is also Wulfram's father. You cannot marry."

Rolfe stepped forward and raised his hand trying to calm down the crowd. "Wait! I've raised Wulfram since birth; it was my pleasure. I love him as though he were my son. But his father was my brother William, Leova's first husband. When he died so suddenly before Wulfram's birth, we all grieved; but because we feared my mother's actions, Leova and I decided to let the world think that the boy was our son, not William's. Even Wulfram did not know." Rolfe was aware of the sudden change in Wulfram's expression as he uttered these last words. "I now realize how wrong we were not to tell him. Truly Wulfram," he gazed at the young man, "I was there at your birth and have always loved you as though you were my blood son." Wulfram continued gazing at the hand that clutched Elene's and made no reply.

Ethel looked at him with concern. "Even if Wulfram is William's child, the relationship between these young people is too close. They are cousins."

Rolfe, suddenly weary, shook his head. "No. Even if Elene were my daughter—and in truth, that cannot be—she and Wulfram would not be cousins. William and I do not share blood. My mother, Allmana—who even today seems to be able to bring pain to my life—brought about the evil that has infected our family. William wasn't my brother; his father was a very distant relative of my father, but when William's mother died in childbirth, his father married Allmana, my mother. With that marriage, my father became William's legal guardian until he came of age. William was entitled to the land and everything on it, but my father was a weak man married to a woman who would do anything to ensure her own sons' future. He let her commit William to the monastery and later just accepted her claim that he had died. The estate fell to our family. My brothers and I had some memory of an older child, but that child simply disappeared and we assumed that he was not one of us. William learned the secret of his birth from one of the nuns years later, but kept it secret since he was content at the abbey and pleased to know that my brothers and I would be the heirs to property he had no desire to inherit."

Rolfe stopped his account as though he were suffering pain, drawing deep breaths as he looked into Leova's face and into the bewildered silent faces of his listening audience. "Continue," she whispered.

Rolfe took a final deep breath, "After William married Leova, he told her his story and after he died, she, in turn, told me."

He shook his head ruefully. "We could see no reason for revealing the truth to others; we always felt we truly were brothers." Rolfe paused again, but then continued with a stronger voice. "Yet this answers only one part of the accusation. How can Elene be my daughter? And how can you know this?"

Ethel looked lovingly from Elene to Rolfe and said gently, "I know because I put the mark on Elene's foot the day she was born. She was conceived when you served as Brother John at Buxton."

Rolfe's face drained of color, and he began to take deep breaths. "How can this be?"

Elene, overwhelmed by her emotions and—like everyone else badly confused by these revelation—broke away from Wulfram and ran to Bryna, who surrounded the young girl with her arms, stroked her hair, and tried to find some words of comfort.

But Elene had no intention of just being comforted. She looked at Rolfe, a spirited defiance shining on her tear-streaked face, "If you are my father, then who is my mother?"

"I am," said a strong voice close beside her.

Hilda rose from her seat on the bench. Removing her wimple and shaking out her long dark curls, Hilda stood up and repeated firmly, "I am Elene's mother."

Pandemonium filled the hall. Leova gasped. Rolfe paled even further. Elene stared at Hilda from the safety of Bryna's arms. Bertram grasped Pagany's arm and guided her to the nearest bench. Only Wulfram stood alone, feeling as though the earth had disappeared from under his feet.

Olaf, horrified by the set of events his conversation with Ethel and Caedmon had engendered, stood up beside his abbess and tried to quiet the crowd. "Please, please. Those who most need to know the truth can gather in the hall. All of you as guests please find places to wait."

Reluctantly, the guests dispersed, talking with one other, offering possible solutions to the strange mystery that was disrupting the festivities. Then Hilda took charge of the family. "Now that Elene's and Wulfram's parentage has been revealed, the marriage can proceed. But before vows are said, I need to seek forgiveness from all here."

Hilda led her friends and family back into the hall, past the planks set up for the wedding feast, and into the family rooms. When everyone had found a place to rest, Hilda spoke.

"Many years ago, Father Jerome, a very wise priest who acted as my confessor, told me that I must live in the air of complete truth."

She brushed her hand across her eyes, "Try as I might, I have not followed his counsel. Only Caedmon and Ethel know of...my secret...and they have guarded it fiercely in the years since I was a girl." She nodded at the two, who smiled back with sad recognition of what she was about to do. "Now I want to live in the air of that old truth, and I think it may at last be possible to be glad of it."

In a quiet, but firm voice, Hilda began, "I didn't want to be a nun. I didn't want to be at Buxton, but my mother's obsession put me there. Only one thing kept me from despair—the books and the learning, and eventually," she smiled at Rolfe, "my teacher, who became my love through the words on the parchment."

As she told the story of her stay at Buxton, her gaze moved from Leona's shaking body leaning against Rolfe, to the faces of those others whom she loved, to Ethel and Caedmon, and to the daughter she had never expected to be reunited with. Finally, as she came to the end of her story, her strength began to fade and her voice shake. "The baby to whom I gave birth was taken from me, and I never knew its fate. I did not even know whether my child was a boy or a girl." She stopped briefly before continuing in an even quieter voice. "Ethel, who nursed me through that hard birth as lovingly as when she nursed me as a child, has brought my baby back to me."

After Hilda's recitation, the only sound came from Elene, who cried quietly, her head on Bryna's lap. Everyone else remained uncomfortably silent, unwilling to risk creating further pain by asking the questions which Hilda's story raised. At last Bryna spoke, trying to piece together her memories with the story she had just heard. "Then you were with child that first time we met?"

Hilda nodded. Finally, she forced herself to look at Leova. Her friend, her sister in life, stared at her through a steady stream of tears. She had disengaged herself from Rolfe, and in bewilderment—after briefly looking back and forth from her husband to her friend—she, too, sought a mother's solace and buried her face in Pagany's lap.

As Pagany stroked her daughter's hair, she looked around and offered her own wise counsel. "Perhaps," she said, her old-country accent coming to the fore as it always did when she was emotional, "Hilda, Rolfe, and Leova need to be alone."

The others recognized the authority of that suggestion and slowly dispersed, Elene supported by the arms of her adopted mother and followed by her male protectors, Wulfram with his grandparents. When the three of them were alone, Rolfe turned to Leova. "I've wronged you by not telling you that Hilda and I were lovers. I had no excuse except that I love you, have always loved you, and will always love you. We feared you would come to hate both of us if you knew." He looked at Hilda for confirmation, and she nodded in agreement. Then he turned back to Leova, "I did not know about the child! You must believe that!"

"I do, I do," stammered Leova, —but...."

"Rolfe, whom I no longer think of as Brother John, and I are both to blame," Hilda said. "The two of us decided at our first meeting at Buxton not to tell you about our one encounter—and it was only one impulsive coming together—and I decided not to tell him about the baby. It seemed cruel to bring up something no one could change."

Leova still remained silent, her face drawn in sorrow.

Leova," Hilda moved to her friend and reached her arms toward her, "Whatever love Rolfe and I shared was engendered by our love of words and manuscripts; that is what remains, naught else. I can't regret it—especially now that I know I have a beautiful daughter. I've long lived with a black spot in my life. Rolfe and I bear responsibility for that, but fate and war, violence and men's desire for power all played a part. God forgave me years ago and the church, through Father Jerome, has forgiven me also. But, can you forgive me, Leova?"

Leova moved back from Hilda's embrace, and thinking it a rejection, Hilda broke into sobs, her hands covering her face, her body shaking. The room remained still, the air charged with Hilda's words.

Leova drew herself up and looked at the other two, first at Rolfe then at Hilda and back again at Rolfe, sensing within herself her own mother's strength. Pausing only a moment, first turning to

Rolfe, she cradled his face in her hands and bent down to kiss his forehead. Then she swiftly turned to Hilda, led her to the bench where Rolfe sat and, placing herself between them, pulled Hilda's hands from her friend's face, and used her own wedding handkerchief to dry up the tears. Hilda gratefully laid her head on Leova's shoulder—Leova, for now, was the strong one.

"Of course I forgive you, but I'm not sure you need to be forgiven. Both of you sought comfort at the time; neither of you can now be held responsible for the way you came together. Your history does not need to torment you. The three of us will go on," she concluded. "We'll live for now, for our children. Call the children! Let's tell them the story so that they can marry and move our tale on to new and better times."

Hilda squeezed her friend's hand and faced the two people who had most influenced her life. "How is it that we three entered some kind of a maze many, many years ago—a maze each of us has traversed differently—and yet, wonder of wonders, God has allowed us to arrive at the same exit at the same time." She found herself almost smiling, "Our lives would assuredly make a tale worthy of the ones that the ancients tell!"

"Yes," Rolfe said, "but we must tell it once more for Elene and Wulfram. I'll go fetch them."

Hilda—this time aided by Rolfe—filled in their story, each answering questions and holding nothing back—no matter how painful. She kept her eyes on Elene, and at last, when all questions had been answered, she added what she hoped would be reassurance.

"Elene, I may be the woman who gave birth to you, but you have been raised by a devoted loving mother who with her sons rescued you and helped you grow into the admirable woman you now are. They can never be replaced and deserve the gratitude of everyone here."

Elene smiled shyly, and kissed Hilda's cheek, confident in her continued love for Bryna.

Hilda hugged her briefly, and her emotion almost spent, tried to tell her daughter how she felt. "For many years, I dreamed at night of my child resting somewhere far beyond my reach. It took even more years before I reconciled myself to your loss and found a place for myself and an occupation that I loved—one that I succeed at. Nevertheless, the other night when you fell asleep on my shoulder, I felt a strange connection to you. I remembered that dream of a lost child, and thought that if I had a daughter, I would want her to be you." She reached out to Elene hesitantly. "Perhaps God spoke to me? Who understands these things? And, now, here you are, a gentle, yet strong and loving young woman who has found a man who loves her. I can ask for no more. I can only hope that you will come to visit me or let me visit you once in a while."

Elene, who had stood beside Wulfram as their parents revealed the past, approached her newly found mother, kneeled down beside her, and placed her head on her lap, just as she had earlier placed it on Bryna's. "I, too, felt the connection. How fortunate I am to have two mothers—one whom I already love dearly and another I know I will learn to love. Visit as often as you wish, and I will come to visit you. Perhaps, one day, we can read together those manuscripts you love so much!" She then turned to Rolfe. "I often wondered about and wished for a father. Now I have one, one who has always treated me with kindness. I could not have a better man for a father."

Rolfe, his eyes a bit watery, bent down to embrace his daughter. "I am truly blessed in you."

Hilda could only smile. "Shall we now speak to that generous woman who raised you and to those hulking guardian angels who love you so dearly?"

"Yes," Elene smiled, and Rolfe again went to the doorway and beckoned to Elene's adopted family. As quickly as they could, they told the story to those gathered around them. Garamond, roaring with laughter shared by his brothers, grabbed his sister and whirled her around, "We always called you Pryncess—now we discover you really are! I guess this makes us your servants! As if we weren't already."

Elene laughed. "You are as little my servants as you've always been! I could not wish for a better family. As my..." Elene hesitated, now even more unsure of how to address Hilda, "as my Mother Abbess said not too many nights ago, 'nobility is not inherited through the blood.' I am who I have always been."

Rolfe looked fondly at his new-found daughter. "I hope I can be the father you never had; I am honored to try and be so." He added, almost as an afterthought, "You now are an heir to my estate here and a princess of Highhear which gives you quite a bit of land and power in your own right. As my rightful heir, you may well bring as much, or even more, to the marriage as William's son does!"

Elene laughed. "Must we think about that now? I want to get married!"

"And so you shall be," Hilda said. And opened the door to the hall to lead them outside.

Postscript: Eighteen Months Later

They stood under the tapestry that Leova and Hilda had created so many years ago, and laughed happily at their granddaughter. "Can any baby be blessed with more grandmothers than this one?" Hilda laughed, looking at the bright-eyed child in her arms.

"No," said Leova, "but you must share her with them! Ethel hasn't had a chance to see her."

Hilda obediently handled over the agreeable child, and smiled broadly at Pagany, Iona, Ethel, Gwynedd, and Bryna. She felt the child blessed to have all of them in attendance.

"When she rules, our Rhiannon will have the strength and courage of ages on her side," Leova declared.

"That's why I suggested naming her for one of my people's great queens," Pagany added.

Wulfram and Elene, who—with her five brothers—had been watching as the women gloried in their newborn daughter, smiled happily. The proud mother, grasping her husband's hand, looked around at all those there. "Rhiannon enters the world blessed; she inherits the wisdom and love of all of us: what a lucky little girl, though it may take her years to straighten all this out." "Yes, yes, indeed," was the reply of all those there.

Leova and Hilda grasped hands and looked at the women who had nurtured them and their children, and now—in ways they had never expected—would care for their granddaughter. "May she find a friend as faithful as you," Hilda said.

"May they create a tapestry of the heart as we did," Leova replied.

Hilda looked up at the worn weaving with its oddly shaped bird in the corner. Thinking back on her girlhood struggle to create the little lark, she said, "We'll hope she takes her weaving skills from you!"

Leova gave Hilda an affectionate hug, then smiled. "And the passion for living from us both."

www.ingramcontent.com/pod-product-compliance
Lightning Source LLC
Chambersburg PA
CBHW051430260626
47162CB00001B/23